TABOO

BLOOD OF KAOS SERIES

BOOK 4

NESA MILLER

ACKNOWLEDGMENTS

A SPECIAL THANK YOU TO

Daniel, my incredible husband

Amy Briggs – Editor Extraordinaire

@rebecacovers on Fiverr

Daniel Palfrey – the talented artist who designed the beautiful roses strewn throughout the series.

My Beta readers and friends who have advised and provided their invaluable assistance along the way.

Many years ago,
a small group came together in the spirit of community.
They called themselves superheroes.
Super they were and super they remain.
Thank you for your super ways, support, and continued friendships.

Long live all you Superdudes!

To my children and grandchildren, who love me despite my odd ways.

I love you!

PURSUIT

Concern for the safety of his wife foremost in his thoughts, Dar spread his great white wings wide as he swept over the town of Laugharne, stretching his senses further and further in search of Etain. The fact she did not respond troubled him. He should have known her predicament long before Swee showed up with the boy.

He circled over the alleyway to assess the situation and spotted her Black Blades escorts surrounded by *Bok'Na'Ra*. Swooping into the mélange of the enemy, he flattened several of the soldiers with a snap of his wings as he touched ground and drew his black scimitars, Burning Heart and Day Star. With his wings retracted, he shoved in between Taurnil and Eol, forming a triangular fighting force.

"Dar! You are here." The light-haired Taurnil yelled over the noise. "E is up the alley. We have been trying to get to her," he grunted as he slashed his sword, "but these demons keep multiplying."

The three slowly progressed through the enclosure. "I will take care of that." Dar chanted as he continued slashing through the horde. "*Deamhan an dorchadais, níl aon chumhacht agat anseo. Glaoim ar na flaithis chun do bhealach a dhéanamh chun ifreann.* (Demons of the dark, you have no power here. I call on the heavens to light your way to hell)."

His eyes on the attackers, Dar stopped and spoke out of the side of his mouth. "When I give the signal, drop to the ground."

Taurnil turned to him, brow furrowed.

"Drop!"

Trained as Black Blades, Taurnil and Eol obeyed the order immediately and all three dropped flat onto the cobblestones.

Thunder rolled through the alleyway. The ground shook furiously, followed by a cosmic electric force. Within seconds, demons and *Bok* alike succumbed to the energy field, disintegrating into ash.

Dar waited a few moments before raising his head and shook the ashy remnants from his blond hair and black leathers. Satisfied with the results, he jumped to his feet. "Let's move."

The other two followed his lead amidst a wind sweeping through the alley and swirling the ash away. The three stopped when a scream rang out.

"Etain. I have to get to her." Dar ran up the alley. At the end, he found another formation of *Bok* pushing their way through the tight space. Unable to see his wife or even her silver-haired head, his anger took over. When she screamed again, his bloodlust exploded.

In the Welsh sector at Castle Laugharne, all heads turned when Spirit came into the dining hall. Donned in her purple leather armor, her light brown hair swept back into a ponytail, and crossbow on her back, she carried her husband's sword on her hip. As the wife of the fallen UWS (United We Stand) chieftain, she informed the group why they'd been called together.

Linq, a lithe, blond-haired Elf, who looked more like a Viking savage, was the first she met at the doors. "Linq. Yer with me." The stress of the situation brought out more of her English country accent. She turned to the others in the room. "Thank you for coming so quickly. The demon, Dathmet, has shown his bloody face. The Black Blades guarding Etain's brother are dead, and he's missing. And the bastard *Bok* have attacked our people in town. We don't know why, but if they're involved, it can't be good. Dar left not long ago." Her gaze went to a lass with long, brown hair, the resident healer. "Swee, was it just the three of ya?"

The young woman furrowed her brows. "Three?"

"You, Etain, and Taurnil in town."

Swee's expression cleared. "Oh! Yes. I mean, no. There were two Black Blades with us. As far as I know, they're still there."

Spirit turned to a fellow clansman. "Zorn, I know ya want to go, lad, but yer not up for it yet. Give the wound on yer back more time to heal." She placed a hand on his arm and softened her voice. "Stay here and see over the children. Help Swee do what she can for the Elven lass."

She turned to the chieftain of the Dragon clan, dressed in brown leather armor befitting his status, and his clansman, Ra. "Aramis, are you two comin' with us?"

"We are," Ra answered on his behalf, a toothpick between his teeth and tipping his cowboy hat.

"Good." She turned to Linq. "Where are those two Blades who—"

"Here, milady," said a dark-headed Elf. He and his blond-haired comrade stepped into the room, outfitted in uniforms as black as their blades. "Riko and Sion. How may we be of service?"

"Yer needed in town. The bloody *Bok's* stirring up a ruckus."

Riko glanced at his friend. "Shit stirring. Our specialty."

"Spirit," Zorn said. "There's something I should tell you." His gaze encompassed everyone in the room. "All of you, before you go."

Spirit sighed, anxious to be on the move. "Make it quick, lad. We haven't much time."

"While we've been recovering..." He placed a hand on the black head of Spirit's Irish Wolfhound, Felix. Zorn and the hound had become inseparable after returning, injured, from their mysterious disappearance at Etain and Dar's wedding. "Since I've had to put aside my recruiting duties for the clan, I've tried to help out wherever I could. It hasn't been much, but I've done a few things."

Spirit shifted, her lips pursed and a glare in her eyes.

Zorn cleared his throat. "Yes. Sorry." He glanced at Swee. "With Etain's brother not feeling well, I've tried to help if only to see if he needed anything." The healer tilted her head. "I *did* try, Swee." He turned to Spirit. "But every time I tried to go into his room, Felix growled and bared his teeth. If I persisted, he'd block the door and growl at *me*. He does it every time we go up the stairs. Even if I'm just walking down the hall, he blocks the door and growls until I've passed."

Spirit, as well as the others in the room, eyed one another. Although she wasn't sure in what way, Zorn's story was significant. The nasty gash across his back told of his unsavory encounter with an opposing sword, but the young man had yet to share any details.

Spirit nodded at Riko and Sion. Without further instructions, they dashed out of the castle.

"Ta, Zorn. I wish you'd said something sooner. Have the Blades take the bodies to the forge and send them to town. Put the rest of the clan on high alert. Remain vigilant." She turned to the healer. "Swee, make the lass as comfortable as you can. We know she won't last much longer. Let's go."

Only one remained standing. Unbeknownst to Dar, it was the sergeant who attempted to arrest Etain earlier for her decimation of a *Bok* patrol.

Having discovered her brother was alive, she'd gone to find him in Deudraeth but she, Linq, and her brother ended up surrounded by the *Bok*. When Robert suffered an injury, she'd lost control of the demon inside her and disintegrated the entire patrol with a single *solar*.

Covered in blood, Dar towered over the defiant *Bok* officer and held the tip of Burning Heart under the man's chin.

"Where is my wife?"

The sergeant sneered. "I don't mix with the riffraff in town. How would I know?"

"Do not test my patience, *Bok*." The tip of Dar's blade nicked into his skin, causing a trickle of blood to run down the man's neck. "Neither of us are strangers to your kind. Where is she?"

The sergeant eyed him for a long moment. "As you can see," he spread his arms wide, "I don't have her."

"Arrogance will gain you nothing." Dar clenched his jaw and leaned into his face. "I will ask again with great restraint. If you tell me, I may let you live. Where. In Tartarus. Is my wife?"

The man's eyes cut to Eol and Taurnil. Finding no assistance from either of the stone-faced Elves, he released a long sigh. "Dathmet has her."

"Do not lie to me." Dar forced the man's head back with the tip of his sword, eliciting a cry from the cornered soldier.

"He might not be lying, Dar," Spirit said from behind him. "The demon's come back. He tore through Robert's room, killed the Blades on guard, and took the boy with him."

Dar turned slightly. Consumed by his efforts to get to Etain, he had not heard the group from Laugharne approach. The realization tightened his grip on the deadly blade. "Did you see him? Any of you? With your own eyes?"

"*We* didn't see the demon," she said. "It was the lass, Renme, who told us."

Staring at the soldier, Dar lowered Burning Heart. The man visibly relaxed but Dar stepped back, brought up Day Star and slashed his throat. He walked to the entrance of the alley as the man slid down the wall.

"Blades, stack the bodies." He turned to the others. "As Black Blades are honor-bound to the High Lord, they will go with me. I do not expect the rest of you to endanger your lives in this quest. I guarantee it will be ugly."

Linq shoved his blade into its sheath. "We may not be bound to *you*, High Lord," he waved an arm toward the others, "but we *are* honor-bound to a friend in need. Etain is as much our responsibility as yours. There will be no rest in Laugharne, or anywhere else, as long as she is held captive."

"Well said, Linq." Spirit stood next to him, flanked on either side by her clansmen and a handful of Elven Royal Guard. "He took me husband. He can't have her."

Dar cast an appreciative eye over the group. "You are all welcomed assets."

"That brings it around to us," Aramis said. "You've become a great friend and ally to the Dragon clan, Dar. Ra and I ride with you wherever you choose to go. Our blades are at your disposal."

"Thank you." He turned to Taurnil. "And you, little cousin, should return to Laugharne until you have recovered from your injuries."

"Who do you think you are talking to?" Taurnil's face turned red. "E is every bit as important to me as she is to you, *cousin*."

"I doubt that, and for your sake, you best hope I *keep* thinking that way." He relented somewhat and reminded the Elf of his status. "Does the fact you are the Prince of Nunnehi, heir to the throne, strike a chord, little cousin? Your people cannot afford their future king risking his life in a private matter."

Taurnil clenched his hands. "Stop calling me *little cousin*. I am damn near as big as you and am just as capable of handling myself in such matters. What would my people think of a king who allows the High Lady to be kidnapped and not fight with all his might to get her back? I will go with or without your blessing."

Just as Dar opened his mouth, another Black Blade holding a bloody *Nim'Na'Sharr* interrupted. "High Lord, sir," said Dalos. "I found this. It belongs to the High Lady, yes?" Gingerly, he handed over the now dim crystal sword.

Dar checked the blade for any damage. "Show me where, Blade."

The group followed Dalos into the alley and to the brick wall where he had found Etain's sword. Dar crouched, dragged his fingers through the splattered blood on the ground and brought them to his lips. With but a touch, he knew the blood belonged to his wife. Its song pierced his heart. A quick flick of his tongue cleansed the stain from his fingertips as he stood.

"She is injured, but not mortally. The children are well. I can sense their energies, as well as that of Dathmet. But there is something else. An energy I do not recognize." He turned to Spirit. "Did you say *all* his guards were killed?"

Spirit frowned. "Aye. I'm sure Renme has passed by now."

"Damn." Dar pursed his lips.

"I called in the clan and set the remaining Blades to cleaning up the carnage." Spirit lowered her voice. "Alatariel will see the dead get the proper transport to Nunnehi. Once they've moved the bodies, the Blades will join us."

Linq turned to Taurnil. "Your mother sends her blessings. Be safe and fight well." He looked at Dar. "She charges you with the complete destruction of the bastard, her words, and to bring Etain safely home."

The great warrior raised his hand toward the pile of dead *Bok.* "*Kela.*" Flames exploded around the bodies and consumed the mass in seconds. The allies backed into the street away from the intense flames.

"Royal Guard, take the injured to Laugharne and stay with them," Dar ordered. "The rest of you, please forgive me, but I must have a moment alone. I—"

"We will wait here," Linq said. "It was the same with Etain when we searched for you after the battle."

Dar broke away to quiet his mind and communicate with his wife. Walking up the street, he recognized the pub where they danced, and she sang to him. The need to be close to her propelled him inside. Ale in hand, he headed to the booth they shared on that memorable day.

She had let down her guard. The depth and power of her emotions drew him in and fused their hearts as one. The only thing stronger had been her loyalty to Inferno.

Dar grabbed his mug and downed half his ale.

Every day since, her love effectively peeled away the layers of pain and indifference in his soul, giving him hope that the life he had dreamt of for so long could be his. He leaned back against the cool leather of the seat and closed his eyes.

"I love you with all my heart and soul, *a chuisle*," he whispered. "This demon will be destroyed."

Dar breathed in and calmed his thoughts before reaching out to his precious wife. After a time, his mind connected with hers, but her chaotic thoughts confused him. Flashes of her brother, Robert, soon changed into Dathmet, instantly morphing into Midir, Dar's dead brother. He saw his own image flutter through, followed by glimpses of the young boy who rode into Laugharne with Swee. He pulled back from the chaos and placed his head in his hands.

What does the boy have to do with this? Is he the reason the Bok turned on Etain? Was he part of a trap set by Dathmet?

He raised his head, gulped a mouthful of ale, and changed tactics.

An attempt to reach his children proved futile. Realizing he had scared them, he softened his aura and tried again.

This time, his tiny daughter answered.

"How are you, little one?" He sensed her hesitation and further softened his tone. *"It is Da, baby girl. I am coming to get you."*

"Da?"

"How is your brother? I can feel his energy but no more than that."

"He sleeps, like Mama."

"Good. How is Mama?"

"Scared, Da."

"Stay strong, little one. Da is coming."

Linq slid into the other side of the booth, pulling him away from the communication.

"Sorry to bother you. We are ready to go." He paused. "What is it?"

One corner of Dar's mouth lifted. "Your intuition is uncanny, Linq."

He shrugged. "It is more a matter of knowing you for so long. What is going on?"

"She is scared out of her mind." Dar's shoulders slumped. Dragging his arms to his sides, he gripped the edge of the bench. "I cannot get through to her."

"Perhaps her fear for the children is the force behind it."

"That may be a part of it, but we both know she is a fighter. She uses her fear to make her stronger. Something else is in the mix here. We must get to them soon, or we will not get them out alive."

"Do you know where they are?"

"No." Dar closed his eyes, clenching and unclenching his jaw, mulling over locations in his head. "Etain destroyed the blood castle. I ripped Midir's castle apart. There is another..."

He heard the Elf shift in his seat.

"Shall we start there?" Linq asked.

Dar opened his eyes, but turned away, his mind's eye on the practice yard where Etain tried to end his life. Midir had taken her there, polluted her with his poison, and tricked her into believing Dar was Midir. Fortunately, Etain's crystal sword, *Nim,* cleansed her mistress of the poison and gave Dar the opportunity to kill his dark brother.

"No. It is in another realm."

"No surprise there." Linq tilted his head. "Why do you hesitate?"

He focused on the Elf. "She cannot leave this realm without me."

Linq raised a brow and sat back.

"After Etain's destruction of the blood castle, I bound her to me to keep her safe."

"To keep her safe," the Elf echoed, a smirk on his lips. "That may be *one* of the reasons." He brought his hands up from his lap and placed the black blade for Taurnil's sword on the table. "Be that as it may, if we are to go into hell, we will need everyone in this small clan as strong as possible. I say it is time this be completed and put to good use."

Dar appraised the workmanship of the blade. It was some of his best work. Its edges gleamed; the blade well-balanced. He reached into his shirt and brought out the piece of black jade he rummaged from Inferno's stash earlier that morning.

"I was going to carve the hilt tonight, but you are right, old friend. We need everyone as strong as possible. It is time Taurnil became an official Blade."

The jade in one hand and the tang of the blade in the other, he brought the two together. Dar closed his eyes and called on the power of his *ultimá solar*, concentrating the incredible force into his palms.

Linq turned his head from the intense light.

Several minutes passed as the heat of Dar's hands melded stone and metal into a cohesive unit. Once done, he placed the sword flat on the table to cool.

"I will not be much longer. Meet me at the edge of town."

"Right." Linq stood. "Make sure you show. She is *your* wife, but she is *our* High Lady, and friend. Give us the chance to get her back and take him out."

He held his gaze for a moment. "Aye."

With that said, Linq was gone.

Dar braced himself and mentally reached out in search of his wife's mind. Softly, he spoke words only he would use.

"A chuisle, lig isteach mé (My love, let me in)."

When he did not receive a response, he pushed a little harder, reverting to English.

"Let me in, my love. I need your help to find you."

The utter silence shook him to his core. He slammed his hand on the table, making several patrons in the pub jump.

"Damn it, Etain," he growled. "He cannot have you."

Dar pushed out of the booth, grabbed the black blade, and stormed out of the pub. He walked straight toward Taurnil, who involuntarily stepped back from the pulsing force in front of him.

"To be a Blade does not require a great ceremony." He tapped the young Elf on the chest. "It is in the heart, and you have plenty of it." He held up the handcrafted katana. "This sword was made especially for you. Use it for the good of the Elves, the Alamir, and in memory of the Krymerians.

It will serve you well. Taurnil of Nunnehi, you are no longer a novice. You are now a Black Blade. Serve *me* well."

The young Elf held his gaze for a long moment before accepting the sword. His eyes widened as he held the hilt in his hand and tested the balance. "I will, milord."

Dar turned to the group. "Time to kill a demon."

Too Late

E tain breathed in, trying to calm her heart. She kept her eyes closed and engaged her other senses.

I remember the blood red skin of his arm. Dathmet.

She forced herself to take a steady breath.

Don't panic. You can't be too far from Laugharne. Dar made sure of that.

Sweat covered her body at the thought of her husband.

Dar. I have to block our mindspeak. He can't come here. The demon will kill him. You're on your own, girl. Figure out how you're gonna save yourself.

She heard heavy breathing to the left and right of her, but nothing more. Whether it was one, two, or an entire troop, their hot, putrid breath made her gag.

I'm in a chair. A remarkably comfortable chair. Maybe I dreamed it all?

Etain opened her eyes. The room with its tasteful gray walls, white trim, and plush rugs was almost cozy, but she didn't recognize it. Unlike Dathmet's blood castle, there were no weapons or chains displayed on the walls.

A demon, his skin as red as blood and hair of flames, stepped in from an adjoining room and walked toward her, his hands clasped behind his back. She blinked several times, thrown off by his black suit and tie.

"Lady Etain. Welcome to my temporary abode." Dathmet waved a hand around the large room as he turned. "Since you and your illustrious friends destroyed my beautiful castle, I have been obliged to go underground for a time."

Although she'd seen the ridge along his back before, the sight of it bulging out from his suit jacket surprised her. She hid her shock by glaring into his red-flamed gaze. "Where you belong."

He grunted a small laugh and crouched in front of her, mischief in his eyes. "Feisty. I like it."

When he glanced at whatever stood behind her, large, rough hands grabbed each of her arms, pinning her to the chair. She glared at one and the other. Dressed in dirty gray armor, the only flesh visible were their ugly faces, both the color of puke.

She struggled against their hold. "What are you doing? Let me go." The demon to her right ripped the sleeve from her white, billowy shirt and twisted her arm, making her grimace, and offered the soft underside to his master.

"Please struggle all you want. The more pain I can give you, the better." He brought his other hand forward, holding a hypodermic syringe filled with a greenish liquid. "We can't have you pulling any of your tricks, *mon petit*."

"What is that?" She fought harder, her mind searching for a protection spell.

"Something to make you compliant. Help you see things from my perspective."

"No! I'm pregnant."

"Do you think I care about the brat you carry?" he sneered.

Brat? She stared at him. *He doesn't know I carry twins.*

"My baby is innocent. Please don't do anything to hurt—"

"Innocent?" He leaned into her face. "For how long? I wager by the age of six, your bull of a husband'll have it well on its way to planning my demise. No!" He straightened. "It will suffer as its mother suffers."

Great goddess of infinite light, protect us with all your might. Great goddess of infinite light, protect us with all your might. Great goddess of infinite light, protect us with all your might.

Feeling the needle slide into her arm, she sucked in a breath and cried out as the heavy liquid slowly entered her veins, its effects taking hold immediately.

Great goddess of infinite...

A light mist fogged her brain. Her body slumped in the chair. The room blurred and concentration moved beyond her capacity. In slow motion, Dathmet removed the syringe, speaking in a distorted voice.

"That should make you more pliable. We'll give it a few minutes to take full effect."

She closed her eyes and slipped into darkness.

⁂

Having left Laugharne on such short notice, Spirit had negotiated just enough horses for herself, her two clansmen, Wolfe and Elfin, and the other Alamir. With the Black Blades consisting of Elves, she knew they would keep pace with their party.

"Dar, I'll send me boys back to Laugharne. You and Taurnil can have their mounts."

He considered the group around him. There were no more discussions to be had. What could he say that would stop them from following him? Etain meant as much to them as she did to him.

"Thank you, Spirit."

He took the reins of a large, black stallion. Standing fifteen hands, the impressive horse's well-rounded hindquarters were testament to its strength, and the tail, like the mane, was thick and long. Dressed in black leathers, Dar's body seemed to meld with the great horse, making them appear as one creature with two heads—one dark, one light.

He glanced at those standing around him. "Am I doing this alone?"

Spirit ordered her clansmen back to Laugharne, despite their protests, while the others scrambled for a mount.

"You can't go in alone, milady!" argued Wolfe, looking every bit the part of his namesake.

"Absolutely not!" agreed Elfin, the tips of his ears red. "We must go with you to make sure you are safe."

"Lads, I'm surrounded by Blades." Spirit waved a hand at the group. "And who better to protect me than our good friend Linq, not to mention the High Lord of Kaos himself?" She linked arms with her clansmen and lowered her voice. "I need you at Laugharne in case this bastard decides to attack again. The clan needs you more than I do."

Wolfe shared a frowned with Elfin. "When you put it that way, milady..."

"How can we refuse," finished the Elf.

"Good. Keep an eye on Zorn. Don't let him do too much. Thank you, lads."

Wolfe gave an order of his own. "Come home safe, milady."

Just before midday, the band rode west prepared to engage in battle as the High Lord followed the tiny beacons sent out by his children.

Linq caught up to Dar. "Have you contacted Etain?"

"Hmph."

"Any idea where they have gone?"

They rode a little farther before Dar answered. "He must know by now he cannot take her to another realm. My guess is he is eager to take what he wants and be on his way."

"What does he want?"

"Her life."

They rode hard through the lush countryside without a break. After a few hours, Dar relented in his dogged pursuit when they came across a stream flowing into a small lake and allowed both riders and horses a short respite.

"Do we have a location?" asked Linq, walking along the water's edge with his friend.

"Not yet." Dar sighed. "All I can do is follow their heartbeats."

"Etain?"

Dar shook his head.

Linq gazed across the water. "Is there anything significant in the west?"

Dar stopped and picked up a stone, turning it over in his hands as he watched the clouds drift across the blue sky.

"Not that I know of." He closed one eye, aimed, and skipped the rock over the water's surface—one, two, three, four before it disappeared.

"So we ride blindly into the night?"

Dar turned to his friend. "If that is what it takes to find my family."

"It is important we get to Etain as soon as possible, yes, but consider who rides with you. The Blades spent the better part of the day cleaning up the remains of their comrades. Taurnil and Eol are exhausted. Wait until morning, at least."

"Blades have the training. They are prepared. Taurnil had the option to go back."

"Oh aye." Linq placed his hands on his hips. "You treated him like a proper boy instead of the man he has become. Most generous, High Lord."

Dar practically growled at the Elf. "We leave at dark."

"And you..." Linq eyed him from head to toe. "What good will you be to Etain in your current state?"

Jaw clenched, he vibrated with restraint. "We will follow where my children lead until she is found."

Linq's nostrils flared. "No matter the cost."

"Thank you for seeing it my way." Dar walked away, relaxing his fisted hands.

Linq yelled after him. "What if that cost is the life of every one of these people? Or worse, your children? Are you prepared to watch everyone you know and love die because you are too bullheaded to listen to common sense, VonNeshta? Do you plan to spend another quarter turn alone?" Dar kept walking. "Did you learn nothing from what happened at the blood castle?"

Dar stopped in his tracks and turned with great deliberation. "Be careful with your words, *Elf*."

Linq strode toward him. "These brave souls will follow you to hell and back, High Lord. You best hold them in as high regard as they hold you and not exploit their loyalty."

"Do as you wish. The Blades and I leave at dusk." With that, he turned and walked off.

Aramis stepped next to Linq. "He's strung pretty tight. I wouldn't go pushing him too hard."

"He is acting like an idiot," Linq grumbled turning his back on the Krymerian. "He needs rest to beat this demon. We *all* need rest, and he damn well knows it."

The Alamir patted him on the shoulder. "Give him some time to think it over. He'll come to his senses. In the meantime, we'll set up camp."

"I have not seen him like this in a long time. Frankly, it scares the hell out of me."

A hard slap to the face nearly knocked her out of the chair, jolting her from unconsciousness into a blind fury. Her tormentor grabbed her by the chin and forced her to look at him.

"There will be none of that, sis," a green-eyed, dark-haired Robert cooed. "But now I have your attention, we can get to business."

Her mind whirled as he pushed her back into the chair. "R—Robert?" Dressed in a black suit and tie, he seemed more like a businessman than an apothecary. Hope blossomed in her heart. "We need to get out of here. Help me up. I think I can find the way out."

"No. We have things to discuss, and depending on your viewpoint, I may or may not allow you to live."

Etain licked her lips, tasting blood. "We're family. Why would you want to hurt me or my baby?" She tried to rise from the chair, but a demon claw grabbed her by the shoulder.

Robert's green eyes flared red as he leaned over her and placed his hands on the armrests, his nose millimeters from hers. "I will *never* recognize the spawn of the demon who murdered my father." Etain tilted her head trying to distance herself from his outburst. "If I didn't have a use for you, you'd already be dead, along with your shit of a husband."

She frowned. "Are you talking about Dar? He didn't kill Dad. Midir had our parents killed."

"Are you really that stupid, Etain?" He pushed from the chair and walked away a few steps. "Can't you see the *lack* of family resemblance between James and me?" He stormed back to her. "Your precious Dar killed *my* father, not yours."

"I—I don't understand."

He almost laughed as he crouched in front of her and stroked her cheek. "Sweet little Etain, living your life oblivious to what was going on around you. You were the favored one, even by our mother."

"That's not true," she whispered. "Mom and Dad gave you everything. They cared for both of us. Why are you blaming Dar for their deaths?"

"Fuck, you are thick." He stood. "*My* father was Midir, you twit." Grabbing her by the arms, he jerked her out of the chair and transformed into the blood-skinned demon, Dathmet. "I have the pure blood of Krymerian kings in my veins," he declared, holding her aloft. "I am destined to inherit the power my father dreamed of and tried so hard to attain. And you will take me there, sister. Your blood will take me there!" he bellowed, shaking her so hard she was certain her brain rattled. Just as suddenly, he let go.

Etain fell to the floor, her legs buckling beneath her. A grunt escaped when she hit hard. Pushing up on one hand, she ran the other protectively over her belly and glared at the demon. "You may have Midir's blood, but even I know half-breeds can't rule in the Krymerian realm. Besides, who are you going to rule? The Krymerians are dead."

Dathmet slapped her so hard her head hit the floor. Stars danced in her vision as she fought to stay conscious.

"*I* am full-blooded Krymerian. *You* are the half-breed."

Before she could recover, the demon guards dragged her to the other end of the room. Yanking her arms overhead, they clamped shackles around her wrists and pulled the chain until the toes of her boots barely touched the floor. With great effort, she tried to bring the red demon into focus but only saw her brother.

"Me?"

He moved closer, his green eyes filled with hate. "Our mother was a Krymerian princess, Etain."

She breathed in and closed her eyes, trying to regain her senses. "Did Midir tell you that?"

"She kept it a secret, thinking she wouldn't see him again. But, for all the trouble you've caused me, I suppose I should be thankful. If you hadn't been born, my father wouldn't have come into my life."

"Wait." Taken aback by his statement, she forgot her predicament and tried to step toward him. The movement put her body into a spin. She cried out at the pain of the shackles pulling her wrists and jerking her shoulders. She sucked in a breath and was just able to stop herself. "Why are you doing this? How can Midir be your father?"

Dathmet moved closer. "Your birth woke the desire in him." His breath was hot against her skin. "He knew he couldn't have our mother, so he set his sights on you. How he planned and plotted, biding his time, waiting for the right moment." He backed away. "It was through his lust for you that he discovered I was his son. Mother never told him, not until she was confronted with the truth. In the end, she could not lie to him."

Etain's stomach churned, her heart beating like thunder. "I don't believe you. Mom was good and loving. How could she ever—"

"You've experienced the charms of Midir," he spat. "Had Dar not interfered, you would be his now and my life would be different. I would be living like the king I am, rather than hiding in a hole." He walked to a nearby table and picked up a dagger, continuing his story as he inspected its deadly edges.

"He said she was older than him, but young by Krymerian standards." Slowly approaching Etain, his eyes remained on the jagged edge of the dagger until he stood in front of her. "She loved him and was ready to marry him." He dragged the tip along her jaw to her chin and down her throat, resting it for a moment in the hollow at the base of her neck. "Until her parents found out about the affair." His eyes moved up to hers as he pressed the dagger's tip into her flesh. "They would have none of it. What they didn't know was the couple had already consummated their relationship. She was pregnant when they sent her away."

She breathed in light, shallow breaths, the blade cold against her skin. "More of Midir's bullshit."

The tip pressed deeper into the soft flesh.

"Why would he lie?" he asked.

A thin line of blood trailed down her chest.

"Because he was a manipulating sadist who twisted everything to his advantage."

Dathmet bared his fangs. "If it weren't for you, I wouldn't need to go to all this bother. The power would be mine, and the Alamir, as well as those annoying Elves, would be history." He dragged the tip of the blade through the small line of blood, tracing it to the scooped neckline of her top. "But we're here now, so shall we move on?"

"Mom loved Dad." Her eyes followed the blade as it traveled over her body.

He emitted a small, humorless grunt. "Yes, I suppose she did, even to the point of dying for him." He popped the first button of her top. "That news, along with discovering he'd been deprived of his son, drove Midir into a deadly rage." With a deft flick of his wrist, the second and third buttons flew to the floor.

"Robert..." she strained to keep a civil tone, "stop this. Somewhere in that red-skinned demon is the boy I grew up with. The one who loved me and protected me as a little girl. My big brother. Please, let me go."

"Too late," he whispered in return. "The blood of the half-breed changes everything. I will rule the *Bok* and destroy those Alamir who will not follow me. I must ensure the status of the Krymerians is restored." He slashed into the delicate fabric of her shirt. With the dagger between his teeth, he grabbed the open edges and ripped it apart. He tucked the dagger into his belt and licked the stream of blood.

"Stop!"

Etain tried to pull away, but the chains didn't allow her much movement. She slammed into the demon. Disgusted by the brush with pure evil, her stomach roiled, and her body heaved. Dathmet stepped away just as the bile gurgled up, issuing out onto the floor and down her partially exposed body.

"You are disgusting." He turned to the guards, "Clean this mess," and stalked to the door. "Let me know when she's decent again."

GAME CHANGER

Dar walked to the other side of the lake in search of a secluded spot to gather his thoughts. Seated beneath a copse of trees, he found comfort in the sound of the water gently rolling onto shore. After quickly washing his boots, he removed them, and fully clothed, walked into the cool water, washing away as much of the dried blood from his clothing as possible.

Piece by piece, he stripped off each layer and tossed them onto the bank. Naked, he spread his arms and fell back into the clear water, allowing his body to sink beneath the rippling surface. The sensations of the water replaced all thoughts as his muscles released the stress of the past few hours.

Linq's words came back to him. He knew he spoke the truth. The rest would do them all good, but Etain needed him.

What good is anything if she is gone?

How many more must sacrifice their lives to this horrible demon?

Clear your thoughts. Push away the emotions, the anger. Let go of the personal aspect.

Tartarus! It is personal! The bastard has taken my wife, my children, my life.

Stop. Do not let the demon push you into doing something stupid. Your family is alive. They are fighting, just as Etain said they would. Keep calm, man. Keep your cool. Become the silent warrior once again. Step into his world and tear it to pieces.

"Dar?" A voice invaded his thoughts.

He dipped under the water, his feet touching the soft sand of the lakebed, pushed off and returned to the surface. Dar shook the water from his eyes. "Taurnil. What do you want?"

The Elf glared at him. "Sorry to interrupt, but I didn't think I'd get another chance to thank you."

"For what?"

"A second chance."

Dar briefly closed his eyes and dove under the surface. When he bobbed up again, he found Taurnil patiently waiting for him. Although annoyed, he decided his solitude was at an end and walked toward the bank. "Second chance at what?"

"Although Etain was taken, you made me a Blade. I should have been more cautious, more aware."

"I fast-tracked your induction *because* of my wife. I know you two have spent time together and have become fond of each other. If you have learned anything, you know she has a mind of her own, and uses it often."

Despite the circumstances, Taurnil laughed. "The lady *is* strong-minded."

Once out of the water, Dar shook his head, sending droplets in every direction, including onto the Elf. "I am afraid her penchant for rescuing the underdog will be her undoing, and mine."

"What makes you say that?"

He grabbed his clothes and spread them out to dry in the sun. "The boy Swee brought with her to Laugharne. I first thought he was used as bait to lay a trap for Etain. But he did not act like a guilty accomplice. Rather than run, he stayed with Spirit's children."

"He could be gone by now."

"True but I doubt it."

"Why is that?"

"My contact with him was brief but enough to tell me he is like Freeblood."

Taurnil raised his brows. "How so?"

"Something Etain said before I met him. Freeblood, that is." Dar motioned toward a patch of grass beneath the trees and sat. "She said he does not tolerate evil and never will. I have to admit, I did not think much of it at the time. But now I understand. That boy is the same. I would very much like to meet his parents."

"So you believe she was saving the day when the *Bok* showed up?"

"Aye." Dar shifted, but with the move, had to adjust his balls. "Damn, grass, gets in places it shouldn't. Back to your induction. You have worked hard and have earned your right as a Blade. I promise, once this is over you will have a proper ceremony. For now, sit and tell me of your experience with a sword."

Taurnil joined him and told his story, from becoming a novice Blade up to the day he met the incredible Etain. "Her moves were impeccable. Just when we thought the master had outwitted her, she waved her dagger over his balls and was in control once again."

Dar chuckled. "She always has a backup plan."

Taurnil's laugh faded into a frown. "Does she have one this time?"

Dar stared out toward the water, thinking of his resourceful wife. "I have no idea what she is up to. I cannot get through to her."

"Is it necessarily a bad thing?"

"I do not like it. It leaves too many implications, too many possibilities, none of them appealing." Dar reached for his leather pants, working them up his legs.

"If you are not able to reach her, how is it you know where she is?"

He growled. "Blast this leather. It is hell when wet." Dar stood and struggled to pull his pants all the way up, carefully tucking away his privates. "There. My children. They are my tiny lighthouses showing me the way."

"I see. Do they tell you of E's situation?"

"They tell me to hurry."

Taurnil stood. "So we leave tonight?"

The big warrior sighed. "No. I hate she has to spend even a moment more in his presence, but these brave souls deserve a rest. We must reserve our strength for when it will be most effective. I will not allow this demon to dictate our actions. If he intended to take her life, he would have done so by now and be gone."

Dar picked up Burning Heart and brandished the blade through the air. "For now, be my distraction. Show me how good you are with your new sword, Black Blade. Perhaps I can teach you a few tricks."

Etain sputtered and gasped at the cold water splashing over her. One demon mopped up the water on the floor while the other stripped off the shreds of her shirt and leggings. Goosebumps covered her chilled skin as she fought to keep her teeth from chattering. Once the guards finished their work, they left her alone.

She used the solitude to systematically call on each of her powers, trying to free herself from the shackles around her wrists. One by one, her electrical charge, her *solar*, her shimmer, even her ability to transform failed, but she kept pushing, again and again.

At last, a small voice echoed in her frenzied brain.

"Save your strength, Mama. Da is coming."

"No," she whispered. "He cannot come here. They will kill him."

"Mama..." Her daughter sounded so sweet. *"Da is strong now. He is coming and will take us home. Save your strength, Mama."*

Tears slid down Etain's cheeks. "I am so sorry, my sweet—"

This time, her son spoke. *"Mama, his magic cannot touch us. Be strong."*

"No need to apologize to your brat. It won't feel a thing." Dathmet stepped into the room, minus his coat and tie. His twisted smile revealed two rows of evenly spaced pointed teeth gleaming against his red skin. A cat o' nine in his hand, he swished the tails against his legs. "I'm afraid I can't say the same for you. Before we start, I need another taste of your delicious blood."

She struggled to avoid his grasp, but his arm wrapped around her waist, pressing her body against his. The whip dropped to the floor.

"Sweet, sweet little sister, you are so beautiful." She bent back as he leaned in to taste her lips. "No, no, no. Come here, bitch." He grabbed a handful of hair and jerked her face to him. "*I* am in control." He slid his tongue over her lips and squeezed a breast before moving down her rounded belly and around to her bottom, pulling her hips to his. "Mmm, I think you would feel nice beneath me, belly and all."

Caught up in his passion, he failed to block a well-placed knee to the groin. With a loud grunt, he pulled back and doubled over, grabbing his crotch.

"Don't touch me again, you fucking bastard." Her knee came up into his head. "I'll cut off your cock before you have the chance to use it."

The demon stumbled into the wall. After a shake of his head, he came at her and backhanded her across the face. "You'll be begging me to fuck you before this is over, cunt. It will be the least of your tortures."

Talons extended from one of his hands and slashed out, catching her across the breasts, slicing her lace bra into pieces. Etain screamed at the sharp tips cutting into her flesh. Dathmet retracted the deadly instruments and moved close to her again, mindful to protect himself.

"Shall we remove your boots and strap those legs?"

A snap of his fingers set one guard in motion. He lifted a leather strap from the nearby table and handed it to his master. Dathmet slid his hands over her hips and down her legs. Using a talon, he sliced through the laces, pulled each boot off, and tossed both aside. With her feet bound, he trailed his tongue along her skin as he slowly slinked up her body.

"Your skin... I can see your muscles flex when I touch you."

When he reached the blood oozing over her breasts, he cupped each one and licked a long line as she squirmed, trying to pull away. His tongue dragged up the next line, taking a blood-soaked nipple between his teeth and sucking it clean.

"No!" she screamed. "Stop it!" Her struggles only encouraged him further as he moved his mouth to the other breast, drinking her blood. "I'm your *sister*! Stop!"

He lifted his head, his eyes heavy with lust. "Your body is nothing more than my toy to do with as I please, so shut up and let me enjoy you." He returned to the blood that flowed more freely with his manipulations.

Etain called upon her most commanding voice. "Robert. You will stop. It is disgusting."

His body vibrated as an evil laugh rolled up from his gut and his ugly grin pressed against her breast. "I told you to shut up, bitch." Extending a single talon, he clipped the thin elastic band of her panties on one side, then the other, and slid the fabric from between her legs.

"No! No!"

The talon retracted as he brought the small piece of fabric to his nose and inhaled. "The female scent. Intoxicating. Not much to this pair, but I think they'll do the trick." He shoved the destroyed underwear into her mouth. "Yes, they work nicely."

Etain grunted her indignation as he unbuttoned his shirt, pulling the tails from his trousers and revealing a tightly muscled torso. She squirmed as he methodically sliced into her skin, drinking her blood. He stroked and tasted every inch of her body, all the time instructing her on how to give and take pleasure from a woman. Her body's betrayal made her cringe as it submitted to his ministrations, the heat building in her belly.

She shook her head to push away the rising primal desires, desperately trying to disassociate from the experience and hoping to stay in control, but Dathmet proved to be a master at the art of manipulation. Mixing pleasure with pain, he slid a hand between her thighs and stroked her as he bit into her neck, pressing his growing desire against her hip.

His fingers moved faster as he whispered into her ear, "Tell me the secrets of the Krymerian vault."

Lost in the sensations of an oncoming climax, she ignored his words.

"You are the half-breed, Etain. Tell me how to change everything."

Again, she shook her head, wanting to place her mind in another place with another man. Suddenly, the pleasure disappeared.

Her body on fire, she screamed her hate for him, and her weakness, struggling to breathe without swallowing the gag. To be taken so far into the realm of pleasure only to have it ripped away before reaching her peak was a torture she never dreamed possible.

The blood trickling over her hips and down the length of her legs made her want to vomit.

He met her hate filled gaze and licked his fingers. "I understand how you turned such a powerful warrior into a whipped dog." A muffled curse came from her lips. He cupped an ear and leaned toward her. "What's that? I can't understand a word, half-breed." He ripped the gag from her mouth. "What did you say?"

"You. Won't touch him. Again."

He undid his belt and opened his trousers exposing his hard member where only she could see. His hand slid between her thighs again, running his fingers through her wetness, making her moan as he grabbed a handful of silver hair and pulled her head back. "Always the little protector. Remember who is in charge here."

Their eyes locked in a battle of wills as his fingers continued to stroke, his cock pressed against her. Revulsion, shame, and need rose inside of her, blending into a miasma that threatened to steal her sanity. This time, he stroked until the tingles took over and her body jerked. At the time she cried out her release, the demon found his personal deliverance against her skin.

She slowly came back to herself and whispered, "I will kill you for everything you have done."

Breathless, he laughed and pushed away. "We've only just begun." Dathmet tucked himself into his trousers and zipped. "As for your revenge, you kid yourself. You have a huge debt to repay to me, and it will be paid in full."

"What the hell have I ever done to you?" She licked her lips to ease their dryness, but it was useless.

"You were born." He scooped the cat o' nine from the floor. "Everything given to you will be mine." A sneer on his face, he circled her. "Your blood, your body, your power. Tell me about the Krymerian vault."

She closed her eyes. "If it is Krymerian... I imagine it would be in Krymeria. Dar would know better than me."

He shook his head, continuing to circle. "You don't learn, do you?" The whip lashed across the back of her thighs.

Etain gritted her teeth and sucked in a breath. "Maybe if you hadn't beat the shit out of him—"

He lashed again, striking her back. "*You* are the half-breed, bitch. Your blood holds the secrets to change. We just have to find a way to open the door."

"You're the precious pure blood. Open your own damn door."

"Unfortunately, being of pure blood doesn't help in this case. The prophecy requires tainted blood." He smirked. "Yours is about as polluted as it gets."

"Polluted or not..." She eyed him from head to toe as he passed in front of her. "*You* are not worthy to be called Krymerian, much less wield the power."

The whip lashed around her waist, forcing a gasp from her lips. Pleased by the song of her pain, he snarled, "Someday you will learn to keep your opinions to yourself." He walked around to face her. "Did I mention it's the human aspect that unlocks it all?"

She lifted her head, determined to keep her wits. "How could I forget, Einstein? You keep reminding me."

"Your blood will give me access to the vault. Then I will change the past and ensure our future together." He moved to her side. "Your dog will fail to exist."

A ragged laugh came from her lips. "My half-breed blood has addled your half-assed brain."

With the flick of his wrist, the whip struck across her shoulder blades, making her suck in another breath. "Sweet little sister... The vault will take me back to the past where I will destroy the boy before he has a chance to become a man." Circling her suspended body, he continued to lash her delicate skin.

Etain tried not to cry out, but eventually, the assault proved too much. Exhausted, she hung by her wrists, the pain from the whip outweighing any produced by the biting shackles.

"This is getting us nowhere." He tossed the whip aside.

With a grunt of effort, she pulled herself up. "You're a sharp one."

Etain defiantly watched him raise his hand, but he stopped, turned, and strolled out of the room.

She blew out a weary breath. Every inch of her body ached, the scratches, cuts, and lashes from the whip burned. The stink of him on her skin made her sick. But she gained some satisfaction in the fact she couldn't give him what he wanted. Her smirk dissolved into a grimace from the cut on her lip stinging.

"Fuck you," she whispered, licking her lips.

Within minutes, the red demon returned, his teeth glistening in the light. "Since you refuse to help me on your own behalf, perhaps I can persuade you in another way."

"I told you I don't know anything about your stupid vault."

He snapped his fingers.

"But I *do* know..." Her words trailed off when the guards escorted Freeblood into the room, a huge purple bruise on one side of his face, his brown curls matted, and hands bound. If only she could infuse her venomous thoughts into her blood, watch the demon writhe in pain as he choked on it.

"Etain!" Freeblood's brown eyes widened at the sight of her. "What the hell?"

He grunted when the guard pushed him deeper into the room, causing him to fall on his knees at her feet. Rather than cry out, he bit down on his bottom lip. His hands bound behind his back, he couldn't reach out, but leaned toward her, exchanging a sad gaze.

Dathmet cut off his show of solidarity with a swift kick in the ribs.

A resulting "Oof" whooshed from Freeblood when he hit the floor.

"I haven't done a damn thing. This is *her* doing." Dathmet turned on Etain. "What was that you said?"

She breathed in to calm her screaming heart, standing as tall as her battered body would allow. "Let him go."

Dathmet merely laughed and slapped her hard across the face. "You have no power here. *What* do you know?"

A bloodied smile added to her defiant stare. "Not so stupid now. Huh?"

He smirked as he slammed Freeblood's head into the floor with his boot.

"Shit," the boy groaned.

"If you value his life—"

"Dar and Midir are the same!" She closed her eyes against the pull of the shackles. "To kill one is to kill them both."

Dathmet ground his boot into the side of Freeblood's face, who grunted in pain. "I am not a fool, Etain. Dar clearly lives without Midir."

"Now, but not when they were small." Etain heard the boy's labored gasps as he struggled to breathe. "Were you able to best my Dar, even as a child, you would kill Midir, and yourself." The momentary surprise on his face was a satisfying win for her.

"How do I know you speak the truth?"

She leaned her head against her arm. "Why would I lie?"

"To save your man."

"I wouldn't risk my friend for your twisted fantasies."

He released Freeblood and walked toward her. "I won't take your word for it."

She shrugged as best she could. "Then please, go the fuck ahead. It'll save me the effort of killing you later."

"You make me laugh." He leaned into her face. "I'll merely change my target."

In the center of a Los Angeles backstreet crossroads stood three horses, tails swishing, an occasional shake of a head, and droplets of water dripping from their shaggy manes. The streetlights flickered, popped, and went dark.

A pale rider astride a dark horse gazed up the road, her light eyes piercing through the night. "I'm not liking this place. It's too noisy." Her voice sounded musical with its soft Irish lilt.

On the other side, a dark rider shifted on the bare back of a pale horse, her eyes as light as her sister's, peered down the road. "Noisy, but the lights are enchantin'."

A third rider in between the two sat atop a painted horse of dark and light. She stared straight ahead. Like her mount, she was a mix, the dark and light of her skin constantly shifting. The light streak at her right temple aglow, she shook her wet, dark hair.

"The demon moved prior to what we agreed. Otherwise, we would have come at our favorite time in the dead of night. Focus, sisters. Our client expects a quick delivery."

"Alive or dead?" asked the pale rider, who continued watching her part of the road.

"Alive," sighed the painted rider. "But he didn't say in what condition."

The dark one sucked in a breath and licked her lips. "I can taste her. She's a strong one."

The pale sister sniffed the air. "I can smell her. She isn't far."

"I feel her power." The sister of dark and light smirked. "She'll not make this easy. She will fight."

The three smiled.

"He'll pay a high price for this one." The third rider glanced at one. "Phee." Then the other. "Phoe. Are you ready, sisters?"

Demon Brother

As the sun set and darkness fell over the camp, the swordplay between Dar and Taurnil came to an end with no apparent champion. The group broke apart, some arguing over who the actual winner was, others remarking on the attacks and parries used, while others prepared for the night's meal. Over a light dinner of meat, cheese, and bread washed down with warm ale, the talk turned to plans for the next day.

"We are not sure of where we go yet," Dar shared with the group. "I have every faith it will become clear tomorrow. However it turns out, it will be a hard ride." His gaze passed over each person. "Other than my Black Blades, if you cannot keep up or feel it is too much, please turn back now. Any breaks we take will be just long enough to water the horses."

Not one blinked or made a sound. A momentary pang filled Dar's heart. Everyone was in for the long haul.

"I am honored by your loyalty. Thank you. Any questions?" With none forthcoming, he stood. "Let's get some rest. We have a lady to save and a demon to kill."

As they broke apart, Spirit and Linq approached him. "Dar." Spirit kept her voice low. "May we have a word?"

With a tilt of his head, he waved a hand toward the fire and sat. "What is this about?"

They huddled close, sitting on either side of him. "There are a few things you need to know before we head out," Linq said.

Dar's gaze slid from one to the other. "You should have spoken earlier."

Spirit leaned forward. "If I'm wrong... I'm almost certain I'm not, but if I am, I didn't want to alarm the others."

"I am listening."

"What Renme said after..." Spirit's breath caught. "Sorry."

Linq gave her an understanding nod. "Take your time."

She swallowed and tried again. "Renme mentioned Dathmet and Etain's brother in almost the same breath."

Dar shrugged. "As you said, the demon has her brother. It makes sense."

Spirit pursed her lips. "It's more the *way* she said it. Swee and I thought she meant he took her brother. But the more I think about it, and considering a few other things that happened, I think she was telling us that Robert *is* Dathmet."

Dar leaned back, stretching his legs out in front of him. "What other things?"

Her eyes widened. "You've been there for most of 'em."

He crossed his arms over his chest. "I know. I want to hear your point of view."

"Oh, well. All right." She seemed to settle at that. "There's the mark that appeared on his torso after a fall nobody witnessed or heard." She leaned in close. "A mark that matches the one Inferno and Linq made for the two of you."

"Which happened after Etain left for the blood castle," Linq added.

Dar glanced from one to the other. "What does that have to do with the mark?"

"Our girl blasted that nasty place to hell," Spirit continued. "That's how it happened. She left her mark on him, just like she did you." Her cheeks reddened at Dar's smug expression. "Well, not for the same reasons, naturally. The place was built on blood. Some of it hers, some yours, and some me husband's." Her voice caught. Taking a deep breath, she carried on. "Zorn and Felix too. By destroying *it*, she demolished part of his foundation."

Both men stared at her.

"Zorn and Felix?" Linq asked.

"There was a stranger at your wedding, Dar." The men glanced at one another and shrugged. "Danced with Swee and tried to take her with him, until Zorn stepped in. It's why the dogs made such a ruckus and ran off. They were chasing after Zorn, who chased the stranger." She raised a brow. "I believe it was this demon Dathmet."

Dar scrubbed his knuckles along his jawline. "The dogs I remember, but there were several strangers at the wedding. Well, strangers to me."

"The bastard killed our Ruby. Between her and Felix, she was the protective one. I think she's the reason Zorn and Felix made it back."

Linq cocked his head. "Why?"

"Because it was her head leading the snake of weapons chasing our girl at that bleedin' castle. I saw the atrocity with me own eyes just before she vaporized it. I lent me own magic so she'd get out in time."

The hairs rose on his body. "A *snake* of weapons?"

"Freeblood tested some hairbrained theory and dripped a few drops of his blood on the floor in the great hall. Where they found you, Dar. The bloody place drank it up like a dying man in the desert. After that, it threw everything it had at him."

Dar stared at her.

Spirit furrowed her brows. "She didn't tell you?"

His throat tightened, making it difficult to speak. "She did not nor did Freeblood."

She bit her lip. "Maybe I shouldn't—"

"You have to finish the story." Dar stood and stepped away. "What does Freeblood have to do with the snake?"

She glanced at Linq before continuing. "It went after him first. We couldn't get out of the hall because of the locked doors. Etain had to use her *solar* to get them open. Before we could get out, a dagger came from nowhere and stabbed into her arm. The lass made sure *we* got through the gates and were safe." Her voice became thick as she swiped at her eyes. "I'm sure some of her blood hit the ground. The bleedin' gates slammed shut before she could get out." Her gaze met Dar's. "Then came the snake."

Deep in thought, he stroked his chin. "It explains a few things that happened after your return. She left again in search of the demon."

"Why?" Spirit asked.

"So I would not need to give my blood to save Taurnil."

Her lips tight, she narrowed her eyes. "What're you saying, Dar?"

He shifted on his feet, unable to meet either gaze. "Dathmet is Midir's son, which makes us..." he sucked in a breath and forced himself to look at them, "family. My blood was sufficient."

Spirit jumped up from her seat and took hold of his arm. "It doesn't make him family, love. Blood relation, that's all!"

Linq climbed to his feet. "She is right, Dar. Where Midir was concerned, blood did not mean anything. He never gave two shits about anyone but himself."

Dar's gaze snapped to him. "Except Etain's brother... *Tartarus*! It makes sense now."

"What's that?" Linq asked.

"Something she told me not long ago." Dar raised a hand, stabbing his index finger into the air. "Midir murdered her parents and took the boy. He raised him as his own because he is." Dar turned to Spirit. "You are right. Robert *is* Midir's son, Dathmet."

She gasped, making both men turn. Dar caught her just as her knees buckled. "Spirit!" Linq snatched his canteen, unscrewed the cap, and held it out as Dar helped her sit.

Her hands shaking, she accepted the canteen, but Linq kept hold of it crouching next to her. After a couple of sips, she wiped her mouth with the back of her hand. "Ta. Sorry."

Dar squatted in front of her. "What is wrong, Spirit?"

"He sat at our table." Her gaze met his. "Met people he shouldn't have met."

"None of us knew at the time," Linq said.

"Me husband did. From the moment he met the boy, Inferno knew something was wrong, but I didn't listen. Etain was so happy to have him back, I ignored me husband's instincts."

Dar placed his hands on her shoulders. "The fault lies with Midir and his conniving son, not you. They took advantage of your decency and our faith in family. Linq is right. He duped us all."

"Speaking of duped, let us not forget this morning," Linq added.

Dar released the mage and stood. "What?"

"Etain was surprised to see me in the forge, remember?" Linq's gaze went to Spirit. "She came in to tell us she was going to town and was certain she had run into me upstairs."

Dar crossed his arms. "A few days ago, we woke later than usual. I went to the kitchen to make us breakfast. Freeblood showed up not long after, so we made something for him and Faux as well. He went on his merry way, but when I walked back into our bedroom, it was a mess. I found a man dragging Etain out the balcony doors."

Spirit raised a hand to her mouth. "Oh, Dar!"

"I recognized him. Hell knows, I have seen enough of the man to know him anywhere." He shook his head. "It was Midir's righthand man, Raum."

"But Midir is dead," Linq said.

Dar shrugged. "Aye. So now the son is the master."

"How did you stop him, Dar?" Spirit appeared ready to cry.

"A blood binding," he said, sitting on the ground in front of the two, "to keep her from crossing realms without me."

She touched his arm. "But the protection spell. How'd he get past it?"

Dar blew out a breath. "Raum must have entered while it was weak and at Robert's invitation." He waved a disgruntled hand. "The entire debacle when Faux tried to destroy the protection spell around Laugharne. And stayed until after it was strengthened. It is the only way he could come and go at will."

"By the stars! You believe this Raum impersonated me?"

"I do. It explains her morning sickness, something she has not had. Thinking he was you, she was not prepared for what lay beneath the glamour."

"There's something else I've wondered about all this time." Spirit reached for the canteen, sipped again, and replaced the cap. "When you came back from Nunnehi, after Midir's attempt to drive you mad, you went to LOKI. Why?"

Dar raised a brow, surprised by the question. "I felt her leave from Nunnehi. At the time, it infuriated me." Guilt washed over him, knowing he treated her badly. He thought she left him because of it. "My head was a mess," he said apologetically. Although his friends knew of Midir's attempt to drive him mad, neither was aware of how he blamed Etain. "But when I returned with Wolfe and Elfin, I could not locate her, which seemed strange. Then I remembered Savage's threat to make Etain pay for her interference when the High Council attempted to arrest me."

"Aye, well..." Spirit murmured. "I'd have liked to see her try." She looked Dar in the eyes. "Swee told me about the day you returned from Nunnehi. Etain was at the house but didn't know until Wolfe and Elfin told her. They weren't sure where you'd gone but caught a glimpse of what was on the other side of the portal you opened. When they described the golden doors, she knew where you'd gone."

"The misconnection has happened on several occasions."

"I'm telling you, it's that demon. He's blocking you from each other," Spirit said. "If you'd known she was in trouble this morning, you wouldn't have needed Swee to tell you."

Dar watched the others settle in for the night. "At the end of the day, he is still Etain's brother. I have to be careful."

"How much do you know of her parents? If Midir's *his* father but not Etain's, how did Midir know the mother?" Linq asked. "It bears investigating."

Dar came to his feet. "Well, it is not happening tonight, and I do not want one word of this shared with anyone, not even the Queen of the Elves." He raised a brow at Linq. "I will do my own investigating. Should I need assistance, I will do the asking."

Linq raised both hands as he stood. "Whatever you say, boss. I am off to sleep. Good night."

Spirit and Dar spoke at the same time, wishing him a good night in return.

"You know, Dar," Spirit said quietly. "Robert's not been seen since this happened. I think it reinforces the idea that he and Dathmet are the same person."

"Robert may be gone for good, Spirit. It is our job to ensure Etain does not share the same fate."

Krymerian Vault

Freeblood squirmed, trying to free his hands, which resulted in a fist to his bruised face.

"Is that necessary?" Etain asked in disgust. "Killing him isn't going to get you anything."

"It will pleasure me deeply, watching the horror on your face as his life slips away because of you," Dathmet cooed, coming close behind her.

Further appalled, she tried to distance her body from his, but the movement encouraged him to tighten his hold, biting into her shoulder as he caressed her breasts. She arched away, fighting the urge to scream. Intent on his pleasures, he drank deeply. His excitement vibrated through his body and bloomed against her buttocks. She desperately needed to distract him.

"This is between me and you, Robert. Let the boy go."

He laughed at her persistence. "The *boy* will run straight to Dar. No. He's in as deep as you." He turned her to face him. "One more thing." He brought his face to hers. "My name is Dathmet. Your Robert is gone. Dead. Any family ties you held with *him* mean nothing to me."

"Keep your demon hands off the lady," Freeblood hissed from behind, rolling to the side to avoid a kick aimed at his head.

"Shut up, Alamir," Dathmet snarled. Cupping her face in his hands, he slipped his tongue over her lips, licking the fresh blood oozing from the reopened cut. Disgusted, her body jerked. With an evil smirk, he said to Freeblood. "Watch and learn, little man, the proper way to use a woman." He sank his teeth into her neck and grabbed her buttocks, pulling her hard against him.

Freeblood rolled toward the wall, pushed up to his feet, and ran at the demon but the guard rushed at him from the side. Their impact slammed Freeblood into the opposite wall, knocking him unconscious.

Tears burned in Etain's eyes at the sound of the gruesome thud and Freeblood's body dropping to the floor. "*Stop,*" she whispered through clenched teeth.

"Give me what I want, and all this will end," he whispered gently, his red eyes soft as he stroked her hair. "The vault, *mon petit*, and all will be set free."

She could hardly believe what she heard. "You will let us go?"

"From your miseries, yes. From this place, no." He sneered, gliding a finger along the side of her face. "Of course, I may change my mind about you. Your blood increases in richness by the moment. I believe I'm becoming an addict."

"I would guess it has more to do with the shit you put in my blood than the blood itself."

He smirked. "Then we move on to the next phase."

A snap of his fingers set the guards in motion. Etain stole a glance at Freeblood. Panic ripped through her, seeing him slumped against the wall. She closed her eyes for a moment and focused on his form again. This time, she noticed the rise and fall of his chest and sighed in relief.

A commotion coming from beyond the large doors raised the hairs on the back of her neck. Dread filled her heart when she recognized the scream.

The guards burst into the room, an angry Faux pinned between them. Seeing Etain, she screamed again, trying with all her might to escape. "Etain!" Her gaze went to the other form beyond her sister. "Freeblood!" Her black eyes flashed at Dathmet. "You lying asshole."

"Strap her up, boys," he commanded.

"Dathmet," Etain said sternly, "she has nothing to do with this."

He whirled around and slapped her. "Doesn't she? With her demon powers stripped, her only use is to persuade you to my cause. Now tell me, or little sister will suffer greater than you can imagine."

One of the guards held Faux as the other tossed a set of shackles over a large wooden beam across the ceiling. Her wrists were bound, and she, like Etain, was left to dangle.

Etain noticed how her belly had grown considerably since she'd last seen her and wondered if the child belonged to Freeblood, or if Spirit miscalculated the death of Dar's seed.

Dathmet walked across the room and grabbed a handful of hair on the frightened girl. "Now, High Lady, what price will this one pay for your silence?" Faux hissed at him when he yanked her head back.

Etain realized her mind was less fuzzy. A plus on the one hand, but a negative on the pain scale. "Let me ask *you* a question." She ran her tongue over her lips. "How do you know this so-called prophecy to be true?"

He seemed intrigued but didn't loosen his hold on Faux. "My father's library holds the keys to many secrets."

"There's a book that tells of this Krymerian vault? Yet it says nothing of its power?"

He shoved Faux's head forward and stalked toward Etain. "Of course, it does. I merely needed a distraction to contain my giddiness over the implications." After another hard slap, he wrapped his hands around her throat.

Etain straightened and lengthened her neck as best she could, but her position made it difficult.

"The prophecy claims the blood of the half-breed changes everything." His fingers tightened. "*You* are the only half-assed Krymerian to be born in over five hundred years. The secret lies in you, not some stupid book."

"You don't know sh—" Her air supply cut off by his grip, blackness crept in.

Just as her body went lax, Freeblood yelled, "Hey, asshole!" taking the inflamed demon by surprise, running into him from the side, and ripping his hands from around Etain's throat. Freeblood didn't stop until Dathmet hit the wall. The Alamir dodged the hands that grabbed at him and ducked just out of reach.

Etain coughed as the air returned to her lungs. A spark of power came alive in her belly, deepening her focus and building the fire. While Freeblood ran for his life, the heat inside of her rose, her eyes lighting up just as a demon guard reached out for the crazed man. With every drop of energy available, she blasted a straight line of *solar* at the demon, disintegrating him on the spot. Recovered from his impact with the wall, Dathmet dashed to Faux and yanked her head back, placing a dagger at her throat.

"I'll kill her now if you don't stop."

Freeblood froze. Etain's eyes turned dark, and she collapsed against her bonds. Dathmet turned to the other guard. "Get another injection." The demon guard turned to leave. "Make sure this one is stronger. And that one..." his gaze flashed on Freeblood, "send in another guard to truss him up like a pig to market. I want no more surprises."

"As you wish, milord." The guard disappeared through the door.

Within moments, another demon soldier entered the room, ropes in hand. He grabbed Freeblood by the collar of his shirt and dragged him to a corner.

"Now, little mama," Dathmet said. "Let's see what we can do to entice your sister to open that luscious mouth of hers."

"She won't tell you anything, fucker," Faux spat.

He laughed. "I can get her to open up in ways she has never dreamed."

The guard returned with the syringe and vial of green liquid. Freeblood and Faux watched him pass it to Dathmet, who filled the hypodermic and injected the green serum into Etain's arm.

"We'll wait a few moments and begin again." He set his instruments on the table. "Quil, while we wait for Lady Etain, fetch the commander and bring him here."

"Yes, your lordship." He saluted and left the room.

Dathmet sat in the chair where Etain's introduction into hell began. "Someone get a bucket of cold water."

Just as the other demon guard dashed out the door, a man with close-cropped gray hair, dressed smartly in a dark military uniform, stepped into the room. "Yes, my lord?"

"Thamuz." The demon stood. "I need a full report on the whereabouts of the good lady's bothersome husband."

"I have riders scoping the countryside." His gaze ventured to the lady, taking in the state of her. "There is no sign of him yet. We should know more by nightfall."

"Excellent. She'll be ready soon, so it's back to work for me. You are dismissed, but at the first hint of the bastard, I want to know."

"Milord." Thamuz raised a brow. "A word in private?"

"You are dismissed, Thamuz."

"At the risk of your anger, milord, we must talk."

Dathmet raised a brow but tipped his head and walked with him to the door. Before stepping out, he turned to the guard. "Quil, watch that one there." He pointed at Freeblood. "When Nergal returns with the bucket, tell him he will have the pleasure of performing my wishes on the dark one."

In the hallway, the men stepped away from the door. "What game are you playing, Dathmet? We spread the stories amongst the men to keep them on board, but that's all they were meant to be. Stories. You were not to mistreat the lady."

"She drove me to it. The woman is infuriating!" He clenched a hand, one eye twitching. "She refuses to cooperate or tell me what I need to know. She actually believes she can get through to Robert, bring out his humanity." His grin carried a lethal edge. "I have to *show* her the boy she knew is dead and *know* with every fiber of her being she is *mine*. That *this* is her life from this point on."

"How little you understand, boy. You risk losing everything by bringing her to this place and double the odds with your games."

"I had no choice!" He lunged at the commander, who stepped back. "They... *She* ripped apart my foundation, my support system. The annihilation of my blood castle nearly ended me. Then having to fight my way out of that Laugharne hellhole. I should have burned it to the ground. My resources are spent, Thamuz. I came here to recoup, and her blood will revitalize me."

Thamuz pursed his lips. "You have backed her into a corner and left her with no options." He walked away a few steps, placing much needed space between himself and the out-of-control demon.

"Options? She has plenty. Her friends can either live or die—her option. That brat she carries can be easily disposed of or it can live—her option."

Thamuz whipped around. "She's *pregnant*?"

For the first time in a long time, Dathmet resembled the boy he used to be—unsure, nervous.

Thamuz's eyes nearly bulged out of his head. "The daughter of a Krymerian princess pregnant with a Krymerian babe. And you treat her like this? Fill her veins with that vile poison! Have you no sense left, boy?"

Dathmet's flaming hair lashed out, his eyes flared, but still, he stepped back from the angry man. "It belongs to *him*."

"It does not matter who the father is! The child is *Krymerian*. Once born, it can be molded to our own designs, raised in the old ways of the Krymerians. None of this camaraderie with worthless races." Thamuz walked toward him. "But for that to happen, you cannot treat the mother like a whore. Do what you want with the other one, but Etain... Release her, clean her up, and treat her with respect."

The demon glared at his commander. "I will not suffer the bastard of that shit. All I need is her blood. I do not wish to share my throne with anyone, not even her."

Thamuz breathed in and released it slowly. "When that child is born, it won't have any idea who its father is. Who better to step in his place than one who is as Krymerian as he? That babe is the future you speak of. Raise it as your own, teach it the old ways, make it the conduit with which to expand your control. Kill the man but honor the woman. The child will need its mother."

Dathmet crossed his arms over his chest. "How is it you know of her history?"

Thamuz lifted his chin. "Our benefactor filled me in for this very reason. You must step back. Give her room to breathe."

"How do you propose we control *her*? Even if he's dead, *she'll* remember who the father is. She'll make sure it doesn't forget."

"Leverage. If the two you have in there aren't enough to persuade her to your way of thinking, I have another who will assuredly sway her loyalties. Do what you wish with them but stop torturing her. You will not win her over with such treatment. Show her the respect she deserves."

Dathmet snorted again. "And the mindspeak?"

"Use the gifts your father gave you. Block it. It worked wonders between her and him. It should be just as effective with the child."

"You're dismissed, Thamuz." He turned toward the door.

The commander saluted, hopeful he would do as he asked, and left his master to his interrogations.

Dathmet returned to the room, picked up the bucket at Etain's feet, and doused her with the cold water. Amidst her sputters, spits, and gasps, the demon hastened her consciousness with a back-handed slap.

Freeblood growled and jerked against his bonds. Faux screamed obscenities. Dathmet grippe Etain's chin, shaking her head from side to side.

"Wake up, sunshine. You're holding us up." Shaking a bit harder, he deepened his voice. "Wake up, Etain."

Her eyes rolled, trying to focus on his twisted, red face, but it proved too much. Her head lolled to the side.

"Perhaps I'm being too rough, milady," he said softly. "You prefer a gentle touch?" Supporting her against his body, his hand glided lightly over her skin, raising gooseflesh. "That feels nice, doesn't it?" His hand roamed over her curves and moved around to her backside while his lips caressed her ear. "Such a nice ass. You make me hunger for you." His breathing grew heavier with each touch. "Now, wake up, or I'll have to tear that brat right out of little sister's belly."

It took a moment for his words to sink in. "What?"

Dathmet spoke over his shoulder. "Nergal, would you do the honors?"

Freeblood jerked against his guard but was helplessly bound. Faux screamed when the demon displayed his dagger and cut across her belly, leaving a long, bloody mark in its wake.

Etain forced her head up. "Faux?"

Dathmet answered on her behalf. "She wants you to tell me where the vault is and how to open it."

"Vault?" Her eyes rolled.

"Etain, don't listen to him!" Freeblood yelled. His demon guard punched him in the face and kicked him in the ribs several times forcing a moan from his lips as he curled into a ball.

"Yes, *mon petit.*" Dathmet pressed his body to hers while his hands continued to stroke her body. A thumb rubbed over a nipple as the other hand massaged her shoulder. "We need you to open up to us." His hand moved lower. "Open up and let me in." A single finger slipped between her nether lips, making her jerk.

"Stop." She tried to push him away, whimpering at the pull of her arms. "What have you done to me?"

"Nothing like I'm going to do to your little sister. Look. It's already started." He leaned his head against hers and turned, giving her a clear view of a crying Faux, her blood trickling from her belly and down her legs.

"Etain!" Her demon guard sliced again, forming an *x* on her belly. "No! Stop it! Stop it!"

Dathmet licked her neck as he continued his strokes. "Come now, little cunt. Give in to me."

Etain moaned as his rhythm increased and his teeth sank into her skin again. "Stop," she panted. "Please. Stop."

"Your sister bleeds for you."

She rolled her eyes in Faux's direction, barely able to hold up her head, and leaned heavily against him. "Let her go."

"Tell me what I want to hear, little bit, and she will suffer no more."

The voice sounded like her brother's.

"But I told you."

He pushed away, making her cry out at the pull of the shackles on her wrists. Dathmet raised a finger. "Kill her."

"No!" Freeblood's howl sounded as though it had come from deep within his gut.

Nergal raised his blade.

Tears in her eyes, Etain whispered, "Let them go. I'll—"

"No, Etain!" Freeblood yelled. "He'll kill us anyway."

The double doors burst open, their hinges screaming as though they too suffered from the pain within the room. Etain heard Faux jerk against her shackles and Freeblood struggle against his ropes. Lost in her pain, she did not respond, but heard the scuffle of feet as they crossed the stone floor. A muffled voice made her cringe.

Please, not Spirit.

She forced her head up and supported it against her upstretched arm but saw only shapes and shadows, squinting to make out the faint outline of a person.

A whiff of perfume made her heart beat faster. She remembered the fragrance. As a child, she'd associated it with friendship, love, and comfort. A safe haven. Someone she trusted. Someone she knew she could still trust, although the woman had only recently come back into her life.

Etain trembled. *It can't be.* But the five-foot-ten frame with auburn curls told her otherwise. *The Alamir world is not a place for humans.* She squeezed her eyes shut and opened them, the hairs on her body rising. Baring her teeth, she hissed.

Bound and gagged, her arm grasped tightly by a gray-haired man Etain had not seen before, was a bedraggled and bloody Jackie P.

Deal with the Demon

His brain fabricating various scenarios his wife must be enduring, Dar retired to his secluded part of the lake. His rational mind knew such thoughts were senseless distractions caused by his fears, yet the irrational persisted. He had to overcome them to save her.

Seated at the water's edge, he fingered the necklace she had given him—two dragons, nose to nose, their tails intertwined. The memory brought a slight smile to his lips, but quickly faded. "I think it would be better suited for you right now, *a chuisle*."

Dar spread his wings and wrapped himself within their warmth. *She is strong. Our children are strong. I know they fight.*

Assured by his new mantra, he eventually closed his eyes and drifted into sleep.

A great white unicorn with golden eyes galloped into the clearing just beyond where Dar slept, followed by a sleek, red panther, the moonlight sparkling in her deep blue eyes. They jumped about, laughing and chasing each other until Dar woke. Seeing his children at play made him smile.

The play became more intense with the jabs of the unicorn's horn coming closer to the panther's skin, while the claws of the big cat sliced threateningly toward her brother's flanks. Dar showed no concern. He understood the rough play between Krymerian children, so he settled back, his eyes slowly closing again.

The smell of blood...

Dar awoke, his senses alert. His children were still at play, but something had changed. The white coat of the unicorn was marred by claw marks, blood oozing from the wounds. Dar sat up and found the panther across the clearing, crouched, teeth bared, ready to pounce. The unicorn's head lowered, prepared to charge. Dar scrambled to his feet and was in between the two before further harm could be inflicted.

"What is all this? You play too rough, children. This will stop."

The panther roared. "She has given up, Da."

The unicorn neighed. "She still fights."

"What are you talking about, children?"

"She grows weak, brother," the panther cried, her voice becoming more of a young girl's than an animal's growl. "She cannot fight him much longer. We must help."

"I want to help too, but you know we cannot." The unicorn's voice changed to that of a young boy. "That would mean exposing us to his magic. We are not ready."

"Children, tell me what is happening."

Tears in his eyes, the unicorn shook his great head. "I cannot say the words, Da."

"Da must know, brother," the panther screamed.

His heart thundering in his chest, Dar forced himself to speak calmly. "Son, tell me. Help me so I can save Mama."

The unicorn stomped his forelegs and snorted. "He touches her in ways he shouldn't. He is a bad man. He won't leave her alone."

Dar's anger came to the surface. "Who? Who does this?"

His son ducked his head, shaking it again.

His daughter uttered the unspeakable words. "The big, red man, Da. The one who hurt you. He is doing bad things to Mama. She is so weak."

"Tartarus!"

"Da!" his son screamed. "We need you. You must wake! Da..."

A deep voice penetrated his dream, bringing him back to reality.

"Dar, wake up. It is time to go."

He opened his eyes. *Why is Taurnil here?* Dar glanced at his surroundings. Although it was a dream, he knew the message was real.

"Be right there," he croaked, his throat dry and raw.

He retracted his wings as he stood, strapped on his swords, and joined the group on the other side of the lake where he handed his pack to a Black Blade. "Prepare my horse. We ride in ten." The sun on the rise, Dar walked to the others, accepting bread and cheese from Linq. "Taurnil, are you ready to be the High Lord this morning?"

The young Elf furrowed his brows. "Excuse me?"

"Hang on," said Linq. "Where are we going? Did you get through to Etain?"

"I believe he has taken her to the town where she found her brother."

Linq swallowed a mouthful of bread. "Deudraeth? If we push hard, we can be there day after tomorrow."

"No time for that." Dar popped a bit of cheese into his mouth. "Things have worsened."

"The Blades and I can keep up, but neither the Alamir nor the horses can. How do you propose—"

"A portal."

Linq washed down his food with a gulp of coffee. "Clean up and move people."

"What do you need me to do, Dar?" Taurnil asked humbly.

"You shall lead them in as the High Lord of Kaos." He winked more as a way to keep himself in check rather than calm the Elf. If he lost his cool at this stage, everything would be lost.

Taurnil appeared stunned but saluted his superior. "I will not disappoint you, milord."

"Do it for Etain, not me." He finished his coffee and turned to Linq. "Tell us the layout of the town while we load up."

"The main part is somewhat of a grid."

Dar raised a brow. "Somewhat?"

"Her brother's apothecary is a block over from the main street at the north end of town."

"Does the main street run straight through?"

"It does."

Dar turned to Aramis and Ra. "We will portal just outside of Deudraeth. Take half the Blades with you, Taurnil in the lead. They know we are coming but will not expect us to split. Make a big show of riding through town. I want them to know we have arrived and are ready for a fight. Head toward the apothecary at the other end of town."

Ra picked up his saddle. "And if they resist?"

"Kill 'em."

Taurnil bristled. "What if they are citizens protecting their town?"

Spirit cleared her throat, turning the men toward her. "If they attack, they're against us. None of them deserve to live."

Although taken aback by Spirit's passion, Dar agreed with everything she said. He faced Taurnil. "Are you up for this?"

The Elf stared at her for a short time and dragged his gaze to the High Lord. "*Ég er tilbúinn* (I am ready)."

Dar clapped his hands. "Let's move out."

Once the all-clear was given, Dar chanted a portal spell and waited until everyone passed through before joining them on the Deudraeth side.

Linq noted the skies as the portal closed. "Typical northern weather—gray clouds and cold wind." He rubbed his arms briskly. "Is she here?"

Goosebumps raised on Dar's arms. "The link is strong. They are not far away." He turned to the others. "Eol, take six of your best Blades and head toward the north side of town. Come in slow and meet Taurnil's group in the center. We will rendezvous at the apothecary." He turned. "Riko, take the east side with another group. Hold your position there. Sion, with me." His gaze stopped on every person in turn. "I want this place surrounded. I will not tolerate surprises."

The Dragon patrol headed for the south end, riding at a quick clip. Eol's crew rode with Dar to the west while Riko moved to the east, all skirting around the edges of town. Once Dar was in position, Eol rode on to come in from the north.

Dar turned to Spirit and Linq. "You two come with me. Sion, remain here and hold the perimeter. No one gets through."

Dalos held up a hand. "Permission to speak, sir?"

"What is it, soldier?"

"What if someone tries to leave?"

"*No one*, soldier. Not until I have my wife."

Dalos saluted and stepped back.

"I expect the townsfolk will keep to their own business. I am counting on Taurnil and the others to keep Dathmet's dogs busy while we investigate the apothecary. The way to my wife is there."

Dathmet carried Etain into his private chambers and gently slipped her into a freestanding tub filled with hot, soapy water, fragrant with the scent of lavender. She cried out when it touched the wounds on her body.

"Take care with her, Lilith."

At first glance, the small, dark-haired servant appeared human, nothing notable until she smiled. Her exaggerated incisors gave her away for the demon she was. "Yes, milord. I've been practicing ever since you told me she was coming. You tend to yourself, sir. I'll have her cleaned up in no time and waiting for you in your bed."

"Make sure she drinks the wine."

"Yes, milord."

He stepped across the tunnel and into a luxurious study with leather sofas, a rich Persian rug, simple fireplace, and paneled walls. It wasn't the room he would have chosen to deal with this unexpected matter, but there wasn't time to shuffle the intrusion to another.

"Ladies!" His eyes on the sisters, he quietly closed the door behind him. Although his heart beat a little too fast, he kept his flames in check and his tone light. He couldn't afford to show his hand to these Banshee. "What are you doing here? We agreed we would—"

Phie, the sister of dark and light, smirked as she sauntered around a sofa. "We have a problem only you can solve."

Dathmet avoided her advance by stepping in the opposite direction. "I have my own problems. What can I possibly do for you?"

She stopped, the smirk still on her lips. "Yer aware of our Trodaire Games?"

Noticing the movement of the other two, he turned to Phie. "I don't have time—"

She walked toward him as her sisters closed in from their opposing directions. "The last games were," she looked away as though searching for the right word, "brutal. We lost our best fighter."

Dathmet raised a brow and shrugged. "Hard times."

A sternness flashed over her features, then melted into a serene smile that made his skin crawl. "We'll need payment sooner than discussed."

He laughed despite his uneasiness. "That's not possible. You'll have to wait."

Phie's gaze slid to her sisters as she drew a dagger from her belt. Quick as a stinging bee, she pounced on the demon, her sisters moving in with her. The tip of the blade hovered just below his chin. "I must disagree with ya. However, we're willing to forego our previous agreement and take our payment in flesh."

His senses screamed to lash out with his flames, but he dragged in a slow, deep breath and forced himself to remain calm. He was good at negotiation. He would negotiate.

"There are three in the lounge. Take them. The one you brought should do well enough, and the Alamir looks to be a fair fighter. His woman would make an excellent breeder."

Phie's deadly smile reminded him of the warnings he'd heard when dealing with the Banshee. Damn Thamuz for putting him in this position.

"Oh, aye. The lady is a *trodaire láidir*, a strong fighter, but human. The Alamir might last a few hours. Both would serve as an interesting intro, but no, we need someone with the resilience and fortitude to reign over the games. A new champion." She pressed her face into his. "A half-breed."

He pushed away from her and stepped back. "Either take the three and go or abide by the original agreement."

Phoe pushed past her sisters. "We'll take the one across the hall. She has the Krymerian blood and that of Dra—"

"Dreaded humans," Phie spoke over her. "It's what makes her lethal." She glared at the other two. "We'll take her and be done with you."

"She is *my* prize, not yours. Get out before I call my—"

One by one, the Banshee joined in their keening, the volume rising to an unbearable screech. Dathmet covered his ears and burst into flames, dashing toward one, then another, trying to set any one of them alight. Anything to silence them. After several failed attempts, he realized each stood in a puddle of water. Wherever they moved, it moved with them. They would never burn.

"All right!" he shouted. "All right! Stop!" Once the noise ceased, he lowered his hands. "I will not give *her* to you." All three opened their mouths to resume the keening, but he held up a hand. "I have an alternative. It isn't a quick fix, but one I believe will prove more profitable in the long run."

Phie nodded to her sisters, whose mouths snapped closed as they moved to stand on either side of her. "What's yer proposal?"

"The one you desire is pregnant. Its father is Krymerian. You can have it once it's born, a month or two, which is nothing in the demon world. Raise it in your ways, train it to fight, teach it that fighting is all there is. No bad habits to break, no barriers to overcome. Nothing but a slave to your games. A true champion. A half-breed."

Phie turned to consult with her sisters. Dathmet glanced at the clock over the fireplace. He had to get rid of the Banshee before the Krymerian showed.

The sister of dark and light turned to him. "We accept."

He closed his eyes for a moment. "I will be in touch when the child is born."

"We will attend the *breithe*, initiate our champion in the way of the Banshee. We will be watchin'." In an instant, they were gone, leaving three puddles in their wake.

⁂

"Lilith, please, you must help me," Etain pleaded.

"Of course, milady. The master would not be happy if I didn't help you in any way I can." She gingerly washed the lash marks across her back and on her arms.

Her words encouraged Etain. "I must get out of here. You have to show me the way out."

The maid didn't falter in her duties. "Be patient, milady. He won't leave you here alone. He's taken a great liking to you."

Etain ran her hands through her hair as she breathed out, trying to get her head straight. "No, Lilith. I must go now."

"Why would you want to leave without the master?" she asked good-naturedly. "I admit, he's been a bit rough with you today, but once you submit to his wishes, you will learn he is quite generous."

"I don't belong here. This isn't right. I'm married to Dar."

Lilith laughed lightly, washing her hair. "Oh, we all make mistakes, milady. The master is aware of how young you are and is willing to overlook it. You will see." She rinsed out the shampoo and applied a sweet-smelling conditioner, working it through the silver tangles. "Things will be better after tonight."

"Tonight?" Etain tensed as she fought the fog in her brain. "What's tonight?"

"Tsk, tsk," the maid clucked. "You are so impatient, milady. The master is in control. Do not worry."

Etain moaned as the water cascaded over her head. Her body shook from a combination of the abuses suffered earlier in the day, lack of food, and the constant struggle to keep Dar blocked.

"I know what you need, miss." Lilith hurried out of the room and returned with a glass of red wine. "This will calm your nerves." She handed the deep tawny drink to Etain. "You're lucky to have caught the interest of the master," she said in a dreamy voice. "He is so magnificent." She sighed. "If only he would see me the way he..." Catching herself, she cleared her throat and reached for a towel.

Etain viewed the liquid with a wary eye, swirled it in the glass, and sniffed it before taking a small sip. Lilith noticed her hesitation. "It is safe to drink, milady." Seeing the doubt in her eyes, she reached for the glass, which Etain gladly handed to her. The young demon took a good-sized sip. "See? Nothing to worry about."

She motioned for Etain to stand as she held out an oversized towel to wrap around her. Reassured, Etain enjoyed a drink of the dark liquid. Its richness warmed her insides and helped her relax. She finished the glass as Lilith towel dried her hair.

With Etain seated in front of the mirror, the maid combed the tangles from her hair. "Another glass, milady?"

"No."

Lilith smoothed the last few tangles, placed the comb on the counter, and reached for a jar.

"What's that for?" Etain asked.

A deep voice startled both women. "Hand me the balm, Lilith. I'll take care of the rest." The demon servant placed a hand over her heart as Dathmet stepped into the steamy room.

"Oh, you scared the life out of me, milord."

"You've done an exquisite job, my dear. You are dismissed."

"Thank you, sir." With a curtsy to her master, she patted Etain lightly on the shoulder, "All will be well, milady," and hurried out of the room.

Etain met his gaze in the mirror. "How does someone like *you* evoke such devotion?"

He laughed lightly as he removed the lid of the jar and dipped his fingers into the salve. "I treat my minions quite well." He rubbed the concoction between his hands. "I'm sure you find it hard to believe that I have a soft spot for my household servants. They take good care of me, and I return the gesture in kind." Electric shocks ran through her body when his hands touched her shoulders, working down her back. His gentle touch surprised her. "If you wouldn't fight me so hard, you would see that side of me."

"I don't care to see *any* part of you. You disgust me."

He smiled into the mirror. "As long as you're here, that's all that matters."

She stood, wrapping the towel tightly around her, and stalked into the bedroom. "I will fight you with everything I have even if it kills me."

Wiping his hands with a towel, he casually walked into the room behind her. "Fight all you want. I welcome your struggles," he said in a cool voice. "It makes the conquest that much sweeter. And you won't die. I won't allow it."

"God!" Holding her towel with one hand, she threw the other into the air as she paced the room. "Take my blood and find your fucking secret but stop with this seduction."

"Seduction?" He circled around her.

"This game." A flush crept over her skin, her heart beating faster as he neared. "This wasn't part of the deal." She pushed her hair behind an ear. *Why is it so warm in here?*

"There'll be no need for seduction, milady. You'll be quite willing in a few moments." He slithered up behind her, gently combing his fingers through her hair.

"Shut up," she whispered, jerking her head. "Dar is my heart."

He swept her hair to one side and kissed her shoulder, slowly moving up to her neck. "You will forget him. You are mine."

"No," she breathed, cringing from his touch. "You didn't want me before."

"I've not experienced anyone like you. It seems our families are eternally linked." He wrapped an arm around her and placed his hand over hers grasping the towel. "I am surrendering to the legacy."

She shook her head to clear her thoughts. "What legacy? Let me go."

"Not until we are satisfied." He leaned his head against hers and spoke softly, making her skin crawl. "We are descended from Lyoness and are meant to be together. We will rebuild the Krymerian race with my pure blood and your human taint. They will be stronger than ever before, and I will rule over all."

"*I* chose Dar."

"Lyoness was meant for him. You are meant for me." Moving her hair to the other side, he trailed kisses along her shoulder to her other ear.

"Fuck your prophecies. Dar is—"

"Stop saying his name!" He grasped a handful of hair and pulled her head back sharply. "He will be dead long before he gets close to this place. Once I take you, he will be dead to you."

She fought against the fire inside of her. "You will *never* take him from me."

"You are wrong, Lady Etain. I've taken precautions to ensure your complete submission." He rubbed his cheek against hers while his free hand joined the other, taking hold of the towel and slowly loosening her grip.

"The wine," he panted. "The luscious, deep wine." He cupped each breast, gently massaging as he pressed his growing desire against her. "It was laced with an effective aphrodisiac. I know you're feeling it. Let go. Give in to it. I will show you pleasures you've never experienced."

"I've heard this garbage before." Her mind raced. There was something she must remember. *Something with the wine. What was it?* "Lilith drank the wine."

He whispered into her ear, "It has no effect on demons. It is meant for humans. I can feel your body's submission. It wants me."

Betrayed by her body's response to his touch, she worked harder to resist.

If only I could reach my demon. Forget that, use your brain. Hit him where it hurts.

"As long as you don't mind sloppy thirds."

He stiffened behind her. "What are you talking about?"

She smiled, knowing she'd struck a nerve. "First Dar, then Midir. Now you. It seems the VonNeshta men *have* made me their whore, after all."

He grabbed her roughly by the shoulders and turned her to face him. "Midir didn't have you."

She raised a brow. "Were you there?"

The confusion was clear on his face. "He told me... He said he surprised himself that day."

Etain laughed. "You believed the craftiest liar in the world?" Turning the tables on him felt positively evil. "I suppose you think this baby inside me is Dar's?"

He pushed away from her.

She laughed at the doubt on his face, happy to push harder. "You don't measure up to either man."

His hair a torrent of flames, he grabbed her hand and forced her to touch his hard cock. "Enough to rip you from asshole to navel, you ungrateful cunt."

Her heart skipped a beat, feeling his large member pulsing against her palm. After a hard swallow, she responded with a sarcastic air. "Little boy."

He knocked her across the room and was on her in two strides, throwing her onto the bed. She kicked at him, trying to squirm away, but he caught her ankles in each hand and pulled her toward him. Dathmet leaned in and bit the inside of her thigh, holding her hips in a death grip as he drank her blood.

"Stop!" she screamed.

He licked the trickles of blood, moving closer to the V between her legs, and nuzzled briefly into the blonde nest. His tongue flicked between her lips. She arched her back, her hands fisting in the sheets at the jolt of white heat streaking through her.

"You said you would do anything."

She wished she could calm her screaming heart and rip off his head. "Where are Faux and Freeblood?"

"Where we left them. Did you think I'd let them go before payment was made in full?"

Etain wanted to kick him, but his ironlike grip allowed no movement whatsoever. "Why Jackie? She shouldn't be in this realm."

He laughed. "That was pure genius. I wish I could take credit for it, but I cannot. Thamuz came up with that ploy. He knew her presence would seal your compliance. You will pay for their freedom with your own."

"You lied to me," she said through clenched teeth.

"As I recall..." He climbed onto the bed between her legs. "I didn't agree to anything. I merely accepted your offer."

"Get off me!" she screamed, raking her nails down his face.

He sucked in a breath and pressed his body into hers. "For that, you will suffer several times over."

THE HIGH LORD

As Aramis and his group entered the south end of Deudraeth, Taurnil moved to the forefront, making sure his blond hair covered his ears and his black blade was visible. He was relying heavily on the hope that none of the *Bok* knew Dar or his face. Shop owners opening their stores for the day's business gave them only a cursory glance as they passed.

At a slow pace, they walked their horses along the cobbled main street and came face to face with a *Bok* patrol. The man in the lead, dressed in the uniform of a captain, held up a hand. "Halt. What is your business?"

Ra glanced at Taurnil. The Elven prince reined in his horse and regally raised his hand, bringing his men to a halt. He sneered at the captain. "Our business is none of your concern."

"Bringing a patrol of Black Blades into my town becomes my business," stated the captain.

The young Elf laughed. "*Your* town? I was under the impression people in this land were free. Who are you?"

"I am the captain of the *Bok* in this region. You will not pass until you speak your business."

Ra nudged his horse forward, shifting the toothpick to the other side of his mouth. "We're here for supplies. Shouldn't be too long."

The captain motioned to his men, who moved across the square and blocked the road. "As I said, you will not pass until you speak your business."

Taurnil's rising anxiety transferred to his horse, his steed stamping its hooves and shaking its head. "The sooner you let us pass, the sooner we will be gone."

⁓⊹⊹⊹⁓

At the other end of town, Dar peeked around the corner of the apothecary. Unable to see how things were progressing on the main road, he had to trust his men to carry out his plan.

"Let's go." He stepped around the corner and headed toward the shop, his thoughts turning inward in search of his wife. At the wood and glass door, he ducked as he stepped inside to avoid bumping his head.

The salesclerk turned at the sound of the bell, a smile on his face. "Good morning, sir. How may I be of service?"

Dar blinked a few times to adjust to the dimness of the shop.

What were her impressions when she first entered? Was she enchanted by the smells? Did the tiny, colored bottles sparkle in her beautiful eyes?

Spirit and Linq followed him inside and positioned themselves where they could keep watch on the door and the goings-on outside.

The dark-haired clerk spoke again, watching the big man eye the amulets on the far wall. "Are you looking for something in particular, sir? A gift for a special someone?"

Dar turned and eyed the floor to ceiling shelves stocked with every kind and color of bottle.

As he approached the counter, the clerk's smile widened. "Ah, you must be the husband."

Dar narrowed his eyes. "What did you say?"

The young man stepped back. "The n-necklace you wear, s-sir. It's unforgettable, as was the lady. S-She said it was for her husband."

"Where is my wife?"

"S-Sir? She was here only the one time."

"She is here now." Dar placed his hands on the glass counter and leaned toward him. "Take me to her."

The clerk glanced at Spirit and Linq, who offered no assistance. His eyes came back to Dar. "Sir, I assure you, I have not seen the lady since that day."

Dar reached over the counter and grabbed the young man by the throat, lifting him off the floor. "Where the hell is my wife?"

The clerk tugged at the huge hand wrapped around his throat. "Sir, I swear to you—"

Dar squeezed harder. "My *wife*."

"Sir, please, I do not know..."

When Etain's will shattered, her screams slammed into Dar, filling his mind with her terror. He no longer heard the clerk's words, nor was he aware of his surroundings. With her defenses obliterated, everything flooded into him.

He shared her degradation, smelled the demon's stench on her body, saw him tasting her blood as it flowed from the wounds inflicted. Her weakness burned into his soul and inflamed his anger. So incensed by the cruelty shown his wife, he crushed the young man's larynx and snapped his neck.

"Dar!" Linq yelled.

The warrior dropped his victim, leaving him in a heap behind the counter, and walked toward the back room.

Linq ran after him and blocked his way. "Keep a clear head, Dar. Your rage will not help her."

He grabbed him by the throat and slammed him into the wall, bits of plaster scattering on the floor. "Do *not* get in my way, Elf. I will *not* lose this family."

Spirit rushed over. "Killing your best friend won't save them either."

"You are either with me or against me. If you choose the later, you are already dead."

Upon his release, Linq landed hard on his feet, coughing as the air rushed into his lungs.

Spirit placed a hand on his shoulder. "Are you all right, man?"

Linq wheezed in a breath. "That will teach me to argue with a pissed-off Krymerian."

Dar continued into the back room, his precious wife's pain ringing in his ears.

Hidden amongst the goods of a local shop, a white-haired boy watched the goings on in the square. It appeared the blond man finally admitted his real intent—a woman. Another liar in his town. She probably wasn't even his wife. Just a poor local girl who'd made him mad in some way.

He understood the *Bok*, knew their dirty ways and how to work around them. These strangers were not people he wanted to get to know. Best if the *Bok* disposed of them before they caused trouble for him, his brother, and the town.

In the face of the demands, the *Bok* captain, Togor, drew his sword as did his men. The opposition brandished their weapons in response. Not long after, another group of soldiers rushed in, attacking the *Bok* from the rear.

The boy sneaked along the adjoining shops with his eyes on the action. He had to warn Dathmet. Maybe his show of loyalty would make the asshole leave them alone for a while.

As he rushed past a gap between the buildings, an arm shot out, knocking him onto his back. Before he could move, a grinning Elf had him pinned to the ground and raised a fist.

"I do not know where you are headed, boy, but I bet it is not in our best interests." Dalos checked the area, making sure no one saw what happened, stood, and tossed the boy over his shoulder.

Freeblood used all his effort to wriggle free of his bindings, or at least free the hand with the blue gem. The dim light cast shadows around the room allowing him to make out Faux but not the other woman. "We'll be fine, babe. Just gotta. Get out. Of these..."

A dark force entered his consciousness, making him pause.

Faux's chains jingled. "What is it? Are you still there? You didn't leave me, did you?"

"I'm here, Faux. Just behind the chair. I thought I heard something." He focused on the ropes, trying to ignore the intense evil coming toward them. *We can't be here.*

"Lady, I don't know who you are or why you're here, but you're going with us. I'm Freeblood." The ropes loosened just enough on the one hand. He lit the blue gem in his palm and extended it into a dagger, cutting into the ropes.

He heard a grunt and mumbling as the woman shifted. Not hearing chains jingle made him happy. He wasn't sure he had the strength to break through two sets.

Freeblood cut through the last bit of rope around his ankles, then dashed to the woman and removed the gag from her mouth.

"Thanks," she panted. "I'm Jackie."

Just as he cut her free, the doors flew open, banging against the walls. The full force of evil nearly bowled him over. Faux screamed.

"Stay down, Jackie." He transformed the blue jewel into a sword. "I gotta save my girl."

At the door, light eyes glowed. Striking at what he feared was a death squad, a counterattack blocked his blade. The impact turned his stomach, but he stood his ground and lifted his sword. His blue-jeweled blade cast a faint glow over three faces. The young man fell to his knees, placing a hand on his chest. "Jesus God!"

These were beings he'd never seen before. Faces of dark and light, fair enough to turn a head, but their empty eyes made him tremble.

The one in the middle raised her light-colored brow. "Not quite." She grabbed him by the wrist and twisted. "Put it away."

With gritted teeth he extinguished the blue sword and retracted it into his hand.

"Phee, get the pregnant one."

"Don't hurt her!" Freeblood yelled, twisting to watch as the light one released Faux, who fell to her knees and screamed in pain when her arms collapsed to her sides. "Hey!"

His tormentor slapped him on the head. "Shut up."

"What about this she-cat over here?" Phoe headed toward Jackie in the corner.

"Leave her. She's too old and human." The sisters laughed. "She won't last long here."

Phoe grinned at the woman. "I think I'll save her the effort." She pulled a wooden baton from her belt.

"No!" Freeblood yelled but couldn't break free of Phie's grip.

Jackie lunged from the corner, grabbing for the baton as she knocked the Banshee back. Both fell to the floor, Jackie doing all she could to wrench the weapon from the other's hand.

"Phie! Help!"

"Bitch never learns." Phie glanced at her other sister. "Phee, watch this one." She sauntered toward the fighting women, jammed a hand into

Jackie's auburn hair, and pulled back hard. Jackie clawed at the hand that held her, yelling obscenities that shocked even Freeblood. Phoe recovered, jumped up, and punched the woman, laughing when she slumped to the floor.

"Is she dead?" Phoe asked.

"Does it matter? We have to go."

Dar pounded the wall in the back room with both fists, bits of plaster and stone clattering onto the floor. It felt bloody good to hit something. He imagined the wall as the demon's face, every punch bruising the grotesque red skin, every impact disintegrating another bone.

I will rip him apart.

Once the opening was large enough, he ducked through and rushed up a rough-hewn tunnel. Occasional torches gave just enough light to keep from wandering into a wall.

Coming to a turn, he forced himself to stop and breathe, sweat trickling off his brow. *Please hold on.* He inched toward the corner. A faint light across the floor of the tunnel indicated an open doorway. He drew his dagger as he rounded the turn.

At the doorway, he listened for an indication of what may await inside, but it remained quiet. He twisted away from the tunnel wall and into a set of circular stairs leading deeper into the earth.

Dar bounded down the steps, the chill from above warming the deeper he went. After several turns, he stepped into another dimly lit tunnel and inched along the wall toward an open doorway. Dagger ready, he stepped into the room.

Energies bombarded him from every angle. More than one living being had been in this room, and not long ago. Although he could not distinguish from whom the energies came, there was one that cut through them all. His gaze went to the other end of the room where a set of shackles dangled from the rafters. Drawn to the spot, his focus remained on the metal cuffs as he walked toward them, remembering how they had cut into his skin and kept him compliant. Jaw clenched, he crouched and dragged a finger through the puddle of blood beneath them, then touched it to his tongue.

"Something more to block her powers as if the cuffs were not enough. Too much of a coward to play on an even field."

He looked around the room and noticed a discarded cat o' nine in the corner, its bloody tips a screaming testament to the tortures his lady suffered. As he stood, the chair caught his eye but more importantly, the torn sleeve draped across its back and the empty hypodermic on the side table.

Dar returned the dagger to his belt and closed his tear-rimmed eyes. With a shake of his head, he swiped them away with a sleeve, and drew his black scimitars. His eyes glowed as his lips moved with quiet words, weaving a magical spell of death over his blades.

He returned to the blood, tucked his swords away, and disintegrated the shackles with a glance. At the other end of the room, he did the same. "You will not restrain another being."

One last scan of the room showed him the blood of those who had been here with her. People who witnessed her pain and tears. From all appearances, people who suffered the same as she. He did not know who they were, but he would make the demon pay for their pain as well.

A sound from behind made him stop. In an instant, a rather strong creature jumped on his back and snaked an arm around his throat, doing its best to cut off his air supply. Dar struggled to get a hold on the being before he lost consciousness. He gained purchase of the arm, and as he pried it away from his neck, reached back flipping the nuisance over his head and onto the floor.

Dar furrowed his brows. "Who are *you,* and what the *hell* are you doing here?"

The woman glared at him. "I could ask the same."

Sass was not what he expected, but the nasty bruise on her forehead told him she was not the enemy. "I am here for my wife. How did a human come to be here?"

The hardness in her features softened, the glare in her eyes turning to more of a drunken dullness. "I doubt you would believe..." She trailed off as her eyes closed.

Dar checked for a pulse. Fortunately, it was strong. "You have been through it, milady." Anxious to find Etain, he scooped her into his arms and carried her into the tunnel. "Do not worry. She is not far."

A burning sensation across his chest made him stop. He stepped under one of the few torches lining the wall, placed the woman on the floor, and lifted his shirt. Blood oozed from the edges of the mark he shared with Etain. Their time was short. If she gave up, his children's magic would fail, and they would pass with her.

"I must leave you alone for a time, milady. If you wake, I pray you have the sense to keep quiet." He moved her into the shadows and headed up the tunnel.

Recovered from the argument with the High Lord, Linq and Spirit stepped through the demolished wall into the dimly lit tunnel and quietly followed it until they found a stairway.

Linq took the lead, winding down toward its end. Halfway, he stopped.

"What is it?" Spirit whispered.

He held a finger to his lips. "A scuffle. Shall we find out?"

At the bottom of the stairs, they inched along the wall to a corner. Linq peered into the adjoining tunnel but saw nothing. Halfway down the corridor, a faint light washed across the floor.

Linq motioned Spirit to stay put while he peeked around the door jamb. Unable to see much of anything, he jumped to the other side and scanned the room, noting the chains flung across the rafters. The smell of blood put his senses on high alert. "By the stars..." He drew his sword.

At his muttered words, Spirit did the same as she followed him into the room. "The bloody bastard. I'll nail his balls to the floor and turn this place into an ice coffin."

Linq picked up a red-stained dagger from the floor. "I doubt they have gone far. Dar said she could not leave this realm without him." He walked to a pile of cut ropes. "There were others here." And noticed the other pile. "There are two sets of ropes."

"And two sets of chains." Spirit stood at the set just inside the door, then walked to the other. "Etain must have been here. These are her boots." She picked up one and found the other lying in the corner. "Should we leave Dar to get Etain and see if we can find the others?"

A commotion made them turn. "We should check that first." Linq led the way into the tunnel.

SHOWDOWN

Dathmet's righthand man rode toward Deudraeth having returned from an errand for his master. As he neared the northern quarter, Raum heard a skirmish and stopped, quietly sliding out of his saddle. He trekked far enough out of the perimeter not to be detected, yet still able to see the action. He hadn't expected the High Lord to arrive so quickly or with a patrol of Black Blades. From the stories he'd heard, the Krymerian worked alone. Intrigued, he searched the crowd for the man.

"Release my wife," he heard a voice bellow over the mélange.

Raum's gaze went to the tall, blond figure, who he knew to be an Elf. Had he not seen him before, he would have been fooled like the captain.

"She is not *your* wife," he mumbled. "I must warn Togor."

"You will leave, now," the captain yelled. His sword in the air, his horse reared up. "Your wife is not here."

Raum pressed his back against a wall. From his vantage point, he noticed a Black Blade across the way. Experienced enough to know where you see one more linger nearby, he closed his eyes and opened his mind, pushing his essence out into the mass of *Bok* soldiers. One by one, he glided through their consciousness until he reached the one closest to the captain. The soldier's eyes glazed over but cleared as Raum seized control and moved closer to the leader.

The manservant called him by name. "Togor."

"Soldier! We are engaged in—"

"That is not the High Lord." Raum pointed at the Elf.

Hearing the voice, the rage in the captain's eyes turned to recognition. "Raum? What are you doing here?"

"That *Elf* is an imposter sent by the Krymerian to distract you. I would guess the man is on his way to the master."

Togor eyed him. "Are you sure?"

"The Krymerian carries a set of black scimitars, not a katana. And he's bigger."

"Get to the master, Raum. I will keep the demons here to distract the imposter and send my men after you."

"Watch yourself. Every entrance into town is covered by Black Blades. Use the tunnel beneath the grocer."

Togor turned to block an oncoming blade. "We'll meet you there."

Once his essence returned to his body, Raum slumped against the wall, catching his breath. With the main road so closely watched, he changed direction and headed toward the small grocery down the road. He was certain neither the Krymerian nor his minions knew of *that* tunnel entrance.

His never-ending exploration of her body continued. Sliding his hand down her bare back and over the curve of her hip, he breathed into her ear. "You are perfection. You make me hunger for more."

"No," she murmured into the pillow. "Let me rest."

He moved his hand between her thighs, making her cry out.

"On your knees."

"Go to hell."

"I see this will take some time." He extended his talons, pressing them against her rounded belly. "If you don't cooperate, I will cut that brat out right now."

She welcomed his threats. They ignited her anger and gave her strength. "And kill me in the process." She peered over her shoulder. "Save us all the trouble and cut my throat."

Fire in his eyes, he sank his fangs into her flesh.

She clenched her teeth and sucked in a breath.

"Shall we bring your little human friend in to join us?" he asked, a bloody sheen on his lips. "Maybe a few of my best men? They deserve a reward for their service. She's not as—"

A loud crash against the door made him turn. "What the hell?" He glanced at Etain. "Do not move."

As if I have a choice.

"Lilith!" he called out. "What have you done now?" He opened the door.

A powerful fist in the face knocked him back into the room.

"I have come for my wife." Dar transformed, growing to over eight feet tall as he stalked toward the fiend picking himself up from the floor. Just as Dathmet regained his feet, Dar swung with a left uppercut and immediate right cross, followed by a knee to the groin. The demon crashed to the floor again, curled into a ball, and held himself, writhing in pain.

"You dare touch my lady." He kicked Etain's assailant in the stomach. "You threaten my children." He grabbed a handful of black hair. "You murder my Black Blades..." He punched him again and again. "All the time claiming to be her brother."

Dathmet found the wherewithal to extend his own talons and swiped at Dar, catching him across the midriff, which gave him the opportunity to scramble away. "*Children*?" His gaze darted to Etain. "You lying bitch." He stumbled to his feet and lit the flames on his head.

"You are a sorry coward." Dar stalked toward him with his fists clenched.

The demon lashed out with his talons again. "She screamed for me several times."

"Screams of *pain*." Dar engaged his own talons. "Her heart told me everything."

Dathmet faked to the right and spun to his left. Dar's deadly talons raked his side. "Aagh! You can't conquer me now. Her blood will heal me. We are brothers in her blood."

Dar grabbed the closest thing available—a six-foot armoire. He lifted the piece with ease and heaved it at Dathmet. The demon turned as his spiked ridge rose from his back splintering the armoire, but the impact made him stumble forward. Shaking it off, he turned and charged, smashing his shoulder into Dar's abdomen, and ramming him back into the wall. A large crack inched toward the ceiling.

Dar stilled to catch his breath but kept his eyes on the demon, waiting for his next move.

Dathmet jumped away, grabbed a nearby curio cabinet, and slung it at him. Just in time, Dar dropped to the floor amidst a shower of wood, glass, and porcelain, then rolled, coming up on his feet in front of Midir's spawn. He slashed out with a clawed hand, but his adversary burst into flames and Dar's talons breezed through their mark.

When the red-skinned demon materialized again, Dar twisted and clipped him with his foot, knocking him flat onto his back. He pounced, fist first.

The slippery Dathmet rolled away at the last moment. Dar's fist plowed into the floor sending a spray of stone chips in all directions. Shock from the impact reeled through his body.

Dathmet jumped to his feet and grabbed him by the arm with a flamed hand, slamming him into the stone wall again.

Dar came at him taking him by surprise. "Dying time has come."

"For once, you're right." The demon sneered. "Happy death day."

He slashed at Dar, who tried to lean back but banged into the wall. The sharp tips grazed his upper chest. He shook off the pain and pushed from the wall bashing his head into Dathmet's face. The satisfying crunch and explosion of warm blood told Dar he had the upper hand.

Dathmet stumbled away, blood streaming from his broken nose. Dar rushed in and shoved him back embedding the demon's ridge into a bedpost. Amused by the turn of the tables, he dragged his tongue through the fresh blood.

"Salty... But your heart will taste sweet."

Dar's attention turned elsewhere when a trembling Etain raised her head from the pillow. He barely recognized his wife. Her face was bruised and swollen and the usual spark in her eyes was gone. There were bite marks all over her body.

Eyes wide, her voice was rough. "Don't do this."

Dathmet laughed. "You see? It's not you she desires."

"Shut up." Dar punched the demon in the face and moved toward Etain.

She moaned as she scrambled to the other side of the bed. "No! Go away! I cannot go! There are others..."

Dar reached for her as she rolled off the bed. Dathmet made a grab for her as she passed him, but with his ridge deeply embedded in the wood, she easily sidestepped him.

Dar twisted away from the bed and caught her around the waist, lifting her off her feet. "Be still, Etain. I am here to help you."

She kicked and squirmed against him. "They'll die if I go with you! They will *all* die."

"Etain!" With a forceful jerk, he tightened his hold on her, his heart crashing in his chest. "There are no others. If you stay, your death and the death of our children will be for nothing."

She turned within his arms and stared at him. The terror in her eyes further inflamed his anger. "No! They're here!" Her tearful glare fell on the demon. "In the big room. The shackles."

Dar fought to keep his voice steady. "I destroyed them. Both sets. No one was there, Etain."

Again, she glared at the demon, her body shaking. "What did you do with them? I *will* kill you." She passed out in Dar's arms.

"You won't get out of here alive." Dathmet laughed, rocking his body to get free from the post. "Once you're dead, I'll reclaim the bitch and kill everyone you know."

Dar's eyes flashed with the light of his *ultimá solar*. "Your reign of terror is over."

At that moment, the door burst open. Someone he had not seen in years, not since the man murdered several Alamir in retaliation for the massacre of his clan, stared back at him.

Dar's light disappeared as quickly as it had shone.

"VonNeshta!"

Dar's voice caught in his throat. A single word from the commander would have them surrounded in seconds. All he could muster was a croak. "Thamuz."

"Thamuz!" Dathmet screamed. "We can end this here. Kill him! *Kill* him!"

The commander glanced at the demon and came back to the couple. Dar's heart thundered, his mind racing to figure out how he and Etain were going to get out of this one. He held Thamuz's gaze for a moment, then lowered it to his wife, who was limp in his arms, broken and bleeding. Dar raised his head with a fierce glare in his eyes.

"Thamuz! Thamuz!" A frantic Dathmet bounced on his feet, determined to intervene. "Kill him! Kill him now!"

The move was subtle, no more than a slight cock of his head, but enough to tell Dar he would not stop him. Dar skirted around the commander and rushed out the door just as Dathmet pulled free from the bedpost. The last he heard was the demon and his commander in a heated argument.

Afraid Thamuz's backup plan might engage at any moment, Dar moved down the dark hallway and stopped when he reached the spot where he had left the woman. Footsteps echoed in the tunnel. He pressed his back to the wall straining to control his breath. He prayed neither Etain nor the woman at his feet would wake.

As the footsteps neared, he recognized the soft-spoken voices and stepped out from the shadows.

Spirit and Linq stopped, hands going to the hilts of their blades. "By the sea... Dar!"

Spirit's gaze went to Etain. "Oh, lass."

Dar shifted her closer to his body as though she needed protection from these precious people they both loved. "I was not sure if we would see any of you again."

Quick footsteps from the other end of the tunnel told of the enemy's advance.

Linq partially drew his sword. "Damn. There is another entrance."

"You should go now," said Spirit. "We'll take care of things here."

Dar's gaze turned to the human woman on the floor, who stirred. "I do not know who she is, but she must have something to do with all this. Linq, would you carry her through?"

He scratched his head. "Aye, but with reservations."

Dar opened a portal to their home and waited until Linq deposited his charge on the other side.

"I have her boots, Dar," Spirit said, holding them up. "She'll be glad to have them." She handed the boots to Linq, who placed them on the other side of the portal.

"Thank you, milady. Linq." Dar stepped through as a troop of *Bok* appeared around the corner. The last thing he saw were his friends turning to meet the enemy.

After a time, Taurnil scanned the battery of fighting men and cut his way to Aramis. "Where are the *Bok*?"

"I don't know. Have you seen Ra?"

The Elf shrugged. "He can take care of himself, right?"

Aramis peered over his shoulder. "I'm sure he'll show up."

Eol rushed up at that point voicing a question about the *Bok*.

"The soldiers must have slinked away." Taurnil sucked in a breath. "By the sea and stars! I should've realized sooner. You are in charge of these demons, Eol. Dar will need us."

Taurnil, Aramis, and a handful of Blades mimicked their evil counterparts and broke away one by one, moving shop to shop toward the apothecary.

Halfway there, Taurnil met up with Sion. "Take three Blades and head around the back. We will go through the front. Hopefully we get there in time to help Dar."

With a nod, Sion and his group moved out. Taurnil and his men sprinted up the main street and over one block from the main road. He cautiously approached the door and pushed it open. After a nod over his shoulder, two Blades entered to clear the room, each one claiming a portion of the shop. In a short time, they gave the all clear for their prince to enter. A Blade returned to the door and motioned the others in, leaving two to stand guard.

Taurnil and his men quietly moved into the back room where they found the jagged hole in the wall. He listened for a long moment but heard only indistinct noises. The warriors glanced at one another, breathed in, and stepped into the abyss.

Although prepared to face the oncoming *Bok*, Linq stayed Spirit's move with a hand on her arm and stepped into the shadows. Dar remained hidden until he chose to be seen. If it worked for him, it should work for them. Spirit furrowed her brows but followed suit and joined the Elf in the darkness. They had a perfect view of anyone coming through the tunnel.

Within moments, the first line of soldiers arrived at the doorway and stopped. Linq was certain they stared right at him and Spirit. Afraid he had miscalculated the viability of their hiding place his hand went to his sword. But the soldiers turned toward the room.

Linq exchanged a glance with Spirit at the sounds of a scuffle followed by a muffled scream.

A lone soldier pushed through the *Bok* and rushed into the room. There were more screams, as well as the smell of burning flesh, which triggered the remaining soldiers into action. Spirit glared at Linq, who shook his head and held a finger to his lips.

A flaming figure exited the room and pushed through the soldiers, setting several alight. It ran up the tunnel but stopped within a few feet. Linq saw another man meet the flame before the two disappeared into the darkness.

One soldier, smoldering from his apparent encounter with the flame, staggered out of the room. "We can't let him get away." As he raced after whatever had escaped, the men turned and ran after him.

Spirit and Linq coughed from the stench of burning flesh. Painful moans drew them toward the room. Linq jumped to one side of the door while Spirit stood on the other. They turned at the same time and saw a mass of burned bodies lying atop one another, except for one. Distinguished by his uniform, he stood at a bedpost, his flesh roasted and a sword through his heart.

"I'm guessing this is what the soldier boys weren't too happy about," Spirit said, eyeing the corpse.

"Let us get out of here before someone blames us for this mess." Linq joined Spirit on her side of the door. As they turned to leave, Taurnil and his men appeared in the tunnel.

"Linq! Are we too late?"

"No time to chat. I think we just got lucky," replied the older Elf. "We must get out of here." At the stairs, he turned. "Taurnil, do you know the sealing spell?"

"I do."

He nodded toward the stairs. "Get everyone up and out. Destroy the stairs when you get to the top."

Taurnil opened his mouth, but Spirit spoke, "I can do that."

"Good. Once everyone clears the opening in the shop, Taurnil, speak the sealing spell so no one passes that way again."

"Are you not coming with us?" he asked.

"There is another entrance. I must follow the tunnel to find it. I will meet you up top."

Taurnil turned to the others. "Move out." As his men raced up the stairs, he turned to Linq. "What happened in there?"

"Nothing good." Linq moved past him.

Taurnil turned as he passed. "Where is Dar? Where is E? Why are we not fighting for our lives?"

Linq stopped and turned to face him. "Is it not enough that we get out of here with our lives?"

"No."

He considered the stoic young Elf and what he had experienced since meeting Dar and Etain. Linq accused Dar of underestimating him, but perhaps he had done the same. The realization Taurnil was no longer the boy he had known for so long hit hard. This was a young man on his way to becoming king. He deserved to know the truth.

Linq walked back to him. "Dathmet and Robert are one in the same." He ignored the devastation on his face. "The demon has betrayed his kind and is on the run. That is the only reason you and I are standing here gabbing like two old ladies."

The devastation turned into concern. "E?"

Linq shook his head. "It is bad, Taurnil. Dar has taken her home to *Sôlskin*."

The struggle to come to grips with the situation showed on his face. "They will need our support."

Come Back to Me

I n the courtyard of their home, Dar closed the portal and phased directly to the bedroom created for her. He hoped the sage and purple colors would soothe her tortured soul and give her comfort. With her in his arms, he gently sat on the huge bed. She awoke with a jerk, eyes wide, turning her head in every direction.

He breathed in to gain control of his emotions. Holding onto her, he tried to ignore the abuse visible on her body. "Etain, we are home."

"Don't touch me," she screamed, pushing away. "I can't be *here*. I can't. Not after what he did to me. Please let me go."

He shifted and set her on the bed. Crouched before her, he peered into her bruised face and noted more bruises around her throat. "*A chuisle*, you are home," he said tenderly. "You are safe. He cannot reach you here."

She avoided his gaze, tears cascading from her eyes. "Don't you see? I can't be *here* with you. He'll come for me. He will kill *everyone*."

"Where should you be?" He gently rubbed her arms. The warmth of his hands slowly removed the chill on her skin.

She hid her face in her hands. "I *don't* know. I don't *know*. But he will come for me."

"My love, you are exhausted. Have you eaten anything?"

She shook her head. "My stomach hurts. My throat hurts. Everything hurts."

He wrapped his arms around her and held her tightly. "It will pass. I promise. I will take care of you, my precious one." His heart broke when her body stiffened in his embrace.

"The children!" Her voice shook as she placed her hands on her stomach. "I can't feel them."

"They are weak, my love. The three of you need food and rest." He kissed her head, doing his best to keep himself together. "A little broth to start." He pulled back the covers and helped her into the bed. "Rest while I prepare you something. I will not be long."

She rolled away from him and curled into a ball. It was all he could do to keep his rage in check seeing the lashes and bruises across her back, but-tocks, and upper thighs as well as the countless bite marks. He swallowed a gasp at the traces of blood between her abused thighs. Tucking her in, he stroked her tangled mass of curls and left a light kiss on her temple.

"Rest, my sweet lady. You are safe."

He hated to leave her alone, but she needed sustenance, and he had to see to the human. Dar headed downstairs hoping he could get the woman situated and find something worthwhile in the cupboards.

He found her sitting on the ground next to Etain's boots, head in her hands. "Where the hell am I?"

"Apologies, milady," he said, grabbing the boots. "You were—*are* an unexpected turn."

"I've been called worse." She lifted her head. "*What* is going on?"

Dar held out a hand. "Come with me. We can share our stories while I tend to your head and get Etain something to eat."

"Etain?" She groaned, her hand going to her head.

Dar scooped her into his arms and carried her into the kitchen. Dropping the boots, he laid her on the island. "Do not move." He grabbed a tea towel, doused it with cold water, and gently placed it across her forehead. "How did you get such a nasty bruise?"

"Can we do this later? I'm not feeling so good." She closed her eyes.

"May I at least have a name?"

"Jackie," she whispered.

"Hello, Jackie. I am Dar, Etain's husband."

"Nice to meet..." Her voice trailed off as she slipped into unconsciousness.

He sighed and ran a hand over his face. "This day gets better by the second."

Once again, he scooped the woman into his arms and carried her upstairs to a room not far from Etain's. As he lay her on the bed, he spoke a healing spell, hoping it was strong enough to start the process, yet not overwhelm her human senses.

"Forgive me, milady. I have another who needs my attention."

Back in the kitchen, his rage took over. H smashed a fist through the first wall he encountered, leaving a huge hole. He did his best to replace his emotional pain with physical pain—something he could deal with. He slammed his head into the refrigerator, crushing the front panel and smearing blood over the surface.

He turned and lashed out at the overhanging pot rack, ramming his fists into the pans, each one flying across the room and clanging loudly against the stone floor. His anger not yet sated, he grabbed the large rack, and with a loud grunt, pulled. The beams creaked, screamed, and finally released the deep-seated bolts. The wood ripped away in splinters. Dar threw it at the back door.

The bastard tortured her. Had his hands around her throat. By the gods, I should have torn out his heart and eaten it in front of her eyes. Shown her I had avenged her shame.

He picked up a discarded pan and threw it at the large bay window of the breakfast nook. Shattering glass echoed throughout the room. At the battered back door, he slammed both hands against it and stared out into the garden.

A slight thud broke through the noise in his head. He held his breath and listened for another. Just as he decided it was nothing, he heard blood-curdling screams.

Dar burst into the room to find the bed sheets shredded and shards of a broken lamp scattered on the floor.

"Tartarus."

A noise from the bathroom had him opening the door to a steam-filled room. "Etain?" Unable to see much, he made his way to the shower and opened the glass door. Intense heat forced him back a step. "Etain."

He waved a hand through the steam and saw her on the floor, fiercely scrubbing her skin with a soaped loofah.

Aghast at the rawness of her skin and blood red water swirling down the drain, he stepped into the shower fully clothed, and turned down the hot tap, letting cool water run in its place.

He reached for the loofah. She scrunched it between her hands and pulled it close to her battered body. "No! I have to wash him off me."

Dar swallowed hard, fighting back his tears. "*A chuisle*, let me help you."

"You can't touch me!" She screamed and turned her back to him.

"Etain..."

He forced himself to stop. His sudden fury was not from her actions, but those of another. Someone he would deal with after Etain was whole again.

He sat next to her and pulled her trembling body onto his lap. "Let me help you, my love." When he wrenched the loofah from her hands, she screamed and tried to break free. "Etain, you must stop. You are only hurting yourself. Please."

She arched her back and pushed hard. "Let me *go*! You cannot touch me like this!" With that, she went limp and mumbled, "I am cursed. Death will find us. I am cursed. He won't let me go. I am cursed. Cursed..."

At his wits' end, he listened to her insane murmurings, her tears tearing at his heart. "I love you, *a chuisle*. I love you." He hugged her tighter and rocked back and forth, their tears mixing with the cool water washing over their joined heads "We are here together. My sweet, sweet lady, come back to me."

⁂

Once Taurnil and the others stepped outside the apothecary, they found a bloody Ra astride his mount and a smiling Dalos, who held the collar of a boy. "See what I found?"

"Dalos! I thought you were with me." Taurnil eyed the captive. "Who do we have here?"

"Don't you touch me, Elf," the boy hollered, kicking at him. "I'll kill all of you. I won't let you destroy my town. I won't!"

Ra grabbed the boy by the hair. "You'll mind your manners. Your town hasn't been touched."

"Liars!"

"Gag him, Dalos," Linq said upon his approach. "Please tell us why you thought we needed another miscreant in our league." He turned to the battered Ra. "You holding up, friend?"

Ra's white teeth gleamed in his blood-smeared face. "Quite well, thank you."

"Mission accomplished?" Taurnil asked Linq as Dalos shoved the boy toward him.

Linq grinned. "Done."

Dalos turned to Ra and ripped off a tattered bit of cloth hanging from his shirt. Taurnil held the boy still while Dalos forced the length of cloth between his lips and tied the ends behind his head.

"I caught him making a run for the shop." Dalos double-checked the bindings. He relieved Taurnil of the burden and tucked the boy under his arm like a sack of potatoes. "He was on his way to tell the demon of our arrival. Weren't you, boy?"

An angry glare was his answer.

"Dar can decide what to do with him." Linq climbed onto his horse and settled in the saddle. "Shall we get back?"

Riding out the north end of town, they joined the Black Blades left behind as guards on the west side and circled around to Eol at the south end. After Aramis released a fire blast to clean up the carnage of dead demons, the allies headed home.

Upon arrival at Laugharne, the Blades situated the wounded in the large dining room where Swee and her team could administer to each one.

Ra dismounted and nudged Dalos with his shoulder. "You might wanna git that gag off the boy before the healer shows."

Just as Swee stepped into the courtyard, Ra shifted, blocking her view of the boy while Dalos removed the gag and slipped it into his pocket as he turned to face her.

Swee walked toward the boy, her eyes widening. "You poor thing." She kneeled in front of him checking the shiner of his right eye. "Where did you get this from?"

With a pout, his eyes went to the Elf standing next to him. "Stay right here." She straightened and turned. "Dalos! What on earth were you thinking? Striking a boy? You could've caused serious injury."

"H-He would not cooperate." Dalos paled to some degree and blustered a few huffs at her responding glare. "He would have blown the whole operation." He turned on the boy. "You are lucky that was all you got. Our orders were to—"

Taurnil grabbed his friend by the arm. "Shall we get you inside, Dalos?" As they walked toward the house, he leaned closer to his friend so only he could hear. "It is just a black eye. You did the right thing."

Swee held the boy's hand and walked him into the house where she washed his face and checked his eye. They all soon learned he was the brother of the boy Etain rescued in town. But their reunion proved to be less than brotherly.

"What're you doing here?" yelled the bigger of the two, hitting him over the head.

The smaller boy raised his arms in defense. "I didn't do nothing!"

"You must've done something 'cause here we are in the middle of it."

"Stop hitting me." The smaller boy pushed into his brother and sucker punched him in the belly. He doubled over with his arms wrapped around his middle but retaliated with a forceable head butt. The two bumped into Swee and knocked her off her feet.

"Stop this!" she hollered.

Wolfe and Ra came to her rescue. Wolfe grabbed the smaller of the two while Ra dragged the other away. All four left the dining room, the brothers yelling at each other.

Swee climbed to her feet, caught her breath, and straightened her hair. She walked straight toward Dalos.

He glanced at Taurnil and shifted in his seat.

"I'm sorry about earlier. I was a bit harsh." She waited until the commotion down the hallway quieted. "Next time, just make sure it's not an eye."

A vindicated Dalos grinned. "Yes, milady."

Tucked away in a slate cavern northeast of Deudraeth, Raum paced at the opening. "We cannot go to the castle. They've both been there. After the stunt with Thamuz, his men will be hunting your ass too."

Seated deeper within the cave, Dathmet leaned against the rock wall, favoring one side. "Her blood runs in my veins, give me a few days and I'll be strong enough to go back—"

"*You* are not going *back* to anything!" Raum stormed toward the demon. "We're moving on."

Dathmet groaned at the man. "Either she will go with us, or we won't go at all."

"Don't be a twat like your father. Drop it." He tapped him on the head. "Use your flame-headed melon to think."

Flames flared but petered out. "Watch your mouth, servant."

"I've stood back for too long." Raum loomed over him. "I'm all you have, boy. It's time you listened to someone who isn't swayed by the blood or cowed by your station. He won't take her to the Alamir."

"Where else would they go?" Dathmet struggled to his feet. "They can't hide from me. I'll take them—"

"Wherever they end up, VonNeshta is sure to raise the spell of all spells for protection. You're going to take your red ass somewhere no one can find you, heal, and make a plan."

"Hmph. He isn't that smart."

Raum pushed the demon, making him lose his balance and fall back. "While you're at it, learn some respect. Midir did you a disservice with his trash talking. I have no use for VonNeshta, but he *is* an accomplished warrior. If you want to beat him, you have to acknowledge his strengths and exploit his weaknesses." He grabbed Dathmet's arm and pulled him up. "Let's get out of here before someone comes. Do you have the strength to open a portal?"

The demon coughed, holding his ribs. "To where?"

Raum wrapped an arm around his waist while resting one of the demon's arms over his shoulders. "The last place they'd think of—the Alamir realm."

The days proved to be busy for the inhabitants of Castle Laugharne. Taurnil gathered the Blades to tell them of Dar's plan for an Academy of Black Blades and extended the High Lord's invitation to any who wished to take a different path from that of Nunnehi.

"This will not be like your previous training. Much like the Blade Gathering, you must present your best to be accepted."

The young, single Blades showed great enthusiasm for the adventure and signed up without hesitation. Most of the seasoned Blades, having families to consider, advised they would think on it. Their prince knew well the sacrifice it would take to leave their homes.

"The door will be open if you decide to join us later."

However, coming face to face with the Queen of the Elves a short time later proved to be a different story.

Taurnil met his mother at the top of the stairs on his way to her room and her way to find him. She wasted no time in speaking her mind.

"Not only is he turning an honored organization into a laughingstock, he takes half of my men. I will not stand for it. These are *my* Black Blades."

"Mother..." He slipped his arm through hers, turning her away from the stairs. "Shall we not do this in the hallway?"

After a few steps, she pulled away. "Do not be flippant with me. He has gone too far."

"I did not intend to insult you, *módir*. But the Black Blades are *his* creation." He moved toward her bedroom and opened the door. "They have sworn an oath to the High Lord of Kaos, not the Queen of the Elves."

"Nonetheless, he cannot take them away from Nunnehi."

With a sweep of his hand, he motioned toward the room. "He did not coerce the Blades in any way. Merely gave them a choice."

Her eyebrows raised over wide eyes. "Coercion is not required by the High Lord of Kaos." She lifted her skirts and stepped through the door with great aplomb. "The moment he walks into a room, any young soldier with a heart for adventure hangs on his every word. Who could resist? *Orð mín* (My word)!" She threw a hand into the air. "*I* would follow him if I could!"

Taurnil almost laughed, but his mother's glare wiped the smile from his face. "Well, yes, I have to agree."

Her glare turned into disbelief. "By the sea and stars..."

He quietly closed the door. "*Móðir*, please."

"You cannot be serious. Not you too." She turned with a flourish and walked to the large window in her room. "How can you abandon your people as well as your queen?"

He closed his eyes for a moment and shook his head. Taking a breath, he joined her at the window. "I am not abandoning anyone. He tried to send me back to hide behind your skirts, but I would not have it. I will not hide behind another, queen or otherwise. If I am to rule our people, I must be worthy of the honor."

She huffed. "How can you learn anything from a man who disrespects you in that way?"

Taken aback, he narrowed his eyes. "He is scared, *móðir*. I would not say this to anyone but you."

"Dar, scared?" She scoffed. "Nothing scares that man."

He was tempted to bare his teeth and hiss but maintained a dignified air. "This man who claimed to be Etain's brother is the demon who abducted her. He *hurt* her. Linq would not tell me any more than that." He leaned into her face. "So, yes, Dar is terrified, and you should be too. I know I am. How do you fight something like that? How do you save someone who has been betrayed by a person they trusted with their life?"

Alatariel blinked as Taurnil turned and stalked toward the door.

"I am leaving with the others for *Sôlskin*. I expect you to honor my wishes." Taurnil quietly closed the door behind him.

For the UWS clan, life returned to something akin to normal. With Spirit as chieftain, they were assured a smooth transition, but she put aside making any immediate changes. It would take time for her and the clan to adjust to the loss of Inferno.

She found solace working with Swee in getting everyone healthy for the trip to *Sôlskin*. Since the young healer would be responsible for two expectant mothers, Faux and Etain, Spirit spent part of her time training her to be a midwife.

"Under normal circumstances, I'd expect Dar to have a room prepared," Spirit said. "But after what's happened, it will be on you to make sure everything's ready. Both of these girls carry unusual babes. Lord knows when they'll decide to be born."

"Do you think they would deliver so soon?"

She shrugged. "Hard to tell. According to Dar, Krymerian babes usually don't go past the sixth month, and Etain carries twins. I'd bet she doesn't get much past the fourth month."

"Oh my." Tilting her head, she asked, "What's so unusual about Faux's baby?"

"Have you ever noticed Freeblood's speed? I suspect it's in his blood. If that's the case, his child will grow more quickly than a normal babe."

"Speaking of Faux, have you seen her lately? I wanted to check on her and the baby."

Spirit stared at her. "I've not seen the lass for days. Nor the lad."

Swee covered her mouth with her hand. "Should we be concerned?"

"I don't think so. If memory serves, they were gone before Etain was taken. Otherwise, Freeblood would be in the middle of it."

"But where would they go in her condition?"

"My first guess is Dar's place. I'm sure Freeblood would want to get settled in before everyone else shows up."

Having discussed the move in great detail with Dar before the Dathmet incident, Linq confirmed all those moving to the Krymerian estate and booked passage on a transport ship set to sail within a couple of weeks. He asked after Faux and Freeblood, but having no reason to disagree with Spirit's assumptions the couple had gone to *Sôlskin*, he moved on with his plans.

Along with the livestock needed for a large estate, he included the horses of the Black Blades who elected to move.

The newest additions to the mix, brothers Cloud and Austin, were kept separated for the time being. Cloud, the older of the two, became Swee's shadow, following her everywhere, drinking in every word uttered from her magical lips. Fascinated by the stories of Dar and her time in the LOKI clan, it wasn't long before he joined her in training to be a healer.

Austin shadowed Dalos wherever he went. The Elf did his best to include him in as much as was possible for a nine-year-old boy. He believed their interaction would eventually change his opinion of the Alamir, the Elves, and quite possibly, the Krymerian.

Aramis and Ra outlined a plan to move the Dragon clan to the island and hoped to have everyone settled not too long after the first of the new year. As an afterthought, it was decided they should see it for themselves before making the final arrangements.

Alaster and his townsfolk set Spirit's kitchen in order and prepared to head back to Deudraeth as soon as the main group left for Dar's estate. They offered to take Cloud and Austin, but Linq decided it best they travel with him since they had no other family, and he was certain Dar would want to speak with them.

Taurnil spent most of his afternoons with Dalos, which also included Austin, building his strength and fine-tuning his moves. At the same time, the practice helped Dalos improve his skills in preparation for acquiring official Black Blade status.

Alatariel, her Royal Guard, and remaining Black Blades left late one night, their dead included, without saying farewell.

IRRECONCILABLE DIFFERENCES

Etain tossed and turned, talking in her sleep, but did not wake for three days. On the first day, Dar fretted, applying various oils enhanced by a healing spell to her injuries. He sat for long periods, watching her, waiting for her beautiful ice blue eyes to open and see her smile. Only briefly did he leave her side to administer to Jackie, who also slept. Her pulse strong and color improved, the bruise on her forehead appeared to be fading.

Come the second day, he dared to leave Etain for short periods to handle business required by the manor. Supplies such as beams, lumber, nails, and other building materials had to be ordered for the construction of the stables and the academy, the stables being the more urgent of the two.

On day three, he considered going into town to find a healer, or at the least, a housekeeper who could help keep an eye on both women. In the end, he decided to give them one more day.

At night, he lay beside Etain and told her of what he had accomplished during the day.

"We start on the stables tomorrow, *a chuisle*." He smoothed the hair from her face. "I hope you do not mind that I left you for a time. It was important. I cannot build this place by myself." He chuckled. "Aye, I admit it. I need help. So I hired a... How would you say it? Construction crew? They will build the stables first, then the academy. Linq and the others should leave Laugharne soon so the stables must be ready before they arrive."

He rolled onto his back and tucked his hands behind his head. "I suppose the barn will suffice for a time. But not for long. Our horses deserve the best." His eyes heavy, he yawned. "Maybe tomorrow..." With one last peek at his wife, he fell asleep.

✦✦✦

Etain woke early, her eyes darting around the room. *Where am I?* The colors were soothing and made her feel safe. To her left, a slight opening between wall-to-wall drapes revealed a small portion of a window, the weak sunlight shining through the panes of glass. She released a soft breath. The room had been a haven. A place where nothing wicked could ever touch her.

What she couldn't remember was how she got there. Her last memory was of being in Nunnehi with Spirit and Swee, visiting the queen, Alatariel. Had Dar been there? Her brain ran through the files in her head. Sorting, deciphering, eliminating different scenarios. *No. He had been fighting. At Laugharne. Against the Bok.*

She rolled onto her side and closed her eyes. Something registered at the last possible second and her eyes popped open again. Adrenaline exploded into her bloodstream, her instincts telling her to run. A set of golden eyes heavy with sleep opened. The blond brows furrowed.

She scrambled away but fell off the bed and onto the floor. Her throat was tight making it difficult to speak. "Who the hell are you?"

"Etain?" The strange man reached for her, his fingers lightly brushing her arm.

Her skin burned like acid where he touched her. Her throat opened up and let out a blood-curdling scream. The farther she shuffled from the bed, the more she realized how her body ached. When she looked down, not only was she naked, the bruises on her arms and torso made her want to vomit.

Eyes wide, she stared at him. "What have you done to me?" With great effort, she climbed to her feet. "Get out!"

He sat up, acting as though he were as shocked as she.

What a horrible man! To do these things and sleep with me!

"You are safe, Etain," he lied. "You are home."

Her gaze darted around the room again. "This is not my home." She hunched over wrapping her arms around her waist and backed away. It hurt too much to stand straight. "How can I be safe with you?"

"It is me... Dar."

"No!" she shrieked. "You're a monster! Look what you've done to me!"

He shuffled from the bed, grabbed a pair of leather trousers from the floor, and wiggled into them.

Who the hell wears leather pants? She ran a hand through her hair as she turned her back. *Is he a musician?*

At that moment, the door burst open. Etain turned, ready to scream again, but saw a familiar face. She blinked several times, trying to make sense of why the woman was there.

"Jackie? What're you doing here? What has he done to you?"

The man turned. "Jackie—"

Etain's eyes widened. "Don't speak to her!"

He ignored her protests. "What are you doing up? You should be in bed." The infuriating man walked over to Jackie. "You took a hard hit."

"Hey." Jackie's gaze left Etain's for his. "I thought I'd better check on her."

Etain felt awkward watching the Dar impersonator help her friend to a chair. *How can she stand his touch after what he's done to us?*

Jackie frowned at her. "Dar, give her that comforter. She's gotta be cold."

The man pushed his hands through his hair. "She is none too happy with me right now. As you can tell." He grabbed the duvet from the bed and approached Etain, holding the cover in front of him. "Jackie is right. You must be cold. Let me wrap this around you."

"No!" She stepped into the curtains just behind her and realized she was shivering. She hadn't noticed the chill in the room until Jackie mentioned it. Her eyes darted to her friend, then to the man. "Put it on the floor and back away." He did as she asked. Slowly, she walked toward the discarded duvet, her gaze on him. Once close enough, she crouched, cringing from the pain, grabbed the cover, and wrapped it around her as she stood.

He watches me like a hawk waiting to swoop in on its prey.

"You should not be up either," said the fake Dar. "I am sure the babies could use the rest as much as you."

Like hell. "I am *not* getting back into that bed so you can abuse me more." She wrapped her arms tighter around her. "How do you know about the babies? I haven't told anyone."

The man shook his head. "I do not understand. *I* did not hurt you. I *saved* you."

"Saved me? I was in Nunnehi. Dar left me there."

"Nunnehi?"

"Me, Spirit, and Swee were visiting with Alatariel, the queen."

He furrowed his brows. "Don't you know who I am?"

"You're a monster."

"*A chuisle*, please get into bed. I will make you breakfast."

Her gaze sharpened. "What did you say?"

Again, he stared at her as if he didn't have a clue.

She scrutinized him from head to toe and back to... "What the hell is *that*?"

His eyes darted left and right as he raised his hands with a shrug. "I didn't do it."

Etain pointed a finger at him.

His hand went to his chest. "The necklace? You ga—"

"No!" she shrieked, pointing more fervently. "*That,* on your chest! The mark I share with my husband." Etain pointed at the identical mark on her chest. "The proof we belong together."

She rushed at him but stopped just short of pushing him. *Man, I want to hurt you!*

"Why?" Angry tears filled her eyes. "Is this another form of torture? Your way of telling me I belong to *you?* I *don't*! I won't *ever* belong to you!" She turned and stormed away as far as the room would allow. "And don't you *dare* use those words. *A chuisle*. Only my Dar ever called me that."

Jackie sighed, pinching the bridge of her nose. "Why don't you give us a few minutes, Dar. Maybe get breakfast started?"

"Hmph. I am sorry, milady. It is not my intention to upset you." He moved toward Etain, but she retreated toward the curtains. "All right." He raised his hands in surrender. "Please get back into bed. You and the babies need to rest. I promise, you are safe here."

She gathered the duvet around her but didn't move otherwise. "Go away."

He bowed his infuriating blond head.

"As you wish. I will return with breakfast."

"Don't bother. I'm not hungry."

"Etain..."

"Get out! Get out! *Get. Out!*"

He pursed his lips but left the room.

"Etain." Jackie shifted in her seat.

"Why are you being nice to him?" She shuffled closer to the chair. "What are you even doing here?"

Jackie scooted to the edge of her seat and placed her hands on each arm, ready to push up. "Let's get you into bed. You've been through a lot."

"No more than you by the bruises on your face."

She slumped back, her hand going to her forehead. "Dar didn't do this to me or that to you."

"No, he didn't. That blond man did."

Jackie furrowed her brows. "Dar said he was your husband."

"When did you meet Dar?"

"Not long after Cruella and her sisters bashed my head in."

"Who?"

Jackie waved a hand. "It doesn't matter. That man you call a monster saved me. And you."

Etain shuffled to the bed and crawled in. "I don't want to talk about him."

Jackie slowly stood. "How about we have breakfast in here?"

Silence.

"Etain?"

"Just you," she whispered, pulling the duvet up to her chin. "Keep him away from me."

Dar stood outside the bedroom door not sure of what to do next. *She has no memory of me.* He turned his back to the door. *Well, not as I am now.*

Barefoot, he padded to his own room and dressed, his thoughts on how he could fix this. He knew his children were weak, but they were the only ones who might know what was happening with his wife. He sucked in a breath and slowly blew it out. With a calm heart, he sent a message.

"Hello, my sweet children."

He waited a few moments but received no response.

"It is Da, little ones. Can you hear me?"

Nothing.

He paced the room, then sat on the edge of his bed.

"My precious ones, can you hear me?"

Still no response.

Dar stood and composed himself with another deep breath. "I will fix breakfast. No matter what she says, they must be hungry."

In the kitchen, he focused on the business of making a light meal for his family, himself included, and Jackie. Etain may not want his touch, but she might allow him to share a meal in the same room. With eggs in the skillet and toast in the oven, a small voice spoke to him.

"Da..."

So light, so frail, he almost did not hear it. He froze. Which twin was it?

"Son?"

"Ema."

His eyes widened. *"You know your name, little one?"*

"We. Listen."

"You are so clever."

"Jamie. Likes his. Too."

"Jamie?" Dar chuckled. *"I will have to remember that."*

"Mama. Doesn't know. We know."

A frown came to his face. *"You must be weak."*

"Mama is sick."

His heart skipped a beat. *"Sick?"*

He sensed his daughter's sigh.

"She's forgotten. The red man."

"She has forgotten many things, little one."

"To save herself, Da."

"I know you need to rest, Ema, but how can I help?"

A faint voice joined in the conversation.

"Only the craze man can make her see."

"Jamie, son. The crazy man?"

Silence

"Jamie? Ema?"

"Craze. Da."

No amount of persuasion brought another response. Dar quietly closed his eyes and murmured a healing prayer.

❦

Jackie followed the smell of burnt eggs and walked into the kitchen. Standing at the range, spatula in hand, Dar turned at her entrance.

"Jackie, you should have stayed upstairs. It will not be much longer."

She scrunched her nose and sat at the island, noticing a huge crack through the middle of the granite countertop. "I hope you aren't expecting us to eat that."

He eyed the debacle in the frying pan. "A slight complication. I doubt she would eat them no matter how perfectly they were cooked. But..." He picked up a plate of toast. "This is still good. Cold but palatable with a little jam."

She gave him a slight grin. "Jam is good. You have any coffee?"

"Is that wise?"

"If you want my help with that one..." Jackie pointed toward the ceiling.

Dar chuckled. "Coming right up, milady." He shuffled toward the coffeemaker, grabbed a cup from the cabinet above and poured. "Black?"

"Is there any other way?"

He pushed the cup to her. "Thank you for stepping in and handling the situation upstairs."

Jackie sucked in a breath as she dragged the cup closer. "She's your wife, Dar, not a situation."

Aghast, he stared at her. "That is not—"

"I'm sure." She lifted the cup to her lips and blew at the steam drifting off the top. "I'm sure you have the best of intentions."

Dar huffed and walked to the dented refrigerator. "How would you know? You live in the human world and have no clue what goes on in the Alamir." He returned to the stove with a carton of milk.

The hairs on the back of Jackie's neck rose. "What the *hell* do you know about me?" She pushed off the barstool and walked around the island. Standing in front of the seven-foot Krymerian, she craned her neck to look him in the eyes. "I've known that girl most of her life. I worked with her father in his dealings with the Alamir. I didn't approve, but a man has to provide, and James did quite well. I loved them like my own—James, Auri, Robert, and especially Etain. She was...*is* an angel, just like her mother."

Her intensity forced Dar back a step.

"I swore to her parents I would take care of her and Robert if anything happened to them. James *knew* the time might come, because he'd made the mistake of working with the darker side of the Alamir."

She wanted to poke a finger in his chest, but wasn't quite able to reach, so she poked him in the stomach. "Maybe it's *you* who doesn't know what goes on in the Alamir. Maybe you aren't as smart as you think you are."

Dar frowned. "May I ask a more personal question?" Jackie lifted a hand, palm up, indicating it was okay. "Knowing their parents were dead, did you search for either of the children?"

She narrowed her eyes. "I didn't know they needed findin'. It was Etain who told me her parents were dead."

His brows furrowed. "Etain?"

"One night not so long ago, she showed up in my bar with Krz and Kane. They're Alamir too. The Haluci clan, or so they said." Jackie shrugged and returned to her seat. "She'd joined them on a mission to save some woman politician. Afterward, she came back to the bar for a catch-up. It was then she told me what had happened." She sipped her coffee, staring out the broken window. "Her father had plans to secretly close his business and move away. When I didn't hear from him or Auri, I thought he'd gone through with it, and they were living somewhere safe. It didn't occur to me they'd been murdered. That's why I didn't go looking." She leaned toward him with a hard gaze. "Had I known, those kids would've been my first priority."

"I am sorry I offended you, Jackie."

His comment made her sit back and sip at her coffee. "I tend to get carried away." Dar reached into a cabinet and pulled out a glass, filling it with milk. "Like my Etain, I will know where you stand." He grabbed a tray set on the counter and loaded it with the toast, milk, and a fresh cup of coffee. "Tell me what you think is going on with my lady."

"You saw something she didn't want you to see." She lowered her cup. "Weakness."

"But I am her husband. She has seen me in worse shape."

She raised a brow. "Has she? I didn't see a lot, but I saw enough. That red-skinned animal didn't take her off to have a tea party."

Jackie didn't know Dar well enough to recognize the signs of his anger—a hardened expression, red rings around his pupils, the sudden stillness in his demeanor. He picked up the cast-iron skillet and threw it. She slid off the barstool and ducked under the island just before it hit the wall, plaster and burned eggs flying into the room. A few bits hit her in the process before tapping against the floor.

He stormed out of the room.

Jackie crawled out from her safe spot and pulled herself up. "Damn. I understand a little better now." Turning, she noticed the tray was gone. "Oh, Lord. I best get up there."

A light knock on Etain's door brought no answer. It seemed to be a trend. Balancing the tray in one arm, he slowly pushed the door open. She lay in bed, but was she asleep or plotting? He glanced around the room for any stray daggers.

"Etain?" He stood beside the bed across from her. "I have toast and milk. I know it is not much, but I doubt your stomach could handle more than that."

He heard her sigh from beneath the covers. "Jackie was supposed to bring it, not you."

"I am sure she will make another appearance soon."

"What if I'm not hungry?"

How he would love to grab the covers and give her a good shake. "You have been asleep for three days, milady. I find that hard to believe."

The covers moved and an ice-blue eye peeked out. "*Three* days?"

"Oh, aye. Since I am here, do you mind if I have a cup of coffee while you eat?"

She considered him for a long moment. "As long as you stay," she glanced at the fireplace, "over there."

"I shall do just that after I place the tray closer to you." The blue eyes turned hard. "Just the tray. I promise." He walked to her side of the bed. The covers twisted and turned as she shifted beneath them and peeked out, watching him place the tray on the side table. "I am going to take my coffee and sit in the chair so we can talk. Is that far enough away?"

She held the duvet tight to her as she sat up. What bruises he could see had started to fade. The dark circles under her eyes were pronounced and her cheekbones too prominent, but there was a spark in her eyes that gave him hope she would recover. Her gaze rolled up to meet his. A slight bow of her head gave him permission.

Cup in hand, he moved toward the chair.

"Where's Jackie?" she asked.

When he heard the dishes clink against one another, he stopped, but forced himself to not turn around. He had to let her do it, alone. He didn't answer until he was seated. "The last I saw she was in the kitchen."

"I wanted to have breakfast with her, not you."

Dar shrugged as he tested his coffee. "She needs her rest too."

With the tray settled on the bed, Etain bit into a piece of toast, closing her eyes as she chewed. After a sip of milk, she glared at him. "If we're not your prisoners, why are we here?"

The straightforward question made him choke on his coffee and cough. *Some things never change.* He set the cup aside while his mind raced to come up with a plausible answer that would not cause her or him further distress.

"Pardon me. Just a tad too hot." He gave her a shaky smile. "You ask a good question."

She raised a blonde brow, chewing her toast.

"Well, let's see... You mentioned you were in Nunnehi with Spirit and Swee."

"Aye."

"Then you must remember why you were there."

Her gaze on him, she sipped from the glass of milk. "Laugharne was under attack."

"Aye." *We're going back that far, are we?* "Once it was over, Spirit asked if I would bring you here in case there was another one, to protect you and the babies from further stress."

She set the glass on the side table. "Why you? Why not my Dar?"

He cleared his throat. "She did not say, and I did not ask."

She thought on his words while chewing another bite of toast. "Why Jackie? What does she have to do with all of this?"

He stalled for time by lifting his cup from beside the chair. "Another good question." *For which I have no answer.* "I assume she had come to visit you." It was as close to the truth as he could get without mentioning what actually happened.

"But she's human. How can she be here?"

He shrugged.

A blonde brow rose. "If I choose to contact Spirit, will you try to stop me?"

"Of course not." *Next thing on the list—contact Spirit and fill her in.* "You are not a prisoner, Etain."

"Do I have any clothes?"

"Oh, aye." Dar waved a hand toward the walk-in wardrobe. "There are a few outfits in the closet. The rest will arrive in a few weeks' time. Shall I leave you alone to dress?" He stood.

"I'd like to shower and go for a walk. Alone, if that's okay."

He bowed. "The bath is just through the black door. My home is your home. You are well protected here, but please do not go too far." He smiled to himself as he walked to the door. The spark still burned inside her. Time was what was required. Time would heal her wounds. All he had to do was keep his sanity until that day arrived.

While Etain bathed, Dar reached out to Spirit to apprise her of their conversation and asked that she not share the information with the others at Laugharne.

"What if her memory hasn't returned by the time they get there? You'll have a hard time keeping things under wraps with that lot."

"One thing at a time, milady. I cannot explain it, but the fact she talked to me this morning gives me hope."

"I'm sure there'll be plenty more questions you'll find hard to answer."

"Perhaps, but she remembers you, Swee, and Alatariel. Surely—"

"Aye, and you said she remembers a version of you too. What if what she remembers in her head isn't who we are?"

Dar blew out a breath. *"I do not know, milady. I just do not know."*

"Please, take it slow with her, Dar. And don't mention Inferno. He was alive when she was in Nunnehi."

"Oh, aye. Good idea, Spirit."

"Have you found out who the woman is?"

"She is a friend of Etain's family and has known her since she was a baby."

The silence made him wonder if she was still there.

"Are you with me, Spirit?"

"Aye. I'm here."

"What is it?"

"What're your plans for the demon?"

Dar blew out a breath and scrubbed a hand over his face.

"He will have to wait. Perhaps when Linq arrives we can form a plan, but for now, Etain is my main concern."

"Whatever you do, be careful. He is a devil."

"Believe me, I know." He pinched the bridge of his nose. *"I have to go but will keep in touch."*

Once the big man was gone, Etain finished the toast and milk. Had it really been three days? She threw back the covers and scooted off the bed, noting how much the pain had lessened.

The only protection I need is from you.

She ran a hand through her hair and frowned. "Ick." Proof enough it'd been several days since she'd washed.

Although feeling better, she walked slowly to the bathroom and peeked inside. She raised her brows at the oversized copper bathtub. Something about it seemed ominous.

Maybe it's the contrast between the black tiles and its shiny surface.

She laughed at herself and reached for the tap. "It's just a tub, silly."

With the tub filled, she slipped into its warm comfort and leaned back. Submerged completely in the soothing water, her body floated, weightless, tendrils of hair tickling where it drifted around her. Suspended in a mindless moment, peace came to her.

She languished in the copper tub with no notice of the time. It felt good to just *be* for a while. She wasn't a wife, a mother, or a friend—no conversations, no need to please, no golden eyes full of questions. She sighed, content in her newfound peace.

Noticing her hands white and wrinkled, she laughed. Perhaps she'd been at peace a bit too long. It was time to get back to reality. A walk would be a good start, but the big man was right about not pushing her limits. The house must be big. She couldn't imagine a man as large as him living in a hovel. She could probably explore for days, and hopefully, never see *him*. Maybe Jackie would join her. The outdoors could come later.

She reached for a towel as she stepped out of the tub and caught her reflection in the mirror on the back wall. Her body was a train wreck.

"If he didn't do this to me, who did?" She touched one fading bruise and winced. Still sensitive. She turned and twisted around to view her backside. There were pink welts across her back, bottom, and thighs.

She furrowed her brows in frustration and closed her eyes. "I don't remember."

A blood-skinned face close to hers flashed in her mind.

Her eyes popped open. She stumbled back, grabbing the towel as she turned, and ran to the first door she saw. She ripped it open and stepped into what was obviously a man's room with a large bed, heavy furniture, and weapons displayed on the walls.

"No!" she screamed, terrified she'd returned to his quarters. In a panic, her head swiveled in every direction, afraid he would appear at any moment. She ran into the bathroom, spotted another door, and ran to it.

This room was decorated in purple, red, and black, again with a large bed, yet it was feminine, albeit more gothic than she preferred. The black stone fireplace enticed her to its dark surface. Hand on her chest, she stared into the stone certain she would feel his disgusting touch at any moment. When she heard a young woman's laughter, she turned.

"Hello?"

The room...

Her heart pounded and sweat beaded on her forehead. She couldn't breathe. Something had happened here. Something to do with Faux.

She ran back into the bathroom and slammed the door shut, her breaths coming short and fast.

Three bedrooms attached to the same bath?

She ran through the only open door and sighed in relief to be in the sage and purple room once again. Throwing the towel aside, she went to the wardrobe and dressed in the first thing she found—a purple skirt and matching top. The outfit exposed her protruding belly, but she didn't care. She had to get away from these rooms, out of this house. How could she ever trust a man—a pervert—who had a set-up like this? *He has to be in league with...With...* She growled in frustration. Her mind wouldn't cooperate. With whatever haunted her.

Etain opened the door and stepped into the hallway, looked right, and saw the stairs to her left. She walked as quickly as she could listening for tell-tale signs of the man, tiptoed down the steps, and dashed toward the front doors.

Just as she reached for the handle, the door opened and there he stood, the pervert.

"Milady! I was not expecting to see you."

His cheeks, tinged pink from the cold, accentuated his golden eyes. Add the dark cloak on his shoulders... *He's incredibly handsome.*

She swallowed, eyeing him from head to toe. "You are disgusting."

He stepped back and allowed her through the door. "Where are you going, Etain?"

After a few steps, she stopped and turned. "Don't you follow me."

"You should put on your boots, milady."

She considered her bare feet. The rocks of the courtyard *were* murderous without the proper gear.

"Where are you going now?"

The cheerful glint in his eyes infuriated her even more. "I won't sleep in that room another night." She walked into the house.

"Are you not going for a walk?"

"Not at the moment."

BANSHEE

Faux relaxed back into the fluffy pillows of her luxurious bed, thinking of another time in Mexico. *Mmm, the sexy troubadour.* How she wished her life were that carefree again. No responsibilities, no cares, no interfering Alamir or Krymerians telling her how to live her life. This one seemed to be working out well. Except she had no idea where she was or Freeblood's whereabouts. If he were even alive.

She traced a finger over the bandages on her belly. The people dressed in white—she wasn't sure if they were doctors or nurses, but they seemed to know what they were doing—had taken great care with her, asking if she was in pain, hungry, cold. She'd never been treated like this in her life. As though she was someone special, someone of worth. They'd given her a warm bath, washed her hair, tended to her wounds, and made sure she was comfortable in this amazing room.

This amazingly *white* room. *Too white for my tastes. A splash of purple, red, or even black would help tone it down.* She closed her eyes and let her mind drift. There wasn't much else she could do, and a nap sounded totally irresistible.

Summoned by one of the midwives, Phie entered the pristine breeding facility. No expense was spared on its maintenance or the care of the valuable inhabitants and their spawn. It was these breeders who kept them flush, producing future Trodaithe. Fighters who would draw in the crowds and guarantee their return time and time again.

Coming to the preview chamber where newborns were displayed, she stopped and peered through the window, smiling at the numerous potentials. Which one would prove the grand champion and bring glory to her house? Who would die in their first battle? So many possibilities for her and the gambling house. Her clientele would bet on anything and everything.

As she turned, her reflection in the glass caught her eye. She indulged herself for a few moments, admiring her dark, wavy hair and the glow of light at her temple. Being in their own dimension, the atmosphere provided the hydration necessary for their delicate systems, requiring no additional moisture. It was refreshing not to have a constant puddle at her feet or water running into her eyes. She smirked. *And they wonder why Banshee keen.*

Fluffing her hair, she blew a kiss at her reflection and proceeded down the corridor to the head midwife's office.

"Phie! Come in. Come in. I'm so glad you were free."

"*Maidin maith*, Siobhan." Phie sat in the chair in front of the desk. "What's so important ya needed to speak to me personally?"

A pale, blue-skinned woman dressed in doctor's whites, her dark hair pulled back, settled behind her desk, and peered at Phie from over her spectacles. "There is no need for that today. I have news that should put you in quite the good mood."

Phie brushed away a speck of dust that had landed on her gossamer gown. "Oh?"

"This new one you brought in. She is not human."

Phie raised a dark brow. "Is that so? How can ya tell?"

"Her blood. We run tests on every breeder brought in." She placed her elbows on the desk and leaned toward the Banshee. "The blood holds many secrets." She winked and leaned back in her chair. "Fortunately, we know how to unlock them."

Not particularly interested, she sighed as she inspected her pointed nails. "And why would I give a particular shit about this one?"

The midwife steepled her hands beneath her chin. "Human is in the mix, along with a few other bloodlines."

Phie rolled her eyes, weary of the woman. "Ya said she wasn't human." She had more important things to do, such as test the Alamir. But the doctors told her she must wait for him to heal, which meant she had to save it for another day. *There is the female goblin who has yet to be tested. Perhaps she and the—*

"Phie!"

Her light gaze met the infuriating woman's violet one. "It would help if ya'd get to the point instead of trying to build a story I'm sure will fall as flat as yer chest." The midwife huffed making her smirk. "Ya know it's true."

"You're so hurtful, Phie. I work hard for the Banshee and do my best to provide a strong and sturdy stock for your Trodaire Games. If this doesn't interest you, perhaps I should talk to Commander Phum."

Phie leaned forward, doing her best to appear apologetic. "Let's not bring me father into this. Please, dear Siobhan, tell me yer news."

The woman's wounded expression disappeared into a secretive smile. "She is a mix, as I said earlier." She stood, apparently too excited by her news to remain seated. "There is human, a touch of Elven, some demon, mostly Krymerian—"

Phie sat up straight. "Krymerian?"

Siobhan placed her hands on her desk and leaned toward the Banshee. "That's not the best part." She practically giggled. "The final piece of the puzzle is..." She bit her bottom lip, grinning like the Cheshire cat, "Draconian!"

That brought Phie out of her seat. "Are you sure, Siobhan? Absolutely certain?"

The woman resembled a bobblehead, nodding like a fool. "Absolutely!"

"Ya must keep this under wraps, for now. Do ya hear me?"

The midwife frowned. "But this is the best news we've had in a millennia. Why would we—"

"Because the children of this woman will be priceless. We will match her with our best males." Phie paced in front of the desk. "I wonder if the Krymerian could be caged. If he refused to cooperate, we could harvest his seed, impregnate her—"

"The Krymerian? You mean the Silent Warrior?" Siobhan's eyes widened as she placed a hand over her chest. "How would you ever control a man like that?"

Phie's lips curved into a wicked grin. "It will take time, but we will dominate the Trodaire world." She turned toward the door. *With the Krymerian and the woman that demon covets in our hands. He's mistaken if he thinks I'll be happy with just her brats.* Her hand on the handle, she glanced over her shoulder. "Say nothing to me father. Give me time to devise a plan, Siobhan. Will ya do that?"

"Don't take too long. This one is ready to give birth. Once that happens, the news will spread. I have no power over the babes after they're taken from their mothers."

"Don't be so afeared, lass. It will be fine."

"You best make it soon."

Phie narrowed her eyes. "Do ya agree?"

"Agreed. But you will owe me."

Phie marched out the door, closing it behind her. *I'll not be indebted to anyone, especially an Elf in me service.*

Siobhan left her office not long after the Banshee. She had her own secret and no desire to share it with the heartless Phie. She and her sisters would see the young succubus sold off to the highest bidder, no matter her bloodline, and that would be a waste.

The creature was more valuable here. If Phie could get the Krymerian to cooperate, either willingly or by force, it would be a boost for the games. Especially if she could find a way to manipulate the DNA to produce more succubi. Siobhan rubbed her hands together, excited by the prospect. The power those female warriors would have over the males!

The one problem she'd not been able to sort was why this one didn't have the usual horns, tail, or powers. And how did she become pregnant? She'd not heard of such a thing with the succubi. This was another puzzle worth solving.

She entered the wing of expectant mothers. Some were human, their spawn to be used as fodder for the opening games. They lasted just long enough to whet the appetite of the crowd and get them in a betting mood. Others consisted of faeries, goblins, demons, even a couple of Elves. And now she had a succubus with Krymerian and Draconian blood! Could life get any better?

Siobhan walked the corridor toward the creature's room. She had to know more about her and hoped she would come to trust her enough to share her story.

After a light knock on the door, she slowly opened it to a naked form lounging across the bed. Her gasp opened the creature's eyes—dark and mysterious. The woman sat up.

"Go away. You've taken enough blood." She scooted off the bed and wrapped a plush, white robe around her.

"I'm sorry. Er..." The midwife ducked her head, feeling rather uncomfortable as she closed the door. "I don't know your name."

"Hmph." The succubus pulled the sash of the robe tight under her breasts. "No one seems to give a damn about that. Why now? You weren't interested when you were sticking your stupid needles into me."

"It was necessary." Siobhan thought it important she defend her actions. "It is for your well-being, and ours, to ensure you've not contracted any diseases or carry strains of contagions that could compromise the compound."

"Compound? Where the hell am I?"

"I'm not supposed to say..."

"Seriously?" Placing her hands on her hips, her bandaged, round belly protruded from the folds of the robe.

"Well..." Siobhan shrugged. *What harm could it do?* "You're in Nocturna."

"Is Freeblood here too?"

She swore she noticed a momentary fire light in those fathomless eyes. Siobhan furrowed her brows. She'd not heard the name before.

"My partner. Is he here?"

"Oh, him. Well, yes, he's here..."

She rushed at the midwife. "Can I see him? Is he okay?"

Siobhan stepped back, indignant. "No. That will not be permitted."

"But he's alive?"

"He is in the infirmary, healing from a nasty gash to his head."

Sudden tears brimmed in the dark eyes as she turned away and walked back to the bed, collapsing onto the covers. "Faux. My name is Faux." She raised her head. "Are you sure I can't see him?"

"It is forbidden, I'm afraid, but I can keep you informed of his condition if you'd like."

Faux sat up. "That would be nice."

Siobhan dared to venture closer. "I'd like to know more about you, Faux. Would you mind talking to me?"

"You aren't like the ones who dragged me here. What are you?"

"Phie and her sisters are Banshee. I am Telquessir." At Faux's confused expression, she decided it best to explain. "My people are of a higher order of Elves."

"I'm not stupid." She rolled her eyes. "Elves aren't blue, and your ears aren't pointy."

Siobhan gave her an understanding smile. "Well, not in the usual sense, no. But if you look closely... May I sit?" She indicated the side of the bed next to Faux, who nodded. Taking a seat, she pulled her hair from her face and turned her head to give the girl a better view. She pointed at the tip of her ear. "You can see a slight rise."

Faux squinted and leaned forward. So close, her breath warmed Siobhan's ear. The black gaze held hers for a long moment before Faux leaned back. "If you say so."

"I'm not certain why my skin appears bluish in color. Maybe it's because my blood is blue."

"Your eyes are violet. I like violet."

"I'm told that my father had the same eyes."

Faux crossed her arms over her chest. "Once my baby is born, me and Freeblood will go home."

The midwife didn't have the heart to tell her the only way she would leave Nocturna would be in a coffin.

Siobhan shifted off the bed and pulled up a chair. "How is it you have the workings of a succubus inside, but none of the markers on the outside?"

Faux shrugged. "I pissed someone off."

The midwife raised both brows. "And this someone took away what you are?"

She raised her chin. "I am still me. I'm more than a set of horns and a tail."

Siobhan leaned forward. "What if I could give them back to you?"

Faux seemed to consider what she'd said and laughed. "Leave me alone, you stupid woman. That won't ever happen."

⁕

It was dark, quiet, except for the sound of his own breathing. The sack over his head didn't allow him to see much. He didn't know whether it was because of the woven fabric of the sack itself or the place was dark. His bet was on the latter; some deep, dark hole to break him down.

Whatever those things were that brought him here, he hoped to never see them again. They were ruthless, unemotional bitches who deserved... *No. I would love to see them one more time. Take hold of their slimy, wet heads and stick 'em into an electrical socket. Watch them burn in a blue fire.* Freeblood smiled. Now if he could get out of these ropes.

Lying on his side, he extended his blue gem into a small dirk, just long enough to be manageable against the rope around his wrists. It took some time, but he cut himself free and pulled the sack off his head.

"Damn if it's any better without it."

He brightened the blue gem and sat up. In the next instant, he threw up and fell onto his side, holding his head.

"Shit." The back of his head hurt, and the hair matted to his scalp. He decided another minute or two might stop the spinning sensation. It helped slow it down but didn't prevent the torment in his brain. *Where is Faux? They said something about her being a breeder.*

"Fuck!" Freeblood leaned against the wall for support, using his hands to push up to his feet. "I've got to get to her."

The clang of the opening door turned his attention away from any escape plans. A tall, thin, green creature with a long face and pointy ears extending away from his head entered the room. His clothing appeared medieval, and his large feet were bare.

What in the hell is that?

The creature's long, bony fingers tapered into sharp black nails. It pointed one of its digits at him, grunted, then at the door.

Freeblood glared at the being. "No way." He pointed at the back of his head. "Thanks to some overexuberant asshole, I can't walk on my own."

The green thing stared at him. After a snort, it shuffled out of the cell and grunted again. Within moments, he heard footsteps slapping in the corridor. Two green creatures as ugly as the first, yet bigger, burst into the cell. Each grabbed Freeblood by an arm despite his shouted protests and carried him out of the room.

"Where are you taking me?"

His head ready to explode, he shut his mouth and let them drag him to wherever the hell they wanted. With his eyes closed, he realized the floor was on a grade, gradually sloping upward. At least he was out of the cell. Maybe he'd be able to locate Faux, then find some way to get the hell out.

HOPE RESTORED

L inq pulled a well-used piece of paper from his pocket and unfolded it onto the table, then reached for a small pencil in his vest. "Will the transport for the horses be here tomorrow?"

"In the morning," said Aramis. "That should give plenty of time to get them situated on the ship."

"Especially since we don't leave till the next day. So we have... What? Seventeen horses to load? Not counting the other livestock."

"Make that nineteen horses," Spirit said, standing in the doorway.

"Nineteen?" Linq referred to his notes. "I counted those horses several times. There are seventeen." He scooted out of his chair and motioned her to join them.

Her smile was melancholy as she sat. "Inferno wanted to give Dar and Etain a special wedding gift. He'd planned on going himself, but..." She closed her eyes and shook her head. "I sent Wolfe and Elfin to complete his business."

Linq asked the obvious question. "What business?"

"A couple of Friesians for Dar's breeding stock—a stallion and a mare. She's with foal, so that will be a bonus for his stables."

Taurnil whistled as he sat back. "Nice gift."

They talked on into the wee hours of the morning as old friends do when they know they'll soon be parted.

When the grandfather clock in the hallway announced the time as one a.m., Linq pushed out of his chair, stretching his arms over his head. "Tomorrow will be filled with tying up loose ends, packing, and farewells. We should get to bed."

All were reluctant to break it up but were agreed. One by one, the allies bid each other a good night.

While those at Laugharne Castle prepared for their departure to the Von-Neshta estate, Dar worked diligently to nurse his precious wife back to health. During her waking hours, her mind blocked the trauma of Dathmet as a defense mechanism.

However, nightmares haunted her dreams resulting in terrible screaming fits in the middle of the night. To help her sleep, Dar invoked the powerful Elven sleeping spell the Wizards had used on him in Nunnehi and reversed it at first light so she would wake naturally.

Dar walked on the edge of complete exhaustion. He spent most of his nights wandering the estate in contemplation of new ways to mend his wife's tormented soul. On those rare nights when he was able to find sleep's sweet respite, he collapsed in a chair set close to the bed to be near her.

His attempts to persuade her to take his blood proved futile and ended either with Etain in tears or staring out the window, ignoring him completely.

"What I need is my privacy, not a transfusion." Out of bed and dressed, Etain stormed to the balcony doors of her room.

"Etain, you are so pale. You do not eat enough." Having brought her breakfast, Dar set the tray on the nightstand, unaware of the dark shadows underneath his eyes.

"Have you seen yourself lately? You look like death. *Your* blood is the last thing I need."

He dipped his head in acknowledgment. "I will not mention it again. Please come eat your porridge."

Arms crossed over her chest, she turned. "As soon as you leave, I will eat."

He clenched and unclenched his jaw. "I will leave after you finish your meal."

Her voice increased in volume with each word. "You will go *now*, or I won't eat at all."

"Then it will be a long morning, milady." His voice rose to meet hers. "I am not going anywhere until this bowl is empty."

Etain considered him for a long moment before walking toward the bed. Holding onto the headboard, she stepped up onto the mattress, her defiant gaze locked with his, and walked to the other side, glaring at him as she picked up the bowl.

Jackie stepped into the room just as Etain dropped the bowl. "What the hell is going on in here?"

Dar caught the dish, saving it and the porridge from certain death. "She refuses to eat."

"I haven't refused to eat." Her hard gaze turned on him. "I just don't want *you* here."

"Mother of us all, give me strength." Jackie joined Dar at the bedside. "He's right. You don't eat, girl."

"Because he's always *here*." Her eyes widened on the last word.

Dar stiffened. "You force me to—"

Jackie quieted his retort with a touch on his arm and turned to Etain. "Stop acting like a child, sit your ass down, and eat your breakfast. Dar, you sit in the chair and make sure she eats it all." Her gaze returned to Etain. "And drink the damn milk. This isn't just about you. Those babies need their nourishment."

Dar offered his hand to help Etain sit, but she turned her head and sank to the bed of her own accord. He sat in the chair, watching as Jackie set the tray on her lap.

"Until I know you're eating as you should, Dar will join you for every meal." She held up a hand at Etain's glare. "You don't have to talk. You don't even have to look at him. But you *do* have to keep down the noise. It's not good for any of us."

Etain stabbed her spoon into the porridge. "Fine."

Dar did not smile, but his heart sang Jackie's praises for the small victory. Desperate to save his family, he decided it would be easier to add an extra ingredient to each of her meals in the future, drawing his blood and carefully mixing it into her food. That, in addition to a healing chant, would ensure her recovery.

Forced to watch his wife shun his touch, the days passed slowly for Dar. Yet his love held fast and his heart remained true, two things that would never change. While passing her room one morning, he noticed the door slightly ajar and heard voices. At first, he felt cheated, noting that Etain and Jackie were sharing breakfast. He'd become accustomed to his silent time with his wife.

"I don't understand why I mistrust the man so much. He seems gentle enough, and sweet," Etain said before biting into a piece of toast.

"He's not so bad once you get to know him."

Etain's eyes widened. "Really? He's so domineering."

"That he is." Jackie considered her for a moment. "But I believe his intentions are honorable. And I know he will take good care of you and those babies."

"You sound like you're going somewhere." He heard the alarm in Etain's voice and quietly opened the door to slip inside. She grabbed Jackie's arm. "Please don't leave me alone with him."

The women sat in front of the balcony doors. Jackie was angled just enough to keep an eye on the door. Her eyes widened briefly telling him to keep his distance. The big man acquiesced and stood near the bed where Etain would not see him.

Jackie patted her hand. "I'm not going anywhere for a while. I need to sort out a few things in my head. They're still a little fuzzy, but I also have a bar to run. It'd be nice if I had a sister or someone who could step in while I recover, but—"

Etain let go and leaned back in her chair. "I used to have a sister."

"Used to?" Jackie's gaze darted to Dar, who shrugged.

"Well, I thought of her as a sister." She shook her head, staring out the doors. "She had an unusual beginning. It's complicated."

"What do you mean?"

Dar imagined the rolling of her beautiful eyes as she exhaled heavily. "I knew you were gonna make me explain." She laughed nervously and ran a hand through her hair. "Let's see... It all started with my husband. He's gone now."

Etain's words pierced his heart like a great sword. He stepped back and leaned against the wall. *Gone? What is she saying?* His mind raced. Not that it mattered, but he knew for certain he was her first lover. There was no doubt.

"What're you saying, Etain?" Jackie echoed Dar's question.

"He wasn't my husband at the time." She lowered her head, picking at the armrest of the chair. "That was later. It was kinda weird how we met." She shrugged. "He saved my life and let me stay in his home to recuperate. He was a gracious host, gave me my own room far enough away from his so I would be comfortable. Not like here, where I'm in the one across the hall." She lifted her head. "I'm not sure if it was for *my* privacy or his." Her gaze turned toward the balcony doors. "Anyway, one morning, I woke to a girl with black hair, horns, and a long tail. It was a strange day."

Dar realized she was, in fact, speaking about him and Faux. His jumbled thoughts settled, and he sat on the edge of the bed.

"That *is* strange," Jackie said, unaware of their history. "What happened to your sister?"

"An angel took her away."

Jackie glanced at Dar again.

"She wasn't a bad sort. She just liked to have her fun. The Alamir even banned her for a time." Etain shook her head, a faint smile on her lips. "That girl loved trouble."

"And an angel took her?" Jackie sipped her coffee.

She answered in a wistful voice. "Long, golden hair, great, white wings, and the eyes of a lion."

Jackie choked on the coffee and coughed in response to her general description of Dar. Etain patted her on the back. "I'm okay," she said after a hard swallow. "Why did the angel take her?"

Dar dropped his head into his hands as his worst fears were confirmed. He had been aware of Etain's apparent aloofness, but to hear her say the words ripped his heart in two. He was more foreign to her today than when they first met.

"I guess because I couldn't get her to mend her ways. He stripped her of her powers and took her with him." The sadness in her voice was obvious.

Jackie considered her for a moment. "Tell me what happened to your husband."

Dar wearily raised his head, not wanting to hear it but unable to move.

This time, her voice turned melancholy. "Maybe he's with the angel too, or I wouldn't be here. I'd be with him."

It was not what he expected. He stood abruptly, which made Jackie jump from her chair startling Etain. "The angel, you say?"

"Are you okay?"

"Yes. I'm fine." Jackie patted her on the shoulder. "Sorry. I thought I heard something. Why would an angel take your husband?"

She shrugged. "Hell if I know."

Jackie met Dar's despondent gaze and slightly shook her head. "You don't recognize Dar at all?"

After several moments of silence, Etain whispered, "I just told you, Dar is gone."

Unable to hear any more, he stormed out of the room and slammed the door behind him.

Etain turned.

Jackie shrugged. "Must've been the wind." Etain seemed to accept the explanation with no question. "Well, *this* Dar owns the estate and has graciously allowed us to stay here until the babies are born."

Etain lovingly placed a hand on her growing belly. "He must be a good man if Spirit let me come here."

Jackie tried to remember if she had heard the name before. "Spirit?"

"Oh, aye. Spirit and Inferno. Lovely people. They're my Alamir family."

"I've not had the pleasure. Do they live in the Nunnehi you mentioned?"

"No." Etain shook her head. "They live in Laugharne. Well, Spirit does. Inferno passed not long ago."

Jackie bit her bottom lip. *Am I supposed to know this?* "Oh, well, all this is so new to me." She vaguely remembered hearing Spirit's name, but Laugharne was new. "Dar said he lives here alone, so it's no imposition on him. We're welcome to stay as long as we wish."

"A handsome man like him isn't married?"

Not knowing his past, Jackie fabricated as best she could, hoping the story would gain him some favor. "He *was* married, but she passed."

"That poor man." Her gaze drifted to the outside.

"Etain?" Her attempts to rouse her back into conversation failed. She feared the mention of Dar's previous life may have driven her deeper into her private world, but if so, the damage was done. Jackie hoped she was strong enough to work her way through it and come back to her family. Even though she wasn't sure Etain would hear, she said, "I'll be down the hall should you need me. Just two rooms. Okay?" She breathed a sigh of relief when she acknowledged her with a wave of her hand.

***

Returning to her room, Jackie closed the door and walked to the large window, where she spent a portion of each day watching Dar work his rose garden. It was a peaceful sight. His gentle touch as he went about the task of pruning stems and pulling weeds belied his often hard nature.

She worried about him. In the days she'd been here, she'd not seen him eat enough to sustain an ant and doubted he slept. The only thing she'd seen him consume was coffee, but he never seemed to slow down.

At night, she heard his restless pacing as he moved about the manor, stopping at his precious charge's door. Hoping for what? She wasn't sure.

It was apparent how much he enjoyed time with his wife as brief as it might be. At mealtimes, he went to great lengths to make each one a special occasion, preparing her favorite foods in the hope something would click and bring her back to him. Sometimes Etain would eat, sometimes not. Dar not at all.

She knew he blamed himself for Etain's state of mind, a guilt she saw weighed heavily on his shoulders.

I've only just met the man. He seems a decent sort, and God knows he loves that girl.

As the last thoughts passed through her mind, a sudden movement caught her eye. She watched Dar move through the garden, but something was different today. His actions didn't reflect his normal self-assured grace. They were sluggish as if his mind was a million miles away. His eyes affixed on nothing, he half-heartedly reached for the weeds, pulling mostly at thin air.

She pressed her forehead against the glass, watching him go through the motions of working his garden. A dark fear crept over her that Dar might lose his will to live if something didn't change with Etain soon. If that happened, her life would be altered in a way she feared would be the end of them both. Would he do something foolish? Could he?

He's not the kind of man who gives up that easily.

Another sharp movement made her focus. She watched the great warrior rip the roses from the ground, slinging dirt and flowers in every direction.

Dread tugged at her heart when he fell to his knees, holding his chest. Afraid he'd come to his end, she opened her mouth to yell for Etain, but before she could, he stood. A single rose fell to the ground.

She decided there and then to do whatever she could to bring the two back together.

Moving day was an early start for all. Up at dawn, Alaster and his staff prepared a quick breakfast that could be eaten on the move. Those leaving roamed through the kitchen at various times, everyone too excited to sit for a full meal.

As the sun peeked over the horizon, Linq and Taurnil stood in the courtyard of Laugharne Castle, waiting for those traveling to Dar's estate. Spirit and her clan stood at the bottom of the front steps, wishing their friends farewell. Tears were shed and promises to stay in touch made. Swee and Spirit walked toward the Elves.

"I'll miss you, Spirit." The women hugged, holding onto one another for a long moment.

"I will miss you too, lass." As they separated, Spirit swiped at yet another tear trailing down her cheek. "You remember how to contact me should you need my help?"

Swee sniffled. "Yes, I remember. I may be calling sooner than expected."

"I hope you get there in time. I'd hate to think of Dar and Freeblood scrambling about, trying to deliver a wee babe." Spirit laughed, trying her best not to cry again.

"If that happens, I definitely want to be there in time to see it." Swee chuckled. With one last hug, she turned, taking Taurnil's offered hand.

"Taurnil..." Spirit saying his name made him turn. She smiled and motioned to Wolfe, who held a large carrier in his hand.

The young Elf grinned, raising his brows. "What is this?"

"One last gift for Dar. We'd hoped it would be under better circumstances, but..." She sighed. "The times are what they are. Aye?"

"Aye."

Spirit reached for the carrier, but Wolfe bypassed her, handing it directly to Taurnil. "'Tis a bit heavy, milady."

As Taurnil accepted it, whatever was in the carrier shifted, followed by a small yip. The weight surprised him, and he nearly dropped it. Wolfe laughed, helping steady the carrier.

"He won't fit in this for long." Spirit looked somewhat sheepish. "I'm sure he'll be twice as big by the time you reach Dar's."

"A dog?" Taurnil stared at the box.

"A puppy!" said Wolfe.

The Elf peeked through the door at the light green eyes peering back at him. "*This* is a puppy?"

Spirit laughed. "Inferno believed a man should have someone he can always count on."

"Watch out, Linq." Taurnil laughed. "We have company. I will personally take care of him until we arrive. Thank you, Spirit, Wolfe."

The UWS clan watched as Linq opened a portal and everyone stepped through onto the dock. Spirit released a long sigh.

Zorn came up next to her, Felix by his side. "Why didn't they portal to Dar's and save the long trip?"

"To give Etain time to recover. She's not ready for this lot just yet."

He crossed his arms over his chest. "Why not stay here until she is?"

She gave him a narrowed gaze and mimicked her husband's Irish lilt. "Don't ya have chores ya should be doin'?" She turned to the rest of the clan. "Don't all of ya have chores?"

Felix barked and Zorn snapped to attention. "Uh, yes, ma'am."

She smiled to herself as everyone scurried off. "Shall we meet this afternoon and decide our plans for the future?" she hollered after them. Some answered with a wave of their hands.

Spirit gazed out toward the estuary and turned toward the castle. "It's too quiet already. But I have children to get to school."

After several long minutes, Dar regained his composure and wiped the tears from his eyes. When he stood, the rose he held to his chest fell to the ground. He returned to the house and walked past the stairs, pausing to open the face of the great grandfather clock. The press of a small lever opened a panel at the side of the stairs. Closing the glass, he stepped through to another set of stairs that descended into the depths of the manor.

At the bottom, he touched an electronic panel on the wall, illuminating the room and closing the door above. In the middle of the large room stood a table made of black granite.

Dar walked to the far end and gathered several liquid-filled bottles, boxes of herbs, and other oddities, including a small brazier, iron bowl, and strip of worn leather. With everything laid on the table, he measured the proper amounts of the ingredients, delicately adding each one to the bowl, and lit a fire.

When it glowed white, he positioned the tip of an iron rod in the center of the fire and closed his eyes in silent prayer. Resolved to his task, he opened them again and put the leather strip between his teeth, grabbing his dagger from his belt. He laid his hand on the table and cut off his pinky at the first joint in one swift move. Dar grimaced, sucking in a breath, then added the severed tip to the bowl, and quickly grabbed the rod from the brazier. He clamped his teeth on the leather strip and pressed the red-hot tip to his wound, sealing it amidst a long guttural groan and a few involuntary tears.

Once the pain dulled, he spit out the leather, grabbed one of the bottles, and pulled the cork with his teeth, dabbing oil onto his finger. The relief was instantaneous. He swiped a sleeve over his sweat covered brow and reinserted the cork into the bottle.

From a small drawer in the table, he removed a heart-shaped, silver locket and chain and submerged the pair into the inky black potion. After several minutes, he extracted the necklace from the brew and gently wiped it clean with a soft cloth. Happy with his work, he slipped it into his breast pocket.

Dar burned off the remainder of the potion and returned his tools to their proper place. With a touch to the electronic panel, the hidden door opened, and he climbed the stairs to the grandfather clock. A flick of the lever inside ensured the room remained hidden.

Physically and emotionally exhausted, all he wanted was sleep. Not that he expected to get it, but he hoped it would be so.

He yawned as he entered the dark bedroom, dragging his feet across the floor, and discarded his clothes on his way to the bed. His mind set on a well-deserved sleep, he crawled into bed and cuddled close to his wife.

Etain twitched a few times but soon settled. With her mind at rest, it seemed to set her body free. She leaned back into his warmth. As he had done on so many nights since coming together as soulmates and lovers, he slipped an arm around her, gently cupped a breast, and nuzzled into her neck. The estranged couple found a peaceful solace in each other's embrace during the quiet hours of the night.

As evening faded into early morning, their bodies responded to another memory. She shifted in her sleep and pressed her round buttocks into him. The connection brought his cock to life, comfortably settling between her cheeks. Her skin warmed as his hand slowly caressed her breast, bringing the nipple to a stiff peak against his palm. In a semi-state of consciousness, the hunger grew in his loins. Etain sighed again and shifted onto her back. Her eyes opened briefly as she smiled at her husband. He dipped his head and kissed her perfect breasts, taking his time with each one. His heart sang at her soft moans and the feel of her body responding to his touch.

"Dar," she whispered.

Encouraged, he moved farther down, gently kissing and caressing this woman he loved so dearly.

"How I have missed you, my love." His hand slid over her rounded belly and between her thighs. His mouth followed exploring for more cherished fruits, tasting the sweetness denied him for so long. A brief thought fluttered through his mind. *If she protests, I will stop.*

As if in answer to his resolve, she arched her back, one hand gripping his hair, the other fisting the sheets.

Intimately familiar with her body, he listened to her deep intakes of breath, cherished the quickening beat of her heart as her need rose to meet his. Settling himself between her legs, electric shocks filled his senses, flowing from his cock and through his belly as he entered her. Encased in her wet heat, the sweet friction between them set off explosions throughout his body. Sweat sheened over their skin as her hips moved in concert with his.

With a slight shift, he embraced her in his arms, bringing their flesh together. He reveled in the feel of her nails skimming lightly over his skin, sometimes digging in when a tremor coursed through her, telling him she was as invested as he. Consumed by the vibrations of each thrust, he vaguely acknowledged the blue light around them. Etain's blue light. Once assured of her satisfaction, he found his own sweet release deep within her trembling body.

TRODAIRE

Just as Faux closed her eyes, another contraction hit. She grabbed Siobhan's hand in a death grip, growling through clenched teeth. "This breathing isn't helping."

The midwife cringed and used the pain to bark a command. "Faux! Breathe!" She panted in the way she had instructed until the young woman fell into the same pattern, working through the contraction.

As the peak subsided, Faux loosened her hold. "I want Freeblood."

"Let's not worry about him right now. You have more important—"

She grabbed the midwife's arm. "I don't give a damn what *you* think is important. I want Freeblood."

Siobhan snapped back. "This baby is coming whether he's here or not." Remorseful of the harshness in her reply, she placed a hand over Faux's and softened her voice. "After we're done..." She glanced away and closed her eyes for a moment. "I'll bring him here."

Faux's gaze bored into her. "You swear?"

She couldn't look her in the eye but gave her a halfhearted smile. "I will make it so."

Once the babe is here, she will forget the man. It was the lie she told herself to assuage her guilt.

The girl let go and relaxed back. "He'll be so happy to see his son."

"How do you know it to be a boy?"

Faux smirked. "If you knew Freeblood, you'd understand."

"Well—"

A young Telquessir intern dressed in blue scrubs burst through the door. "Mistress Siobhan! You must come! Phie has demanded your attendance."

"Girl!" she barked. "I have a mother in labor. Tell Phie I will attend once the babe is born."

The young girl's eyes widened, sudden tears welling in her eyes. "Mistress, I thought you liked me."

Siobhan thought she'd made a joke, but the horror in the girl's eyes told her it was not. She sighed. "Jazmeen, I can't leave—"

Wringing her hands, the girl resorted to begging. "Please, Mistress." She lowered her voice. "You know how she is."

Siobhan knew well how brutal Phie could be and realized she used it more often than not, even with her sisters. "Get Mistress Doria to sit with my lady." She turned to an equally anxious Faux. "I won't be long."

"You can't leave me here alone! What if the baby comes?"

"Faux, you will not give birth for a while. And should anything happen, Doria is as experienced as I. She will know what to do."

"What could happen?" Her voice was on the verge of hysteria. "Why do you have to go? I don't know Doria. Please, Siobhan. Don't go."

"Please, Mistress." Jazmeen stood in the doorway. "She was most adamant."

"Get Doria!"

The girl jumped and disappeared out the door.

Siobhan turned to Faux. "Nothing more than a contraction or two will happen. Don't worry. Like I said, I won't be long."

Faux pouted. "This Phie is a real bitch."

"Oh, she's so much more than that, my lovely. I promise, I will be back soon."

Dressed in whites similar to Siobhan's, a tall, slim female with pale green skin followed Jazmeen into the room. Judging by the midwife's easy smile at the woman, Faux figured this was Doria. Her large, yellow eyes made her more imposing than the other two, but she seemed to have a gentle nature.

Siobhan hurried past the woman as she made the introductions. "Faux, Doria. Doria, Faux. Get to know each other." She rushed out the door, Jazmeen behind her.

Doria bowed her head. "Good morrow, Faux."

"You don't look like them." Faux nodded toward the door. "Are you an Elf?"

She moved closer. "I come from Blackwoods, land of the Goblins."

Faux narrowed her eyes. "You're tall enough, but your ears are too small, and your nose seems normal to me."

The midwife laughed and sat in the chair next to the bed. "Because I am of mixed blood. It is why I am here instead of Blackwoods. The Goblin community only recognizes those of pure blood and abhors taint of any kind."

"Prejudicial Goblins?" Faux adjusted her covers. "What's wrong with mixed blood? Everyone knows mutts are smarter, stronger, and much prettier."

Doria laughed. "Mutts?"

Faux shrugged. "It's a compliment. I'm a mutt. Mixed blood and all that. What I should've said is that you're too pretty to be a Goblin."

The Goblin sighed. "And too green to be accepted by anyone else."

"You aren't *that* green. Just a little."

"Thank you." Doria smiled slightly. "It took some time to accept how I look. I suppose it comes from my mother."

"Who is?"

"Was. She passed some time ago."

"What about your father?"

"Ah, well..." Her gaze came back to Faux. "He serves the *Bok* and does not recognize me as his kin."

Faux rolled her eyes. "Well, he's a stupid man. What the hell did he expect?" She leaned forward. "Kin isn't what it's cracked up to be. They can be meaner than any stranger." She reclined back onto her pillows. "I've found it's better to build a family of your choosing. People who accept you for who you are and don't judge. It doesn't mean they won't tell you off, we all need that sometimes. But they do it because they care."

Doria tilted her head. "Where is your family, Faux?"

"One is in the infirmary." She placed a hand over her belly. "Freeblood is this one's father. I hope he's okay." Her eyes met the midwife's. "The rest will come for us."

Doria pursed her lips. "For your sake, I hope they are successful."

Siobhan ran after Jazmeen into the grand courtyard where they found Phie in disarray, her skirts torn and hair more disheveled than usual, dismounting her precious paint kelpie. Her sisters remained seated on their mounts, each with three Trodaire hopefuls behind them, their hands bound and secured to a lead rope. Behind Phie was a large wooden box atop a wheeled cart.

"Siobhan!" The Banshee displayed a cheerful grin. "I'm in too good a mood to be upset about yer tardiness. Come see what I've caught for our games."

"I have mothers in labor, Phie. I can't just come running—"

She spun around. "Don't push yer luck." The frightening grin returned to her face. "Yer going to be quite impressed."

Siobhan's heart skipped a beat at the threat, a daily occurrence since being brought to this place, but she knew the Banshee wouldn't follow through. Siobhan had become too valuable. "It must be impressive if you've gone to this much trouble."

Phie banged on the side of the box, which elicited a growl, several bangs in return, and a rocking of the entire structure. The Banshee laughed, her eyes aglow. "I thought they were near extinct, but Dathmet provided the one ya think more important than my summons, and this one fell into our laps." She winked. "More or less."

What does that mean? Has she found another succubus? How did she find out?

Siobhan stood back, her heart racing. Phie grabbed a crowbar from an approaching soldier, jumped onto the cart, and proceeded to pry the top off, the nails screeching as she forced them from their holds. She made quick work of it and pushed off the lid, letting it fall onto the ground.

"If ya know what's good for ya..." She spoke to whatever was in the box, "You'll behave." In the next instant, she fell off the cart onto her backside when the prize jumped at her but fell back into the box with a grunt.

The soldiers surrounded the cart, their swords drawn. All the others in the courtyard reacted the same as Siobhan and stepped back.

Phie laughed, picking herself up from the ground and brushing the dust from her clothes. "Come out, hellion. Meet yer new life."

Everyone held their breath, waiting for the prize to show itself. Siobhan quietly speculated that the creature must have an enormous stubborn streak.

Phie climbed onto the cart and reached into the crate. The midwife heard a grunt of pain from the creature as the Banshee pulled it up by the roots of its long, dark hair. Her heart nearly stopped when she realized it was female, until she noticed there were no horns or tail. She was certain this wasn't a succubus. There couldn't be another like Faux.

Thank the saints! Her secret was safe.

But if this female wasn't a succubus...

Siobhan rushed back to Faux's side, hoping she had not yet dilated too far. She heard the girl's pain-filled screams long before she got to the room.

"Siobhan! Ooooo! Where have you been?"

"Breathe, Faux. It will help." Siobhan conferred with Doria, keeping her eyes on the succubus. "How far apart are the contractions?"

"They're coming so quickly. I haven't had a chance to time them. Siobhan, I've never seen *any* birth advance this rapidly."

"*Holy hell!*" screamed the patient.

Going to Faux's side, Siobhan held her hand and breathed with her, reminding her to take light breaths until the spasm passed. "I don't understand how or why, but this baby is coming sooner than I expected. Just keep breathing. Doria..." Siobhan glanced over her shoulder. "Let's get her off the bed and into the birthing chair."

"A *chair*?" Faux screamed.

"Faux, you must calm down and breathe. The chair will make it easier, let gravity do its part."

"Can't I have something for the... Holy shit!" Faux grunted with another contraction. "The *pain!*"

"It's too late for that now. You need to be brave and soldier through it." Siobhan held her hand. "Now breathe."

"I *am* fucking breathing!" She squeezed her hand.

"And stop screaming. Save that energy for when you have to push."

"When is that?"

Once the contraction subsided, Siobhan checked her cervix. "Let's get her to the chair." One stood on either side of the soon to be mother and helped her scoot off the bed. "We'll get you into position. When the next contraction comes, push with all you've got."

Faux pushed when they told her to, doing her best to channel everything into the act of giving birth and not scream. Her gown clung to her sweat-drenched body as she gripped the arms of the chair.

"When does gravity kick in?" She clenched her teeth through a long, guttural grunt, ending in a shriek. When the contraction passed, she glared at Siobhan. "The screaming helps."

Said with so much earnest, Siobhan tried not to smile. "Whatever gets the babe out, you go with it." She patted her face with a cool, damp cloth. "You're doing great. Just a few more pushes and we'll have ourselves a baby."

Faux closed her eyes for a moment and gritted her teeth again as a new contraction came on.

After a total of forty-five minutes, Faux gave birth to a healthy baby boy, weighing well over eight pounds.

With mother and son cleaned and settled in bed, Siobhan watched the sleeping pair. It had been an easy birth, despite the fuss from Faux. She named the boy Jake, but Siobhan doubted it would stick. Phie had her own ideas of what to call her Trodaithe. His mother might think of him as Jake, but the Trodaire world would know him as some Irish legend from long ago. Pity. The name suited him.

At that thought, she turned to Doria. "I'm going to check on our patient in the infirmary. Will you call me if she wakes?"

"I will, but I shouldn't. You're going to get your heart broken again. That witch won't let you keep either one."

"You let me worry about my heart." She winked at the other midwife. "I have a sense that things are about to change around here."

"Hmph." Doria settled into the chair next to the bed. "Sense is the one thing you run short on, my love. But like you said, it's no worry of mine."

"You're a dear. Thank you, Doria."

Freeblood stood alone in the arena. His manhandling escort had dragged him here and left him, locking the large wrought iron gates upon their departure. He peered into the stands that strangely resembled a football stadium, wondering if he could shimmy up the wall. *Then what?* He knew Faux was somewhere close but had no clue where.

Then, for the first time since this debacle had started, he thought of Etain. He had so much thrown at him in such a short time, his thoughts had been on surviving and making sure his family did the same. Now he thought of her at the mercy of that dickhead demon. *Where had they gone? Was she still there, or did Dar find her?* It was almost more than he could bear.

"What the hell am I doing—"

The great iron gates squealed as they opened. Freeblood spun around and watched the black and white women enter with a dark-haired woman dressed in red leather armor in the middle of their odd trio. Her amber gaze pierced into his. He didn't know this woman, but his gut said he should.

"Alamir." The bossy two-toned sister seemed to be the alpha of the three. "You'll spar with this one. Show us what ya can do."

"Because you tell me to?"

The alpha hissed, baring her fanged teeth. "Unless ya prefer to die without a fighting chance."

The white sister jerked her head to the right. "Weapons are over there."

He turned and walked to where she'd indicated. A sword and shield lay in the dirt. He stared at the pitiful things and chuckled. *What a joke.* "You expect me to use this piece of shit? If you want me to be a warrior, treat me like one and give me something I can fight with."

The three glared at him, but the amber-eyed woman smirked.

"Ya won't leave the arena until ya fight," said the darkest of the three.

Freeblood eyed the three bitches, the image of their heads consumed in blue fire coming to him. He was tempted to laugh but thought better of it. His head had seen enough action from them. "Then fuck off and let us get to it."

The sisters shared a glance, eyed the dark-haired woman, and walked out of the arena, locking the gates behind them. Freeblood heard their cackles ring in the air.

With them out of the picture, he exchanged a glance with the woman.

"Hey. I'm Freeblood. Looks like we're both having a shit of a day."

She eyed him from head to toe. "It appears so. I am Illiana."

"How'd you end up here?"

"Are you trustworthy, Freeblood?"

A surprised laugh escaped his lips. "If it comes down to either you or me, hell no."

Illiana laughed too. "I am here for a reason. How is it *you* are here?"

He slid his hands into the pockets of his jeans and shrugged. "Outnumbered and thought I was dead."

"But you are not the only one."

He narrowed his eyes. "Why do you say that?"

"I doubt you will believe me."

"Try me."

Illiana tilted her head. She walked toward him, coming almost nose to nose. "In case we have ears that are not our own."

He wasn't sure what it was about the woman—her mannerisms, her scent, or maybe the way she spoke—but he knew one thing for certain. "You're not Alamir, are you?"

The woman grinned. "Hell no."

He chuckled. "For some ungodly reason, you remind me of someone else."

"Do I?"

He furrowed his brows.

"I like you, Freeblood. But if we hope to get out of this horrendous place, we will have to make a good show of trying to kill one another." She brought her fists up.

"I think you're right, but I'm not in the habit of hitting women."

Illiana threw the first punch, knocking him off his feet. "It is time for a new habit."

He swiped a line of blood from the side of his mouth. "That's some right hook."

"If you are that easily impressed, you will love my left." She moved forward, raising a foot. Freeblood rolled away just as she stomped the ground where he'd been.

Scrambling up, he bounced on the balls of his feet, building up the wherewithal to hit her. He swung out with his left, but she leaned out of the way. He tried again, thinking she might expect him to hit with his right, but she avoided him again.

"Not much of a show if I can't get a few punches in."

"Be smarter." They circled one another. "If you cannot be smarter, try harder."

That hit his male pride, but he was damned if he would let her see it. He danced around her, jagged to the right, jigged to the left, and clipped her with a right.

She stumbled to the side and came back with a strong left. Freeblood ducked and jabbed her in the stomach, her whoosh of breath washing over him.

Back and forth the punches landed, neither one getting the upper hand for long. One would fall, the other hoping it was over, until the one on the ground struggled to their feet to throw another punch. Bloody, bruised, and exhausted, the two eventually collapsed, neither able to rise.

Something significant had happened. He didn't know why it came to him so suddenly, but it had, and hadn't left him since he'd awakened. Freeblood sat up in bed. Groaning, his eyes rolled, and head dipped. An inner strength rose to the surface as he forced his shoulders to straighten and lifted his head, but his eyes refused to focus. The whiteness around him brought on a strange sense of déjà vu, reminding him of the first time he'd met Etain. Could the footsteps he heard be hers?

"Hello, Freeblood. I doubt you remember me."

Not Etain. Damn. He lay down again. *Why does my head hurt so bad? Oh yeah. The bitches. Did I hear their names right? Phee... What were the others?* He ignored his visitor as she approached, concentrating instead on the three hellions who had changed his life. *Phie... Yeah, the head bitch. And the other. Phoe.*

"I'm Siobhan. How's your head?"

He narrowed his eyes, finding it difficult to focus on her face. *Siobhan?*

"Headaches?" She lifted each eyelid, inspecting his eyes with a penlight.

"I have too many other aches to worry about my head."

She tucked away the light, checking his heart rate and temperature. "Your sight will clear up in time. I apologize for the rough treatment. Phie and her sisters can get carried away."

"Where's Faux?"

Siobhan paused. "She's fine."

There was something she wasn't telling him. Deception dripped off her. "Are you sure she's okay?"

"Yes. She's tended to quite well. No harm will come to her."

He narrowed his eyes. "Where is she?"

"I... She is fine."

"You know, lady, I've been around enough women to know when one uses the word 'fine,' it usually isn't. What's happened?"

Although he couldn't see her face clearly, he sensed her hesitation. He knew what she wasn't telling him. His Jake had been born, but these bitches had other plans for his family.

At that moment, he heard someone cough from across the room. Freeblood squinted and made out a form in another bed, figures standing on either side of her. *Illiana.* He could see well enough to know she was covered in blood too.

Siobhan touched him on the shoulder. "I have to see to her. We can talk later."

"Yeah. Sure."

It was definitely Illiana. Bruises and scratches covered her face, one eye swollen and knuckles bloody, much like his. They'd made a good enough show of their fight. Her head lolled to the side toward Freeblood and her eyes opened. She gave him a bloody grin and winked.

Pushing away the hands trying to clean her wounds, she slowly sat up. "Give me the cloth. I will do it myself."

Freeblood sat up straighter in his bed. The way she spoke... He'd noticed it before, but it was more pronounced now. He'd heard someone speak like that before. A man. The only one of his kind. He looked more closely at the young woman—dark hair, fine features, amber eyes. Not quite golden, but close enough.

No way!

"Illiana," Siobhan sighed. "The sooner you allow them to do their job, the sooner they'll be gone."

The amber eyes fell on the woman in the white coat. "They will make things worse. This *human,*" her gaze went to Freeblood, "has done his share of damage. I am trying to mitigate further injuries."

Freeblood considered if she meant to herself or the attendants. He may never know the how or why, but he and Faux had an ally. A Krymerian ally.

JACKIE

D ar stirred and woke with a start when he realized where he was and who he held in his arms. The warmth of her skin against his felt like heaven, and the sticky wetness between their bodies made him smile.

"A dream come true," he whispered, nuzzling into her hair. He breathed in her scent, fascinated by her nearness, yet wondered what this could mean. As his mind drifted, it came to him that she hadn't suffered from the usual nightmares or rejected his advances.

"Could you be working your way back to me?"

He dozed, drifting in and out of consciousness until a sharp whisper snapped him wide awake.

"Dar. What do you think you're doin'?"

Careful to keep as still as possible, he turned his head to a set of strange glaring eyes, then remembered who she was.

"Jackie. I am sleeping with my wife. Why are you out of bed?"

"Does your *wife* know you're sleeping with her?"

"She knew it last night."

She narrowed her eyes. "You're playing a dangerous game, mister."

"I am fighting for my life, Jackie."

"Dar." She softened her tone. "I don't begrudge you this bit of happiness, but you gotta tread lightly. Her mind is jumbled right now."

"I don't have to explain myself to you or anyone else." They both held their breath when Etain stirred in her sleep. Dar lowered his voice further. "If you insist on butting in, run her a bath. I am not sure how much she will remember of last night, and I will not risk her finding the evidence. I will place her into the bath and head across the hall."

Jackie shook her head as she walked into the en suite. Dar pulled away and rolled off the bed, reached for his pants on the floor, and pulled them on. He scooped the groggy Etain into his arms and carried her to a morning bath.

Please forgive us the deception, my love. Your waking mind is not in sync with your spirit.

Slipping her into the bath, he exchanged places with Jackie, who effectively blocked the view of the door as Dar quickly stepped out.

Etain lifted her head and narrowed her eyes. "Why are you... Wait. How'd I get here?"

"You dozed off. Quite rude if you ask me. You should go to bed earlier, Etain."

She ran a hand through her hair. "I-I thought I did." *Something doesn't feel right.* But it was just her and Jackie. Despite her initial uneasiness, Etain decided she was all right. With a shrug, she leaned back into the water. "Well, I *did* have the most delicious dream. Maybe that's why I'm so tired this morning."

Jackie raised a brow. "If it was that good, you have to tell me about it."

"I dreamt of my husband."

Her eyes widened. "You dreamt of Dar?"

Etain pursed her lips. "Don't get excited." She lowered the washcloth into the water. "My *husband*, Dar."

"Oh, sorry." Jackie bit her bottom lip. "Don't you find it odd that the man here shares the same name as your husband?"

"I called him Dar, but his name was Darknight. Completely different." She soaped the cloth, speaking in a reverent voice. "It was like he was here, touching me, kissing me. Well... You know."

"It was good?"

"It was magical."

"But he's gone now, isn't he?"

Etain frowned. "Couldn't you let me enjoy it a little longer?" She dunked the cloth, causing water and bubbles to splash over the side and onto Jackie. "It's hard enough knowing I won't see him again."

Jackie stood. "Those kinds of dreams won't do you any good. Your babies need their mama to be strong in body," she leaned into Etain's face and tapped the side of her head, "as well as in mind. Time to leave the past behind and get on with the present."

Jackie straightened and walked toward the door. "Finish up and get dressed. We're going to have a good breakfast this morning." Stepping out, she peeked back inside. "And you're going to eat all of it."

"Fine," Etain muttered as the door closed.

⁘

Enticed into the kitchen by the aroma of freshly brewed coffee, Dar's main goal for the morning switched to a hot cup. Usually, he was the one who made the morning brew, but it appeared someone beat him to it today. Taking a mug from the cupboard, he glanced out the window and noticed Jackie sitting alone in the garden. He opened the cupboard again and placed another mug next to his, filling both with the steaming brew.

He opened the door, grabbed the mugs, and stepped outside. "Good morning, Jackie. How did it go with Etain?"

The sun bright, she squinted at him. "I tiptoed around the sketchy parts. Don't worry. We're good. According to her, it was a *delicious dream.*"

"Well, that sounds promising." His expression cleared as he handed her a cup. "I know you like it black."

"And hot." Jackie placed her hands around the cup, blowing gently across the top. "I hope you aren't planning any more hookups in the near future."

Despite her negative response, Dar felt encouraged. "If you are referring to what happened last night, nothing was planned. The body remembers what the mind forgets."

She raised a brow. "As long as it doesn't backfire on you."

"I agree with you on that point." He sat in the chair next to her. "I am sorry you and I have not had much time to chat. It has been hectic since our return."

"I thought hectic was the way of the Alamir."

Dar chuckled and sipped his coffee. "Then perhaps I should mention that although *this* is Alamir..." He waved a hand, encompassing everything within their sights. "I, myself, am not." He enjoyed another sip.

Jackie turned in her seat. "You're not one of those *Bok* James used to deal with either. I remember how they made me nauseous, and you don't."

Dar tilted his head, a smirk on his lips, and lifted his cup to her. "I will accept that as a compliment. I have had plenty of dealings with the *Bok* myself."

"Like the last piece of work you saved us from?"

He set his cup on the ground next to his chair. "Did he make you nauseous?"

"Most definitely."

"The demon *commands* the *Bok* but is not *of* the *Bok*." Seeing her confused expression, Dar pursed his lips. "He is like me."

She leaned back in her chair, crossing one leg over the other. "I don't understand."

"He is my brother's son." Dar sighed. "Midir was dark, but it appears his son has surpassed him in that area."

"If you aren't *Bok* and you aren't Alamir, what are you?"

His gaze returned to her. "I am Krymerian."

Something changed between them. He was not sure if it was her mouth, a twitch of an eye, or her attitude, but something shifted. Dar waited for her response, not sure which way it would go.

She lifted her mug, tested the temperature against her lips, and swallowed a mouthful. "I met a man named Midir a time or two. He was different from the Alamir. He was usually cordial, but you could feel something pulsating just below the surface. I never liked the man."

Dar's scalp tingled and gooseflesh rose over his body.

"He and James had quite a few business dealings. James knew Midir was a piece of shit." She shrugged. "But the deals were lucrative."

"James was Etain's father, aye?"

Jackie glanced at him. "You didn't meet her parents?"

He shook his head. "Etain and I met a few years after she became Alamir. She did not tell me much of her human existence, only of their deaths, nothing more."

Jackie chuckled. "The girl plays it close to the cuff until she gets comfortable. Once she lets her guard down, you know you're gold." She finished her coffee. "Refill?"

Dar picked up his cup and handed it to her. "Thank you."

She disappeared into the kitchen and soon returned with the mugs.

"Did you meet her parents before or after she was born?" Dar took his from her outstretched hand and blew away the steam before chancing a sip.

"She was just a baby when I met James. I knew people he wanted to be introduced to, so we formed a business partnership. When I met his wife and the kids, well," she shrugged, "I was a goner. Those kids were so darn cute, and Auri was just the sweetest thing. They made me feel like family." A shadow of a smile touched her lips. "Hell, they *made* me family."

"Auri?"

Dar had to wait for Jackie to take a sip.

She winced. "Ooo, hot!" Pursing her lips, she sucked in the cool morning air. "Aurelia. Etain's mom. I called her Auri. That's how close we were."

"I imagine you were devastated when you heard of their passing."

"It was a hard pill to swallow." Jackie sat back. "But hearing she'd found her brother made it a little easier. Where's he in all this?"

Dar debated on whether to tell her the truth or leave it as a mystery. The earnestness in her face made his decision for him. "*He* is the red-skinned bastard."

The mug slipped from her hand and shattered on the ground. "No. No. That can't be. That sweet boy." Jackie sprang from her seat. "Oh, my god. Are you sure?" His answer was in his eyes. She collapsed back onto the chair. "No wonder she's messed up. She worshipped that boy, and vice versa." She hid her face in her hands, muttering through her fingers, "Oh, Etain. You poor, sweet girl."

Dar placed a tentative hand on her back. "She does not remember much of what happened. She thinks he died with her parents."

Jackie swiped at her tears. "She mentioned a place I've never heard of. Nunnehi? And an Elven queen?"

"I sent her to Nunnehi when the *Bok* attacked Castle Laugharne."

She sat up. "Elves are real?"

"You will find out for yourself soon. The ship from Laugharne should be here in a couple of weeks."

"We'll see. I have a bar to get back to." She lowered her voice. "If there's anything to go back to."

"I would appreciate it if you would stay on a while, for Etain's sake. Perhaps we can contact this Krz you mentioned earlier and see if he can cover your bar."

"That might work if he has the time." She seemed to relax. "He and his brother spent a lot of time at his granddad's bar. At least I'll know my people won't suffer. Do you know how to find him?"

"I know people." He winked. "We will locate him."

Jackie stood. "Well, I told Etain she was gonna eat some breakfast this morning."

"Brave effort." Dar stood as well. "One more thing. How is it you came to be in that room where I found you?"

She shifted her weight to one hip, slipping her hands into the back pockets of her jeans. "The bar'd just closed when Siouxsie and her band showed up, claiming I could either go with them or die where I stood."

Dar crossed his arms over his massive chest. "I know of the Banshee, but I have not heard of these particular ones."

She chuckled. "Well, I don't know if that's what they call themselves, but there were three of 'em—female. Dripping wet, just like their horses. Rode 'em right into my bar."

He hoped they were not who first came to mind. "Anything distinctive about the women?"

"Isn't that enough?" She shook her head. "Black on white, white on black. The one in the middle rode a paint and had the same coloring."

Dar rubbed his neck, feeling drained. "The Phums. They are the worst of the Banshee. *Tartarus*. What the hell did he promise those three?"

Jackie shrugged. "Devil only knows."

"One more question, if I may."

"Shoot."

"You were the only one in the room when I arrived, but it was obvious there were others at some point. Did you see anyone else, besides Etain?"

Jackie held his gaze for a long moment. "Oh, my word. There *was* a couple. But I wasn't there for long before the Banshee showed up again. I can't believe I forgot."

"You suffered a hard blow to your head. You are lucky to remember anything. This couple, did you get their names?" He did not want to mention anything mostly in the hope she would not say the names he feared she would. Faux and Freeblood could be anywhere, but with Etain saying her sister was gone and no mention of the boy, his gut told him things were not as they should be.

Jackie shook her head slowly. "I don't remember anything about them. It was so dark. I'm sorry."

"Perhaps it will come back to you in time." He noticed how pale she had become and linked his arm with hers. "Come with me, milady. A dram will set you right."

"It's gonna take more than one."

"I will not argue with that."

Within the hour, Dar showed up at Etain's door to escort the ladies to the dining room.

"Oh, Dar." The smile on Etain's face faded. "I-I thought you were Jackie."

Not even her cool demeanor could bring him down today. "Then we are even. I expected her to open the door." He stood there, smiling, his heart light as a feather.

She raised a brow. "Are you okay?"

"Never been better, milady."

"You seem pretty chipper today."

He laughed. "Pardon?"

"Uh... You're in a good mood."

"Thank you for noticing. It is a beautiful day full of promise." He forced himself to look down the hall. "Is she on her way?"

Etain shifted, one hand on the knob, the other resting on her hip. "I'm sure if she were, you would've seen her by now."

He could not help grinning like an idiot. She was his Etain—sassy and sarcastic. "You speak true, Lady Etain. Would she mind if we went down for breakfast without her?"

The lady frowned again. He stepped back as she leaned into the hallway and peered up the hall toward Jackie's door.

"I am merely concerned about the food getting cold," he added.

"She probably wouldn't mind."

He offered his arm, but seeing the distrust in her face, he dropped it. "Apologies. Old habit."

She turned her head, obviously uncomfortable.

He suddenly blurted, "I have a gift for you." It had not been his plan to do this so soon, but the awkwardness between them drove him to it.

Her eyes widened, surprised. "A gift for me?"

As though a schoolboy offering a prized apple to his beloved teacher, he reached into his breast pocket and dangled the special locket before her eyes. "A gift for a mother-to-be. A locket to hold pictures of your beautiful children."

Her eyes sparkled. "Dar," she breathed. "Dar!" The distress in her voice startled him. She reached for the partially missing digit. "What happened to your finger?"

Relieved and happy she noticed, he smiled. "It is nothing. Mishap in the garden." He moved his hand back and forth. "See? Still works."

"Is that why your garden looks like tornado alley? You should be more careful."

"I will make every effort to do so." He noticed how she continued to stare at his hand. "As long as you do the same, milady."

She touched the ring on his third finger. "Where did you get this?"

He lowered his hand, searching for a plausible lie but told her the truth. "It is my wedding band."

Tears shone in her eyes. "It's identical to the one my husband wore." She raised her hand. "Just like mine."

"Oh, aye. Now that you mention it, they are similar," he agreed, afraid the slip might push her away. "But I am sure not exactly the same."

She held his gaze with her own. "Ours were given us on our wedding day by Queen Alatariel of Nunnehi."

"Ah, that explains it. Our rings were made by the Elves too."

She leaned back. "I hope I'm not too forward, but..."

Dar shifted on his feet.

"You don't say much about your wife. Jackie told me—"

"Excuse me, Lady Etain, but I am sure you are as hungry as I. Could we discuss this another time?"

She blinked. "O-Of course. I-I'm sorry. I didn't mean to..." Her gaze returned to the locket in his hand. "Shouldn't you save this for someone special?"

The change of subject eased the tension between them. "Who is more special than an expectant mother? This way you will always have your children with you."

"You're too thoughtful." Taking the necklace from him, their fingertips touched. She reacted with an involuntary gasp.

Dar stepped back. His heart dropped, thinking he had ruined the moment.

Instead of pulling away, she reached out to him and rested her hand lightly on his arm. "It's okay," she whispered. "It didn't hurt."

He relaxed but was resolved to avoid another incident. "You are feeling better today?"

Admiring her gift, she removed her hand. "I am." Her words strengthened his blossoming hope. "I love it, Dar." She held out the locket. "Would you mind?"

"It would be my pleasure." As she lifted her silver mane, he wanted so badly to take her into his arms and kiss her delicate neck. But he settled for breathing in her scent as he fastened the necklace. "Turn and let me see."

It was as if she moved in slow motion. Her long hair cascaded down her back as her profile came into view, a bright smile on her lovely face and a sparkle in her ice-blue eyes.

"How do I look?"

Bewitched by her innocent seduction, he dropped to one knee.

"What are you doing?"

"Milady." His voice caught in his throat. After a hard swallow, he tried again. "You take my breath away. All else pales in your presence."

Never comfortable with such compliments, she blushed. "Please. I'm nothing special." Her gaze returned to his. "Thank you." Hand on the locket, she slipped past him and rushed down the stairs.

Dar remained on his knee for a few moments, working to calm his emotions.

Jackie, on her way to breakfast, came upon him. "Do you need help?"

He gave her a brilliant smile and rose to his feet. "I believe a momentous bridge has been crossed, milady."

She raised a brow. "Don't let it run away with ya."

He held out an arm to escort her. "I shall take it slow." As they started down the stairs, he asked, "I have an idea I would like to run past you. It has to do with Etain."

"I hope it's a good one."

"Our children will soon be born and we will—"

"Need a nursery." Jackie stopped. "I think it's just what she needs. It'll get her mind off her troubles."

"The sooner, the better. I shall ask her over breakfast."

In the dining room, Etain was already seated in her usual chair, leaving Dar at the head of the table.

"My goodness." Jackie eyeballed the feast as she sat to his left. "Look at all this!"

Their laughter made him happy. It had been far too long since his house was filled with love, laughter, and the faces of people he cared for deeply. Even Jackie, a woman who might not be easy to win over. But if Etain loved her, he would find a way.

As they passed the dishes around the table, Jackie noticed the locket. "What a beautiful necklace, Etain. I don't remember seeing it on you earlier."

She touched the treasured piece. "Thank you. Dar gave it to me this morning. It's a locket so my babies will be with me all the time."

"It's lovely." Jackie winked at him. "Nice work."

Dar quietly sighed as he lifted his coffee cup, unsure of how to broach the subject of his idea. "Etain, speaking of babies." He glanced at Jackie, who gave him an encouraging nod. "I, well... It is time to look toward the future." Seeing her apparent interest, he continued with more confidence. "I have been thinking of creating a nursery. Would you consider taking on the project?"

"Really? You'd let me design it?"

"It would be for your children."

"Well, I have to admit..." Etain fingered her silverware, straightening the knife and adjusting the spoon. "I *have* wandered into your room. Accidently, of course." Her gaze returned to Dar. "I've been mulling over a few ideas. I thought we could move you into the purple room." She chuckled and rolled her eyes. "Well, after it's redone to more, well...you. Then redo that horrid bathroom and add another one. Next to that would be the nursery, which would take up most of your current room, and the next room would be mine." She shrugged. "Just for while we're here if you don't mind."

Dar sat back in his chair, eyeing his industrious wife.

Jackie chuckled. "That's a lot of thinking, girl."

Etain picked up her fork. "There's not much else to do around here."

"Works for me." Dar pushed back his chair and stood. "Draw out your plans and we can work on the details when I get back from town." Before the women could react, he was gone.

Etain laughed. "Did that just happen? Did he really give me free rein?"

"Yes, ma'am, he did." Jackie sat back in her chair. "Something's different with you."

"I *feel* different."

"Because of the dream?"

Etain fiddled with the silver again. "Maybe."

Jackie shook her head. "Whatever gets you back to being you, darlin'. Let's finish our breakfast and get these dishes done, then I'll help you with those plans. Better to move while the iron's hot."

THE SHIMMER

Dar walked out the front doors, contemplating his *modus operandi*, wishing he could go into town on horseback. Since the stables were only partially built, not to mention empty, he opted to drive. A necessity he learned during an excursion into the human realm not long after his alliance with the Alamir. Proud of his new four-bay garage, he climbed into the one vehicle parked inside—a recently refurbished vintage Dodge one-ton pickup. He had requested the restorer keep the rusty, rough finish, but the interior boasted all the modern luxuries, including GPS, not that he needed it. Although a work truck, there was no reason why it could not be comfortable—black leather with silver trim and a Hemi under the hood. He revved the engine and pulled out with a screech.

"Git you some of that," he murmured, chuckling at his version of a Texan accent.

The peacefulness of the drive gave him time to consider the past few weeks. He had not intended to sleep in her bed last night. With yesterday having dragged, his brain switched off and his body did what it had done since they had come together.

At the local grocery, he set up a delivery for later in the week and stopped by the farm store to place an order for equipment and feed. If the weather held, Linq and the others should pull into port in about a week, give or take a few days.

He swung by the flower shop to buy a bouquet of daisies, Etain's favorite, and picked up a few more rose bushes for his garden. With that done, he headed home, looking forward to an evening with his beautiful wife.

The moment he entered the house, her anguish slapped him in the face. Flowers in hand and heart hammering, he ran toward the study and burst into the room, where he found her on the floor, sobbing. He scanned the area as he moved toward her and crouched.

Tears filled her eyes as she lifted her head, cowering from him. "No..."

"My sweet lady," he said softly, pained to see the terror in her eyes. "It is Dar." He placed the flowers on the coffee table.

"Stay away from me," she cried. "I won't go with you. I won't." Her eyes darted around the room as she scrambled onto the sofa, burrowing back into the corner and hugged her legs to her chest. "I won't go."

Dar's baffled mind raced, thinking of something to snap her out of it. He considered the possibility she may be asleep. "Etain," he said more sternly. "It is Dar."

She stared at him with wild eyes, her mouth open, and lips trembling. A war raged within him, fighting the urge to wrap her in his arms, crush his lips to hers, and hold her until the fear subsided.

He held her blue-eyed gaze with his and lowered his voice. "It is only me, *a chuisle*."

Whether from the sincerity of his gaze or his words, he saw the fear drain out of her. "Dar?"

He reached for her, but she shied away. Too late, he realized she saw Dar, the master of the manor, not Dar, her husband.

"Aye. That Dar." He failed miserably at trying to keep the disappointment from his voice, but she did not seem to notice. "You are safe."

She ran a hand through her hair and gave him a shaky smile. "I-I must have fallen asleep." She glanced around the room again. "For a moment, I thought you were an angel come to take me away."

He sat on the other end of the sofa. "Angel?" From the corner of his eye, he noticed Jackie standing at the door. He held up his index finger as a signal to wait.

Etain dropped her gaze. "The one that took my sister. I thought he'd returned to take me too."

This was the second time she had mentioned a lost sister. He was not sure of whom she spoke, but the faint bloom of color in her cheeks told him of her uneasiness.

Etain shrugged, her gaze still lowered. "Faux. That was her name."

Jackie visibly stiffened, drawing Dar's attention away from his wife, and disappeared into the hallway.

"She was either in trouble or causing it. She wasn't a bad person..." Etain lifted her gaze to his, bringing him back to her. "She just enjoyed life." With a nervous laugh, she pushed her hair behind her ear. "Silly me. You don't have wings."

He smiled, despite her words. "No wings today, milady."

Feeling the awkwardness of the moment, he stood. "It has been a busy morning. Have you been out today?"

"No. After we did the dishes, I came in here to read."

Dar grinned. "Then it is time for a walk. Would you like to see the new developments since our return?" He held out his hand.

She hesitated but accepted and unfolded her legs. "I've noticed a few things going on." Wobbly, she lurched off the sofa. He easily caught her, pulling her into a close embrace. She peered up into his face, her lips parted. He leaned toward her, but at the last moment, she dipped her head. "I didn't want to get in the way."

Reluctantly, he released her and stepped back. "As long as we keep our distance, we will not interfere with the work."

"I *would* like to see what you've been up to." She quickly glanced at him. "You're gone most of the day."

"It is a big place, milady," he chuckled, touched to know she had noticed his absence. "My crews are talented, but I still have to oversee their work."

"Shall I get my boots?"

"Let me save you the trouble. While I get your boots," he scooped the flowers from the coffee table and offered them to her, "you can put these in water. I hope you like them."

"They're beautiful." A smile lit her entire face. "I love daisies. How did you know?"

"They reminded me of you—fresh, light, and beautiful."

"Do you have a vase?"

"Let's see what we can find."

Etain followed Dar into the kitchen. "So, what happened in here?" she asked, watching him pilfer through a few dented cabinets. "It must have been a lovely room at one time."

"Renovations. Another room in need of a facelift."

She furrowed her brows. "Wouldn't it be easier if you took everything out before you started the demo?"

"Where is the fun in that?" He chuckled and opened one of the doors in the island. "I do not have a vase." He reached in and popped up with a large glass stein in his hand. "But I have this."

Etain laughed at the triumphant grin on his handsome face. "A worthy vessel, milord." She joined him at the sink and unwrapped the daisies as he filled the makeshift vase with water. "Scissors?"

His brows knitted together. "Scissors?"

She held up a small packet. "Extra flower freshness."

"How could I forget that?" The enigmatic grin returned. "Look in the drawer in front of you."

Opening it, she found what she needed. "Perfect."

"I shall return momentarily with boots and a cloak for milady."

She snipped a corner of the packet and poured the solution into the water, taking her time arranging the flowers. "Beautiful."

Dar stopped for a moment at the kitchen door to admire his lady and her artistic arrangement of her flowers. He found it hard to breathe at the thought of how far they had come in a relatively short amount of time. She no longer stared at him with eyes filled with fear or cringe when he came close. Dare he believe she had warmed to his presence and might soon see him as her husband?

Stop that line of thought else you get ahead of yourself and ruin everything. One step at a time, man. She is here, safe and well. It must be enough for now.

He cleared his throat as he walked into the kitchen. "Shall I help you with your boots?"

She turned with a furrowed brow.

"It cannot be easy bending over."

A mischievous smirk lifted her lips as she touched her belly. "Maybe that's why I don't bother with 'em."

He glanced at his own pair of boots. "Luckily for you, I am an expert. It is not a skill achieved overnight."

Etain laughed. "I suppose not." She walked around the island and maneuvered her bottom onto a stool, swinging her feet. "Did you bring socks?"

He set the boots on the floor and reached behind him, producing a pair of long socks from his back pocket. "I did say I was an expert."

Laughing a little harder, she covered her mouth with her hand. "Purple? Where did you find those?"

He gave her a wink. "Secret stash. Now, give me a leg and we shall get you set for an afternoon outdoors."

Her movements were innocent enough, but Dar thought he would lose his mind when she slowly lifted the skirt of her dress, exposing a shapely leg.

"I love purple." She tilted her head. "You're getting to know me pretty well."

By the Krymerian gods, if he met her beautiful gaze, he was certain he would lose hard-earned ground with the lady. It was all he could do to slide the sock onto one gracefully long leg and the other, without trailing his hands farther up each thigh, kissing her ruby lips, and absconding her to bed.

"Dar? Are you okay?"

One at a time, he set each booted foot on his thigh, his focus on tightening the laces. "Oh, aye. Just making sure they are secure."

Finished, Etain extended both legs and admired her footwear. "They look brand new."

"A good polish and new laces make all the difference."

He helped her off the stool, grabbed the cloak and fanned it out behind her, clasping it at her neck as it settled on her shoulders. His gaze met hers. Those beautiful, ice-blue eyes held his for what felt like a blissful eternity. *I wish you could see me as I am.*

"Thank you." Her gaze left his to linger on his lips as she licked her own.

He wondered if the electricity between them affected her the same as him. How he loved the anticipation but knew where it would end.

His heart ached seeing the magic leave her eyes as she returned to her world.

"What about you, Dar? Don't you need a cloak?"

His hands dropped to his sides. "I come from sturdy stock. Shall we go?"

They walked side by side to the front doors, Dar itching to drape his arm over her shoulders and pull her close. Outside, he found ways to widen the gap between them. Not that he wanted to, but he needed to breathe.

"The stables are almost complete," he said, steering her toward the main gates. "Our horses will live like royalty and be the best in all the worlds."

"I have no doubt." Once through the gates, she swiveled her head, looking across the fields. "Where're you keeping them? Shouldn't they be grazing?"

His heart back to its natural rhythm, he welcomed the distraction. "Well, we do not have any yet."

They walked along a dirt path formed by the work trucks and men traipsing back and forth in the building of the stables. Dar considered paving it into a certified road but decided to keep it natural. It would be better for all the animals—four-legged and two-legged.

"You've built stables without horses?"

"Oh, we have horses. Quite a few. They have not arrived yet."

Coming upon a structure, Dar stopped, taking it all in.

"I thought we were going to see the stables," she said.

He crossed his arms over his chest and leaned toward her. "We are."

Her mouth gaped open. "*This* is a stable?"

"Aye."

She gawked from one end to the other. "Are you sure you aren't from Texas?"

It made him laugh. "Wait right here." He hurried to the far end of the building and disappeared around the corner.

Etain eyed the details of the building. Even she could tell it was crafted by master tradesmen. The width of the structure was outmatched only by its roof that slanted up into a towering peak. She liked the sage green paint on the outer walls, making it blend in with the surrounding landscape.

The huge door at her end slid open. She gasped, experiencing the full impact of the interior, and realized where he'd gone. At the other end was another open doorway that framed a stunning view out to the sea. The man knew how to put on a show.

She breathed in the fragrance of freshly cut timber. "I love that smell."

"As do I." Dar approached, holding out his hand. "Shall we go inside?"

She accepted and walked with him. Just inside the door, she stopped. The overhead windows strategically placed on either side of the roofline filled the interior with natural light. "What kind of wood is that on the ceiling?"

Dar followed her gaze. "Bamboo."

"I like it. Is it safe to have such big windows on the roof?"

"They will not break. I made sure of that." He stepped deeper into the building. "The beams you see are made of steel, but I had them encased in bamboo."

Etain walked to one of the stalls. "Is it built with timber?"

He grinned. "The façade is timber, but the frame is steel and cinder block with a fireproof insulation in between."

"The stalls are incredible." Her hand followed the curve of metal that dipped down to allow the horse to poke its head out from the stall. "Why're they so big?"

"Any horse would rather be outdoors than locked up." He spread his arms as he joined her. "Even in a place as grand as this. These stalls should help put them at ease. Plus, I have a few horses on the large side that will need the extra space."

"Where are they coming from?"

He turned to her. "That is something we need to discuss but the time has not been right."

Etain frowned. "What's it have to do with me?"

"Well, the horses are not coming alone."

She raised a brow. "No?"

"First, let me say, it takes more than what one person can handle to keep a place like this in good nick."

She crossed her arms and leaned against the stall door. "You seem to have plenty of help around here."

"Aye, but they are not here to stay. Once done with whatever jobs they are doing, they will move on to the next one."

"So what're you saying?"

"This is where it gets sticky."

"Why? Is a woman you're interested in coming too?" She shifted onto both feet and dropped her arms. "Is your conscience suddenly bothering you?"

He frowned. "What? No. Where would you get an idea like that?"

"I see things. I know…"

Dar placed his hands on his hips. "What is it you think you know, milady?"

She dragged her teeth over her bottom lip, trying to sort out what she was feeling. *Why wouldn't he have a woman? Look at him. Not my type, but he's easy on the eyes. And that grin…*

"Well, that bathroom for one. Three doors?"

"You have a problem with three bedrooms sharing the same bath?"

It sounded rather ridiculous when he said it. She crossed her arms again. "It's obvious which one is yours. But the ones on either side are decorated to *feminine* tastes. It doesn't take much imagination to come to a conclusion. I appreciate your curtailment of deviant activity while I've been here, but it's merely a matter of time before nature takes over."

Hands still on his hips, he cocked his head. "Did you just accuse me of being a sexual deviant?"

She rolled her eyes and ran a hand through her hair. "It's crossed my mind."

His glare turned into laughter.

Etain blinked, unsure if he'd lost his mind or was genuinely amused by what she'd said. *Should I laugh too? I'm being honest with the man.*

He swiped at the tears in his eyes. "Milady, I have not had such a good laugh in a very long time. Thank you."

"Glad I could amuse you."

He placed a hand over his heart. "Oh, aye. That you did." Lowering his hand, he took on a serious air. "This is not easy to say, so I am going to be straight with you and hope for the best."

She stepped back. "What?"

"We are building an academy for Black Blades. I am sure you have seen the materials at the site just outside the wall."

She had been wondering about it. "You're building a school for warriors?"

Her memory of the Black Blades impressed him. "Aye, but this one is for the best of the best. Not just any swordsman or woman will be accepted."

She shrugged. "Am I supposed to be intimidated by a school?"

"I hope not. But it means there will be more people on the estate and in the house. I do not expect this first session to be a large one, so the novices will stay in the rooms downstairs. Once the academy is complete, we will start on separate housing."

It would be an adjustment, but she didn't plan to stay too long after the babies were born. Once they were big enough to travel, she would go to Laugharne. If Spirit refused them, she'd go home to Texas, or maybe Jackie would let her stay with her in L.A.

"Etain? Did you hear what I said?"

"Oh... Aye. I just won't go to that part of the house."

Dar nodded, pursing his lips. "Perhaps. However, the students are not the only people on the ship."

Her heart skipped a beat. A warm flush crept over her skin and her scalp tingled. "Who else is coming?"

He raised a brow. "Linq."

She shrugged. The name didn't mean anything to her.

"Taurnil."

A solemn blink made him continue.

"Aramis and Ra."

Maybe he would mention someone she knew eventually.

"Eol and Galdor."

She turned her head toward the stall and heard him clear his throat. With a roll of her eyes, she cast her gaze on him.

"Swee."

Finally. She smiled. "Swee is coming?"

He blew out a breath. "Aye. She wants to deliver the babies."

"Anyone else I know?"

He appeared rather consternated. "You do not recognize any of the others?"

"Why would I?"

Rubbing his forehead, he closed his eyes for a moment. "They were at Laugharne. You saved Taurnil's life after you saved mine."

She laughed, waiting for the other shoe to drop, or for him to laugh. It was a sobering moment when he did neither. "What? Seriously? I don't think so." All he did was gape at her with those golden eyes. "How could I? I'm pregnant, *and* I was in Nunnehi. Why would you say such a thing?"

"Because...," he said in a soft, almost apologetic voice, "you have suffered for it, my love. Suffered greatly."

"Stop it!" She jammed her hands into her hair, her eyes darting left and right, anywhere but at him. "You cannot love me. You can*not*. I won't allow it." Searching for an opportunity to escape, she turned.

"Etain, please don't run from me."

From the corner of her eye, she saw him reach for her, but she shrugged away.

"Talk to me. Let me help you find your way back to me... To us."

She covered her ears, her eyes brimming with tears. "No! No. Please stop. I am not who you think I am." She knew the words he would say next. She heard them before he spoke. "Please don't say it. Please."

"*A chuisle...*"

It was either run, which she just couldn't manage right now, or fall to the ground in a blubbering heap... So she shimmered.

"Damn." Closing his eyes, Dar inhaled and blew out the stress of the morning. "I am out of my depth this time." *Better to focus on things I can control.*

He considered each of the large stalls—twenty to be exact, ten on each side. They would allow plenty of room for a draft horse, or if he were lucky, a mare and her foal. He caressed the wood of the first stall, admiring the fine craftsmanship, the perfection of the joints. "Exquisite."

A few more days' work and it would be completed, just in time for its valuable tenants. His gaze roamed up the alleyway to the other set of sliding doors that led to a good-sized corral and on to an open pasture. His heart lifted, thinking of the beauties that would live here and run free, some to be ultimately sold to other horse lovers.

Dar walked along the center aisle, his hands behind his back, peering side to side as he passed each stall. "Should I continue acting as though everything is all right? She has to face the truth."

He stopped. "Why would you forget Linq and Taurnil, but remember Swee and Spirit? I wonder if you know of Inferno's demise at the hands of the demon. What about Freeblood? Will you recognize him?" He rubbed his forehead. "*Tartarus*. She thinks Faux has been taken away by an angel. What happens when they come face to face?"

A noise made him lift his head. "Hello?"

The lights lowered. The hairs on his neck rising, he turned around. Before him stood the image of his first wife, Alexia, dressed in white, the serene smile he remembered on her beautiful face.

"*Dar, my handsome husband.*"

"Alexia? Why are you here?"

She floated toward him but stopped inches away.

"*You are so conflicted, my love. I could not stand back and not come to you.*"

"Why now? Why here? You have been gone for so long. Where were you all those years ago when my heart bled for your loss?"

She had the decency to act contrite. "*You needed to mourn. To let us go. That could not happen if I returned to you. It would have given you false hope or pushed you beyond your limits. The world needed you more than I or the children.*"

His step toward her made her retreat.

"I have been conflicted on many occasions, yet you have not shown. What has changed?"

"*Your Etain is a lovely young woman. You two are well-matched. More so than you and I ever were.*"

"You and the children were my world."

A smirk touched her lips. "*The children were your world.*" She held up a hand to stop his interruption. "*You know it is true, as do I.*" She placed her hand on her chest. "*I did not begrudge you that. We did not marry for love, but you showed me great respect because of our family. It was more than what many Krymerian wives had at that time.*"

"I loved you in my way."

"*This love you have with Etain.*" She bowed her head. "*It is eternal, fierce, and true.*" Her gaze met his. "*You are a different man with her.*"

His shoulders slumped. "How true can our love be if she does not recognize me?"

Alexia moved a tad closer to him. "*She is struggling, fighting her way out of a dark place, my love. If you push too soon, you could lose her. Be patient. She will come back to you in her own time.*"

A sudden tear trailed down his cheek. He had no words to express how his heart ached for his past and future families. He watched her extend a hand and closed his eyes at the coolness against his cheek.

"*Be strong, my love. Be patient.*"

When he opened his eyes, she was gone.

Remembrance

Jackie paced in front of the window in her room. Dar and Etain's conversation in the study brought a harsh reality crashing down on her. *Faux. How could I forget? Holy Jehoshaphat! And...* She bit her bottom lip, trying to remember something else.

As she turned, she bumped into Etain. "Lord, child." Jackie placed a hand on her chest. "You scared the life out of me. I must've been deep in thought. I didn't hear you come in."

"Sorry." Etain stared at her, running a hand through her hair.

Jackie narrowed her eyes. "What's wrong?"

"I don't know *how* I got here."

"Huh?"

Etain glanced at the door. "I was in the stables with Dar. It's like I just disappeared and showed up here."

Hearing the tremble in her voice, Jackie pulled her to a chair. "You should sit, child. You've been under a lot of stress. Obviously, your mind was elsewhere when—"

"No. I was in the *stables* and now I'm *here*. I didn't walk. I didn't run. I just disappeared from there and showed up here."

"Okay. Okay." Jackie crouched in front of her. "I don't think it's anything to be worried about. This Alamir world is a strange place where even stranger things happen."

"Come on, Jackie. I—"

"Let me tell you a story." Jackie paid no mind to the doubtful expression on her face. "Not too long ago, a couple of Alamir showed up in my bar. Brought their clan too."

"Alamir? In your bar?"

"Yes, ma'am. Popped right in outta nowhere."

"Who were they?"

"Well, one was named Krz." She waited a moment, letting the name roll around in that blonde head. "And the other was Kane." She watched her closely, not sure if she had any recognition. "They're brothers."

Etain sat back and rested her chin in her hand, deep in thought. After a time, she whispered, "Haluci."

Jackie covered her excitement by sitting in the chair next to Etain. "Do you know them?"

She shrugged. "Maybe."

"One night, they showed up with another Alamir. Someone I hadn't seen in years."

Etain leaned toward her but didn't say anything.

"There was a woman giving a speech just up the street. Krz got wind that some nasty piece of work had hired assassins to kill her, so he and his brother came through with a friend. Seeing her again took me by complete surprise."

"*Bok*," Etain said. "It was a *Bok* assassin. That's why the Alamir intervened."

She said it so casually, Jackie thought she might continue the story. But she sat there with an expectant gleam in her eyes.

"Okay. Well, they were running a tad behind. I was afraid they wouldn't make it in time, but this girl..." Jackie bit her lip, determined to keep her cool and not rush the story. "This young woman ripped the map outta my hand, grabbed Krz and Kane, and all three disappeared in a blue..." She tried to think of the right word. "Shimmer." It lit a spark in the girl's eyes. "That's it. A blue shimmer."

"So you think that's what I did? Shimmer?" Etain laughed and pushed out of the chair. "I don't recall seeing any 'blue light'," she quipped, using her fingers to air quote. "Oh, Jackie. You had me going for a sec."

Her flippant attitude burned. She was trying to help, and this little miss turned into a smartass. Jackie snapped back without a thought. "I heard you telling Dar about your sister, Faux. That's her name, right?"

Etain frowned. "Aye."

"I know your mom didn't have another child and your dad didn't stray. How is it you have a sister?"

She blinked a few times. "What difference does it make? She's with the angels."

Jackie stared at her. "Faux is who you're talking about, right?"

She appeared unsure. "You talk like you know her."

Jackie stood at this point, wondering how the hell she could forget. They must've bashed her head pretty hard.

Freeblood! That's his name.

She faced Etain. "Does the name Freeblood mean anything to you?"

When all the color drained from her face, Jackie rushed to her side and helped her into a chair. "Sit, girl, before you pass out."

"He was in a motorcycle accident." Etain stared at her as she sat. "I-I took him to the hospital."

"What?" Jackie had no clue what she was talking about. "When did that happen?"

She shrugged. "A long time ago. He was the reason why I went to see Faux."

Jackie crouched in front of her. "Do you remember the last time you saw her?"

She ran a hand through her hair. "On the beach?"

"Is that where you saw the angel take her away?"

Etain bit her bottom lip and shook her head. "No."

"What happened on the beach?"

She stood. "I don't know."

"What does Freeblood have to do with Faux?"

"*I don't know!*" She jammed both hands into her hair. "He's her lover. She was Dar's lover." Etain walked to the window and stared out. "Spirit told me she lost the baby. But I saw her big belly. I saw it!" She glanced over her shoulder. "She betrayed me, and now she's gone."

Jackie stood. "Darlin', you're not making sense."

A memory of a bloody "x" across a pregnant belly flashed in Jackie's mind. *Could she be having Dar's baby too? Maybe that's why Etain's forgotten them.*

"Dar is mine."

Jackie joined her at the window. "Why don't we get you back to your room?"

The women turned and walked to the door. "I'm okay." Etain pulled away. "I think I'll go for a walk."

"Etain—"

She opened the door and stepped out. "No. You go talk to Dar, tell him whatever you need to tell him. I'll see you later."

Jackie let her go, her thoughts on how the hell the girl knew what she'd been thinking. If she knew Dar was on her mind, what else did she know?

A shiver ran up her spine. "Whatever it is, Dar needs to know."

At the bottom of the stairs, a knock on the front door interrupted Etain's thoughts. With a furrowed brow, she opened to...

"Ms. E! Hello!" A man with rich, milk chocolate skin glanced over his shoulder to a large group of people behind him. "I hope you don't mind our showing up unannounced."

She blinked. "Alaster?"

He flashed his whiter than white smile. "Yeah. I'm sorry for this." He glanced at a woman at his side and lowered his voice. "May we speak in private?"

The request pulled Etain's attention away from the group smiling at her. "I'm guessing this is more than a visit?"

Alaster shrugged. "We can go into town if you're hard-pressed for space."

"Space isn't a problem." She stepped aside. "Why don't y'all come in? There are a few rooms down the hall from the kitchen and lots more up the back stairs." As they continued to file in, she politely pushed her way through the group as she spoke. "You'll find linens in a closet at the end of the hallway."

The woman next to Alaster gave her a gentle smile. "We'll take care of everything."

Her deep, warm, southern voice was a comfort. Etain smiled in return when her name came to her. "Welcome to *Sôlskin*, Cherise. We didn't get much of a chance to speak at Laugharne."

"It was just short of mayhem, wasn't it?" Her hearty laugh faded into a frown. "I'm sorry for all of us showing up like this, but we had nowhere else to go."

"We take care of each other. I hope y'all will consider this your home." Standing at the door of the kitchen, Etain's gaze passed over the entire entourage. "Take as many rooms as you need and don't hesitate to tell me if you need anything." She waved a hand toward the hallway she'd mentioned earlier.

"Thank you." Cherise turned to the others. "Let's get busy!"

"While they settle in," Alaster said, "might we have a chat?"

Etain led the way to the study. Closing the door quietly, she motioned the Alamir to one of the sofas as she slipped off her cloak. "What brings you here? I thought you were going home."

"We *did* go home the morning everyone left for the ship." His voice carried a hint of sadness. "Things weren't the same. The *Bok* knew about our involvement in the battle."

She walked around to a table behind the sofa and poured a dram. "Here. You look like you could use it." She made sure he had a good hold of the glass before she released it. "It must've been bad."

He slammed back the drink and held the glass out for a refill. Etain raised a brow but poured him another. "It was horrible," he said, his voice raspy from the Scotch. "They destroyed everything. My shop, our homes. They even hit those who had stayed behind." He sipped the second drink. "We barely made it out."

"Was anyone hurt?"

"We were lucky. Once we found our homes wrecked, I knew our lives would be forfeit. We headed to the coast and opened a portal. I didn't dare go back to Laugharne. Spirit has suffered enough."

"She would've welcomed you with open arms."

"I was afraid we'd bring the lady more trouble."

He stood and walked to the French doors. "I have to confess, we didn't just come here to be safe. When Dar told us about your home..." He turned to her. "I knew you'd need help."

"Wait. You opened a *portal*? Since when do Alamir have that power?"

Alaster grinned. "Not everyone in the clan has it, and it takes two to open one."

She crossed her arms over her chest. "Two?"

"Well, the women are the gate keepers—TGK for short. And the men are the key masters, or TKM."

"So the gatekeeper starts the process, and the key master opens it?"

He nodded enthusiastically. "That's it!"

"Clever. How did you know where to go?"

"I had a few conversations with Freeblood."

There's that name again. What is so important about this guy?

"He gave me a general idea of where the island was so we chanced it. Luckily, fate has taken pity on us today."

"Indeed, she has. Your being here *would* be a great help." She joined the Alamir at the French doors. "I'm sure Dar'll give you part of the garden out there. Just don't mess with his roses."

Alaster squinted through the glass. "Roses?"

She chuckled. "I don't know what happened to them, but they're there."

He pointed at the Scotch with a raised brow. Smiling, she waved a hand and watched as he returned to the table behind the sofa, pouring another glass.

"The stables are almost done. Dar tells me he's building an academy for warriors who wish to become, um...Black Blades. You *will* be busy all the time. Are you up for it?"

He seemed unsure for a moment. "How can I say no to all that?"

She walked toward him and stuck out her hand. "Welcome home."

He laughed, accepting her hand and the offer. "Thank you, Ms. E. I got a quick peek at the kitchen while we were in the entry."

She gave him a half-hearted smile. "Renovations."

"Well... I figure we got here just in time." Alaster headed for the door. "I best get to work on the new design."

"Before you go." Her words stopped him at the door. "I'm not sure how long Dar's construction crew is contracted for. Do you have anyone who does construction? The kitchen isn't the only room that needs work." She rested a hand on her belly. "We could use a nursery too."

"Gordon knows his way around a construction site, and I'm pretty sure Winny is an architect. Shall I send them your way?"

"Oh, aye. I'll put them right to work."

***

Dar spent the rest of his day working with the crew on the stables. Toting lumber, measuring and remeasuring, hammering and sawing. The manual labor made him feel alive and a part of something bigger than himself. He was building a home not just for him, but for his family, friends, and people from all over who dared to venture far from their homes for a new life. The work took his mind off his personal troubles.

Just as the thought entered his mind, he glanced at the sky and realized how late it had become. He turned to the construction foreman. "Shall we call it a day?"

"Works for me, Dar." The man waved him off. "You go ahead. We'll clean up here and head home. See you tomorrow."

Dar gave him a huge grin. "You will! It's been a good day."

Although his mind urged him to rush, his gut said walk. He made himself stop several times, take a deep breath, and start again. Walking through the gates of the house, his instincts told him to veer toward the rear door leading into the kitchen rather than the front doors. As he rounded the corner, he stopped, seeing a new door and wondered if it was the smartest choice, this one being mostly glass. He didn't recognize the workmen but tipped his head nonetheless and slipped inside.

Hearing his wife's laugh, his gaze went directly to her, sitting at the island, an easy smile on her face. She radiated like the sun as she chatted with... *Cherise?*

There were people everywhere—clearing, cleaning, cooking. He searched for Alaster but didn't see him. *What is going on here?*

At the same time, his heart swelled to see the care taken with his wife. He stepped to the side of the door behind the workmen so he wouldn't interrupt this precious moment.

How long before she smiles at me so easily and accepts me as her husband?

He heard a female voice call his name. "Dar! Why're you hiding in the shadows over there? Come here."

Excited she had seen him and wanted him to come to her, he turned toward the voice. But the hand that beckoned him was not hers. It belonged to Cherise. Once again, he searched for Etain's beautiful face.

He wanted to die. Feel his heart explode and fill every cavity of his torso with its blood until his body bloated into a flesh-colored balloon and it too, exploded. Etain was gone. Had she seen him and left? Or had he not even registered with her? Either way, it took what little willpower he had left to drag himself to the woman.

"Cherise..." He tried to sound happy to see her. "I am surprised to see you. Where is Alaster?"

"He's gone into town. That man's always gotta have more." Cherise laughed. "We ran into Etain earlier. As a matter of fact, you just missed her. She was sitting right here, having a good time... But jumped up and left." She seemed not to notice Dar's downtrodden demeanor.

"We've come to lend our capable hands to the cause. Things weren't too great back home, so Alaster decided to bring us here. The missus said it was all right."

Dar turned away, checking to see if perhaps Etain might return.

Cherise leaned into his line of sight. "If it's a problem, we can move on."

"No." He forced himself to focus on the immediate situation. "She is right. You are most welcome here. But I think we are getting the better part of the deal."

"Ms. E warned us." Her laugh was as deep and warm as her blue-black skin. "Alaster's measured everything and went to order what he could. Whatever he can't order, he'll get one of our own to build." Her smile softened into something more serious. "I hope you don't mind us taking over your kitchen."

No matter how relieved he was to have these gifted people here, the best he could manage was a lift of the corner of his mouth. "I built this place for our family *and* friends. Thank you for taking us on. If you'll excuse me—"

"Dar!" A worried Jackie came into the kitchen. "There you are. Do you have time for a chat?" She noticed the other people in the room. "What's going on in here?"

Dar walked her toward the hallway. "I will introduce you later. Does it have to do with Etain?"

"Not directly."

He stopped. If it was not about his wife, the chat could wait. "This is not a good time, Jackie."

She grabbed his arm and pulled him toward the one room that was most likely unoccupied—the study. Once inside, she closed the door. "Faux and Freeblood."

"What about them?"

"So you know them too?"

"Aye."

"Then you know Faux wasn't taken by an angel."

He sighed, crossing his arms over his chest. "What is it, Jackie?"

"The couple in that room, with the chains and ropes..."

Dar felt the color drain from his face. Lightheaded, his arms fell to his sides as he staggered. Although considerably smaller than him, Jackie rushed to his side.

"How about you sit?" With him seated, she poured him a dram and shoved it into his hand. "Drink this."

By the gods, how long has it been? He slammed back the Scotch. "Do you know where they are?"

She took the glass from his hand, poured him another and poured one for herself. "I don't know where, but I know who."

He accepted the glass, swirling the amber liquid. "The *Bok*?"

"Banshee. They no sooner dumped me on the doorstep before they showed up again and damn near bashed my brains outta my head. Hearing Etain mention Faux's name brought it all back to me."

"You asked if I knew them too. Did Etain say anything?"

She sat on the other sofa across from Dar. "Not much that made sense." She raised a brow. "Did you really mess around with Faux?"

Dar drained his glass and set it on the coffee table. "Of all the things to remember..." He stood. "It's old news, Jackie."

"But not so old that the baby she's pregnant with could be yours?"

His gaze hardened. "Freeblood is the father. That's all you need to know." He headed toward the door and opened it. "If you will excuse me, I need to contact a few people. We have lost too much time."

She lifted her glass to him, downed the Scotch and set her glass next to his. "I'm sorry I didn't remember sooner. They seemed like good people." She stood and walked out into the hallway.

"This is not your doing, milady. You are lucky to be alive, and I am glad of it. You have helped my Etain immensely and have probably saved the lives of Faux and Freeblood. I am grateful to you."

"Oh, well..." She appeared taken aback. "Glad I could help."

"I do have a request."

"Shoot."

"Etain was in the kitchen earlier when I came in, but suddenly left. Would you search her out and make sure she is not in distress?"

"Not to add to your worries, but I'm guessing you two had a conversation in the stable earlier?" When he didn't acknowledge or deny, she continued. "That's what she said. Anyway, when she was with Krz and Kane at my bar, she called it a shimmer. It threw her for a loop when she did it this morning."

"I thought she shimmered on purpose."

"Nope."

He rubbed a hand over his face. "Then I doubt she is aware of her other powers."

"Could it be a problem?"

"I do not know, Jackie."

"Well, I'll go find her, make sure she's okay."

"Thank you." He quietly closed the door and turned the lock.

She ran as best she could, having to stop a time or two to catch her breath. Her stamina wasn't what it used to be. Paying no heed to the sun as it dipped lower in the sky or the crisp bite of the evening, she ran toward the seclusion of the trees. She wanted to become lost in their shadows, needing the comfort of their silent serenity. Once within the protection of the forest, her anger slowly ebbed, and she was able to think.

Panting, she sat next to a large tree in the remaining shafts of sunlight shining through the leafy canopy and leaned against the massive trunk. She closed her eyes and rested a hand on her belly.

How can one person be so damn irritating?

She sighed.

Forget about him. Think about the shimmer. Was Jackie serious?

Oh, aye. She was damn serious. If looks could kill...

Etain circled her hand over her belly.

I don't even know how I did it. Maybe I learned it from the girl Jackie spoke of?

She laughed at herself.

Where would I shimmer to anyway? Spirit's? She's the one who sent me here in the first place.

To keep me safe.

How safe can I be with him hovering over me?

Have you considered why he hovers?

Guilt.

What is he guilty of Etain?

Someone gave me these bruises. He was in bed with me.

Spirit wouldn't send you to an abusive man. Jackie wouldn't allow you to stay either.

If not him, then who?

When you're ready, you will remember.

Her body drifted as the heaviness of sleep carried her away.

"*Mama.*"

She smiled, thinking it a dream.

Another tiny voice spoke. "*Mama.*"

My beautiful babies. I imagine you'd sound like that if you could talk.

"*Mama!*"

Startled, she sat up, her eyes darting left and right. "Who's there?"

"*We are with you, Mama,*" said one.

"*Don't be scared, Mama,*" said the other.

"*Don't run from Da.*"

She pushed a hand through her hair. "I can't see you. Where—"

"*It is Ema. Me and brother are here with you. Please don't be scared.*"

Etain's heart raced. "What?"

"*We are better now.*"

"*We are stronger.*"

"*But you are not. Da wants to help you, Mama.*"

Realizing the voices spoke inside her head, Etain touched her belly. "I-I can hear you."

The two giggled.

"*You forgot, Mama. We protected you. I am Ema.*"

"*I told you it was too much magic, Em. Mama, I am Jamie.*"

"How do you know your names?"

The voices fell silent.

"Hello?" Etain caressed her belly with both hands. "Are you there, or have I lost my mind?" She sighed and leaned back against the tree. "It must be true. You *are* Krymerians. Someone told me I am too. He said my mom, your grandmother, was a Krymerian princess. I don't know how that happened. If mom was, why was she in the human world?"

She heard a rustling from the shadows. After a hard swallow, she pulled her bare feet beneath her, prepared to stand, when a white muzzle peeked out into the fading light. Etain held her breath. A wolf, white as snow, emerged from the darkness and sat on its haunches, blue eyes staring at her.

Etain matched the stare. Her rational mind told her she should be wary, but her heart said otherwise. "Hello," she whispered as she slowly placed a hand on her chest. "I am Etain."

The wolf jerked its head as though it understood.

Their staring contest continued for another long moment before the wolf stood, howled, and disappeared into the dark. Etain pushed up onto her feet, her heart racing.

Again, she heard a rustling in the brush just before Jackie burst from the shadows. "Etain!" Her wild gaze darted around the clearing. "Are you all right?"

She saw the concern on her face and heard it in her voice. "I'm okay."

"Was that a wolf I heard?"

"It's all right. She ran off."

"Well, I suggest we get out of here. If she has pups close by, she'll be back."

"She didn't seem dangerous."

"Let's not take that chance, okay? Besides, it's getting late and it's too damn cold to be out." She raised her brows, noticing Etain's bare feet. "With no shoes, no less. Where are your boots?"

"I-I'm sorry." She shivered. "My feet swell later in the day, so I took them off in the kitchen. You're right. It's colder than I expected."

"Here..." Jackie undid the clasp at her neck and shrugged off her cloak. "When I didn't find you in the house, I figured you'd gone outside. Put this on and let's get you back to where it's warm."

She held out the cloak and waited for Etain to come forward. With it securely on her shoulders, Jackie lifted the hood over her head. "Didn't anyone ever tell you of the beasties that come out at night?" Her smile warmed Etain's heart. "It's not safe for civilized people."

"I'm safe then. No one has ever accused me of being civilized."

They turned toward the house, laughing. "You'd think I'd remember that. You and your boots and jeans. Drove your mama nuts."

Etain sighed. "I wish she were here now."

"Me too," Jackie whispered. "Me too."

They walked in silence for a bit before Etain announced, "They spoke to me."

Jackie glanced at her. "The faeries in the forest?"

She grinned and shrugged. "Almost as crazy... My babies."

"Hmph. Is that so?"

"They know their names." She chuckled. "I've only just decided what to call my son, and he's calling himself Jamie instead of James."

"After your dad?"

"I miss him too."

"What're you naming the other one?"

"She's named after my and Dar's mothers. Emalyn Aurelia."

As they walked into the courtyard, Jackie said, "Your parents would be damn proud of you, Etain."

A pout showed on her lips. "I hope so."

"Let's get upstairs, get you warmed up and to bed. You've had a long day."

"A warm bath would be nice."

Upstairs at her bedroom door, Etain waved her off. "You go on to your room. Your day's been no shorter than mine."

"That may be true, but I'm not totin' around extra babbage, am I?"

Caught off guard by the woman's comment, Etain actually giggled. "*Babbage?*"

Jackie grinned as she opened Etain's door. "The mouth doesn't always work the way you want it to. I meant to say *baby baggage.*"

"I hear ya, sister." Etain stepped into her room. "You're right about the bath and straight to bed."

"Let me run it for you. I know it's getting harder to bend over and such."

"Are you sure?"

"It'll be the easiest thing I've done all day."

As Jackie disappeared into the bathroom, Etain ventured into the walk-in wardrobe to find a fresh gown for the night. The first thing to catch her eye was a sword in a golden scabbard. She called out to Jackie, but she didn't answer.

Etain marvelled at the beauty of the scabbard and hilt as she picked it up. She turned and walked out of the wardrobe.

"Whatcha got there?" Jackie asked, drying her hands with a small towel. "The water's running."

"A sword. Where did it come from?"

"Oh, well, it was in the closet across the hall. It's so darn pretty, I figured it was yours. Dar wouldn't own a sword like that."

She pulled the sword from its scabbard and gasped. As did Jackie.

"It's beautiful," Etain whispered.

"Looks like crystal."

Her brows furrowed. "Who would make a sword out of crystal? Maybe it's a display piece. I'll ask Dar about it tomorrow. If he can have swords on his walls, why can't I?"

After a shared laugh, Jackie pointed toward the bath. "You best get in there, girl. It should be ready. Hand me the sword. I'll put it back."

"Thanks, Jackie." She left a kiss on her cheek. "I'll see you in the morning."

"Night, darlin'."

THE CRYSTAL SWORD

D ar knew it would be a long, tedious night. Sequestered in his study, he reached out to Linq to apprise him of the situation.

Linq's response was immediate. *"My guess would be Nocturna. We both know of the Phums love for the Trodaire."*

"Oh, aye. I have not paid much attention to their antics through the years. I am ashamed to say I have not cared much until now."

"Well, Dar, it is easier to ignore the damn Banshee than take them on."

"They will find they have messed with the wrong Krymerian."

"What I do not understand is why they took Faux. She is not a fighter."

Dar gazed at the fire ablaze in the fireplace. *"Perhaps as leverage."*

"Ah. Keep the boy fighting to save the girl."

"Gods know how long he will last, though. Freeblood is tough, but I think even I would find it hard to keep up."

"You know, I think this goes deeper than the Trodaire."

"What are you thinking, Linq?"

"As if Faux and Freeblood were not enough, these Banshee searched out Etain's family friend—her human *friend—brought her to this world and marched her into the same room as Etain."* Linq paused. *"What do you think that did to her?"*

Dar did not answer right away. He pictured the room as he had found it and recreated the scene in his mind as best he could. He hoped what he imagined was worse than what she had experienced, but remembering the blood and the bruises, he doubted he was far off.

"She was horrified." He pinched the bridge of his nose. *"The bastard used every angle he could to break her. For what?"*

He heard Linq blow out a breath. *"We may never know."*

"How soon till you get here?"

"Another week, at least."

Dar closed his eyes. The last thing he wanted to do was leave Etain. Even though she did her best to avoid him right now, he knew she was working her way back. *By the gods, I wanted to be here when she returned!*

He stood and paced the room, contemplating how long it might take to rescue the couple, wondering if he could do it in a matter of days rather than weeks. Days would mean total annihilation of the Banshee and whoever stood with them. Weeks could mean the death of Faux and Freeblood.

Linq interrupted his thoughts. *"Dar, stop. You cannot go. You must be there for Etain."*

"Who the hell else is willing to go into that hellhole?"

"You leave that to us."

Dropping it for now, Dar moved on to another problem.

"Do you know an Alamir named Krz?" He sensed the Elf's hesitation.

"I have met the man. He showed up at Laugharne a few times. Why?"

"Etain's friend, Jackie, has a bar in Los Angeles in the human realm. He and his clan have visited a few times. It must be a portal link."

"Back when COL was attacked, he and his brother showed up at Inferno's speaking of a new entry point they had found. That must be it. Do we need to protect it?"

"Jackie's worried about the business and her people. Apparently, the man has experience in working a bar. Can we get it covered for a while?"

"If Aramis or Ra cannot find him, they will know someone who can."

"Good, good. Now, back to the other problem... It has to be now, Linq. We cannot wait another week."

"Leave it to us, Dar. You take care of your family, help Etain heal, and get ready for those beautiful babies."

"Linq—"

"We will speak again soon."

With that, he cut off the conversation.

"Tartarus!" Dar picked up a glass and threw it at the fireplace. *"Linq. Linq!"*

Unable to raise him again, he stormed to the door, ripped it open, and marched toward the kitchen. Despite being upset with his friend, hunger pangs twisted in his stomach. He had not eaten much at breakfast and worked hard most of the day. Maybe with a full belly, he would be able to concentrate and come up with a plan, or at least get the damn Elf to talk to him.

He stalked into the kitchen, his mind on what might be readily available, and stopped short, unsure of what to say. Or if he should say anything. He stared at Etain as she stared at him, a spoonful of cereal suspended in midair.

She slowly lowered the spoon into the bowl. "I-I'm sorry. I'll leave you—"

"No. You stay and finish your meal. I will leave you in peace." He turned to go.

"Dar. Wait."

He heard the barstool scrape across the stone floor and the pad of bare feet before she came around to stand in front of him. Dressed in her white nightgown, she looked delicate and fragile. How he wanted to wrap her in his arms and assure her she had no reason to fear him. Tell her how much he loved her.

"You must be starving."

The concern on her face touched him, but he knew it was nothing personal. "It has been a long day. I am sorry I disturbed you. I was not expecting—"

Etain gave him a slight smile and shrugged. "Me either. I figured everyone was in bed and thought I'd slip down here for a little something. I'm sorry—"

His gaze met hers. "No, my lo—" He bit his tongue. "No, milady. You do not eat enough. Please, finish. I will come back later."

She reached out and touched his arm. "Let me fix you something to eat. Please. It won't be fancy, but it'll taste better than anything you can make." She smirked.

Dar relaxed. "I stand here, a starving man, and she makes jokes."

Etain's laugh was the music to his life.

"Sit. I'll fix you a sandwich."

He sat at the island, watching her walk back and forth from the refrigerator, an array of items in her arms, most of which had nothing to do with a sandwich. But the essentials were in the mix.

She placed three pieces of bread on a plate. Dar raised a brow, intrigued, until he realized her ice blues were on him.

"Mustard, mayo, or cream cheese?"

"Pardon?"

She pointed the tip of the knife at the bread. "Or are you one of those *butter* people?"

"Inspire me with your creativity."

Holding his gaze, she tilted her head, raised a brow, and picked up the cream cheese, slathering it over all three pieces of bread. Bit by bit, she added lettuce on one, sliced pickles, tomatoes, and smoked ham on two, then stacked them one on top of the other. With a large knife, she sliced it on the diagonal.

"I hope you enjoy," she said, sliding the plate toward him.

He leaned over, meeting her halfway. "At the risk of ruining the moment..." He eyed the stacked sandwich as he sat back. "Have you forgiven me for this morning?"

Etain shrugged, focused on putting things away. For once, Dar decided not to push and concentrated on the treat in front of him. It took both hands to get a hold of the half, but it disappeared in a few bites. As he eyed the other, Etain sat on the barstool next to him.

"I think it's me who should ask for forgiveness." She placed her arms on the island, her right dangerously close to his left. "You've proven to be an honorable man."

He could not move. Her being this close made his heart sing and bleed at the same time. How long before she flipped into someone he did not recognize and run away? He doubted he had much more in him, but this was his family. He had to find it from somewhere deep inside.

"I see your struggle, Dar. I *feel* it, as if we're connected in some way. Maybe we were kindred souls in another life or something."

"It *was* another life," he whispered. *Maybe this is all we have now.*

Wanting to change the mood, he asked, "Care to tell me why you are awake?"

She gazed at him for a few moments and glanced at the door as though deciding whether to carry on with the conversation or disappear like she had done so many times before. "I've had an interesting evening."

"How so?"

"I was in the bath, warming up from my escape into the cold." Etain rolled her eyes, her expression telling him she was aware how ludicrous her actions had been. "When I heard someone call my name. I thought Jackie'd come back to chat, but it wasn't her. It was a feminine voice, so I knew it wasn't you either."

Intrigued, he turned to her. "Could it have been Cherise?"

She shook her head, the fragrance of her freshly washed hair teasing his nostrils. "It crossed my mind, but no. This is going to sound ridiculous, and I don't even know why I'm telling you this." She laughed, embarrassed. "It was coming from the wardrobe. So, I thought it was one of the children from Alaster's group playing a joke on me." Her expression turned more serious. "It was a crystal sword that glowed like the aurora borealis."

She stopped, waiting for him to say something. But he did not know what to say without saying too much.

"Okay, well..." She twisted in her seat. "She said her name is *Nim'Na'Sharr* and I am her mistress." Etain laid a hand on her chest. "She belongs to me. Weird, huh?"

He shifted and turned away from her, placing his arms on the island around the plate in front of him. She had forgotten the beautiful sword he risked his life to forge for her. He could not tell her the story as it happened. It would be too much for her to take in. But his next words were just as hard for him to say. "It *is* your sword. Your Dar made it for you."

Silence hung in the air for a long moment. Then he heard her chuckle. *She's laughing?*

"Why would he make me a sword like that? It's pretty, but not practical. And I'm not one to hang swords on the walls." She smirked. "No offense. But what do I do with it?"

If Nim can't get through to her...

He did not have the heart to continue the conversation.

"Lady Etain..." He pulled his hands into his lap. "I do not mean to be rude, but may I finish this delicious meal you have made for me so I might go to bed?"

"I-I'm sorry." She leaned back and slid off the stool, bending down to pick up her boots. "You came in here to eat, not chat. I should get to bed myself. Good night."

Dar slightly turned his head toward her, his eyes lowered. "Good night, milady."

He listened to her move through the hall, waiting for the familiar creak of the stairs that told him she had gone to her room. Focused on the food in front of him, he ate the sandwich, rinsed the dish, and finished with a cool glass of water. He followed in her footsteps down the hall and up the stairs, going to his own room with the hope sleep would take over before his thoughts drove him mad.

Linq wasted no time in meeting with the others to bring them up to date on the happenings at *Sólskin* and the Banshee situation.

"From what you have told us..." Taurnil circled the table in one of the ship's conference rooms, "the Banshee kidnapped Faux and Freeblood and have taken them to Nocturna for their Trodaire circuit..." He turned to the Alamir sitting on the other side of the table. "Or gladiator games, for Aramis and Ra. And left Etain's friend for dead."

Slouched back in his seat, Ra raised a brow, taking the toothpick from between his lips. "Banshees? Gladiators?"

Linq nodded. "Oh, aye. They have been around for a long time. I have heard stories in passing, but this is the first time someone I know has been directly affected."

"This is insane." Aramis shook his head. "It's the twenty-first century."

Ra shifted in the seat and leaned forward. "How Romanesque."

"They have been doing this longer than the Romans," Taurnil said, leaning against the wall. "It is the Banshee who started the whole thing. The Romans borrowed the idea from them."

"What do we do, gentlemen?" Aramis asked. "Are we slipping in to get them out, or taking on the Banshee nation?"

Linq raised his brows as he blew out a breath. "If they get wind of what we are doing, there will not be much difference."

Ra exchanged a glance with Aramis. "You two know where this Nocturna is?"

"*I* do," said Linq.

"Are we doing this quiet?" Ra put the toothpick back into his mouth and clamped it between his teeth, speaking around it. "Or are we going in guns blazin', so to speak."

The older Elf sat a butt cheek on the edge of the conference table with one foot on the floor. "We do not know if they are aware of who Faux and Freeblood are attached to. I think it best we go in quietly and not make it obvious."

Ra nodded as he scratched the scruff along his jawline. "These Banshee went to the human realm and grabbed someone who means somethin' to Lady E."

If his conversation with Dar had not been through the mindspeak, Linq would have accused Ra of eavesdropping.

"For all we know, they abducted the other two and delivered 'em all to that rat bastard, Dathmet." Ra chewed on the toothpick for a moment. "I think they know who they got and what it means. And…" he held up a hand, pointing toward the ceiling, "they ain't finished."

Taurnil pushed away from the wall curling his hands into fists. "What makes you say that?"

Ra turned his head to the young Elf. "By their standards—not that I know what they are, but since these Banshee kidnap and force people into service, I doubt I'm far off. Wouldn't it be a coup to catch them a Kry-mer-ian? How many folks you figure *he'd* draw in for their games?"

"That is one reason why I want him out of it." Linq slid off the table. "It is on us, boys. Etain needs the man more than we do."

Aramis stood. "Does Dar know this?"

"Aye. We had a long conversation that ended with me telling the man to focus on his wife."

Ra laughed as he stood, running his hands down his thighs to straighten his jeans, and shook out his floor-length leather coat. "Good man. Let's do this before he ruins our plans."

"Hold on a minute." Taurnil held up a hand. "I am assuming we four are going." The three stared back at him. "I thought so. We have no idea how long this is going to take. Who is going to meet Dar when the ship docks?"

"I am perfectly capable." The men turned toward the door where Swee stood, leaning against the jamb. She shrugged. "Sorry. I knocked." She stepped into the room and closed the door. "Not that I mind, but why am *I* meeting Dar instead of Linq?"

"Hello, Swee." Linq turned to the men. "Aramis, do you know how to get in touch with Krz of the Haluci?"

"If I can't, Angel of FWH can."

"While I explain the situation to Swee, would you get in touch? Tell him Jackie needs someone to watch the bar."

Aramis furrowed his brows.

"He will understand. I will meet you in the hold when we are done here."

The other three said their goodbyes to Swee as they filed out of the room. Once they were alone, Linq turned to her.

"You might want to sit for this."

BLACK SAND

Swee and Dalos stood at the railing of the great ship, anxiously awaiting the moment they would disembark. They spotted Dar's blond head towering over the others on the dock and watched as he instructed the animal transporters to the proper location for unloading the livestock. Finally, the ship came to a halt and the gangplank put in place.

"Dar! It's great to see you." Swee grinned, rushing off the ship with Dalos.

"Good day, High Lord!" Dalos' smile was twice as big. "What a glorious place."

Dar laughed as he hugged Swee and shook hands with the Elf. "Welcome to my island. Dalos, there should be plenty to keep the likes of you busy and out of trouble."

"How much trouble can I get into without my partner in crime?"

"Oh, aye." Dar stroked his chin. "How much indeed? I think loading the luggage onto the buses is a good start."

"But—" Dalos started.

"No more talk. You have work to do." He pointed toward the loading ramp. "I want to be on the road within the hour."

"By the stars," Dalos muttered, walking off. "Me and my mouth."

Dar grinned at Swee. "How was the trip?"

"I didn't find my sea legs for a few days, but for the most part, it was good." Her expression changed to concern. "How's Etain?"

"Ready to give birth." He chuckled. "Now if the children would cooperate."

"Have you heard from Taurnil or Linq?" she asked as they walked toward the buses waiting to take them to the manor.

"I have not, but communication is too risky. Do not worry, Swee. They know what they are doing. Do you know if Linq was successful in contacting Krz?"

"Aramis got the message to him through Angel of FWH. The bar is in good hands." She leaned closer. "Does Etain know about any of this?"

Before he could answer, Eol and Galdor, followed by two boys, joined them. Everyone sported huge smiles, exchanging handshakes with Dar. Except the smaller boy, who stood apart, disgust on his face and arms crossed over his chest. Dar welcomed each one personally and received an official introduction to Cloud.

At the scowling boy, Dar stepped back and assumed the same stance. "Who do we have here?"

"This is my—" Cloud started.

"You ain't near as big as I thought. Where's the blood?"

Dar stifled his grin, not wanting to disappoint the young boy further, and raised a brow. "You came looking for blood?"

"Yeah. They said you're a great warrior who eats the hearts of your victims." He lowered his arms and placed his hands on his hips. "I wanna do that."

Barely able to contain his laughter, Dar turned to Eol to avoid embarrassing the naïve warrior. "Who do we have to thank for this?"

"That would be Ra, milord."

He stole a peek at the scowling boy. "It sounds like he told quite the story, aye?"

Eol glared at the small hellion. "In Ra's defense, it is not easy to keep this one quiet. He is a wild child."

Dar turned to the boy. "You have come to be a warrior, have you?" The child nodded, a spark of interest in his dark green eyes. "Well, what is your name, boy?"

He puffed out his chest. "I'm Austin of Deudraeth, come to kill the assholes who killed my Da."

"Austin!" his brother yelled.

"Killed your Da?" Dar echoed.

Cloud tried to interrupt. "Sir, please ignore my brother. He's just a kid."

"Shut up, Cloud!" Austin yelled, balling his hands into fists.

"You don't walk up to strangers and say asshole or tell them you want to eat hearts. Didn't you learn anything from Da?"

"I'll show you what I learned." Austin swung, but thanks to a quick-thinking Galdor, who grabbed Cloud out of the line of fire, he missed his brother's face. Dar picked up the fighter by the scruff of his shirt. Already in mid-swing, he landed a good blow to his jaw.

"Now you've done it!" Cloud yelled. "He'll probably eat your heart *and* your head!"

"I'd like to see him try!"

"That's some punch you have there, young warrior." Dar held the struggling boy out of range as he adjusted his jaw. "There is not much call for the eating of hearts nowadays, but I believe we can teach you a few other useful things. If you settle down, I will show you some Krymerian fighting moves when we get to the manor. Deal?"

He struggled a bit longer, albeit halfheartedly, as he considered the offer, and crossed his arms again, the scowl returning to his face. "They better be good ones. No baby stuff."

Dar set the boy on his feet. "Welcome to my home, Austin of Deudraeth. Let's load up and get moving."

His eyes on the boy as he followed the others, Dar leaned toward Eol. "How has it been?"

"It has been different."

"What happened after we left? Since I have not had news, I assumed it went well."

"There were a few bumps and bruises from the encounter with the *Bok*, but other than that, none of ours died. How has it been with you, High Lord?"

"Rough, but with you lot here, things are looking up."

With Dar gone to meet the ship from Laugharne, Etain showered, found a dress that allowed room for her belly without fitting like a sack on the rest of her, leggings for warmth, and her boots. If she was expected to face so many unknowns, she needed to take a walk to help her cope.

Walking down the stairs, she noticed something white draped over the banister at the bottom. Upon closer inspection, she realized it was a cloak. A heavy, warm one that might be her size. There were interior sleeves to cover the arms and slits in the fabric for the hands so the cloak could remain fastened to keep out the cold. The hood was lined in deep purple velvet. Beneath the cloak was a pair of soft, white leather gloves.

She returned the cloak to the banister, thinking it belonged to Cherise, and walked into the kitchen.

Alaster turned as she entered. "Good morning, Lady E! How're you feeling this fine day?"

His bright smile and unusual greeting lifted her spirits, making her chuckle. She took a seat at the island. "I'm good. How are you?"

"Mighty fine. Hungry?"

"Maybe an egg and some toast?"

"Comin' right up, milady."

She watched him work. "I found a cloak on the stairs. Does it belong to Cherise?"

He glanced over his shoulder. "No, no. Dar left it for you. He said it's getting too cold to be wandering outside without something to keep you warm." He turned to her. "Please tell me you have shoes on today."

Etain grinned, slipped off the barstool, and walked around the island. She clicked her heels three times. "In case I wanna go to Kansas."

Alaster's laugh filled the kitchen. "You crack me up, Lady E. Kansas." He shook his head with a chuckle as he returned to his cooking.

She walked back to her seat. "I wanted to take a walk before those people arrive, get myself prepared."

"*Those people* are as much your friends as they are Dar's. Matter of fact, you and Taurnil were pretty tight."

She tilted her head. "We were? Why is it I don't remember him?"

He shrugged. "Things like that are hard to tell."

"Well, maybe things will change once I see him."

Alaster grabbed the toast, placed it next to the sunny-side-up egg on the plate, turned, and pushed it across the island toward her. "I wouldn't worry too much about it. The mind is a wild and wonderful thing. You'll remember when you need to." He returned to whatever he'd been preparing before she walked in.

Etain buttered the toast, thinking of what he'd said. "Alaster?"

"Yes, ma'am?"

"What did *I* do at Laugharne?" She folded the toast, breaking it into two pieces.

He lifted a lid on a tall stockpot, picked up a large spoon, and stirred the contents. "Do?"

"Yeah. I mean, you're an amazing chef. Cherise ran Laugharne even better than Spirit and seems to have everything in hand here. Spirit is a talented mage. Swee's a wonderful healer. And Dar, well... He's busy with stuff all day." She fingered the fork next to her plate. "What did *I* do?"

Alaster set the spoon on the countertop and turned. "You're a good friend. You gave us an opportunity to be true Alamir and fight for something we believe in." His voice caught, but he cleared his throat and continued. "You protected us and Laugharne. Hell, you saved Dar's life, as well as Taurnil's. *That's* what you do."

She stared at him, her mind desperately trying to place his words in the right context within her memories. Her gaze dropped to her hand, toying with the fork, and to her belly. She let go of the fork and rested her hand over her babies. "Alamir," she whispered. "Krymerian."

He tilted his head. "The babies?"

"Me."

Alaster lifted his brows. "Who told you that, Lady E?"

"He did."

"Dar?"

She stood. "I've got to go. Thanks for breakfast." She walked out without answering his question.

"Lady E!" he called after her. "You didn't eat anything!"

The walls closing in on her, she hurried to the stairs and stopped at the cloak. She luxuriated in its comfortable warmth on her shoulders. The gloves were the softest leather she'd ever touched. Dressed for the weather, she stepped outside and breathed in the crisp, morning air.

Etain bypassed her sacred forest, following a new path she'd not noticed before. After walking a good twenty minutes, she found herself on a beach of black sand with water the color of turquoise gently rolling onto shore.

She pulled off the leather gloves and unfastened the clasp of her cloak, dropping everything onto the ground. The air was fragrant with the smell of the earth and sea. She ran her hands through her hair and gave her scalp a good scratch. With a laugh, she sat on the sand, unlaced and kicked off her boots, removed her socks, and pushed her toes into the sparkly blackness. Next to go was her dress. She'd not bothered with underclothes today. They had become too uncomfortable to wear.

Standing, her hands moved over her protruding belly.

Shall we go for a swim, my lovelies?

Etain walked into the water and dove under the surface. The sea warmed her skin. Everything seemed to flow away from her—the awkwardness since coming back from Nunnehi, the strange feelings Dar brought with him, the black holes in her memories.

Floating to the surface, she let her thoughts do the same, humming to herself as random memories flitted across her mind. Light, inconsequential ones that raised no alarms.

After a while, one in particular surfaced.

The dark of night at the ocean's edge. No. She frowned. *Not like this ocean's edge that comes straight up to the shore. It was an estuary.* She smiled. *That's right... Laugharne estuary.*

She saw two demons in the water—one with black wings, the other with white, their tips darkening into crimson. Her brows furrowed as her mind's eye tried to determine what they were doing. Those same brows rose as she slipped beneath the surface and splashed up, spluttering.

She swam to shore and walked across the beach toward her discarded clothing. By the time she reached them, her body and hair were dry. After she dressed, it took three tries to get the laces right on her boots, but once tied, she stood and picked up the cloak and gloves. As she turned to leave, she saw the white wolf standing at the top of the path, watching her. She had the odd sensation the animal had something to say.

When Etain blinked, it was gone. With a shrug, she walked up the path and noticed how the air turned colder with each step. By the time she reached the top of the path, she draped the cloak over her shoulders and slipped her hands into the gloves.

Then she heard the sounds of large vehicles and sighed. There was no use in delaying the inevitable. If she didn't show, someone would come looking for her, and she had nowhere else to go. Her peace had come to an end.

Passing the forest, she came face to face with a brown-haired young woman and a dog. The dog yapped, wagging his tail, but the woman stopped and tightened her hold on the leash.

Etain tilted her head and lifted a hand to shade her eyes from the morning sun. "Swee? It's you, right? Cause if you aren't her, you gotta be her twin."

Swee's shoulders relaxed, as did her hold on the leash. The red dog broke free and ran straight to Etain, who leaned over to meet him. Licking her hands, he did his best to get to her face.

"Red Dog!" Swee barked. "Down!" She walked closer. "You have better manners than that."

Etain straightened. "It *is* you. Why are you being so awkward?"

"Sorry. It's been a long trip and, well... I wasn't expecting to run into you out here."

"I take a walk every morning. Dar said you were coming."

"How are you doing? Oh, my gosh, the babies have grown."

Etain placed a hand on her belly and laughed. "I've become a house." Her smile returned to the red-haired, green-eyed beast at her feet, tongue hanging out the side of his mouth. "Who is this?"

Swee laughed. "Well, he doesn't have a name yet. That's for Dar to do, once I find him. Taurnil called him Red Dog on the voyage. He's a puppy."

"Are you sure?" Etain grinned.

"That's what I said." Her smile faded. "A gift from Inferno."

Etain crossed her hands over her heart, feeling a momentary pang and sudden tears. "Hello, Red Dog. You are most welcome." He gave her a soft yip and stood, nuzzling her outstretched hand. "You're a good boy."

She accepted Swee's offered arm as they strolled to the manor. "How was the trip?"

"It was a great adventure. I've not been out to sea before." Her eyes sparkled. "Me and Dalos had a little trouble, but once I found my sea legs, I was in heaven. The skies are like nothing you've ever seen, and the waters are dark and mysterious. I imagine it would take days to reach the bottom."

Etain laughed at the excitement in her voice. "I imagine it would."

Swee grinned, but her eyes betrayed her concern. "You didn't answer my question. How are *you*?"

She shrugged. "Not bad, I guess. I'm tired most of the time."

"For good reason." Her gaze went to Etain's belly. "Have you chosen names for your little ones?"

"I have." A spark entered her voice as she spoke of her children. "Our daughter will be Emalyn Aurelia, after both our mothers."

"Both?"

"Mine and Dar's. His mother was Emalyn."

"But I thought..." Swee shook her head. "It doesn't matter. It's a beautiful name. Do you think she'll be blonde?"

"I haven't thought about it much. As long as she and her brother are healthy."

"And what have you decided for the other?"

"Well, I have one, but I haven't told anyone yet." After a few steps, she stopped again, out of breath. "Damn. I must've walked farther than I thought. Every day seems to take more out of me."

"Please. You're having twins."

"I'm so glad you're here, Swee." She pushed her hair from her face. "Let's get to the house. I'm not feeling so hot right now."

They began walking again but didn't get far. Etain swooned into the healer, who helped her sit beneath a tree. "You stay right here. I'm going to get someone who can carry you back."

"No, Swee." She pushed against the tree, trying to lift herself off the ground. "I don't need to be carried."

Swee put a hand on her shoulder. "Stop." Her authoritative voice made Etain plop down on her bottom. "Do not get up and don't you move until I return. Red Dog, stay."

He trotted over to Etain, licked her face, and sat next to her. She closed her eyes as Swee walked away. Not long after, the puppy nosed into her hair and snorted. When she opened her eyes, he licked her face again, making her laugh.

"Hi, Red. I'm okay, little man." She stroked his head, rubbing his ears. "I guess I'm not as Krymerian as some believe." She rubbed her nose against his. "Krymerians are brave and strong. Me? I'm tired and afraid of what comes next."

It wasn't long before Swee returned with none other than the man of every infernal hour. Dar walked straight to her. Without a word, he scooped her into his arms, despite Red Dog's barked protest.

She didn't flinch, didn't fight. It was a relief to let someone else take control. Why not him?

"You are pale, Etain." Dar eyed the barking dog. "Hush."

Red whimpered and ran to Swee, standing behind her legs, but kept his eyes on the big man.

Etain swept her hair behind an ear. "I'm okay. Maybe I stayed out too long. But the beach and the water were so beautiful, I had to go for a swim."

"Beach?"

"Just back there, past the forest." She waved a hand in the general direction as Dar walked. "The one with black sand. It's amazing how warm it is down there compared to how cold it is up here."

"I have not seen one like that and cannot imagine the water being warm this time of year."

There were beaches all along the coast of the island, some brown, some white, but he could not recall one near the forest.

"I'll take you there one day if you'd like." She placed her arms around his neck. "You don't mind, do you?"

A faint smile touched his lips. "I would like it very much."

"Oh…" Etain swiveled her head. "Have you met our new friend?"

"We have a new friend, do we?" If he closed his eyes, it would be easy to believe she was herself again.

"His name is Red Dog." She lowered her voice. "He's a gift from Inferno."

Dar sucked in a breath. "Inferno?"

"Oh, aye. Just proves he loved you."

He raised a sardonic brow. "I doubt he would agree with your choice of words."

"Maybe not, but he did."

He narrowed his eyes, but his voice was light. "How would you know?"

"Because *I* lo—" She pressed her lips together, cutting off what she had started to say. "Uh, well… Because I knew his heart. He would only give a gift like Red to someone he respected and cared about."

Past tense. She remembers his passing.

Swee caught up to them. "Red Dog's not the only gift." Dar kept walking but peered at her. "He sent a stallion and a mare." Her gaze flicked to Etain and back to Dar. "She's expecting too."

Etain's mouth dropped open. "See?"

He gave Swee a sideways glance. "Are you sure about the horses?"

She laughed. "Are you telling me you didn't count the animals when they loaded them into the transport?"

Her question made him grin. "I did not. For once, I left that detail to Linq."

"Watch out, Dar. You're starting to slip," Swee joked.

They walked into the courtyard, past the buses, luggage, and general chaos to the open front doors. Dar ducked into the study and placed Etain on the sofa.

Swee and Red Dog stayed at the door. "I'll get you something to drink. Do you have tea?"

"There should be some in the kitchen. It's back that way." Etain pointed in the general direction.

Dar made a move toward the door. "Shall I show you—"

"No, no." Swee held up a hand. "I'm sure I can find it." Her gaze went to Etain. "No getting up, you hear? Red Dog, come."

As the door closed, Dar sat on the edge of the coffee table. "In your best interests, milady, I think you should stay closer to the house. The weather can turn nasty in an instant at this time of year, and while I have explored a good portion of the island, I have not seen it all. I heard a wolf's howl not long ago. I had not noticed it before, so I am curious as to where it came from."

"I can't stay cooped up in this house. I need my exercise."

"That is not what I said. Stroll down to the stables or come to the academy and watch the men at work." He leaned toward her. "Please do not go too far, at least until the babies are born."

Swee and her escort returned, a full tray in hand. Dar moved across to the other sofa as the healer set it on the coffee table and sat with Etain. Swee picked up a damp washcloth and applied it to her forehead.

"That's nice. You're so thoughtful, Swee."

Red Dog watched her ministrations and lay on the floor, tail wagging, eyes darting back and forth between the women and Dar.

"I had a lot of practice during our voyage. There were a few who didn't do so well."

Etain tilted her head. "They were lucky to have you."

"Tea?" Dar leaned forward and poured a cup for his wife. Without asking, he added sugar but held back on the milk and handed it to Swee. Etain pushed up and leaned against the arm of the sofa, taking the cup.

He turned his attention to the pup. "Swee, introduce me to this strapping young man."

Red Dog seemed to shrink beneath the big man's scrutiny. Standing slowly, he slinked toward the women, his green eyes on Dar.

Swee patted him on the head. "Inferno wanted you to have someone you could count on."

"Did he?" He contemplated the man's intentions as he stared at the young pup and held out a hand. "Come."

Red Dog eyed the women. Etain grinned. "He's a little scary at first, but he's okay."

The pup lowered his head, tail between his legs as he approached Dar, but his gaze did not waver. The big man petted his head. "There's a good boy. Pit?"

"That would be my guess," Swee said.

"Does he have a name?"

She shrugged. "Nothing official. Taurnil called him Red Dog, so we have too."

Dar laughed. At the sound, Red Dog's tail came up, wagging, and his tongue lolled out the side of his mouth, giving his own version of a smile.

"Red Dog. Good name." He scratched the dog's ears and pulled his front paws up onto his lap. "I wonder how much growing you have left. Any idea how old he is?"

"He was about three months when we left."

Dar's gaze returned to the pup. "So we will have us a monster in a few more weeks." He laughed again when Red licked his face. "Good boy."

Etain yawned. "Sorry."

"It has been a day, has it not, milady?"

"You should rest." Swee took the cup from her and placed it on the table. "Do you want me to help you upstairs?"

"No," said Dar as he set the puppy's feet on the floor and stood. "Stay here. I need to ensure the horses are situated and see if my Black Blades are settled. No one will disturb you." He turned to the healer. "Swee, let's give her some peace and quiet."

"Uh, well... Okay." She touched Etain's shoulder and joined Dar. "You holler if you need anything."

Etain yawned again. "Don't worry. I'm not going anywhere."

At the door, Dar stopped. "Red Dog, come." He heard a whimper and Etain's encouragement to the puppy.

"Go on, little man," she whispered. "It's okay."

In the next moment, he heard the pad of paws on the floor and smiled when Red Dog appeared, his head low. "That's a good boy. Let me show you around."

JAIL BREAK

Freeblood watched attendants run out of the room in the face of Illiana yelling to leave her in peace. During her tirade, she glanced at him and scowled. At first, he wasn't sure what her message was, but when she included him in her glare, he slid down and pulled the covers over his head. In the next few minutes, he heard footsteps come toward his bed. Breathing steady, he hoped they would leave him to his dreams.

A few minutes later, Illiana pulled his sheet away.

"Are you feeling better?"

He blinked. "I'll live."

The woman sat on the edge of his bed. "We do not have long, so let's make this quick. I have come to take you out of this place. Are you well enough to move?"

Freeblood slowly pushed up, leaning back on his pillows. "Why would I go anywhere with you? Maybe you're here to take me somewhere worse."

"There is nowhere worse." She shrugged. "Well, that is not completely true. There are demon realms where they would have thrown you into the pit as food for their beasts." She grasped his shoulder and pulled him forward for a look at the back of his head. "No infirmaries in that hell."

He pushed her away. "We're close enough. Are you gonna tell me who you are and why you're here?"

"We do not have time for the long story, but the short version is I am on your side. It is in your best interests, and that of my family, to see you safely out of here."

"*Your* family? I have my own family to worry about."

"They will not be yours much longer unless we make a move."

"Kinda convenient, don't you think?"

"Not convenient. Connected. Do you know where your Faux is?"

"She's not far."

"Can you make it there without being seen?"

"The tough part is getting out of here. They check pretty often."

She grinned. "I will take care of that part. Your job is to get her out."

"What about my son?"

She frowned. "Son?"

"That doctor came in here today acting a little weird. I know Faux was close to having our son."

Illiana blew out a breath and stood, pacing beside the bed. "A baby. By the sea... We must get him out as soon as possible. They do not allow the mothers to keep their babies for long. Once the babe has fed on the first milk, they will take him away."

He pushed out of the bed. "No one is taking my son *or* my girl. Hand me my Converse." Her confused expression made him stop.

"Converse?"

"Uh, sneakers."

She shook her head, clearly at a loss.

"My *shoes*. The green ones at the end of the bed. I'm going now."

"Not yet." She placed her hand on his shoulder. "It will not be long now, Freeblood. "We will get them out."

Hearing footsteps in the hallway, Illiana dashed back to her bed and slipped under the covers. Freeblood did the same, but his brain raced, envisioning where Faux and Jake could be. With any luck, they'd be together.

The portal opened a few miles outside the city of Nocturna. Linq had been here many turns ago. Although he did not attend the Trodaire, his business involved its machinations—a blood oath from the Banshee to stay out of Nunnehi and the entire Elven realm. Alatariel wanted to protect *all* Elves from their brutality but aware she did not have the power to enforce it outside their own lands, she compromised with an agreement that any Elves found elsewhere not engaged in Nunnehi business would be fair game. In return, the Elves would not interfere in Banshee business. As far as Linq knew, the Banshee had honored the oath.

"We have to stay out of sight at all costs," he instructed his three cohorts.

"Shouldn't be too hard in the dark." Sitting on a tree stump, Ra leaned forward placing his elbows on his thighs, and the ever-present toothpick at the side of his mouth. "Is that *carte blanche* on silencing anyone who isn't with us?"

"Aye."

"Is that wise?" asked Taurnil.

Linq's gaze slid to the younger Elf. "Wisdom was lost when the Banshee decided to play Dathmet's game. Either way we do this, we all lose."

Taurnil considered his words. "I do not follow."

"I got this one, Linq." Ra leaned back, turning his gaze to Taurnil. "If we *don't* take back what's ours, they'll think they can take whatever they want, whenever they want." He stood and sighed. "And if we *do* take back what's ours..." He pulled the toothpick from between his lips, pointing it at Taurnil. "Whether they know you Elves are involved or not, it'll be war. They know Faux and Freeblood have something to do with Etain, and most likely know Etain is attached to Dar. Either way we work this, we're fucked."

Taurnil swallowed, his face pale. "Thank you for the clarification, Ra."

"Do we know where this Trodaire is?" asked Aramis.

"That is why we are on the outskirts." Linq walked to the edge of the cliff overlooking Nocturna. "It should not be hard to find. The town will have a concentration of lights. The compound will not. As I remember, it lies to the south."

Taurnil joined him. "Is Nocturna a major Banshee city?"

"It belongs to the Phums," Linq explained as the other two stood along the edge. "I would describe them more as rogue Banshee. They keen like the others, but not to warn of impending death. Their captives usually end up dead in the Trodaire."

"How are we going to do this then?" Taurnil asked.

"It is a plan in progress," Linq admitted. "Locate the Trodaire, spot the entrance, wait until dark, slip in and out, and run like hell."

Ra chuckled. "You make it sound easy."

"The easy part was getting here." Linq smiled halfheartedly.

The four eyed the city before them. It was not long before Aramis pointed to the left.

"Look. There's a large dark area over there with a few lights. It's about the size of a football field."

Linq zeroed in with his enhanced sight and spotted it nestled near three large buildings. "That is it. The buildings next to it would be where they house the Trodaithe, the fighters, and in another is where they keep expectant mothers and newly born babes."

"But which is which?" asked Taurnil.

"I just realized that I haven't met Faux," said Aramis. "If I find her, how will she know to go with me?"

Ra shook his head and shrugged.

Taurnil's eyes widened. "I have not met the lady either."

Linq sighed. "Let's hope I am the one who finds her. Once we enter the area, no noise whatsoever. Aramis, Ra, do you understand *te shingō?*"

"We've been around the block a few times." Ra adjusted his hat. "You *te shingō* away, pardner."

⁓ ❦ ⁓

Freeblood waited until the last of the attendants made their evening rounds. The moment the door closed, he threw back the covers and reached for his Converse. Fortunately, they didn't use hospital gowns, so he didn't have to waste time getting dressed.

Illiana rushed to the door to ensure they weren't surprised. "I will divert their attention if needed. It would be best if you did not need it."

"Yeah, thanks for the pep talk."

"The courtyard is full of shadows. Make sure you stick to them."

"I'm not an amateur, you know."

Illiana shrugged. "May you find them quickly."

He turned off the lights in the foyer and opened the door. After a search of the courtyard, he dashed into the darkest shadows he could find. Bit by bit, he made his way toward a building he'd not been in, but the closer he got, the stronger the pull. He didn't know if this building held the mothers and babies, but it had Faux. His speed made short work of the last stretch.

He pressed his back against the brick wall, listening for anything out of the ordinary. *I'm good, but not this good.* He warily opened the door. *Who knows, maybe they're that arrogant. Stupid little Alamir can't find his way out of a paper bag.*

On second thought, he closed the door and moved farther along and around the corner. Spying a long line of windows, he tried each one. Eventually, he found an open one and climbed inside.

Freeblood zig-zagged across the hall, dashing from door to door, cautiously peeking inside each room. At the end of the hall and his patience, he knew he had found her. The heat in his blood suddenly cranked to a level he hadn't felt since they'd been separated.

After a thankful sigh, he slipped inside, quietly closed the door, and tip-toed to the bed. He placed a hand over her mouth and leaned into her face. She surprised him when she pulled him on top of her before opening her eyes.

"Where the hell have you been?" she whispered harshly. "You look like shit."

"Just over there." He nodded in the direction of the infirmary. "I've been a little under the weather."

"Well, while you've been lazing around, I gave birth to our son."

"I thought so." He held her close, relieved they were together again. "How are you? How's Jake?"

She cocked a brow. "Oh, you remember."

He crushed his lips to hers. "I didn't think I'd see you again. Did they hurt you? Is he big, small? I know he's handsome." Tears burned in his eyes.

She laughed. "He is. Would you like to hold him?"

He swiped at his eyes and rolled over to her side and sat up. "He's here?"

She scooted off the bed and leaned over a small crib. A black bundle in her arms, she handed it to Freeblood. "He's a special kid. No crying, no fussing... But he eats like a demon."

His heart pounded, cradling the tiny body. "That's my boy. Black?"

She shrugged. "These bitches are crazy. White for girls, black for boys."

He lifted the edge of the blanket and lost his heart. Jake's tiny face was the most beautiful thing he'd ever seen. Wisps of dark hair covered his head, and his little lips were heart-shaped, like his mother's. "Hello, little man.

I'm your dad." He sniffled as he kissed the baby's forehead. "We're going to get you home."

"We're leaving?"

"That's why I'm here. To get you two out."

Faux met his gaze but didn't say anything.

He watched her for a few moments as he rocked the baby, noting her melancholy perusal of the room. "What is it, Faux? Do you not want to go?"

"I don't know." She wouldn't look at him. "They treat me like I'm someone special."

He reached out and grasped her hand. "Babe, it's not a good place. They suck the life out of everyone who comes through here."

She crossed her arms, hugging herself.

"I've been told once the babies drink their mother's milk the first time, they take the little ones away." He stood and moved closer to her. "Faux, if you stay, you'll never see him or me again."

She placed a hand on the blanket. "You're right. We need to go."

"It'll be different once we get back. I promise."

They heard footsteps in the hallway coming closer.

"Shit." Freeblood glanced around the room. "We gotta go. Now. The window."

"Doesn't open. I've tried."

"Is there another way out of here?"

She turned to the crib and grabbed an extra diaper along with Jake's pacifier. "Do you *see* another way out?"

"Faux, I can't be found in here."

"You stay put." She shoved the diaper into Jake's blanket and tucked the pacifier next to his head. "I'll see if I can get rid of them." She went to the door.

"No..."

She opened it a crack and peered into the hallway. "The hall's clear." She stepped out and reappeared. "Come on. They must've gone into a room. It's probably the last check of the night."

Freeblood followed her through the door and down the hall. When they heard a door open, Faux pushed him into the baby ward, watching him through the glass until she knew he was hidden.

"What are you doing out here?"

Faux turned. She didn't recognize the woman. She wasn't blue like Siobhan or green like Doria, but she wore the same uniform.

"I-I'm sorry. I was just admiring my little one." Faux admired the babies through the glass. "I could stare at her all night."

166

NESA MILLER

The woman stood next to her at the viewing window. "They're irresistible, aren't they?"

"Yes."

"Which one is yours?"

Faux pointed at a white blanket and hoped the woman was clueless as to which baby belonged to which mother. "Right there. I can't believe she's mine."

"Precious." The woman turned to her. "But you must go back to your room."

Faux pouted. "Can't I stay while you finish your rounds? Please? Just a little longer. The nights are so long without her."

She stared at her for a few moments. "As long as you stay right here. I have a few more rooms to check, but you have to go back to yours."

"Thank you!" Faux gave her the biggest smile she could muster. "You're so kind. I won't go anywhere. I swear."

The woman checked the hall.

Faux held her breath, heart hammering in her chest. From the corner of her eye, she saw Freeblood peer from around the corner of a wall inside the baby ward. Her eyes widened as she shook her head. He ducked back just as the woman turned and peered into the room.

Faux couldn't be sure if the midwife saw him or not. "On second thought, it's been a long day and I'm pretty tired. Would you walk me back to my room?"

The woman cocked her head. "Are you sure?"

"I'd hate to get you into trouble. I'll see her in the morning, won't I?"

"Yes, you will. Thank you, miss." She stepped away and moved up the hall. "You coming?"

Faux peered through the glass one last time, a tear trailing down her cheek, and blew a kiss. "Mommy's tired tonight, little one. I'll see you..." her voice caught in her throat, "later."

***

Freeblood watched Faux press her fingers to her lips and blow a kiss. He wanted to shout at her to come with him. But if he was to get his son out, he had to remain quiet, wait until the two were gone, and run to the infirmary. Maybe Plan B would come to him between here and there.

He stepped out from behind the wall, creeping quietly across the floor with his eyes on the viewing window. A sudden noise in the hallway made him stop. His son cradled in his arm, he listened and waited. Hearing the noise again, he concluded it was the nurse continuing her rounds. She seemed to have moved farther down the hall from Faux's room.

Maybe I can backtrack and take her with us?

Emboldened by the idea, he continued his quiet trek. As he neared the door, his foot caught the leg of the end crib, giving it a good jolt. He stopped and sucked in a breath as he watched the white blanket wiggle. His heart hammered in his chest as he pulled up the end of his shirt and swiped away the sweat on his forehead.

When no sound came, he blew out the breath and whispered to his son, "Close call."

He slipped into the hallway and quietly pulled the door closed, the click no more than a whisper. As he turned, a lone, shrill cry pierced the silence. He froze.

"Holy shit."

Another piercing cry joined the first. And another. And another. In moments, the entire ward joined in a choir of screaming babies.

All was clear to his right. He planned to rush to Faux's room, lie low for a while, then slip out with her and Jake once everything quieted.

He checked his left. At the end of the hall stood the nurse, staring at him. His heart sank.

So much for that.

She pointed at him and added her own scream to the chorus.

The hairs on his neck prickled. In the blink of an eye, a squad of goblin soldiers rounded the corner.

Freeblood looked at his son, who blinked and lifted his tiny arms in a stretch.

"Time to go, bud."

He turned in the opposite direction and ran as fast as he could, bypassing Faux's room. Their shouts of "Stop!" and "Get him!" compelled him to run even faster.

At the end of the hallway, he turned the corner, his Converse losing their grip on the tiled floor. He pulled Jake to his chest, his head cradled in one hand, and shielded him with both arms. Shoulder first, Freeblood bounced off one wall, and the other, but kept his footing and barreled toward the front doors, shoving them open, thankful they weren't locked.

Once outside, he raced across the courtyard, shadows be damned.

Illiana met him at the infirmary door. "Where's Faux?"

He shook his head, breathless, and ducked inside. "She couldn't get out. Without exposing me and Jake."

She turned the lock. "Then why are you out of breath?"

Freeblood tried to slow his racing heart. "Things didn't go according to plan. The goblins'll be here any minute." He spoke quickly as he carried the baby to a bed. "Jake has to get out. If they take him, he'll be gone forever."

"And Faux?"

"I'm going back for her while you take my son to Etain and Dar." He laid Jake on the bed and tucked his blanket tightly around him.

"What do you propose to do about the goblins?" she asked, peeking through a window.

"I'll worry about that once Jake is safe. If you're what I think you are, you can open a portal, right?" He lifted the baby, holding him close to his chest.

"I can."

Without any consideration of whether or not she knew the Krymerian, he asked, "Do you know where the island is?"

"I have an idea." She walked toward him. "We won't know until it opens."

"As long as you're on the island. *Sôlskin* is on the south end. Walk until you see a massive white wall with a huge house behind it." He shoved Jake into her arms. "Tell Dar about this place. Tell him what they're doing."

Illiana reluctantly accepted the tiny bundle. "I am not good with babies."

"All you have to do is get him to Dar." Hearing heavy footsteps, he glanced at the door. "They'll take over from there."

The woman shook her head. "No—"

"Illiana, Faux is *my* family, *my* responsibility. I can't ask you to risk your life."

"I do not recall you asking me for anything." She pushed the baby back into his arms. "You are a great fighter, Freeblood. You have one hell of a punch, but as strong as you are, you will not last long here. This place will kill you, and your family. Your people will never know what happened."

"They *will* know because you're gonna tell them." He held the baby out to her, but she backed away. "Please, Illiana. I can't leave without her."

"It is *your* job to take your son to a safe place. We will come as soon as we can."

She opened a portal with a sweep of a hand. Freeblood blew out a breath at the familiar landscape as the shimmering slice widened.

"Wow. It's daytime there." Yet his excitement was tempered by guilt at leaving these brave women behind. It wasn't right by his standards.

I'm the man. I should be the hero.

"Times differ from place to place."

He shoved Jake at her again. "I'm stronger than you think. Just head south. You can't miss it."

The goblins had arrived, testing the lock on the front door.

She reached out as if to accept the small bundle. Instead, she grabbed Freeblood by the shoulders and pushed him through.

"Illiana!"

He stepped toward her, but she held up a hand and pointed at him.

"Go. Get Jake to safety. I will get Faux." An eerily familiar grin curved her lips. "They will not see me coming."

He couldn't comprehend her willingness to sacrifice so much for people she'd just met. "Why would you do this?"

Brow cocked, she asked, "How else would you get home?" Freeblood heard the door give way. "I have company."

The last thing he saw before the portal snapped shut was dark hair waving through the air. Stunned by the realization of what she'd said,

Freeblood stared at the landscape in front of him. Had she taken his son, he and Faux would have been trapped forever.

Outside the Trodaire, Linq motioned to Aramis and Ra to take the building to their left, while he and Taurnil went for the one on the right. They agreed if they found their appointed building did not have what they were looking for, the team would move on to the one in the middle.

Linq and Taurnil split, each making their way around their chosen target, and met in the rear. Although there were no guards stationed, they decided to avoid the doors and entered through an open window. Taurnil being the first to enter growled a curse when he ran into something large and heavy.

"By the bloody stars..."

Linq slipped in without mishap. "What is it?"

"A desk," Taurnil groaned.

"If they did not know we were here before, they do now."

Taurnil growled again. "I do not hear anything. Maybe she is not in this one."

Linq walked to the door and turned the knob. "Locked. Check the drawers. There could be a spare key."

"In the dark?" The younger Elf limped toward him. "Run your hand along the top of the door."

Linq raised a brow but dragged his fingers across the trim. He grinned and held out a key. "How did you know?"

"In case of emergencies."

Once unlocked, Linq opened the door. "Emergencies? In Nunnehi?"

Taurnil returned his grin. "Of varying degrees."

Linq held a finger to his lips as he slipped into the hallway. Going from room to room, each Elf checked every other one, finding each one locked.

As they passed the newborn viewing room, Taurnil stopped. Eyes wide, he stared at the precious babes wrapped in their black or white blankets.

Linq nudged him to move on, but he did not budge. He tapped his wrist to indicate the passing time. Taurnil shook his head and pointed at the babies, cradled his arms, then tapped his right fist with his thumb up against his left palm. Linq shook his head and tapped his wrist again. When Taurnil shook his head once more, the older Elf threw his hands into the air.

Taurnil closed his eyes but opened them when Linq shoved him to the floor.

"Be quiet."

"What is it?" Taurnil whispered.

"A nurse in the nursery. Hands and knees, let us get out of here."

Crawling from underneath the viewing window, the two quietly stood.

Linq whispered, "With the babes here, we know it is the right place, but short of bursting through every door—"

"We need a diversion. Something that will force them to open the doors."

"I will not put these women or their babes at risk."

"What *will* you do?" Taurnil growled.

Linq narrowed his eyes, but before he could speak, a noise from up the hall shattered the silence. He turned his head. "What is that?"

"Rattling. Someone wants out."

Linq grinned. "She is not known for her patience."

"Shall we assist the lady?"

Taurnil passed him and followed the sound along the hallway. Before he could locate the actual door, all went silent.

"Damn," he muttered. Undeterred, he lightly tapped on one door, and the next. At the last door, he finally heard a voice from the other side.

"Are you there? Can you hear me?"

Taurnil glanced over his shoulder and motioned to Linq.

"Freeblood? Are you here?" the voice asked.

Linq slipped up next to the younger Elf, pulled out his dagger, and slowly worked it between the door and the jamb, being as quiet as possible. It was not long before the door popped open.

Taurnil placed a finger over his lips as he pushed his way inside. The woman backed away from the door until she saw the one behind him.

"Linq!"

"Shhh," he whispered as she rushed at him, throwing her arms around his neck.

"I never thought I'd be so happy to see you!"

He placed a hand over her mouth. "You have to be quiet, Faux. Neither did I."

She pulled his hand away. "Did Freeblood make it out?"

Linq furrowed his brows.

"Freeblood has Jake."

"Jake?"

"Our son."

Linq sighed and glanced at Taurnil. "Maybe Aramis and Ra have him. Let us get out of here while we can."

⁓ ❦ ⁓

Illiana dove under the covers and pulled them over her head, desperately trying to slow her breathing. She wondered if Faux had betrayed her partner and son. The story of Laugharne at risk of succumbing to the *Bok* had spread quickly through Nunnehi. It was the thing that had piqued her interest in the Alamir and the Krymerian who saved them.

Suddenly, someone ripped the sheet from her. She stared at a man in a hat and a toothpick between his teeth. He was not green or ugly nor was he a Banshee.

Simultaneously, they both asked, "Who the hell are you?"

He was Alamir. She could tell that much. A little rough around the edges, but maybe that was a good thing. She sat up, making him step back. Then the other one stepped forward—more refined, regal.

"Are you here for Freeblood?" she blurted.

The rough one eyed her head to toe. "What's it to you?"

She swung her booted feet over the side of the bed and stood. "Because he is not here."

"Where'd he go? Are you one of those Banshee?" His hand went to the hilt of a sword inside his long coat.

"We must get Faux out before the Banshee realize it was him in the nursery." She bypassed the men and walked to the window for a peek through the blinds. "Where did the goblins go?"

"Are your buddies gonna sideswipe us?"

Illiana turned sharply. "I am the one who helped Freeblood escape. Are you going to help me save Faux or not?"

The regal man was pale. "Goblins... Big, green, and ugly?"

"So you *did* see them."

"They marched to the middle of the courtyard, turned, and headed out of the compound."

"We tried the main door, but couldn't get it open, so swung around back and found another way in," said the man with the hat.

She placed her hands on her hips. "Do you have an extra sword?"

He raised both brows and chuckled at his friend. "I doubt Linq knows about her."

"Linq?" Under other circumstances, she would not reveal her hand, but there was not time for such games. "An Elf with blond hair and tattoos on his head?"

Both men eyed her with respect. "You know Linq?" asked the regal one.

"She does." The man himself walked into the room, followed by Prince Taurnil and a dark-haired young woman.

The other two whirled, surprised by their appearance.

"Illiana. What are you doing here?" asked Linq.

"Illiana?" Taurnil raised his brows opposed to Linq's cool expression.

"Your Grace." She bowed her head.

The cowboy tipped his hat. "How'd you get in?"

Linq twirled his dagger and tucked it into his belt. "The locks around here are mainly for looks."

The woman considered Illiana for a moment before she spoke. "Where's Freeblood?"

"Are you Faux?"

"I am."

Illiana's gaze roamed over each of them. "Freeblood has gone to Dar's island. I suggest we do the same before—"

Quick footsteps from outside made her stop.

"Shit!" exclaimed the man with the hat, who unsheathed an immaculate broadsword from inside his overcoat. "Must've tripped an alarm somewhere."

The refined man also brandished an impressive sword. They came prepared to fight. The woman did not appear to be a fighter, but since she was part of Dar's family, Illiana was determined to protect her at all costs. The men could take on the others.

"Faux, get behind me."

"Why would I—"

Linq pushed her toward Illiana. "Do as she says, Faux, and maybe we will all get out of here alive."

DELIVERANCE

Etain woke with a start. The rising hairs on her skin felt as though bugs crawled over her body. She pushed up and peered over the back of the sofa.

What was that? Has he found me?

She twisted around as best she could, placed her feet on the floor, and looked at her clothes. *I thought he...* She pulled the top of her dress down enough to see the mark she shared with her husband. It was whole. There was no wound.

But... He stabbed me.

She heard the front door open and close, which set her heart into over-drive. Tears in her eyes, her stomach roiled. She had to find someone who would help her and her family escape. She couldn't let them die.

Etain bit her bottom lip and pushed onto her feet. Her knees wobbled, but she forced one foot in front of the other. Hand on the doorknob, she turned it ever so slowly and opened it enough to see the entryway. It appeared to be empty. She sighed and slipped out of the room. Without another glance, she took the stairs as quickly as she could, stopping halfway to catch her breath.

A sound from downstairs urged her back into motion. The pad of a footstep on the stairs sent her into a panic. Regardless of her condition, she raced up the remainder of the stairs and into her bedroom. Her back pressed against the door, she listened for her pursuer.

Footsteps came from within the room. She wasn't alone. *Damn.* When she turned her head, she saw Dar standing in the doorway to his private bath, a towel wrapped around his hips, another in his hand, drying the ends of his hair. She hadn't seen his hair loose in a such long time. He seemed thinner than she remembered. *Has he been ill?*

⁘

"Etain." He stopped just inside the bedroom. "Is there something you need?" He recognized the fear in her eyes but did not move toward her lest she bolt out the door or worse.

"Dar!" She ran to him.

"What is wrong?" He dropped the towel in his hand and wrapped his arms around her. "You are safe. No one can hurt you."

She pulled away, her trembling hands on his bare chest. "Save me, angel," she pleaded and grabbed one of his hands placing it on her cheek. "I remember."

Wary, he was not sure what to think. She would say things one minute, then flip a switch and destroy all his hope the next. "What do you remember?"

"I don't know why I didn't see it before now." Her eyes held a wild glint. "You were there when I changed. It was *you* who spoke to me, told me to calm my heart, to hide. It was *you*."

The situation turned downright uncomfortable. "Etain... What has happened?" He tried to pull his hand away, but she refused to let go.

"You have to replace his vile touch with yours." Fear made her voice waver. "I can*not* live with this any longer. Please, take it away. It hurts too much."

He searched her eyes, expecting to see the blankness he had seen in them before, but her gaze seemed clear, coherent.

"You are my angel. *Please* remove his taint. Make me yours again."

"My lady..." he breathed.

Her mouth hovered a breath from his as she pushed him back, surprising him with her strength. She took his mouth with such passion, her firm breasts pressed against his chest, he moaned, forgetting their current situation. Her erect nipples taunted him through the fabric of her dress. Her rounded belly rubbed against him. Consumed by her desire, he hardly noticed her slide down and remove the towel from his hips.

Heat seared through him when her mouth engulfed his cock, taking him in long, hot strokes, her hands touching him in places he had not been touched in a long time. His body craved hers. Thoughts tumbled through his head, melding into one as she drove him toward an explosive moment.

Just able to gather his wits, he reached for her. "That will not do, milady."

Her gaze pierced through him. "I need you." Rising to her feet, she pulled the dress over her head.

Stunned by his wife's clarity, he pulled her close, his hands caressing her back and over her hips, and lifted her. Dar enjoyed the weight of her against him, her breath on his skin, her warm flesh pressed to his. Grasping her hips, he drove into her heat, wanting to lose himself in her.

She ravaged his lips, their tongues meeting amongst the chaos. Their souls reconnected; two hearts united in a single rhythm. Encased within a blue glow, they clung to one another, reveling in their shared ecstasy.

In time, he carried her to the bed. Lying next to his wife, he gave her a gentle kiss. "I love you more than life itself, *a chuisle*."

Drifting toward sleep, her eyelids fluttered closed. "You have saved me, my sweet savage."

Tartarus was his first thought in the early hours as he woke to a set of smiling blue eyes.

She laughed and lightly caressed his face. "You're home."

"Pardon?"

"From the battles." She kissed his mouth. "My heart told me you were safe, but it confused me. If you were okay, why weren't you here?"

Groggy with sleep, he stumbled over his words. "B-Battles? I-I—"

"With the *Bok*," she said patiently. "Were you able to save Laugharne?"

"Laugharne is safe. Do you not remember? You were there."

"In the beginning, but you sent me to Nunnehi." She kissed him again. "You sent me there with Spirit and Swee. Don't *you* remember?"

"You know who I am?"

She laughed. "Of course." Sadness flashed over her beautiful features as she pulled away. "Unless this is your way of telling me you no longer love me."

"No!" he blurted and crushed her to his chest. "No..." He breathed deeply and whispered into her ear, "I thought I had lost you."

"Why would I be lost?"

Sinking into her fathomless ice-blue eyes, he decided not to tell her everything just yet. It was obvious her mind still blocked several events, but his heart swelled knowing she recognized him. He would worry about the rest later.

"I... Well, I was not aware you had come home. I went to Nunnehi and they told me you had left."

Her brows furrowed. "I think the fighting has addled your brain, my sweet man." She lovingly stroked his hair. "You told Alatariel to send me home."

For a moment, he wondered if perhaps he had lost his mind. But all doubts vanished when her mouth met his with heated lips and pressed her body to his.

"I have missed you terribly, my sexy savage," she whispered into his mouth, holding his gaze prisoner with hers. "Make love to me."

"Milady..." He groaned softly. "Welcome home."

Afraid it had been a dream, Dar dawdled, reluctant to leave her and made excuses to not to get out of bed.

Etain turned onto her side and propped her head on her hand. "Don't you have things to do?"

"But I have only just returned." He moved toward her, wanting to be as close as possible. He had missed these quiet moments with her. "We have lost time to make up for."

She kissed his lips. "What about the stables?"

"They are completed, and the horses are settled."

She raised a brow. "Okay... What about the academy? Has that started yet?"

Her ability to seamlessly return to the flow of their life impressed him. "Next week. I thought I would give everyone a chance to rest after their long trip."

"Aww. Aren't you the sweetest man?" She leaned forward for a kiss, but furrowed her brows and jerked, her hand going to her stomach. "Oh!"

"What is it?" Dar sat up. "Are you in pain?"

"No." She laughed, rubbing her belly. "One of the babies kicked. It feels so weird." She grabbed his hand and placed it over the area. "Here. Push here and see if he kicks again."

Dar grinned and held his breath, letting her guide his hand to the spot. When nothing happened, he pressed down, but did not get a response. Disappointed, he applied both hands, prodding and poking, trying to invoke some sort of reaction from his precious children.

"Dar, that tickles!"

"I want to feel it."

His frustrated expression made her laugh. She placed her hands on top of his and held his gaze as they waited. Eventually, a tiny something bumped against his palm.

"Oh!" they said at the same time, grinning like idiots.

"A good, strong kick." Dar leaned toward her stomach. "Hello, my sweet, precious babies. Mama and Da are here." He pressed his face closer to her belly, his voice filled with love. "Soon, little ones, you will be in our arms."

"James Harley VonNeshta," she said, stroking his hair.

Dar lifted his head. "Another distant cousin I have not been told of?"

"Our son, my love." She shrugged. "If you like the name."

"James Harley." A grin spread over his face. "I thought the name Harley was not to your taste."

"Let's just say it grew on me. I want to make you happy."

He leaned in and kissed her softly. "You make me happy by being here with me. You are everything I have ever wanted."

"I love you." She caressed his cheek. "Now, about trying to get rid of you. I've been thinking about the renovations of our rooms to include a nursery. I hope you don't mind, but I've consulted with an architect to get started. Me and Jackie are meeting with her this morning."

He raised a brow. "What have you decided, my love?"

"My plan is to turn Faux's bedroom into ours. Your room and the room that was mine will become the nursery and a schoolroom. For when the children are old enough. The room on the other side will be updated and an adjoining door installed to be used as a sitting room—at least until Faux and Freeblood show up."

"Interesting plans."

"You haven't heard the best part yet." She grinned. "Your decadent bathroom is history. We'll keep the copper tub and add a shower, but the room will be split into two separate bathrooms. The other side will be for the children. And the rooms will be light, bright, and airy—no black tiles, no weapons on the walls, and one door per bathroom." She playfully tapped the tip of his nose with a finger. "No more sleepovers for you."

Dar chuckled. "Where will *we* be during these upgrades?"

"We can move into the room across the hall. Surely, you can slum it for a short time."

He pulled her close. "As long as I am with you, *a chuisle*, I will sleep anywhere."

To give Etain time to shower and dress, Dar agreed to meet her downstairs for breakfast. Along the way, he happily informed those he passed of her recovery and introduced Red Dog to those who had not met him yet. His day was further blessed when he walked into the kitchen. Alaster not only had fresh coffee ready, he also introduced him to a landscape architect—Ali, short for Alison—and a couple of others with landscaping experience. Once the chef and his wife were informed of Etain's recovery, Dar showed the landscapers the grounds.

"This is *my* garden," he said in a serious tone.

"Yes, boss." Ali was about five-foot-six, brown hair, blue eyes, and a pleasant demeanor. "Alaster told us about *your* garden as well as the herb garden."

"Herb garden?"

"He loves growing his own herbs, so he put dibs on this bit next to yours."

Dar understood the man's passion. "Fresh ingredients would be a welcome treat. Perhaps we could expand our garden facilities to include more than herbs." Seeing her face brighten, he knew they were kindred spirits.

"In the old days, they called it a kitchen garden," she said.

The two other landscapers eyeballed the area. "They'd build a big ol' wall around it," one explained.

"That'd keep anyone from tramping through," said the other.

"And easier to install a watering system," added Ali.

The two men exchanged huge grins. "A watering system," they said in unison.

"Oh, aye. A watering system," Dar agreed, wondering if he had unleashed a three-headed beast. He was not sure what the job would entail, but they seemed up for the challenge.

One clapped his hands. "Yes, boss!" He reached for Dar's hand, pumping it profusely, then Ali's. "Thank you, Mr. Dar, Ms. Ali. Those roses are gonna love it. And Alaster's gonna have the best herbs on the island."

As soon as one released him, the other grabbed his hand, shaking it with the same enthusiasm. "And fruit trees. Thank ye, Mr. Dar. We'll put a nice little fence 'round your beauties to keep them separated from the rest of the garden."

Dar laughed. "Thank you... I'm sorry. I did not ask your names."

"This here's Jon and I'm Tony. Good to meet you, Mr. Dar."

"We are all fellow gardeners here. Just call me Dar."

"You got it, boss."

Laughing, Ali shook his hand, as well. "I'll draw up the plans and get back to you in a couple of days. Is that all right?"

"Sounds good to me. If we are done here, I have a breakfast date with a beautiful blonde. Thank you, Ali." He turned to the men. "Thank you, Jon, Tony. We will build a beautiful sanctuary for everyone who comes to *Sôlskin*."

Jake squirmed in his arms and began to cry. "Damn her!" Freeblood cuddled him closer, tightening the blanket around him. "It's okay, little guy. We'll be out of this in no time." The day was bright and sunny, but cold. He shivered as he rocked the baby. "I hope she's as good as she thinks she is."

He scanned the area, and although he'd never ventured far from the manor, he knew it to be Dar's island. The beautiful landscape gave him an appreciation of why the man had come here as well as the fact it was an island. He supposed, in time, the entire place would become a fortress.

He shifted Jake to his shoulder, patting him on the back. "Any idea which way is south, bud?" He turned around. "I guess this is as good a direction as any."

After several steps, he noticed something in the path. "What is that?" He squinted and lifted a hand to shield his eyes from the glare of the sun.

Whatever it was, moved. And it was white.

"What's it doing?"

Freeblood squeezed his eyes shut, and opened them as wide as he could, blinking several times as he peered down the road again. "Is that a wolf? Shit. Dar never mentioned wolves."

He turned in the opposite direction and walked away as calmly as possible. *You're not supposed to run, right?* After several steps, he peeked over his shoulder. The wolf was still there, moving toward them, but not in any great rush. Thinking it rather odd, he turned to face it.

The wolf stopped, close enough that Freeblood could see its blue eyes. He took a step. The wolf bared its teeth and growled fiercely.

"Trust me, you don't want a piece of this, buster." He shifted Jake, cradling him close to his chest. "But I'm more than happy to leave this part of the island to you. We'll go the other way and hope like hell there aren't more like you."

He turned and headed in the opposite direction. After walking for several minutes, he dared to peek over his shoulder. Happy to see the wolf was gone, he blew out a relieved breath. But was that good or bad?

Just as he decided to backtrack, he heard a small *mew*. A tiny kitten waddled out from behind one of the larger rocks strewn along the path, followed by two others. The first was solid black with bright green eyes, another was white with amber eyes, and the last was gray with blue eyes.

Freeblood expected the mother to pop out but when none showed, he said, "What are you little guys doing out here alone? There's a big bad wolf not far away. Maybe you're why he was hanging around. Not that you'd be much more than an appetizer. You'd better come with us."

He did his best to round them up, but they kept wandering in the other direction.

"I think providence is trying to tell us something." He peeked at Jake. "Shall we follow?" The small boy yawned and stretched, then returned to his sleep. "You're missing all the fun, bud."

Freeblood hoped it was the right direction as he and Jake trailed after their three escorts.

In time, the troop came upon a rise in the land. Down the road, Freeblood noticed a large structure. Glowing, white walls spanned from one side of the island to the other with a grand manor behind them. Tears filled his eyes as a thankful smile spread across his face and squeezed his son tight to him.

"That's it, bud. We're home."

HOMECOMING

———————

Halfway through breakfast, Austin ran into the manor, yelling, "Dar! Ya gotta come!"

Red Dog scrambled to his feet, barking. Dar jumped up, his mouth full of eggs, and dashed into the hallway, his napkin in hand. He ran into the boy, knocking him off his feet.

"Austin. What's all this?"

Sprawled on the floor and his cheeks bright pink from the cold, Austin grinned at his mentor as he clambered to his feet. "Sorry, Dar! Hi, Red!" He laughed, petting the dog and pointing at the front doors. "Someone's coming!"

His enthusiasm made Dar laugh. "Take a breath, boy. What is coming?"

"Not what. *Who*." Austin had become a fixture at the stables, going back and forth between it and the house. There was not much he did not see around the estate. "You gotta get out there. Hurry!" He spun on his heels and ran back the way he had come, Red Dog barking and chasing after him.

"Austin!" From the way he moved, it was obvious he was out of earshot.

Eol and Galdor joined Dar in the hallway. "Could it be Linq and the others?" Eol asked as they followed the boy.

Dar stepped out the front doors just as the person Austin had announced walked through the large gates, looking the worse for wear and carrying something in his arms. He frowned at the bandage around his head, and as he neared, the bruises on his face and arms.

"Freeblood."

"Dar! Oh, my god! You're here." He walked straight up to him, shoved his bundle into his arms, and hugged him.

"Er, well..." Dar held the blanket to his chest as he endured the hug, realizing there was something solid within its folds. "I am glad to see you too." He struggled to disentangle himself from the boy's hold.

Freeblood stepped back and swiped his eyes. "We gotta go back, get Faux out. Once they know we're gone, they're going to be really pissed." His gaze roamed over everyone around him. "Hi, Eol, Galdor. Damn, I didn't think we'd ever see anyone again."

His eyes on the blanket, Dar asked, "Who do we have here?"

"This is Jake." Freeblood uncovered his little face.

Dar grinned. "Your son?"

"He's just a day old, but isn't he incredible?"

The men congratulated the new father. At this point, Red Dog trotted up to Dar and sat at his feet, tongue lolling out the side of his mouth.

"Who is this?" Freeblood crouched and gave the puppy a scratch behind the ears. "Hi. Aren't you a beaut?" He laughed when Red Dog slurped his tongue across his face.

"This is Red Dog. A gift from Inferno." Dar smiled. "He's a good boy."

"Where's Linq? I thought he'd be here."

Dar glanced at Eol. "Let's go inside."

Freeblood jumped up, making the dog bark and skitter back to Dar. "What about Faux? She can't stay there."

"That is what we need to talk about." Baby Jake in one arm, Dar draped the other over the young man's shoulders and walked him toward the house. "Linq led a team into Nocturna to get you out. It worries me that he did not make contact before you left."

"How did you know where we were?"

"Etain's friend, Jackie."

Freeblood furrowed his brows. "A friend of Etain's?"

They stepped through the front doors and into the study. "The other woman in the room with you and Faux."

His eyes widened. "Jackie... I'd forgotten about her. Is she—"

"Who do we have here?"

The men turned to Etain standing at the study door. Jackie, having also attended the meeting with the architect, stood just behind her, but held back.

Damn. In the excitement, Dar had forgotten she was back in the flow. His heart sank. *Does she not recognize the boy?*

On her way toward her husband, she glanced at Freeblood.

"What happened to you? You look horrible."

He smirked. "Well, I feel pretty good."

A tiny squeak came from the blanket in Dar's arms.

"Who is this, my love?" She moved closer and peeked inside. Dar sucked in a breath, unsure of what to say. Wonder in her eyes, she smiled at her husband. "A baby?" She reached for the tiny bundle and cast her eyes on the new father. "Is this your son?"

Freeblood watched her, seemingly mesmerized by her presence. "J-Jake. His name is Jake."

She rocked the baby in her arms. "Hello, sweetheart. Aren't you the sweetest thing?" She glanced at Freeblood. "Where's Faux? Surely she can't stand being apart from this little darlin'."

"S-She wasn't feeling well and needed a few days to recover. So I brought Jake with me to keep him from getting sick." He grinned at his son. "What do you think of him?"

Dar relaxed, impressed by the young man's quick thinking. Happy and content for the moment, he smiled seeing this part of his family reunited. It occurred to him that the last time Etain had seen her sister was under great duress with no time for conversation. *How does she know the baby is a boy?* He shrugged the thought away. Who was he to doubt the bond between sisters? Especially sisters such as these.

"Pure magic." Her gaze returned to the baby. "He's perfect."

Before someone thought to ask the question of Faux's actual whereabouts, Dar steered the conversation in another direction. "Rest is what both of you need. We will get Swee to—"

"Did I hear right? Is there a baby in here?" Swee pushed her way through the group. Seeing Freeblood, she stopped short. "Heavens!"

"Swee! Just who I was thinking of. Meet my son, Jake." He gestured toward Etain. "He's been through a lot. Would you mind checking him out, make sure he's okay?"

Swee held her arms out to Etain. "Hello, little one. Welcome home. Let's see how you are." She touched Freeblood on the arm. "You'd better come too."

Dar draped an arm over his shoulders. "You take care of Junior." He glanced at Eol and Galdor. "We will take care of dad."

Swee hesitated. "Are you sure?"

"Aye, milady." Eol answered before Dar had the chance. "We have had plenty of first aid training as Black Blades."

She shrugged as she turned to Etain. "Would you like to come? Get in some practice with a real live baby?"

"It's not like I don't know what to do, but it would be more fun than listening to these old women catch up." She winked at the men and followed the healer out of the study.

By this time, a small crowd was gathered in the entryway. As Swee and Etain maneuvered through the group, several came forward, patting Freeblood on the back, telling him how glad they were to see him.

"Shall we get you settled?" Dar noticed a small critter attempting to crawl onto the toe of his boot. "Did these kittens come with you?"

Freeblood laughed. "We found them on the way." He leaned close so only Dar would hear. "That reminds me. Did you know there's a wolf out there?"

Dar raised a brow.

"Just north of the forest."

"Oh, aye." Although he had not seen any, he had heard its howls. "Would someone take care of the kittens? They can live in the barn. It will not hurt to have a few mousers."

Austin pushed his way through and eyed the new face yet kept his opinions to himself. Still, Dar knew what he was thinking. His expressions were like an open book. When the boy saw the kittens, though, his whole demeanor changed.

"Kitties!" He plopped down on the floor, giggling like the child he was, and let them crawl into his lap. Stroking their soft fur, he laughed even harder when Red Dog sniffed at the strange little creatures. They meowed in his face and patted his nose, which made him sneeze, and in turn, knocked them off their tiny paws. "I'll take care of 'em, Dar."

"Thank you, Austin."

As people moved on to start their day, Dar steered Freeblood back into the entryway. "Pardon us, my friends, but the boy needs medical attention." The group allowed the men through and slowly dispersed. Closer to the kitchen, Dar called out, "Alaster!"

He did not see the man but heard his answer. "We're on it, boss. It'll be a grand dinner. Cherise! Get the man something to clean the boy's injuries."

Dar grinned at Freeblood. "Good man."

"How'd that happen?"

"Sheer luck on my part. They needed a home, and we needed organization. He, Cherise, and their clan have made a huge difference."

Dar led the way to a small den toward the back of the house. Eol and Galdor stood as sentries outside the door. Inside, Dar motioned the young Alamir to sit while he poured a dram for each of them. Within minutes, Noah, Cherise's son, and another young boy were at the door, a tray in hand.

"What is this, Noah?" Dar asked as the boys entered the room.

"Mama sent these for you to use on Mr. Freeblood, sir." He set the tray on the coffee table. "The bowl has warmed chamomile for cleaning, and the little bottle's Arnica oil that'll help with the bruises." He turned to Freeblood. "Put a little on a couple times a day. It'll help with the pain. Oh, and there are scissors and bandages."

"Thank you," Freeblood said, leaning back into the sofa. "Please thank your mom."

"I will." The boys left the men alone.

"Get a mouthful of Scotch down you while I take a peek at your head. That rag has seen better days."

Freeblood touched the bandage as he spoke. "Oh yeah. I'd forgotten about it. Those Banshee dinged me a good one." He knocked back the dram, set down the glass, and leaned forward.

Dar snipped the bandage at the side and slowly rolled it off his head. The gash at the base of his skull was ugly but had been stitched by a skilled hand. He picked up a cloth, doused it in the warmed chamomile, and dabbed at the wound.

"Someone mended this with great care."

Freeblood snorted. "Gotta get their money's worth."

"Did they cause these bruises?"

"Some. A few came from Dathmet's goons. But I can thank Illiana for the fresh ones."

Dar stopped for a moment. Where had he heard that name before? Mulling it over, he doused the cloth with the solution again and continued to wash away the dirt around the wound and the back of his neck.

"Who is this Illiana?"

"Another sucker taken for their stupid games. The Banshee made us face off in the arena. But... Ow. It's really tender."

Dar tossed the used cloth onto the tray, picked up the small vial of Arnica oil, and dabbed a small amount onto the wound. "This should help with the pain. If you have any headaches, ask Alaster to boil some white willow bark and make a tea for you." Dar handed the oil to the young man and returned to the Scotch. "Clean your face and apply oil on the bruises. You should see an improvement by morning."

He poured another glass for each of them as Freeblood washed his face and arms, being careful with the shiner around his left eye.

Dar sat and leaned back, sipping his drink. "Tell me how you and Faux ended up in that room with Étain."

"First, tell me how she is." He put the cloth on the tray and grabbed his dram. "She looks a lot better than when I last saw her, but something's off."

Dar tilted his head. "Why do you say that?"

Freeblood sipped his drink and gritted his teeth as he swallowed. "Ho. That's smooth." He met Dar's gaze. "She's Etain, but at the same time she isn't." He shrugged. "I can't explain it."

A pang in his heart made him realize what he had said was true. He was so grateful to have any part of her back, he had ignored it. "She has only just returned to me."

"What do you mean?"

Dar breathed in, reluctant to tell him things he preferred not to discuss, but he understood that to bring her back one hundred percent would take everyone working together.

"She does not remember any of it—not her brother, the demon, or that either of you were there." He finished his drink. "When we came here, she did not know who I was. She thought Faux was dead." He leaned forward, placing his elbows on his knees and staring at the glass in his hands. "I do not believe she knew anyone other than Jackie, Swee, and Spirit."

"Damn, Dar. That must've been tough."

He set the glass on the table. "Then last night, she came to my room. She knew *me*." He touched his chest. "As I am now, not some Dar from long ago. And this morning..." He sat back, rubbing his fingers over his lips in remembrance of her kiss. "When she woke, the sparkle in her eyes, the way she kissed me." Tears burned in his eyes. "She was my Etain."

"We'll be careful with her, Dar," Freeblood said softly. "We'll get her back all the way."

He swiped his eyes and gave him a partial grin. "Now, tell me your story."

Freeblood spent the next hour telling of his and Faux's plans for a vacation before heading off to *Sólskin* and their initial kidnapping by a group of *Bok*. He moved on to tell another side of what happened in Deudraeth and their second kidnapping.

After several more drams, Dar walked him upstairs to rest.

With Freeblood tucked away, Dar stopped by his bedroom, hoping to find Etain either there or in one of the other rooms. To his surprise, demolition had started on every room, the one designated as the nursery being the furthest along. Dar thought it providence at its best. Jake and Freeblood could move in upon completion, and he was sure it would not be long before his own children arrived.

He turned to the room across the hall where he heard laughter and baby talk. Seeing Etain, Swee, and Jackie having a merry visit with Jake touched his heart.

"Sounds like a party in here," he joked, standing at the door.

Etain looked up from the baby on the bed. He swore her face brightened even more seeing him there. Yet he was reluctant to go to her. What if it wasn't—

"Dar." She straightened and walked toward him, extending her hand to take his. "There you are. Come give Jake a proper hello."

He pulled her to him and kissed her. Her lips were warm, soft, and responsive.

"Are you okay? You've been acting kinda weird," she said when he pulled away.

"I am now," he whispered, wishing the others were in another room.

"It's good to be home, isn't it?"

"Aye."

She took his hand again. "Come say hi, then you can get back to whatever intrigues you were up to."

"Good morning, Jackie." Dar dipped his head. "I saw you briefly in the foyer earlier." He wondered if his wife had shared any details of their night together with the lady.

"I didn't want to interfere in what seemed to be a family reunion."

Etain brought her head up from playing with the baby. "Jackie, you're family too. Don't ever think you're not. I'll introduce you to Freeblood later. Okay?"

Jackie stole a glance at Dar and shrugged before she answered, "That'd be nice."

Dar cleared his throat. "Is the baby all right?" he asked Swee. "It appears we have had a bath."

"He's a little underweight, but we can fix that." She wrapped the baby in a light blue blanket. "And yes, he's had a bath. Poor thing was in need of a fresh diaper, but he's a little trooper. Aren't you, sweetie? Didn't fuss once."

She handed Jake to Etain, who carried him to a chair and settled in, offering him a bottle.

Swee leaned close to Dar, her voice low. "Anything on Faux?"

"Nothing. I hope Linq and the others find her soon."

"Shall I check on Freeblood?"

He shook his head. "He is sound asleep. Half a bottle of Scotch made sure of that. We will not see him until morning."

"Poor kid. Let's hope we can get his family back together."

"Thank you for taking care of them, Swee. We would be lost without you."

"Go spend time with the baby and your wife." She turned to Jackie. "You also need a checkup. How about we go to your room, or have you other things to do?"

"I have the time," she said.

On their way to the door, Swee stopped. "I'll check in on you two later if that's okay, Étain."

"Take your time. Catch you later, Jackie."

Once the ladies were gone, Dar crouched next to his wife. "Since it appears I have lost you to another man, I need to go into town for a few things. Will you be all right?"

"There's no other man for me, my love. You go ahead. I think we'll take a nap after this."

He grinned, gazing at Jake, who drank greedily. "She says I am her only man, then admits to sleeping with another. Shameless."

She nudged him with her shoulder. "He's not as demanding as you."

Dar feigned insult. "I never ask for more than a lady is willing to give."

Etain narrowed her eyes, handed the bottle to Dar, and shifted Jake to her shoulder. "Yet you seem to get more than what she intends."

He set the bottle on the floor and grasped one of her hands in his, turning it palm up. "Who am I to question the intentions of my lady?" He brought it to his lips, leaving a kiss in the center. "I will not be long."

"Be careful. Oh, and pick up some baby onesies?"

Dar cleared his throat. "What?"

"Uh, pajamas. Cherise said there's a baby shop in town with everything. Just stop by and tell the ladies he's a good-sized newborn. They'll do the rest."

"As you wish, milady."

⁕⁕⁕

Cloud ran up as Dar walked toward the garage. "Hi, Red." He patted the puppy's head. "Are you going to town, Dar?"

"I am."

"Can I go with you? Ms. Swee gave me a list of things I need for my classes, and I want to pick 'em out myself. That is, if you don't mind me going."

"What do you say, Red?" Dar opened his door. The puppy yipped and jumped into the cab. "As long as you do not mind a stop by the baby shop. Hop in, Cloud."

"Baby shop?"

Dar grinned. "Our friend Freeblood brought home his new son today and needs a few things."

"Okay." Cloud climbed into the truck. His eyes widened as he checked out the interior. "Wow! Cool truck, Dar. It's so big."

"Big truck for a big man."

Driving through the main gates, he sensed the boy wanted to say something. "What's on your mind, Cloud?"

The boy gazed out his window as though trying to find the right words. Dar kept quiet and waited for him to sort it out.

Cloud turned suddenly, a serious expression on his face. "Have you really eaten the hearts of your enemies?"

Dar gave him a sideways glance. "I have."

Red Dog sniffed at the boy, sticking his nose into his ear and making him laugh. "Stop it, Red." He put his arm around the puppy and hugged him close, giving Dar a tentative glance. "Why?"

No one had ever asked. He wanted to be honest, but at the same time, did not want to delve too deep into the spiritual. "I do not go into battle with the thought of doing so. It is impulsive." He glanced at the boy. "Not a good thing to be when facing an enemy. We train so we will be prepared and *not* lose focus." His eyes on the road again, he sighed. "In those first moments, it is the satisfaction of knowing you are the victor. But it is not always enough." Dar paused, reflecting on his encounter with the *Bok* before they attacked Laugharne. "Rage can take over and consume you, heart and soul. It leaves you vulnerable."

Cloud buried his face in the puppy's red fur. "You lose your focus," he lifted his head, "and it could get you killed."

Dar gave him a cursory glance, impressed by how quickly he grasped the implications. "Aye."

"So you won't be teaching Austin how to do it?"

Now he understood why he had asked. Despite their constant fighting, they were still brothers. Perhaps his lengthy explanation had been a touch overkill. "I will not."

Cloud's green eyes were filled with sincere appreciation. "Thank you."

Once in town, the three stopped by the print shop to order announcements for the opening of the academy and walked to the apothecary for Cloud's supplies. Next on the list was baby supplies. He told the ladies what Etain had told him and sure enough, he and Cloud walked out with baby pajamas, shirts and pants, diapers, bottles, and a new pacifier.

Before they left the store, one of the ladies said, "When you're ready, we have baby furniture too."

Dar widened his eyes at Cloud. "Thank you for your help, ladies. I will keep it in mind."

Once the shopping was done, Dar offered to treat the boy to lunch at the local diner. "We can get to know each other."

"Well, I *am* hungry. Do you know what a hamburger is?"

At first, Dar thought it a joke, but when he glanced at the boy, his expression was too serious to be anything but genuine concern. "I prefer mine rare and juicy with bacon piled on top."

Cloud relaxed and grinned. "I like mine with ketchup. I've never had one with bacon."

Dar held the diner door open as Cloud walked in, followed by Red Dog. "I strongly suggest it. Bacon makes everything taste better."

After they sat and ordered, Dar leaned back, while Red Dog lay at his feet, his red nose peeking out from beneath the table. "Tell me about your family, Cloud. Where do you come from?"

The boy squirmed in his seat. "Well, uh... Our grandfather was a great Alamir warrior. He was the chieftain of the Krath clan."

Dar leaned forward. "Your grandfather was Jodoc Andrazia?"

Cloud stared at him. "Y-you knew my g-grandfather?"

"Judas Priest. I fought many a battle with Jodoc." He gained a new appreciation for the boy. "He *was* a great warrior *and* chieftain. The Krath clan was not the same after his death." His brows furrowed. "But you could not have possibly known the man. How old are you? Twelve? Thirteen? I know he died many years ago."

"Yeah... I mean, no, I never met him. Da told us stories and showed us pictures of him and Grandma."

"Your grandmother has passed as well?" The boy nodded silently. "I do not believe I ever met your da."

"Prolly not." He shrugged, picking at a scratch on the table surface. "He, uh... Well... He didn't believe in all that stuff."

Dar leaned back when the waitress brought their food. Once she walked away, he picked up the conversation again. "What stuff?"

Cloud eyed the burger in front of him. "Huh? Stuff?"

"You said your da did not believe in all that stuff. Are you talking about the Alamir way of life?"

Concentrating on his fries to make sure he applied the correct amount of ketchup, he said, "Oh, yeah. Da wasn't into any of it. My da used words to fight his battles. The *Bok* didn't scare him."

"He was an intellectual?"

Cloud's face screwed up. "No... Whatever that is. Da was a printer and a writer, but mostly a printer." He lowered his voice. "He fought the *Bok* that way."

The conversation lulled as they enjoyed their meals. Dar contemplated what he learned of the young boy as he shared bits of beef and bacon with Red Dog, who inhaled every morsel. He dared to venture into the unknown again.

"Tell me how your father died, Cloud."

The fry in his hand dropped onto the plate. He sat back, placed his hands in his lap, and dropped his head. Dar respectfully waited; afraid he had gone too far. Just as he was ready to tell him not to worry about it, the lad spoke in a raspy tone, the tears apparent in his voice.

"They came one night while we were asleep." He paused for a breath. "The *Bok* took my da." His voice cracked, but he continued. "And my mom." Tears glistened in his eyes. "She made me and Austin hide in the crawlspace."

"Cloud..."

The boy shook his head. "I need to tell you. I-I *want* to tell you."

Dar appreciated his resolve and sat quietly.

Cloud swiped his napkin across his eyes and blew his nose. Another deep breath seemed to give him the fortitude he needed to continue. "We could see through the slats." He glanced at Dar and lowered his head. "They strung them up right in our home. My da wouldn't tell those bastards a damn thing. He wouldn't betray his sources." He clenched his jaw, his anger rising. "When he wouldn't talk, they tortured my mom. She spit in their faces and told them to go to hell." He slammed his hand on the table. "Da told the world what scum they are, and they killed him for it."

Dar reached across the table and gripped the boy's hand. "I understand."

He pulled free and glared at him. "How would you know anything? You didn't see what they did."

Dar's gaze did not waver from Cloud's. "Strap 'em down, string 'em up. Doesn't matter. The result is the same. Slice into the first layer of flesh, peel it back inch by inch, their victim screaming while the others are forced to watch." The boy's mouth fell open. Dar leaned back. "I was not there when your parents were murdered..." His voice caught but he swallowed it away. "The same happened to my family many years ago."

"Oh... I'm sorry."

Hearing a whimper from Red Dog, Dar comforted the puppy with a scratch behind an ear while he and Cloud shared several moments of silence in remembrance of their families.

Dar tossed a few bills on the table. "How about we head home?"

TO SAVE A SUCCUBUS

The five spread out, taking on the guards who rushed at them. Taurnil glanced at Linq. "Goblins?"

Linq shrugged and engaged the two who came at him. Taurnil blocked an oncoming attack and ducked under another.

Aramis and Ra slashed and dashed, slaying as many as they could without getting themselves killed.

Illiana grabbed a sword from a dead goblin and protected Faux, herding the girl away from danger, hacking at whatever came close.

Amid the chaos, a blue-skinned woman dressed in doctor's whites slipped through the fighters. "Faux!" She made a beeline toward the young woman, dodging away from Illiana. "What are you doing? Why are you with these people? I thought you liked it here."

Faux touched Illiana on the shoulder. "It's okay. I'll take care of this."

The Krymerian turned, blocking an attack, and stabbed a goblin. "I am here if you need me."

Faux eyed the midwife. "These are *my* people. I'm going home."

"Why? I thought we'd made a connection."

"You think I don't know what you're up to?" Faux rolled her eyes. "You took enough blood to fill a family tree." She shoved her face into the midwife's. "I won't be your breeding whore."

The woman blinked, frozen by the anger thrown in her face. "I-I—"

"No. *Me*." Faux leaned back and swung with a scalpel in her hand, slicing Siobhan's throat. Blue blood spurted. Eyes wide, the woman covered the cut with a hand, staring at Faux. In seconds, she collapsed to the floor.

Illiana had no time to acknowledge Faux's actions with more than a raised brow. She realized the goblins had caught on to the fact that the most important person in the room was the young woman.

"Faux, can you wield a blade?"

"Not a sword."

Illiana grabbed a dagger from her boot and shoved it into Faux's hand, pleased to see she knew how to hold it. Now, if she could use it like she did the scalpel...

Before the Elves or Alamir had a chance to react, the goblins rushed at the women. Although the two fought valiantly, one of the enemy swords slipped past Illiana's and sliced Faux on the side of the head. She staggered and stumbled against the wall, her blood splattering the Krymerian.

Illiana turned on the smirking goblin. By the time his putrid eyes met her glare, his head sailed across the room. Each one that challenged her fell to her sword.

Linq was just able to break through her battlelust. "Illiana, we must go. Faux needs medical attention, as do you."

"I am fine. Go! I will cover your backs."

She barely acknowledged the opening of the portal, noting a flash of blue from the corner of her eye. Everything became a blur, seen through a red shroud. The face of a Banshee flashed in her mind. Did she kill her, or was it wishful thinking?

At some point, hands grasped her shoulders, pulling her away from the onslaught of demons. She stumbled into the dark, having the presence of mind to shout, "Where is Faux?"

Someone said she had gone through the portal, but Illiana felt too heavy to move. As long as the young woman was safe, she could rest.

Ra placed two fingers on the side of Faux's neck.

"Is she alive?" asked Aramis, kneeling by his side.

"Yep, but her pulse is weak."

Aramis looked more closely. "The blood appears to be coming from her head. We must be careful."

Ra stood. "Where'd the Elves git off to? And where's that warrior woman?"

"The last I saw they were running toward the portal. Do you think they were intercepted?"

"Hard to say. May whatever god they believe in be with 'em. They're gonna need it." Ra scooped Faux into his arms. "Whatever we're gonna do, we best do it now. She's bleeding pretty bad. Hell knows, I don't want Dar to see her like this."

"Then let's make sure he doesn't."

No sooner had they headed down the road than they heard a vehicle come along.

Ra glanced at Aramis as an old Dodge pickup rolled toward them. "Aw, hell. What're the odds?"

The truck skidded to a stop. Dar jumped out one side, followed by Red Dog, as Cloud jumped out the other. He rushed up to Ra, giving Faux a cursory once-over.

"*Tartarus.* What's happened?"

"We were on our way to the house."

"Give her to me." Dar held out his arms. "Aramis, are you able to drive?"

"Of course, I can drive."

"You're a mite peaked, boss," Ra said. "You sure?"

"No worse than you." He turned to the Krymerian. "Get her to Swee. We'll be right behind you."

Dar nodded and disappeared.

Dar burst into the kitchen. As he hoped, Alaster was there, making notes in his journal.

"We need help."

He put away the book and called for Cherise.

She quickly appeared, assessed the situation, and took charge. "Clear off the island and put her there. Alaster, put water on to boil." She turned to her son, Noah, who stood at her elbow. "Get a sheet, boy. Shred me some bandages and be quick about it!"

"Yes, ma'am." Noah turned to his friends who had followed him and his mother. "Charlie, Missy, come on."

"Where's Swee?" Alaster asked. "I'll go—"

"Don't be bothering Ms. Swee," Cherise barked. "She's got her hands full with Mr. Freeblood and Jake. We can handle this." She spied one of the girls watching. "Shila, get them scissors from the drawer over there." The small girl ran around the island and to the drawer indicated. In seconds, she returned to Cherise, scissors in hand. "Thank you, girl." She lowered her voice. "Go get my bag. You know the one. Bring it quick."

"Yes, ma'am."

"We need to clean up this blood so I can see what I'm working with. Do you have any experience—"

"Warm water and a cloth, Alaster," snapped Dar.

"Thank you, sir. Let's get to it."

Dar gently laid Faux on the island, cradling her head in his hand. Alaster shoved a wet cloth at him, and he proceeded to wipe away as much blood as possible, Cherise bustling around him.

"Lord have mercy! Where has this girl been?" Cherise leaned over the young woman. "I don't see any blood anywhere else. Just her head."

"The top half of her ear is missing." Dar applied pressure to the wound to staunch the flow.

Shila returned with the bag and handed it to Cherise.

"Dar, I'll get to work on her ear if someone will get a room ready."

He switched places with Cherise and assisted with the procedure for a time. Once assured of her ability to stitch the wound, he turned to the sink and washed his hands. "I will see to her room. When it is ready, I will return for her."

"Thank you," Cherise said without looking up, but as he walked off, she called out. "She's going to be fine, Dar."

He stopped at the door. "Thank you."

Busy cleaning the island, Alaster glanced at Etain and Jackie as they walked into the kitchen.

"Hi, Alaster. Have we missed supper?" Etain asked.

"You have not, Lady E." He quickly turned to the sink and rinsed the cloth in his hands. "Supper's not for another couple of hours."

Etain's eyes darted around the room. *Have we walked in on something we shouldn't have?* Nothing looked amiss. "I was hoping we could get something to eat."

He left the cloth in the sink and turned. "Who do we have here?"

"I'm Jackie." She stuck out her hand. "We haven't met, but I've tasted your exquisite cooking. It's good to meet you."

He shook her hand. "Thank you, Jackie. Nice to meet you. I'm Alaster. What can I get you ladies?"

Etain couldn't shake the uneasiness. "Something light."

"Yes, ma'am. I'll warm you up some chicken noodle soup. It should hold you over until supper."

She watched as he pulled out a pan, bowls, and other utensils, then went to the refrigerator for a large tureen. As he poured the cold soup into the pan, Etain asked, "Is everything okay?"

He glanced over his shoulder. "Why do you ask?"

She shrugged. "I feel like we've missed—"

Alaster turned but his gaze went past Etain's shoulder. "Dar!" He pointed his wooden spoon at his guests. "Look who's come for a bite to eat."

Etain turned slightly and watched her husband walk toward her with a disconcerted expression on his face. "What's wrong?"

He sighed and hugged her close. "You know me too well. Hello, Jackie."

"Hey, Dar. Even *I* can feel the tension."

Etain furrowed her brows. "Has something happened?"

"Faux is here."

"What? Where? I want to see her."

"Wait." He held onto her. "She is asleep and will be for at least twenty-four hours, if not longer."

She searched his face, waiting for more. "Why? I want to see her, Dar. Does Freeblood know?"

"No, and we are not going to disturb him. He will know soon enough. Alaster, when it is ready, would you mind bringing it into the dining room?"

The chef waved the wooden spoon. "Don't mind at all, if you'll grab them bowls and spoons on your way out."

Dishes, silver, and napkins in hand, the three moved into the next room, sitting at one end of the large table.

"Why can't I see Faux?" Etain asked.

"We will see her after you eat something, but I want you to be prepared and not expect much for a few days."

"Would you please stop babying me and spit it out? *What* has happened to her?"

It was Jackie who answered. "Those damn Banshee."

Etain's head swiveled toward her. "Banshee?" *What do they have to do with any of this?* She'd not thought of them in ages. Surely, they didn't hold a grudge this long. Etain shook her head, more in shock that Jackie knew about them than the memory of them. "How do you know?"

"They kidnapped me. That's how I met Faux and Freeblood."

Jackie saw Dar close eyes and shake his head.

"You were kidnapped? I don't understand." Etain turned to Dar. "Did you know about this? Is that where they've been all this time? If they had Jackie, how'd she get here if Freeblood's just now shown up?"

Dar sighed. "Aye. Freeblood did not want to upset you by—"

She scooted off her chair, pacing toward the door. "Freeblood? This has you written all over it, Dar. Why did you lie to me?"

He straightened in his seat. "I did not."

She paced back and gripped the back of her chair. "Freeblood said Faux was sick and would follow when she was better. You knew what was going on, yet you said nothing. And neither of you mentioned Jackie's involvement."

He opened his mouth to speak, but Etain cut him off. "How long? How long have you known?"

Dar leaned forward, placing his elbows on the table. "Long enough to send a team to get them out."

"Where's this *team*?"

"I am sure Aramis and Ra are upstairs somewhere, cleaning up."

She glared at him. "You sent Aramis and Ra to face the Banshee?" She picked up the back of the chair, set it hard against the floor, and paced toward the door.

Dar stood. "Linq and Taurnil went with them, but as far as I know, they have not returned yet."

She paced back to him. "This is my fault."

Dar and Jackie spoke at the same time. "What?"

She gripped the back of the chair again, her gaze downcast, thinking of another time. "Well, not *my* fault. More my dad's. But it *is* because of my family. I didn't realize anyone could hold a grudge this long."

Alaster carried in the soup tureen. "Soup's on," he laughed as he set it on the table. "I'll leave this right here. Serve yourselves when you're ready."

Once he was gone, Etain removed the lid of the tureen, served Jackie and herself, and returned to her seat. She stared at her hands in her lap for a moment, gathering her thoughts. "It was a business deal that did not end well."

Dar remained standing, unsure how to respond. He doubted the Banshee's involvement had anything to do with her father's business dealings. They could not possibly know of her parentage. Dathmet might have been stupid to engage their services, but not to the extent he would divulge Etain's or his history. Since Jackie was their original target, he was certain Faux and Freeblood had been taken as payment for services rendered. His one hope now was that Etain not ask more questions about Jackie.

In his silence, Jackie said, "You were just a girl, Etain. Your dad dealt with a lot of different cultures. You can't know if it was the same ones."

Dar turned toward Jackie. *James* did *work with several groups. Surely it was not the same—*

"Once was enough. He refused to deal with any Banshee after that fiasco."

"But still, girl—"

Etain placed her hands on the table, eyes downcast. "I can see them clear as day." She lifted her head, staring into the past. Dar heard Jackie gasp as he was tempted to do when he saw the coldness in his wife's eyes.

"One was dark. One was light. But her light didn't brighten. She was a sinkhole that devoured the light and destroyed all hope." Etain blinked. "The third was the mouthpiece, the worst of the three. A mixture of the dark and the light, one engulfing the other, always shifting. She made me sick. They *all* made me sick. I didn't recover for weeks." She blinked again, picked up her spoon, and delved into the bowl of soup.

Jackie nodded at Dar. "That would be them."

He sat, his mind on Etain's father and how if the man were here today, he would punch him in the face. He exposed his family, his *children*, to creatures that should have been kept in fairy tales and not experienced in real life.

My lady's life was not as picturesque as I thought. She's been through more than I ever imagined.

He watched her swirl her soup and scoop a spoonful to her lips, blowing lightly to cool the liquid before slurping it down. She laughed, covering her mouth with one hand while setting the spoon to the side of her bowl, her eyes wide and mischievous. Her cheeks colored when she caught his gaze on her.

"Sorry. But it *is* good." She lifted her napkin and dabbed at her mouth.

He chuckled, glad to see her moroseness gone. "Perhaps when the children are old enough, we should hire an etiquette coach to avoid such improprieties when at the dinner table."

She returned her napkin to her lap, making sure it was positioned just right. "Hopefully, our etiquette coach will have the patience to teach their *father* that it's impolite," her eyes met his, "to point out their mother's mishaps when at the dinner table." She picked up the bowl and slurped the rest of the soup.

Dar laughed and glanced at Jackie, who was not laughing. "Lord help those poor little souls."

Etain chuckled and dabbed her mouth again. "Oh, Jackie. They'll have perfect manners, despite their rudely obnoxious parents."

"I'm thinking maybe their Aunt Jackie should visit on a regular basis to ensure they survive their raising."

Her comment only encouraged more laughter from the other two, which infected her as well.

"If you ladies are done, shall we go upstairs and see Faux?"

Freeblood opened his eyes the second she entered the house. Sudden tears burned, a warm sensation trickling into his hair. A mixture of relief she was safe, happiness she was home, and excitement he would see her soon overwhelmed him. He tried to sit up, but the pounding in his head made him lay back.

Maybe I'll close my eyes for a few minutes, give my head a chance to settle.

He wiped his eyes as he closed them. He tried to stay awake, but he... Was. Just. So...

The next time he woke, he knew it was late. Silence lay over the house like a blanket of snow. Freeblood wondered why she hadn't come to him by now. Had Dar intervened, making her wait until he was awake?

He slowly sat up and twisted his legs off the side, giving his head time to adjust to being vertical. Once the dizziness passed, he noticed a plush robe at the foot of his bed and a pair of slippers on the floor.

"These people..." He closed his eyes in silent appreciation. "They take such good care of us."

He slipped on the robe and slid his feet into the cozy slippers. How something so simple could change your whole day. Standing slowly, he shuffled to the door but stopped for a moment, holding onto the jamb.

"No need to rush, dude. She isn't going anywhere."

The world steady again, he stepped into the hallway and made his way to the landing. He stopped to get his bearings, then continued to a part of the house he'd not visited before. Since most of the rooms were empty, it was easy to locate her. He shrugged, smiling to himself.

I could find her in Grand Central if I had to.

Quietly, he opened the door and slipped inside. There were two double beds, Swee sitting in a chair between them, asleep. A lamp on a bedside table behind her cast a dim light over the room.

Coming closer, he frowned at the bandage around Faux's head, and noticed Jake beside her, tucked in the curve of her arm. He moved toward Swee and lightly touched her shoulder.

She startled awake, giving him a sleepy smile. "What're you doing out of bed?"

"I had to see my girl." He glanced at Faux and back at Swee. "Go to bed. I'll sit with them."

She yawned and stretched. "You shouldn't."

"I want to be the first face she sees when she wakes."

Swee pursed her lips but stood. "It might not be for a while."

He turned to Faux. "That bad?"

"Depends on how you look at it. They cut off half her ear. Cherise stopped the bleeding and did a beautiful job stitching it up, but..."

"Yeah. This is Faux we're talking about." The two laughed. "She'll be pissed."

Another yawn.

"Go to bed, Swee. We'll be fine."

"There's diapers in the drawer there." She pointed at the bedside table. "And there should be a bottle warming downstairs. He's going to wake pretty soon, ready to eat."

He chuckled. "He *is* my son. We'll see you later."

"Night, Freeblood. Thank you." She headed toward the door. "Oh, and welcome back."

He waved to her and sat in the chair as the door closed. He had a few seconds to admire the picture of Faux and Jake in their sleepy paradise before the boy stirred.

He opened the drawers and found fresh diapers along with a package of wipes, placed them on the bed, and scooped his son into his arms.

"My main man," he whispered. "How's it hanging?" He chuckled when Jake's tiny eyes squinted open, then closed as he yawned and stretched. "Let's get you changed, and we'll go find a snack."

He laid the baby at the foot of the bed, unwrapped his blanket, and unsnapped the bottom of his onesie. Grinning at his son, he loosened the diaper, but didn't remove it.

"You aren't gonna catch me out, boy. I know how the water cannon works."

Opening the wipes, he pulled out two, and warmed them between his hands. As quickly as he could, he switched out the dirty diaper for a clean one, wiped him down, taped him up, and snapped him back into his onesie. "I still got the touch."

Tucked into his father's arm, they returned to the chair. "Let me have a good look at you. I swear you've grown since we got here." Freeblood laughed, rubbing a hand over his son's head. "Is that brown fuzz on your noggin? Gonna take after the old man, aren't you?"

Jake voiced his displeasure.

Dad bounced the boy in his arm. "Okay, okay. Let's go."

In the kitchen, he noticed a bottle warmer on the counter next to the stove. "What the... It's as if they knew we were coming." He removed the bottle and tested the liquid on his wrist. Satisfied it was safe to drink, he offered it to his son, who latched on in a second.

"Oh... That's right. Etain's expecting twins." He laughed at himself. "Of course, they'd have everything."

Amidst the confusion caused by the death of the midwife and Faux's disappearance, Linq and Taurnil dragged Illiana's still form down a dark hallway, hoping they had not been seen.

"Are you sure she is alive, Linq? There is a lot of blood."

"Here." Linq shoved open a door. Spying an examination table in the center of the room, he relinquished his hold on her to Taurnil. After locking the door, he answered, "She was breathing before the portal closed."

Taurnil lifted her onto the table while Linq rifled through various drawers, searching for anything that might help. He found a penlight and turned to the table to illuminate her face. The Elves shared a woeful glance, but neither said a word. Linq leaned down. Feeling her breath, he nodded.

He handed the light to Taurnil. "Hold this while I check for wounds." He ran his fingers through her blood-soaked hair, feeling for lacerations on her scalp and lower neck. "Nothing." Then he inspected each arm and her torso. Aside from the expected cuts and scratches from participating in a fight, none were particularly deep or life-threatening.

"I am not finding anything."

When Taurnil moved the penlight farther down, the two exchanged a frown.

"How did we not see this?" Linq exclaimed, seeing a dagger protruding from her thigh. "Move the light closer."

"Linq, this is *her* dagger."

"By the sea and stars. How the hell did she end up with it there?"

"It was in Faux's hand last time I saw it."

The older Elf sucked in a breath. "Let us not go down that road right now. We have to get her stable and make sure she does not bleed to death before we get out of here. Agreed?"

Taurnil raised a brow. "What do you want me to do?"

"Do *not* remove the dagger. She will bleed out."

"I hate to be the harbinger of bad news, but we cannot stay here. They will search the building."

"I know that, but we cannot afford to move her."

Heavy footsteps sounded in the hall.

"*Helvítis fjandans* (Fucking hell)!" Linq growled.

"I know."

They heard men yelling and doors forced open, the sounds coming closer. Linq glanced around the room. It was either engage the goblins once more, risking the chance they would be taken prisoner and forced into the very thing they were trying to save the others from, or squeeze through a narrow, five-foot-tall window with no latch.

"Taurnil, get that window open. I do not care how you do it. Just do it."

"What about Illiana?"

"We must leave her here." He held up a hand. "They will not hurt her. She is too valuable as a Trodaithe. We will add her to the growing list of poor souls to save, but we cannot do it if we are caught. Get that window open."

Taurnil removed his scabbard, sword and all, stepped back from the window, and threw the scabbard, hilt first, as hard as he could. The window cracked but did not break. "By the stars." He picked it up from the floor, stepped back as far as he could, and threw it again. This time, the glass gave way, the hilt going completely through. He rushed to the window and broke out the remaining glass.

"We can get through if we hold our breath."

Linq leaned close to Illiana's ear. "We will come back for you, milady. I promise."

Her eyes fluttered as she turned her head to him. "Go... Now."

"Linq, we have to move."

"Go. I am right behind you."

Taurnil sucked in a breath and eased through the opening. Bits of glass cut into his leather armor, but he made it through otherwise unscathed. Linq, hearing the doorknob turn, dashed to the window and drew his sword, wielding it in his left hand. He sucked in a breath and squeezed through the opening, mentally counting the seconds to keep focused.

"Here! There's a body on the table." said one of the guards.

Linq glared at Taurnil and whispered, "Help me. Take my arm."

The younger Elf dropped his sword and reached for the older one, pulling with all his might. "Living rough. Might do you. Some. Good." Taurnil placed a foot against the frame of the window for leverage and pulled harder. This time, Linq came free, a piece of glass cutting across his left cheek. "Linq!"

"Go! It is only a scratch."

"Who's that at the window?" they heard from inside the room.

"Don't let them get away!"

Fortunately for the Elves, the goblins proved too large to fit through the opening, no matter how hard they pushed. The two disappeared into the darkness.

An Unexpected Proposition

U p early the next morning, Dar kissed his wife, her belly, and left her to check on Faux first, followed by Freeblood.

He quietly opened the door to Faux's room and peeked inside. Freeblood lay in bed with her and Jake, all three sound asleep. Happy to see the small family together, he walked to the chair between the two beds and sat, inspecting each respective bandage from afar. He noted both suffered from head injuries. It would be important to remember in the future when he faced off with these rogue Banshee. He knew it would happen. He *wanted* it. First, he would hunt down Dathmet and kill him, then turn his full wrath on the ruthless hags.

"Dar?"

So engrossed in his musings, he had not heard Etain, or Red Dog come into the room. He stood as she walked toward him. "*A chuisle...*"

"How is she?" Etain wrapped her arms around his waist as he draped his arm around her, pulling her close.

"Time will tell." He kissed the top of her head.

"Are you going to share your blood?"

He grinned. It was just like her to get straight to the point. "I will leave that decision to her partner. If he wishes to share his, so be it."

"She looks better than she did last night. Maybe he already has, not that he can afford it. I don't understand why the Banshee took *them*."

Dar knew why, but Etain was not ready to hear their story. "The only motivation they require is the blood of others."

"And a nice profit." She shrugged. "Shall we grab the boys for breakfast?"

"Do you think Swee will show before we go down?"

Etain chuckled. "Absolutely."

"Excellent. Let us wake the—" Dar released her. "Well, he is no longer a boy, is he?"

"He is not. He's come a long way. I'm glad you've noticed."

Arm in arm, they walked to the other side of the bed. "In my defense, I have been somewhat preoccupied with other matters."

Etain leaned over the young man and gave his shoulder a shake as she whispered, "Freeblood. How about some breakfast?" When he did not wake, she shook him again. "Freeblood."

Red Dog pushed his way in front of Etain and set his forepaws on the mattress, giving the young man a big lick on the face.

His eyes popped open and slid to her. "It wasn't me. I swear."

Red Dog yipped, wagging his tail, while Etain and Dar laughed softly.

"For once, I have to say I believe you," Dar said. "Are you up for breakfast? You can bring Junior with you."

"What?" Freeblood scrubbed his face with a hand, scratching Red Dog behind the ear with the other and blinked a few times. "Oh... Uh, yeah... It hasn't sunk in yet." He started to throw back the top cover but stopped and let it fall back into place as he sat up. "Let me get dressed."

"Is it all right if Jake goes with us?" Etain asked, already reaching for the baby.

Freeblood ran his hands over his bandaged head. "He'll need a fresh diaper, but yeah, you can take him. I'll see you downstairs."

Breakfast was like a homecoming for several people, especially Etain. There were so many she'd not seen since Laugharne and had to be introduced to Austin and Cloud, which left the smaller boy confused. He couldn't understand why she didn't recognize him when she was the one who rescued him from the *Bok*.

With everyone seated at the table, Dar leaned toward Austin sitting next to him. "She has had a difficult time. Be patient with her."

"I think I know what you mean, Dar. The *Bok* gave me and my brother a hard time. I'll do what I can to help."

Dar patted him on the back. "Trust me, she is a good friend to have."

"And pretty."

Dar laughed. "Oh, aye. She is."

The absence of Linq and Taurnil was noticeable, yet no mention was made of their whereabouts. Not until Etain stood and gazed over the beloved congregation of friends and family.

"I don't usually do stuff like this." An unsure, yet gracious smile came to her lips. "But here I am, doing it."

Laughter tittered through the group. She glanced at Dar, who furrowed his brow. "I'm sure you've noticed that two important people of our family are missing. Well, four, but Freeblood will be here—"

"I'm here!" he said, breathless from his rush down the stairs. "You know me. I don't miss a meal."

There was more laughter as he joined the table and sat across from Dar. "Sorry, Etain. Just getting used to being home. Go on with what you were saying."

"It's so good to have you here with us, Freeblood." She gazed at the others. "Make that three. Faux is upstairs, recovering. But she'll be with us in no time."

Some touched Freeblood on the arm, offering their well-wishes for her quick recovery, while others raised their cups of coffee in a show of support. He turned a tearful eye to Etain and wiped his face with a napkin. "You guys... Look what you're doing to me."

Laughter filled the room, but everyone soon settled down to listen to what their High Lady had to say. It was true when she said she was not one to make speeches, which meant this one was important.

Dar gently tugged the skirt of her dress. "What are you doing?"

She merely glanced at each person around the room as she spoke.

"We have a new family member. Well, aside from Jake." A few laughed while others smiled. "I don't know how many of you have met Jackie."

Etain waved a hand to where she sat midway down the table.

"I've known this lady all my life and am so happy to have her here. If you haven't had the pleasure, please introduce yourself."

Jackie acknowledged the well wishes but appeared rather uncomfortable.

"What many of you may not know is that Linq, Taurnil, Aramis, and Ra risked their lives to rescue my sister from the Phum Banshee, a horrible band of skin traders with no regard for life, other than the notoriety and riches it can bring." Etain turned to Aramis and Ra, who looked more like schoolboys caught in the act than saviors. "Thankfully, they were able to bring Faux home." She pressed her hands together in front of her as though in prayer. "Thank you so much. You are my heroes."

Dar tugged on her dress again, forcing her to lean down to him.

"What. Are. You. Doing?"

"I'm warning them of the disaster that is going to come and I'm to blame."

"But you are not."

"We discussed this last night, my love." She winked at the group. "One sec." And whispered to Dar, "When I became Alamir, I should have made them my first priority and wiped them out then."

He kept his calm, aware of the eyes on them. "*A chuisle—*"

A small voice broke into their private conversation. "Why'd they stay if those Banshee are so mean?" asked Austin, innocently staring at Etain and Dar.

Ra spoke before Etain could answer. "Taurnil wants to save the hostages we had to leave behind—the babies and their mothers."

The boy scrunched his entire face. "What's a hostage?"

Dalos, sitting at his side, answered, "Someone taken by force and held against their will."

Etain furrowed her brows when the boy looked at her with sad eyes. "Are they part of the *Bok*?"

"They are not," Dar said. "But they have been known to work with them."

"Do Banshee have hearts?"

Dar tilted his head. "It is debatable. Why do you ask?"

"Cause I want to help. I want to save those babies and their mamas and eat the Banshee hearts."

"Austin! You're so stupid!" his brother yelled.

Red Dog scrambled from where he lay on the floor, barking.

Jake woke, crying from his makeshift crib of a drawer behind Etain.

"Cloud!" Swee scowled. "Don't speak to your brother like that."

Fortunately, Dalos caught Austin by the collar before he could get to his brother. "Let's go outside, little brother. I cannot teach you how to *eat* hearts, but I can show you how to cut one out."

Swee jumped up. "Dalos! Don't you dare." She grabbed Cloud by the arm. "You're coming with me."

Etain turned to get Jake. "What have you been teaching that boy?" She cuddled the baby close. "It's okay, little one."

"Nothing yet, but I know what his first lesson will be. Red, quiet." He bent down and scratched the puppy behind the ears. "Good dog."

And just like that, the subject of the Banshee was shoved to the back shelf for another day. Conversations soon struck up between the diners, and Etain's attempt to share her confession was forgotten, even by her.

"If you have plans like that for our son..." The thought of her son eating hearts. She loved the man to bits, but sometimes his warrior ways didn't sit well with her. "I have news for you, buster. It ain't happening."

He leaned in close, his lips next to her ear. "Now that you mention it, it *is* a good skill to have. Comes in handy when you need a little pick-me-up in the midst of battle. I think I will teach them both."

She bit the inside of her cheek and rolled her eyes. "You are *not* funny." She pushed away from the table. "I'm going for a walk with the only decent men in the room."

Dar let her go and leaned back.

"Freeblood, Jake is going with me. Jackie, care to go with us?" She cuddled the baby close and called for Red Dog. Her haughty gaze returned to her husband. "I'll leave you to your debauchery."

As she and Jackie walked out the door, the sound of Dar's laughter sent tingles through her.

⁕⁕⁕

After most everyone cleared the dining room, Dar and Freeblood remained, their conversation turning to various orders of business.

"What're you gonna do about Linq and Taurnil?"

Dar shrugged. "They know how to handle themselves. If they need my help, they will let me know."

Freeblood gently scratched his head. "Seriously? No rushing in to save the day?"

"Not this time." He stood and grabbed his coffee cup. "More?"

"Yeah, sure." Freeblood pushed his cup across the table.

"It is important I remain here. They understand that." At the sideboard, he filled both cups as he spoke. "For Etain and our children..." he carried both cups to the table, taking his seat, "and the rest of our family."

Freeblood focused on his coffee.

Dar noticed the young man's discomfort. "Etain told me trouble is coming." He enjoyed a sip. "It will. We must be prepared when the Banshee retaliate. With that in mind, I will not leave Etain. She is still fragile."

Freeblood sipped from his cup. "She didn't sound so fragile this morning."

"She surprised me too. When Austin asked what a hostage was..." Dar blew out a breath. "I was not sure what it would do to her."

"Even if they knew where to come, why would they?"

Dar raised a brow and waggled his finger at him. "Do not question the mind of a woman, especially a Banshee. I thought you would have learned that by now."

"Uh... Yeah."

They shared a moment of silence, both quietly sipping from their cups.

"You know what this place needs, Dar?"

He leaned back in his chair, fingering the handle of his coffee cup. "What is that?"

"I'd like to get this monster of a house wired for twenty-first century technology."

Dar shot him an incredulous glare. "Technology is a nuisance of which I have no need."

"How do you propose to run a business in today's world without it?" Freeblood placed his elbows on the table. "This is something we need. And I want to supply everyone with a cell phone so we can keep in touch."

"They are ridiculous contraptions. If I want to contact someone, I will use the mindspeak."

Freeblood snorted. "Fine for you, but us mere mortals need a little help."

Dar sipped his coffee and patiently set it down. "Answer me this. If you are in the midst of a sword fight, which hand will you use to call for help? Or if you are lost and there is no connection, how will anyone find you?"

Freeblood grinned, not intimidated in the least. "I have a few bugs to work out, but all the phones can be linked, so if someone comes up missing, we can track their phone through any one of the others. Plus, phones have voice recognition. Not quite like your mindspeak, but damn close. Some of us would feel better knowing we had instant contact with our family."

"No phones. They make people lazy. And, if we locate our people via their phones, so will the *Bok*." Dar raised a brow. "But perhaps the other."

He considered the young man for a moment. "You have grown since we first met."

He gave Dar a sideways grin. "About damn time, right?"

"Like the rest of us, you have been through things no one should have to experience. You have handled yourself well."

"I know you think I don't listen, but I hear what you say. I see your sacrifices. It's time I contributed and ensured our family's survival."

Dar leaned forward. "I have a proposition for you."

"Okay..."

"You spent a lot of time at the Laugharne stables. Did you learn anything?"

"I think so," he said apprehensively.

"Tell me what you experienced."

Freeblood blew out a breath. "How do I put it into words?" He gazed out the window. "When I'm with the horses, I'm at peace, in tune with myself. Like I belong." He placed a hand on his chest. "I can breathe and think. Things were so hectic at Laugharne, they helped me cope." A corner of his mouth turned up slightly. "Sounds weird, huh?"

Dar shrugged. "Not to someone who understands."

He perked up at the admission. "You know what I'm talking about?"

"As a boy, when my lessons became too much or I upset my father with something I had done or did not do, I sought refuge in the stables." Dar chuckled at the surprise on the young man's face. "I was not born knowing everything. I had to learn too."

"Sorry, Dar..." Freeblood laughed. "It's hard to imagine you as a kid."

"I thought the same of my father when he would tell me of his life growing up, always with the premise of teaching me a lesson, of course."

"Hmph." Freeblood sat hunched over his cup. "All mine did was beat the hell out of me. No stories from him."

"You have not said much about your family."

"Guess that makes us even." Freeblood smirked. "Neither have you."

"True. I think when all our children are here, we will have plenty of time to share our stories. In the meantime, I want to offer you the management of the stables."

Freeblood stared at him, his mouth open.

"I will teach you everything I know." At his continued silence, Dar added, "Or, if you would prefer, you can work at the academy with Linq."

Freeblood stood. "You want *me*..." he pointed at himself, "to handle the horses? The entire business? Buying and selling?"

The range of emotions on the young man's face struck a chord with Dar and reminded him of when his father had given him the same opportunity. "Along with health, fitness, and well-being, as well as hiring, firing, and financials. There is a lot to it."

"Damn, Dar." He ran a hand over his head and further surprised the Krymerian by rushing around the table and hugging him. "Thank you. No one has *ever*... I don't know what to say. Where do I start?"

Dar stood and clamped a hand on the young man's shoulder. "Let's start by introducing you to the stables and her tenants."

"Good idea."

"Give me a few minutes to speak with Swee."

Before Freeblood could react, Dar was gone. He scratched his head, feeling as though he'd missed his cue, but grinned. "Stable manager."

A million ideas ran through his head, the most important being the installation of a wireless system for the house, stables, and... Hell, he was feeling generous, even the proposed Black Blade Academy. Dar would appreciate it, eventually.

With the nursery nearing completion, Dar and Etain made several trips into town. New furniture was required for every room, including the babies' room. Plus, it gave the couple time to reconnect away from the hustle and bustle of the manor.

"Faux is still Faux, whether or not she has a tail. She'll be wanting help with the baby," Etain said, checking the tag on a crib that caught her eye. "I love this one. And it comes in different colors."

Dar stroked his chin. "She has settled somewhat since the binding. She might surprise you and be the perfect mother."

Etain gave him a patronizing smile. "You're just that special, aren't you?"

He narrowed his eyes. "I know well enough." He stared at the multitude of baby cribs. "Why must they be different colors?"

"I was thinking white for Emalyn and walnut for the boys."

"The boys?"

She walked on through the collection of cribs. "Jamie and Jake."

Dar stopped. "Oh... Aye. I must get used to the name Jamie."

"And Emalyn wants to be called Ema."

"In Krymeria, the *parents* were in charge. Children did what they were told, not the other way around. I do not recall Inferno taking orders from his lot."

She stopped her perusal of the beds. Mentally, he kicked himself for his slip of the tongue, but held her gaze. *Show no fear.*

"They got their way more than you know." She rolled her eyes. "It's not like the babies changed their names completely."

Victory in the face of adversity. "But what if I want to call my son by his middle name?"

She shrugged as she returned to traversing the sea of cribs, waving a hand through the air. "Take it up with your son, but if I were him, I wouldn't answer you."

He chuckled to himself. *If the boy wants to be called Jamie, so be it.*

"Oh, Dar!"

Her sudden outburst jarred him from his thoughts. "What is it?"

She squeezed her belly in between two other beds, heading toward a wooden crib stained light grey. "This is it!" Her eyes sparkled as she circled the piece of furniture. "Not too modern, not too old-fashioned. Even the color is perfect."

He furrowed his brows. "But earlier you said—"

She waved a hand. "Forget that. This is it. Three of these. And..."

His heart skipped a beat, seeing her so happy. By the gods, how he had missed that smile. "And what?"

She pointed toward another corner. "And three of those chests of drawers with the changing attachment. The color matches the beds, and with three babies, they'll get plenty of use."

He crossed his arms over his chest. "Should we get the matching rocking chair?"

Her eyes wide, she looked in the direction he indicated. "Can we get three? That way, no one gets left out."

"Of course," he said, although he had meant it as a joke. "Now, shall we get the odds and ends for Alaster?"

Once she chose the other items required for growing babies, they left the shop and walked toward the butchers.

Several heads turned as the Amazonian couple walked through the door. Already on friendly terms with the butcher, Dar grinned.

"Morning, Dar." He turned to the lady. "You must be Mrs. Dar. Welcome."

Etain smiled. "Morning."

"What will it be today, sir?"

"The usual if you do not mind, Bob."

"Don't mind at all."

Etain watched Bob prepare and hand her husband package after package, Dar filling the cart. "The usual?"

"Oh, aye. My *weekly haul*, as Alaster calls it."

"But... It's all pork. Don't you think it's a bit...obsessive?"

"Just because a man likes to have a little pork on hand does not make him obsessed."

"A *little* pork?" With a raised brow, she picked up two packages. "Two slabs of bacon?"

"Four actually. It tastes better if you slice it yourself."

"I'm surprised you bother." She held up two other packages. "What're these?"

"You are a Texas girl, Etain." He laughed, taking the packages, and returning them to the cart. "You know pork chops."

"Are you sure you haven't confused your T-bone with your pork chops?" She held up two more, raising her brows.

He grinned and pointed to her right hand. "Pork brains." And pointed to the other. "Pig's feet."

Her face turned deathly white as she dropped the packages into the cart. "I'll be right back," she croaked, covering her mouth with one hand and holding her stomach with the other.

Dar noticed a toilet sign off to the side and happily pointed at it. Etain left him at the counter.

He heard her moan as she entered the toilet and smiled to himself. "I may give up eating hearts, but not my pork."

Dreams Do Come True

F aux opened her eyes, blinked, and rolled them closed. She lifted a hand to touch her head, but another grasped it before she could. After a deep breath, she opened her eyes.

"Hey you."

The voice seemed familiar, but she wasn't sure if it was a good thing.

Faux squinted, trying to make out the face. "Where's my baby?"

"Jake's with Freeblood." The woman squeezed her hand. "He'll be back in a little bit."

"What?" She closed her eyes and heard the woman shift in the chair. *How does she know?*

"Faux, it's Etain."

"Etain?" Her eyes popped open, followed by a piercing pain through her head. "Ouch." Again she closed her eyes. *It has to be another ploy by that...* A memory cut through the pain. *Oh. She's dead... Good.*

"Don't try to get up. You've taken a hit to the head."

Faux heard the woman's heavy breathing and the sound of a chair dragging across the floor. She slowly opened her eyes. Now that she sat closer, she relaxed. "Etain... Where are we?"

Etain leaned toward her. "We're at *Sôlskin*. Swee thought it best you have peace and quiet, so we're toward the front of the house away from the noise. There's a lot of construction going on down the hall—a new nursery and rejig of the bedrooms. Can I get you anything?"

"Freeblood and Jake are here?"

"Downstairs, having breakfast."

Faux touched her head. "Why am I wrapped like a mummy?"

Etain held onto her hand. "Leave it alone. Like I said, you took a hard hit. It'll take a while to heal."

"Help me sit up."

Etain moved to the bed, giving her support and fluffing her pillows. As she slowly sat back in the chair, Faux stared at her belly.

"You're about to pop."

"I wish I would." She blew out a breath. "I think the human half has overwhelmed the Krymerian half. They're taking their sweet time."

"Krymerians can be kinda stubborn too. Maybe you should climb in the other bed. Let everyone take care of both of us."

Etain laughed. "A tempting proposition, but I'm overseeing the renovations, so no rest just yet."

The door opened and Freeblood with Jake in his arm walked into the room. Seeing Faux awake, he rushed to the bed. "Babe! You're awake. Hey, Etain. Man, I wanted to be the first face you saw when you woke." His smile spread from ear to ear. "But I'm glad you two got to catch up."

"Freeblood, why don't you give Jake to his mom and help his auntie onto her feet?"

He walked around to the other side of the chair, handed the baby to Faux, and assisted Etain out of the chair. "Where are you off to?"

"I have a few things to do—the nursery, moaning about how miserable I am, stuff like that." She chuckled. "Y'all have a nice visit." Her gaze returned to Faux. "It's good to have you home."

Etain closed the door on her way out.

Faux kissed Jake on the head. "How's she doing? She looks tired."

Freeblood sat in the chair. "She's had it pretty rough, babe. But she seems to be coming on okay."

"Are you sure? She doesn't seem to be herself."

He smirked, leaned forward, and touched her cheek. "I said the same thing to Dar. At least she knows who everyone is now. When she and Dar first came back, she didn't even recognize *him*."

She closed her eyes briefly, enjoying the feel of his touch. "Are Linq and Illiana here?"

"Not that I know of." He dropped his hand, resting his elbows on his thighs. "Ra and Aramis brought you back, but the others haven't returned yet."

Faux raised her brows. "Are they Black Blades?"

"Nah. They're with the Dragon clan. I figure they'll end up moving here."

"Dragon clan? When did they show up?"

Freeblood laughed. "There were at Laugharne, babe. I guess you didn't run into 'em."

She rocked the baby, smiling at his little face. "No big surprise there after Dar's big show. It's a wonder they even bothered to bring me home."

"It's going to be different here." He shifted to the bed, sitting on the edge. "Dar's handed the management of the stables to me." Her eyes widened. "I know! He really did. We have a home here, babe. Jake's going to grow up with Dar and Etain's kids. You two can reconnect, be moms together. We'll be a real family."

As good as it sounded, she wasn't convinced. There were a few wild cards still in play. "What about Dathmet? What's Dar gonna do about him?"

Freeblood ran his hands over his hair. "He didn't say, and I didn't ask."

She raised a brow. "The Banshee?"

He moved back to the chair. "Damn, Faux, can't we just concentrate on us for a minute?"

"You and Jake are the reason I'm asking. We came too close to losing everything." The thought of what could have happened made her shiver. "One thing I learned from all this is I can't let anything happen to either of you. My heart can't take it."

She put Jake on her shoulder and leaned against the pillows. "Climb into bed with us. Let's enjoy the peace while we have it."

As the days passed with no sign of the twins making an appearance, an edgy Etain found it increasingly difficult to check her temper in light of her swollen ankles, aching back, and enormous belly that seemed to weigh a ton and got in the way more often than not.

One morning, as she and Dar prepared to go downstairs for breakfast, she suddenly sat on the edge of the bed. "Why don't you go on without me? I know you have a lot of things to do."

Red Dog trotted to her side of the bed and placed his head on her lap, looking at her with his light green eyes. She patted his head. "Hi, Red."

In an effort to teach the pup who his true master was, Dar had him sleep by his side of the bed. His plan was beginning to show fruit, but he was not too sure if he or Etain was the master.

Dar frowned. "I hate to leave you, *a chuisle*. What if—"

She waved her hand in the air. "I don't feel any different than yesterday. I think you're safe to take care of business without worrying about me."

He crouched in front of her. "I will check on you during the day." He kissed her on the lips and stood. "If you need me—"

"Go. I'll be fine." As he headed to the door, she called out, "Wait! Come help me up, please."

A grin on his face, he returned, giving her a supportive hand. "Are you certain?"

"I'm up. I'm good. Thank you. I'm gonna check on the progress of our rooms, then I'll be down."

"I would be happy to go with you."

"I can take my time if I go alone," she said, adjusting her clothes.

"In other words, I would be in the way."

She grinned. "How well you know me, sir."

He winked. "As you wish, milady." With one last kiss, he was out the door. "Come, Red."

She heard the two bounding down the stairs. "Okay, heifer. Let's get moving."

Just as Dar and Red Dog reached the bottom of the stairs, Austin ran into the manor, flushed and yelling at the top of his lungs. "Dar! She's gonna blow! She's gonna blow!"

"Austin. Have you no volume control, boy?"

Red Dog bounced toward him, barking.

Excited, the boy paid no heed to the question. "It's coming, Dar. Right now!"

Dar laughed. "Who's coming this time?"

"The baby horse! Uh, I mean the foal! You gotta come. Hurry!" He spun and ran out the front doors, Red Dog chasing after him.

"Austin! Where's Freeblood?"

"What a great day," Aramis said, stepping into the hallway, Ra behind him. "Shall we join him?"

A strange sensation crept along the back of Dar's neck. "You two go ahead. I will be along shortly."

"We'll let 'em know you're coming," said Ra as they stepped outside.

As he closed the door, Dar heard her sobs. He took the stairs two at a time and found her halfway up, sitting on a step and leaning against the wall, her cheeks streaked with tears.

His presence made her cry even harder. "I'm so tired. I can't even walk down the blo-ody stairs. D-amn. Now I have the hic-cups." She slapped her hand against the wall.

He sat next to her and wrapped his arms around her shoulders. "This is the hardest time, my love. But I promise, it will soon be over, and we will have our precious babies in our arms."

She buried her face in his chest. "I just want them o-ut of me. You said it would be a f-ew months." She sniffed, then held her breath, which ended with another hiccup. She rolled her eyes. "It's been five now, and I'm tired of l-ooking like a beached whale. Ugh! My ankles are gone, my waist... Ha! What the h-ell is that? My back hurts, and they keep kick-ing and moving. I can't get any sleep. I d-on't want to do this."

He tried to keep a straight face at her forlorn expression.

"My love..." He brushed the hair from her face. "I am afraid the only path is forward. Just a little longer. Once you see their tiny faces, all this will be forgotten." He rocked her gently. "Let's get you back to bed. I think it is time you reserve what strength you have for the births."

"I can't. I can't lug this gro-tesqueness back up those stairs."

He stood, helped her up, and pulled her close, then phased into their bedroom. He helped her into bed. "I will get Swee to send breakfast."

She looked away, a pout on her lips. "I'm not hun-gry."

"Etain, you must keep up your strength."

She rolled onto her side and pulled the covers over her head. "I'm already the size of a house."

"Etain—"

"Go away. I want to be alone."

"If I did not have a mare ready to foal, I would stand here and argue with you, but—"

She threw back the covers and grabbed the bedside lamp. "Then go take care of the bloo-dy horse!"

Dar dodged as the lamp sailed past his ear and shattered against the wall. "Etain! Calm down." He moved toward her, but a perfectly aimed book stayed his advance.

"Go away! Get out!"

Discretion being the better part of valor, he did as she demanded and backed out the door. Blowing out a breath, he turned and bumped into a smirking Swee.

"Need help, big guy?"

"Good morning, Swee." He glanced over his shoulder at the closed door. "Would you please get breakfast for the good lady and see if you can talk some sense into her?"

She laughed, shaking her head. "To a woman pregnant with overdue twins? No way, Dar." The sight of his crestfallen face made her reach out to him. "But I *will* get her breakfast and see if I can get her to eat."

"Thank you." He drew in a breath. "I am afraid she has been pushed to her limits and there is nothing I can do."

"Take care of what you need to do this morning. After she eats, I'll check to see if she's dilated."

He shrugged. "I hate seeing her like this. She said some alarming things."

"Dar." Swee spoke in a soothing voice. "Women say things they don't mean when they're tired and cranky, especially in her condition. Don't worry. Once she sees those babies, all this will fade away."

"I hope so. We are running low on bedside lamps." Reluctant to leave, he said, "Find me immediately if anything happens."

She pulled him toward the stairs. "Dar, I'm a professional. I can handle it."

Her comment made him laugh. "How professional are you at ducking and dodging?"

<hr>

Dar stepped into the stables just as the foal's head crowned. Austin ran out of the stall and grabbed his hand. "This is so cool! Dalos said the little horse'll be standing before the day's over. Did you know that, Dar?" Not waiting for a response, the boy slid to his knees next to Dalos, ready to assist the tiny horse into the world. "Wow."

Dar appreciated the wonder in the boy's eyes. "It amazes me every time, Austin."

"Big day, isn't it?" Freeblood walked in with a smile on his face.

"There you are." Seeing the young man took his responsibilities seriously eased his mind. "How are Faux and Jake?"

"Jake is the coolest kid in the world." His grin turned into a frown. "Faux's ready to get the bandage off her head. But, I gotta tell ya, Dar, I'm not."

"Why is that?"

"Because then she's going to see her mangled ear. You know how proud she is of her looks. I don't know if I can handle the dramafest and everything else at the same time."

Dar thought for a moment, stroking his chin. "What does Swee say?"

"She needs another couple of weeks, at least."

"Hold Faux off as long as you can. I might have something that will take away the drama of losing half her ear."

"Like what?"

Dar shook his head. "You will have to wait."

Once satisfied with the way things were progressing in the stables, the High Lord pulled a small piece of paper and pencil from his pocket, drawing a schematic as he headed toward the academy to check on those developments. Every clan in the Alamir realm, including the Ambassadors, had been notified. He hoped to have at least one full class for the spring session.

"Construction can start on the student dorms soon," he mumbled to himself.

Not expecting a large turnout for the first semester, he planned to house the students in the manor until the dorms were completed. With Alaster and Cherise on board, it would make things easier.

At the garage, he sensed something amiss and changed direction toward the house. Bounding up the stairs two at a time, the bedroom door opened just as he reached for the handle. Swee placed a hand on his chest and pushed him back as she stepped out of the room, closing the door behind her.

"At last." She linked an arm through his and guided him down the hall.

He glanced back at the door. "What is it?"

She patted his arm. "Etain is fine, but weak. The babies are good." Dar visibly relaxed. "But—"

He stopped and grabbed her by both arms. "But what? Spit it out."

"Dar!" She pushed him away, rubbing her upper arms. "Calm down."

"I am sorry, but I cannot bear to lose my family."

Her glare softened. "You're not going to lose anyone. We just need to get those babies here for all their sakes. She's dilated to some degree, but it's been several hours with no change."

"Are you thinking Caesarean birth?"

"Both babies are in the right position. I would prefer a natural birth. I don't relish the thought of putting Etain under after all she's been through, nor would it be good for the babies." A sparkle came to her eyes. "I consulted with Spirit. She told me of an old wives' tale that has proven quite useful with some of her births."

"Does it involve magic?" he asked skeptically. "I do not know of any spell that will help in this case."

"It *is* a spell, of sorts. But only you can invoke its power."

"Me? I just told you—"

Taking his arm again, they paced the hall as she explained what he must do.

"Take it slow. I don't know how responsive she will be in her condition."

His hope restored, he gave her a huge grin and a tight hug. "Thank you, Swee. My babies will be here before morning. I swear it."

She laughed as he quietly slipped into the bedroom, ready to play his part in the birth of his children.

Dressed in an airy gown of white gauze, Etain lay on her side, her back to the door. Dar saw where the fabric clung to her sweat-soaked skin and heard her heavy sigh. Gently, he sat on the side of the bed, running his hand along her hip. "How are you, my precious one?"

"Hanging in there."

He slipped a hand over her taut belly. "Swee told me of a way I can help."

She closed her eyes. "Short of going back in time and me saying no to your advances, I don't know what it could be."

Dar raised his brows. "Interesting proposition, but I think her idea will prove more useful." He turned and removed his boots. "She says Spirit swears by it."

"Spirit's done her share of swearing through the years, but what the heck. Let's give it a try."

He stood and stripped off his clothes.

Her eyes widened. "What the hell are you doing?"

He slid into bed, spooned his body close to hers, and gently slipped a hand underneath her gown.

She stiffened. "This is what got us here."

"*A chuisle*, relax and let me love you." He lightly stroked the length of her back and up again, taking his time. With each caress, his touch moved lower down her back to include her legs and feet.

"It feels so good," she sighed. "But I don't understand."

He shifted over, lying in front of her. "Apparently, she has had many successes when this technique has been used." Opening the front of her gown, he dipped his head to suckle each breast.

"You're lucky I'm too tired to move, otherwise…"

Dar's body reacted as she languished in his attentions, but he made every effort to concentrate on the job at hand—inducing labor. He explained that stimulating the nipples released a hormone within her body that would help start contractions.

She framed his face with her hands and kissed him softly. His gaze held captive by hers, she kissed him more intently as one hand traveled down, stroking his need. The two sighed, her invitation too tempting to ignore.

The couple relished their shared passion and took their time, bringing each other to a smooth and easy release, oblivious to the outside world.

Taking advantage of the quiet in the house, Swee stole away to her room for what she hoped would be a few hours' sleep. This being her first birthing, she wanted to be alert and ready for whatever may come.

Within a few short hours, she was awakened by a frantic knocking on her door. She pulled on her robe and met an agitated Freeblood pacing in the hallway.

"Swee, you gotta come now. Etain's in labor."

Groggy, she passed the nervous young man, and headed toward Dar and Etain's bedroom. "How would you know?"

He rushed along beside her. "I was on my way to bed when Dar stepped out, and, well… I offered to help so he wouldn't have to leave her."

Swee found the door ajar and stepped into the room but turned to Freeblood, placing a hand on his chest. "It would be best if you stayed out here for now."

"Oh. Yeah. Right."

"Thank *Tartarus*, Swee," Dar said as she closed the door. "The contractions are coming close together."

"For how long?" She stared at the dog lying next to Etain on the bed. "If you'll excuse me, Red."

"Red, down," Dar commanded.

Reluctant to leave Etain's side, the puppy whined, but at the glare from his master, he jumped off the bed and padded around to lay at Dar's feet.

"Thank you, Red." Swee checked her patient. "How long have the contractions—"

"Forever," Etain grunted through gritted teeth.

Dar shook his head. "Maybe an hour?"

"I need to check her progress. Would you help her onto her back, Dar?"

Her hands roamed over Etain's belly, double-checking the positions of the babies. She checked her pulse and touched her forehead. Etain grunted when another contraction hit, squeezing Dar's hand as she struggled to breathe through the pain.

"Keep breathing, Etain. I'll be right back."

Etain's eyes widened. "Where. Do. You. Oh hell..."

"Don't talk. Just breathe. I'm just a few steps away."

"I am here, my love," Dar said, doing his best to be the supportive husband. Etain narrowed her eyes and bared clenched teeth.

Swee opened the door to a concerned face. "I need a few things before these babies pop out, Freeblood, and you must get them quickly." After telling him her detailed list, she turned away and called to the puppy. "Red Dog, come." Hearing him pad across the floor, she returned to Freeblood. "Please take Red. All this fuss is upsetting him, and Etain is handful enough."

"Come on, boy." The puppy drooped his head as he stepped out of the room. "I'll be right back. Let's go find Cloud."

Red Dog lifted his head and wagged his tail, his tongue lolling out the side of his mouth, back to his old self. He looked back at Swee and barked.

"I guess you told me." She chuckled, closing the door. When the contraction passed, she checked Etain's cervix. "Well, Lord VonNeshta, as usual, you've made good on your promise. Your children should be here before the sun rises." She couldn't help but laugh at the grin on his face, but another contraction set them in motion. "If you will support her from behind, it'll make it easier for her to push. Etain, remember your breathing."

"I *am* breathing," she growled. "Just get them out."

Swee used her most authoritative voice. "You remember what Spirit taught you and keep breathing. I'll tell you when it's time to push."

Jackie stepped into the room, extra sheets, towels, and a good-sized basin in her arms. "I'm here to help."

In the middle of a contraction, Etain turned her head. "Jackie? Ow!"

"Breathe, Etain. Don't talk," ordered Swee. "Jackie, fill the basin with warm water. Make sure it's *warm*, not hot, and it stays warm."

Jackie set the linens on the edge of the bed and looked around the room. Spying the bedside table, she placed the lamp on the floor and shoved the other items into a drawer, then set the basin on top.

"Spread a sheet over the top and a towel over that," Swee said as she placed a sheet over Etain's legs.

"No need for modesty," Etain grunted. "She's seen it all. What happened to Freeblood?"

Jackie shrugged. "I told him I'd step in. How's it going?"

Another contraction started. "It depends. On which side." Etain panted a few breaths. "Of the contraction. Holy hell!"

Swee checked her again. "It's time, Etain! Push!"

As the sun rose on the first snowfall of the season, James Harley VonNeshta quietly made his appearance. Dar supported his exhausted wife, watching Swee expertly conduct the concert of births.

"Take him, Jackie," she said, handing over the tiny baby. "Get him cleaned up while I help the other one. Make sure the wa—"

"It's warm, like you said." She smiled at the baby as she carried him to the bedside table and gently washed his little face and body. "Hey, bud. We're gonna be great friends."

Not to be left behind, his twin sister, Emalyn Aurelia VonNeshta followed, screaming for all to hear.

"Oh... Yes, ma'am. We hear you!" Swee laughed, seeing the tiny girl's red face. "We have us a red-headed spitfire. Jackie, give yours to Dar and take this one. I need to finish with their mother."

With James Harley wrapped tightly in a soft towel, she walked around the bed and handed him to his father. "*Fáilte, a fhir bhig* (welcome, my little man). I am your da." He held him up so an exhausted Etain could see his face. "This brave, beautiful lady is your mama."

Jackie rushed back to Swee, took the little girl, and performed the same gentle bathing ritual. "Hello, little miss." She beamed, holding the small package in her arms. "They're perfect, Etain."

Swee straightened. "Dar, would you hand your son to Jackie for a moment? I need you to move Etain while I change the sheets, then we'll leave you happy parents alone with your sweet babies."

With the bed freshened and Etain settled against the pillows, Jackie delivered one tiny miracle to her and the other to Dar.

"We'll leave you for now, but I'll be back later to check on everyone." Swee gathered the used sheets and headed to the door. "Jackie, you coming?"

Etain answered for her. "She'll be along in a minute. Thank you, Swee."

Swee gave her a wink and left the room.

Etain held out a hand. "I'm so glad you're here."

Jackie sat on the opposite side of the bed. "Me too. But we can visit later. Spend as much time as you can with these precious babies," her gaze went to Dar, "and your husband. I'll be around for a while."

Dar stood. "Jackie, shall my son and I walk you to the door?"

"Dar!" Etain huffed. "Don't be rude."

Jackie laughed and patted her arm. "It's okay, darlin'. There are a few people downstairs I'd like to chat with. We'll catch up soon."

"Tomorrow we'll have our own chat without any bossy men around."

His son in his arm, Dar walked her to the door and stepped into the hallway with her. "Thank you for your help. I am glad you are here too."

"Enjoy your private time while you can. Once she comes out of that room, life's gonna get pretty complicated."

"Dar, what're you doing?" Etain called out from the bedroom.

"Be right there, my love." He smiled at his son and Jackie. "We will speak in a few days."

Two and Three to Go

The Elves ran until they reached the cover of a forest. Safe within the darkness of the trees, Linq stopped and turned. "It appears we have not been followed."

Taurnil chuckled and joined him, searching the hills for movement. "Who could keep up with the likes of us?"

"Not this time, no, but they know we are here." Linq raised a brow. "They will be ready for us next time."

Taurnil frowned and ventured into the difficult conversation he could not avoid. "That is why you must return to *Sôlskin*."

Linq straightened to his full height. "You know I cannot. *Will* not. You need my—"

"I am your prince and future king." He stood as tall as his friend, meeting his angry gaze. "It is an order, not a request. My focus cannot be compromised. It is paramount that I know you are away from this place and safe."

"Hmph."

Taurnil recognized the doubt and anger in his eyes and followed him deeper into the forest. "Do you think I do not know it will be difficult? If Illiana is who I think she is, how can I walk out of here without her? And I cannot in good conscience leave these women and children to the will of the Banshee."

Linq turned sharply. "Who do you think she is?"

Taurnil breathed in. "Dar's sister."

The older Elf narrowed his eyes. "Dar has never mentioned a sister."

"Call it a hunch."

"By the sea and stars! You are willing to risk your life and that of your kingdom on a hunch? The queen will—"

"This is *my* life." Taurnil forcefully swallowed to keep his calm. "I am no longer a child. The queen, my mother, will not dictate how I live it. You will return to the Alamir and ensure none of this affects Etain or Dar."

"They have already been affected by sending the others home."

"Then you can keep Dar where he is and make sure he does not interfere."

"What do you expect me to do when your mother comes asking questions?"

Taurnil stepped toward him. "You will tell her nothing. The last thing we need is a war between the Elves and the Banshee."

"Your mother will not be the problem. The war begins the moment you step into their camp."

He grinned at Linq. "My war. My rules."

"You have been around the High Lord for too long."

"Perhaps, but it is something I must do. We will part at dawn."

"What is your plan?"

"It is simple. I will offer myself for her release."

"Pardon my abruptness, milord, but if you expect these Banshee to honor your request, you are quite delusional. If she is Dar's sister, they will never suffer the loss of a Krymerian warrior or an Elven Prince. I fear for both of your lives."

"The High Lord has taught me many things, as have you." Taurnil winked. "I will win."

A dark-haired man dressed in black leather armor stood in the middle of the room, his hands clasped behind him. His hair pulled back into a plait revealed a strong jawline, presently clenched. "How is the burn, Togor?"

"Milord." The soldier saluted his commander with a fisted hand over his heart. "Mending well. I was more fortunate than some of my brothers."

"I hear the upstart is on the run."

"Yes, milord, but we have our best trackers on his trail. He won't be able to hide for long."

The commander's blue eyes glowed for a brief moment. "What of Thamuz?"

"His body has been prepared and awaits your command."

"He and the others deserve a proper ceremony. Have the pyres built and ready in two days' time. See if any have family who wish to attend for the calling of the names."

Togor raised both brows, although only one was visible having lost the other and a portion of his face at Thamuz's fiery death. "Mekar, sir..."

His commander gave him a steely eye. "You do not approve?"

"They are not Krymerian, milord." His voice vibrated with indignation. "Most were former Alamir turned *Bok,* and the rest were demons. They do not—"

His superior remained patient. "I appreciate your puritan heart, Togor. The demons will be returned to their respective worlds for whatever burials they deem necessary. But Thamuz and the others *will* have a Krymerian send-off. They were loyal and served me well." He shook his head. "It was my mistake in trusting this bastard of Midir's. Neither he nor his father had the integrity required to see this to its proper end. It seems the sister is made of finer stuff than her brother and might possibly restore my faith in our kind."

Togor cleared his throat. "Half-brother, milord."

His smile as dazzling as any displayed by Dar himself, he winked. "Thank the gods for that small blessing!" Mekar placed a hand on the captain's shoulder. "As soon as we have him contained, we can proceed with our original plans. We have four other stones to attain."

"Three stones, milord."

He dropped his hand. "You have been busy."

"Not I, milord. Thamuz. He handed over the SAF stone before he went to talk sense to the demon."

"Perhaps Dathmet was of some value after all." Mekar walked around his desk. "The sooner we bring those stones together, the sooner we can reverse the damage caused by my brother so long ago. Kaos will return to its proper place, and the Alamir will no longer have a purpose." He sat in his chair and leaned back.

"What of the Banshee, milord? Do you expect retaliation?"

"In time, I expect so. This dark-haired woman—more of a girl if you ask me—has cut them deep."

"Do you think she's significant?"

A thoughtful Mekar stared at nothing in particular. "She reminds me of Nataré, my brother's wife." He snapped out of his reverie and turned to Togor. "We should do our own research and uncover her history. It will be interesting to find how she is involved with the Elves. Phie will look for compensation and possibly a war. Let us make sure they do not go sniffing around our family at *Sólskin*. They can have their games, but not at my expense."

"As you wish, milord." With another salute, the captain turned to leave.

"And Togor..."

He stopped and faced his superior. "Yes, milord?"

"Not you. You cannot be seen by the lady. Understood?"

He tipped his head. "Yes, milord. I will assign my best men to the task."

"Good man. You may go."

After a final salute, he left his commander, who stared at the door for a few long moments and voiced his thoughts aloud. "Where would I go had I murdered a favored commander? Demons?" He shook his head as he swiveled his chair around toward the window. "I think not. They will be searching for your head. You are too noticeable for the Alamir, and there is nothing in Krymeria."

Mekar stroked his chin. "Human? There are parts of that world where you would fit in, no questions asked." He smiled to himself. "Wherever you are, you will not be able to resist her for long. You will make a move and we will have you."

Journey behind the scenes of the Blood of Kaos series - a world of warriors, magic, intrigue, and love. A monthly email will provide you with insights into the series that you won't find anywhere else.

In exchange for sharing your email, I have a special gift for you. It's a quick read that will give you the lowdown of when Dar met Etain.

Scan the QR code and register to access your copy of
Once Upon A Darknight

Coming soon —

Book 5 (Untitled)

Trodaire — A Blood of Kaos Novella

NOTE FROM NESA

If you loved the story or even if it wasn't your cup of tea

It doesn't have to be fancy or a 5-star rating

Scan the QR code for **TABOO** and share your journey into Kaos.

ABOUT THE AUTHOR

After marrying her special someone, Nesa decided life was too short to spend it all in one place. Instead of him moving to Texas (her home), she moved to England (his home). Since then, life has been an adventure!

Nesa is a 'learn as you go' kind of gal, which can be challenging, especially when it comes to writing. Although it took a backseat to raising her three children and work, the desire to write never died. Now that her kids are grown, she can indulge in her fantastical stories.

You can find Nesa Miller here: